# *WORDS OF LOVE— AND DESTINY*

Other men, unable to control their hunger, had grabbed at her. With Richard there was no desperation. He knew where he was going and was in no hurry to get there.

He started with her lips, sliding his fingers round her mouth, caressing her face, then stroking her neck. Lightly, with great skill, he touched her all over until the tingle became a giant surge of desire.

He kissed her. Gently, experimentally, as if she was some delicious fruit and he wanted to savour her taste. . . .

"Now," he whispered.

*Also by Trudi Pacter*

*Kiss & Tell*

Published by
HARPERPAPERBACKS

# SCREEN KISSES

# TRUDI PACTER

HarperPaperbacks
*A Division of HarperCollinsPublishers*

If you purchased this book without a cover, you should be aware that this book is stolen property. It was reported as "unsold and destroyed" to the publisher and neither the author nor the publisher has received any payment for this "stripped book."

This is a work of fiction. The characters, incidents, and dialogues are products of the author's imagination and are not to be construed as real. Any resemblance to actual events or persons, living or dead, is entirely coincidental.

HarperPaperbacks  *A Division of* HarperCollins*Publishers*
10 East 53rd Street, New York, N.Y. 10022

Copyright © 1990 by Trudi Pacter
All rights reserved. No part of this book may be used or reproduced in any manner whatsoever without written permission of the publisher, except in the case of brief quotations embodied in critical articles and reviews. For information address HarperCollins*Publishers*, 10 East 53rd Street, New York, N.Y. 10022.

This book was previously published in 1990 in Great Britain by Grafton Books.

Cover illustration by Maren

First HarperPaperbacks printing: June 1991

Printed in the United States of America

HarperPaperbacks and colophon are trademarks of HarperCollins*Publishers*

10 9 8 7 6 5 4 3 2 1

*For Nigel*

## *Acknowledgments*

I would like to thank Graham Watkins for taking me behind the scenes at the theatre. He showed me what a director goes through when choosing an actor. Jeremy Sinden and Delia Lindsay showed me what the actors go through. The agent's eye view was admirably taken care of by Derrick Marr and by Dennis Selinger, who initiated me into the mysteries of the movie world. Once I grasped the mechanics of the business I was able to talk to Greg Smith, who told me how a film is put together. Finally Richard Loncraine put the whole thing through his director's viewfinder.

To all of these experts I am eternally grateful.

She couldn't take her eyes off his hips. They reminded her of Elvis Presley. Or Mick Jagger. Straight and skinny and born to wear denim.

This is no way to carry on, she thought. Not on a day like today. With an effort she pulled herself together. "How did the audition go?" she asked the unknown man in front of her. He must have been a couple of years older than her, around thirty. And he looked the way she felt. Nervous.

"It was tricky," he said. "To tell the truth, I'm surprised I'm still in one piece." He looked at her curiously. "What are you going up for?"

"Laura Cheveley," she said, "the bitch part." The man gave her a long, appraising stare and started to smile. "With your eyes and all that red hair, you might be what he's looking for. I seem to remember Jeremy Powers' last girl had your kind of look. Sexy in a hungry sort of way."

He smiled some more. "If you play your cards right, you could be in with a chance."

She started to feel angry. There was something about auditions that always reminded her of a meat market. They herded you into crummy little rooms like the one she was in now. All yellowing net curtains and dirty paintwork. They put you through your paces, and at the end of it they picked you for the way you looked. You could read like Vanessa Redgrave and they still picked you for the way you looked.

She glanced across at her companion and wondered where he had gone wrong.

"Tell me," she asked, "what was so tricky about Jeremy Powers?"

"He tried to throw me," said the man sulkily. "To break my nerve. And he did it on purpose."

He walked over to the window. Then he turned round to face her.

"Look at me," he urged. "Take your time. I want an honest opinion. Now tell me, what type do you think I am?"

Now it was her turn to sit in judgement. He's certainly handsome enough, she thought. If you like that old-school-tie sort of look. Though his hair could do with a wash and he really shouldn't wear his jeans so tight. This time she stopped herself staring at his hips. "I think," she said, "that you're the James Dean type. Young, broody, misunderstood. That kind of thing."

## SCREEN KISSES • 3

"Exactly," he said, satisfied. "And that was the part I was going up for. The juvenile lead."

"So what went wrong?" She was intrigued now.

He looked at her. "Powers tried to make me play the old fart."

The laughter started in her stomach, climbed up her throat and, before she could stop it, burst out of her in helpless giggles. "But you're an actor," she spluttered. "You're meant to be other people. That's the whole point of it."

He didn't think it was funny. "You wait till you go in there," he threatened. "I'd like to see how you react when Jeremy throws you one of his little surprises."

She stopped laughing. She hadn't come here to be surprised. She'd come here to play Laura Cheveley. Her stomach twisted into a knot. What if the man in the other room went on playing tricks and decided to cast her as the dowager duchess?

Panic set in. He can't do that, she thought. He mustn't do that. I'll kill him if he tries.

The young man read her mind. "What's the problem?" he asked. "Worried you won't be allowed to play the wicked lady?"

She gritted her teeth. "If Powers thinks he can do me out of it, he'll have a struggle. I've wanted this part for seven years now. Ever since I started in the profession. And to do it with Powers directing—" she paused "—that would be really something."

Now it was her companion who smiled. "Sounds like you're going to have a fun time in there."

He gathered his things together, and headed for

the door. "Here's hoping the best man wins," he said cheerfully. "Good luck with the old bear. You're going to need it."

And he was gone before she could give him her telephone number. She sighed. One down, she thought. And one to go.

The door connecting the two rooms opened and a small, mousy girl carrying a script and some coffee in a paper cup motioned Rachel to come through. She stood up and hauled her heavy tote bag on to her shoulder, then she lifted her chin up, put on a smile and marched in to face Jeremy Powers.

He was smaller than she had expected. And younger. Though if you looked like him, she thought, it didn't matter what age you were. He put her in mind of a small, dark gnome—the kind you read about in the Brothers Grimm—square and bull-like with a shock of black hair and heavy brows. Had he a milder manner certain women might have found him attractive. But Jeremy Powers wasn't looking to win friends that day.

Rachel's smile faded. The first move was up to him. He was sitting behind a large, imposing desk, riffling through a stack of papers. Each sheet, she knew, contained the lives and careers of all the actors who were auditioning that day. Some he would keep; some he would put in the pending file; and some he would throw in the wastepaper basket. She wondered where hers would be in the end.

He lifted his head and stared her full in the face. The smell of the cattle market came back to her.

## SCREEN KISSES • 5

"Rachel Keller," he said softly. "Is that your real name, or did you make it up?"

"I didn't invent it for the stage," she said. "Why do you ask?"

"No reason. It just sounded a bit Jewish, that's all."

She bridled. "Do you have anything against that?"

He looked at her and let out a sigh. "This is a casting session, dear, not a concentration camp. Has Richard Roberts been making you nervous?"

So that was his name. Richard Roberts. She filed it away for future reference, then turned her attention to the man in front of her. "Actually," she said, "he has. He told me you made him switch parts at the last moment."

The dark man grinned, and for a moment he almost looked charming. "He was too pleased with himself, that one. Needed to be shaken up a bit. Don't be taken in by all that moaning, Rachel. It did him the world of good. Who knows, I might even make an actor out of him."

"And me," she asked, "what will you make of me?"

"That depends." He looked down at her résumé lying open in front of him. "You haven't done badly so far. A season at Nottingham. A play with the Royal Shakespeare. Not to mention six years slogging away in the distant provinces. What makes you want to come on this cheap little tour?"

"The part," she said. "Laura Cheveley."

He folded his hands across his chest and leaned

back in his chair. "So she's ambitious as well as beautiful," he said. "I might have known it. What makes you think you'll be a better Laura Cheveley than, say, Vivien Leigh or Sarah Miles?"

"Vivien Leigh is dead," she said. "And Sarah Miles is a screen actress. Anyhow she'd never do this tour. It's too small-time for her."

He looked at her again. "But it isn't for you," he said, "not yet, anyway." There was a pause. Then he said, "Get up, will you, and walk across to the light. I want to see how you move."

She's skinny, he thought, but on her it looks good. There's a lot of pride there. I can see it in the way she holds herself. She'll have to get rid of that. Then he looked at her face. Christ, he thought, she could have been made for the part. He remembered the playwright's description of Laura Cheveley. Dead white skin, long red hair, a throat that went on for ever. This girl's read the book too, he thought. Or her agent has.

"Sit down," he said. "It's time we had a talk. I want to know how you feel about the part."

"Look," she said, "why don't you let me read for it? Then we'll both know."

He scowled. "In this situation, I'm the one who makes the suggestions. Anyway I've seen you act. I saw you in *Private Lives* when it came to Hampstead."

"And what did you think of my Amanda?"

There was a long silence. Then he said, "Do you want the truth? Or are you looking for flattery?"

"Actually I'm looking for a job. So you'd better tell me the truth."

## SCREEN KISSES • 7

He leaned forward across the desk, his eyes holding hers, and despite herself she was mesmerized.

"Okay, you asked for it," he said. "Your problem, Rachel Keller, is you're a selfish actress. You're good, I'm not saying you aren't. But without proper direction you hog the whole of the stage for yourself. The moment you make an entrance, any entrance, none of the other actors stand a chance."

She was furious. Coldly furious. "I think," she said, "the problem lies with the other actors."

"Not in any play I'm directing."

"Meaning . . . ?"

"That if you want me to direct you, and I suspect at this stage in your career you do, then you'd better listen to what I'm going to say. Because it concerns your behaviour.

"When you play Laura Cheveley for me then you'll play her my way. I don't want to see any little bits of business that take the attention from the rest of the cast. There will be no upstaging. No masking. And no missing of cues. Do I make myself understood?"

"Perfectly," she said, standing up. She put her hand out and took her résumé off his desk.

"You won't be needing this any more," she said. "I won't be working for you."

He tipped his chair back against the windowsill and put his feet on the desk. "Why the sudden change of mind?"

"Because I don't take orders from autocrats. You might be able to frighten the likes of Richard Roberts, but you don't impress me."

## 8 • TRUDI PACTER

She stood up, grabbed hold of her heavy leather bag and turned on her heel. "I'd rather be on the dole than work for a bastard like you."

As she walked towards the door she heard the faint sound of applause.

"Wonderful," said Jeremy Powers. "If you go on reacting like that I'll turn you into a great Laura Cheveley."

She had every intention of walking through the door and out of his life. Her pride told her to leave. Her integrity told her not to look back. But in the end she was cut down by her ambition. She needed to make her reputation. She needed to play Laura Cheveley. She needed Jeremy Powers.

She turned round. "Do you mean what you just said?"

He didn't bother to take his feet from the desk. "I meant every word of it. And now that you're coming to work for me there's one more thing you should know. I don't like temperament in my actresses."

Rachel hadn't wanted to go on the stage—not in the beginning, not when she was at school. At Prestwich Comprehensive the careers adviser steered her towards a professional career. If she got her "A" levels she could study to be a doctor or a lawyer, and the prospect intrigued her.

Her parents were less enthusiastic. University? University for Rachel? They recoiled from the prospect. Four extra years of study meant four extra years of paying her bills and watching her grow older. Four more years when she didn't have a husband. No, they

## SCREEN KISSES • 9

decided, better that she leaves school as soon as possible. She can take her "A" levels if she insists, but after that she has to meet her obligations. We can't afford to keep her for ever.

Rachel's parents were poor. Their parents before them had fled the pogroms of Eastern Europe during the 1920s and come to settle in England. They had ended up in Manchester, where the weather was cold and the living was hard. Both generations of Kellers had to struggle for survival.

The first generation, Rachel's grandparents, took it in their stride. They were born having to fight for life. Rachel's parents didn't fare so well. Rachel often thought it was a miracle her father managed to make a living at all. It was as if all the Kellers' energy had been used up breaking free from their oppressors and there was nothing left over.

Rachel's father, Joe, had a hairdressing shop in Prestwich, the suburb where they lived. He chose hairdressing because he liked women. He got on with them. If he had been any good at it, he might have made a fortune, but as it was he came close to starving. There wasn't a perm done by his hand that managed to stay in curl longer than a week, not a cut that didn't look ragged, nor a tint that didn't look false.

Other men would have given up and taken a job in a factory. There were more than enough blue-collar jobs in the industrial north. But Joe Keller wasn't a quitter. His father hadn't fled the Russians for his son to get his hands dirty and his back bowed standing by a conveyor belt. Instead he burned his hands with perm lotion and talked himself hoarse persuading the

## 10 • TRUDI PACTER

local women he could transform them into beauties. The only tool of his trade was optimism, and he used it on himself as well as his clients.

Tomorrow, he told himself and Anna, Rachel's mother, tomorrow would be better. Tomorrow his business would turn the corner. Tomorrow Rachel would meet a nice Jewish boy and get married. Tomorrow there would be one less mouth to feed.

But even Rachel, his only child, was a disappointment to him. She wasn't beautiful. She wasn't interested in the sons of his friends. And they certainly didn't want to know her. Her looks were the problem. She was too thin, all long, skinny legs and no bottom to speak of. And as for her chest—it was better he didn't think about Rachel's chest.

He had never known a woman so unwomanly. Where had he and Anna gone wrong? he asked himself. It wasn't as if they didn't feed the girl. She ate three big meals a day—boiled chicken, fish cooked in the Russian style with tart, sour sauce, red cabbage with raisins, soft, round dumplings. But everything they put into this daughter of theirs, she burned up like an incinerator. She was restless, always on the move. A hyperactive engine, hungry for food, hungry for life. Hungry.

He wished just sometimes she would calm down and come to a stop. Then maybe he could talk some sense into her. He thought about his mother, who was plump, placid, and happy to stay at home. His wife was the same. So where did Rachel get her ideas from? Her energy? Her thinness?

He decided in the end that she must be a throw-

## SCREEN KISSES • 11

back to an earlier generation. No one he could remember in his family looked like her, and certainly no one had her red hair. That was the main bone of contention between him and his daughter—her wild mass of carroty hair. He was always on at her to tie it back or smooth it down. He even offered to cut it for her but she wouldn't hear of it. Her hair, like her flat chest and her thin arms, was something she guarded, and refused to change. When he or her mother discussed Rachel's appearance with her the conversation always ended up with a family row.

"Why are you always trying to change me?" Rachel would protest. "What's wrong with me? Aren't I good enough for you the way I am?"

She wasn't, and she knew it. It troubled her, for she knew one day she would have to make a decision. Either she changed herself to fit her surroundings, or she had to change her surroundings.

When she was eighteen the decision was taken out of her hands. Her father offered to do her hair.

The offer came on her birthday dressed up as a present and Rachel didn't have the heart to turn him down. She knew Joe couldn't afford to buy her a present and, unlike some of her schoolfriends' fathers, he didn't have the skill to make her something. All he could do was style her hair.

So Rachel accepted his offer with one provision—that he wouldn't alter her appearance. She didn't want a perm, a tint or a cut. She didn't want her father to do anything she couldn't put back into place afterwards. Reluctantly he agreed.

She arranged to visit her father's salon on the

## 12 • TRUDI PACTER

Monday after her birthday. It was a quiet day. There were so few customers at the beginning of the week that Joe often took Mondays off. At least, Rachel thought, she was guaranteed privacy. If her father made her look a mess the rest of the world wouldn't see it. Not on a Monday.

She called into the salon on her way home after school. As she had anticipated it was completely empty. There was an air of neglect, of giving up. The round-backed leatherette chairs were shabbier than she remembered, and some of them had stuffing leaking out underneath. The mirror that ran the length of the shop was smeary and spotted with lacquer. She stroked her hair possessively as she waited for her father to come out.

This is mine, she thought, running her hands through the thick, red curls. This is my pride, my glory. I don't want anybody to touch it, least of all my father. But she knew she had no choice. And when Joe appeared from the back of the shop carrying a pair of scissors, there was no going back.

He pointed at a chair in the middle of the row. "Take that one," he said. "We've got the place to ourselves, we might as well use the space."

Warily, Rachel sat down with her back to the long mirror, and felt afraid. There was something about her father, the way he stood, the scissors in his hand. There was something not quite right about the whole situation.

"What are you planning to do?" she asked, looking at the scissors. "I don't want it any shorter."

## SCREEN KISSES • 13

"Calm down, darling, I'm not going to make it any shorter. Trust me."

She was unconvinced. "Then what are you doing with those scissors?"

He looked at the scissors then he looked at his daughter and smiled. It was a professional smile, the sort he gave to the local women when he was trying to convince them he could make them beautiful.

"These scissors," he told her, "are not what you think. They may look as if they could cut your hair off, but they do no such thing."

"Then what do they do? Tell me." Now she started to worry in earnest. She had washed her hair that morning, and in the mirror she could see it shining and gleaming under the strip lighting. She had never loved it more.

She was seized by the temptation to get out of the chair and make a run for it. But Joe caught the alarm in his daughter's eyes and handed her the scissors. "Don't be frightened," he said. "They're harmless. They don't do anything."

Close up they didn't look like scissors at all. They were more like two steel combs fastened together. They had long steel teeth, each one ending in a serrated edge. Rachel stared at them with curiosity. "How do they work?" she asked.

"They're thinning scissors," said her father. "They pass through your hair, taking out the bulk that makes it look like a bush. I'm going to thin your hair, the way I would thin a rose bush. At the end it will be sleeker and much healthier, I promise you."

Before Rachel could say anything, Joe took the

## 14 • TRUDI PACTER

scissors out of her hand and pushed them deep into the mass of her hair. He snipped away. Twice, three times, four times. Then he took the scissors away. "Shake your head," he commanded.

Rachel did as she was told. Nothing happened. Then she ran her fingers through her hair. Handfuls of red curls came away in her grasp.

Horrified she turned to her father.

"What have you done to me?" she demanded. "You said you weren't going to cut it."

Joe took Rachel by the shoulders and swung her round in the chair until she faced the mirror. "Look at yourself," he said. "Does it look as if I've cut your hair?"

Fearfully she raised her eyes. Then she stared in surprise, for she looked exactly the same as she had before her father had gone to work with his scissors. Her hair still came down to her elbows. It still curled and bounced. Experimentally she shook her head, and as she did her hair moved with it in a shining red curtain. Her shining red curtain.

She swung her chair round away from the mirror so she faced her father. "You didn't do anything," she said, astounded. "How could you snip snip away and do nothing at all?"

Her father smiled his hairdresser's smile.

"Trade secrets," he said.

She laughed, relieved. "I won't ask what they are," she said. Then she added, "Can I go home now?"

"Of course you can, darling. Just give me a cou-

## SCREEN KISSES • 15

ple of minutes to tidy up what I've done. Then it's all over."

He walked behind her, obscuring even her back view from the long, neon-lit mirror. Then he brushed her hair back behind her ears and started to snip slowly and methodically.

Rachel stared into space and wondered what her mother was making for supper. She remembered there was a chicken in the fridge. Maybe she boiled it up today, thought Rachel. Her mouth watered at the prospect. She loved the way her mother did chicken in the pot with carrots and onions and great juicy dumplings.

Her father brought her back to the present. "I've finished," he said. "Let me turn you round so you can take a look at yourself."

Once more Rachel saw herself in the mirror. But the girl who stared back wasn't her at all. She couldn't be. She had hardly any hair to speak of. Slowly, almost in a trance, she lifted her hands to her head. The hair she touched was short and springy, like a lawn that had just been mowed.

She got up from the chair and walked towards the mirror to take a closer inspection. She knew she had a thin face but without her hair it had a pinched quality she hadn't seen before. She turned to the side, then she turned her back to the mirror and looked over her shoulder. Now it was short and thinned out, she noticed with surprise, her hair didn't curl at all. Instead it sat obediently on her head in a wispy Eton crop.

Joe Keller regarded his only daughter carefully. "Do you like it?" he asked.

## 16 • TRUDI PACTER

Rachel ignored the question. "How did you do it?" she asked. "You said you were using the thinning scissors."

"Okay, so I had to lie a little. I changed over half way through. If you knew what I was doing you might have stopped me."

"Stopped you?" she screamed. "Of course I would have stopped you. You, you butcher."

Before he knew what she was doing, Rachel grabbed the scissors he had left lying on the counter and threw them half way across the salon. Then she took hold of a can of hair lacquer and hurled it at the mirror. The glass splintered and cracked, reflecting thousands of tiny images of her, shorn and ragged.

Joe felt like shaking her, but pity stopped him. "I'm sorry," he said haltingly. "I didn't know it meant so much."

She stared at him in disbelief.

"Look at me," she demanded. "I'm skinny. I'm plain. I've always known that. It was only my hair that saved me and made me special. Now you've taken it away I look like everyone else in this godforsaken place."

She turned away from him and walked to the battered Morris Minor waiting outside. And for the whole of the drive home neither of them spoke a word. As they walked through the front door Rachel put her hands up over her head in an attempt to cover her hair.

"So you finally got rid of that mop," said her mother. "About time. Now at least you look normal."

But Rachel wasn't listening. She ran up to her

## SCREEN KISSES • 17

room and reappeared ten minutes later with a scarf draped peasant-style around her head. For the next few days she appeared in a variety of scarves, all artistically arranged. Sometimes she was a peasant, sometimes a gypsy. She even attempted an Indian turban.

Her father was not amused. "You look as if you're off to a fancy-dress party," he protested. "How long is this going on for?"

She didn't answer him. Instead she went out and bought a felt sombrero which she wore to school. There was no way she was going to let anyone see her new haircut.

In the weeks that followed Rachel refused to discuss what had happened in her father's salon. Her mother and her friends at school all tried to pump her about it and they all got nowhere. As far as she was concerned the subject was closed. It was as if she had taken a magic marker and erased the episode from her life.

One day Rachel's mother went into her room when she was out at school. Over her dressing-table mirror Rachel had draped a towel. Dear God, thought Anna, not only does she want to hide from the world, she wants to hide from herself. If I don't do something about this soon, the girl's going to make herself ill.

She thought of sending Rachel away. But where to? A spa? A tour of Europe? They didn't have that kind of money. In the end she consulted her brother, Albert, an influential accountant living in London—the only successful member of her family. He came up with a plan. One of his responsibilities was the Central School of Speech and Drama, where he sat on the

## 18 • TRUDI PACTER

board. Its chief function was to turn awkward young men and women into actors by teaching them walking, talking, charm . . .

"That's what Rachel needs," said Anna. "She's not much to look at. But with a bit of charm, something to say for herself, she could make a man want her."

Then she learned how much the fees were. "Forget it," she said.

Anna didn't think about the Central School until two months later when her mother died, leaving a small legacy. Normally the money would have gone into the shop. Now she could see a better use for it.

"But it's a waste," said Joe. "How do we know anything will come of it?"

"We don't," said Anna. "But do you have any better ideas? If you refuse to send her, she'll go on moping around the house and we'll never get her off our hands. Consider this an investment in the future."

Joe handed his wife's money over. But it didn't make him happy. The Kellers didn't have money to spend. They didn't have money to burn. And they certainly didn't have money to invest.

It wasn't that Rachel didn't like the Central School, or London. She loved them both. The problem lay with the acting lessons.

She hated reading plays, with their endless stage directions and footnotes, but that was only the beginning. She soon discovered that even the footnotes had footnotes. Everything she read had a hidden meaning. A simple request such as, "Take me to your leader"

## SCREEN KISSES • 19

was explored and taken apart. Why did the character want to go? Who was the leader? How did the character feel about the leader?

At the end of the first few weeks her head was reeling. She had never imagined people were so complex. It made her feel uncomfortable. If the man in the street was a mass of fears, phobias and hidden motivations, what did that make her? It wasn't something she wanted to think about. Yet she was compelled to. Every day there was another class forcing her to focus on some aspect of herself. There were voice lessons that made her feel inadequate because of her flat, northern accent, movement classes that made her conscious of her skinny legs, and mime sessions that simply made her feel a fool.

Rachel had come to London to get away from her family and make a fresh start. She had no intention of spending her time contemplating her navel.

Her uncle, Albert Finer, had taken responsibility for her and she was given the spare room in his comfortable semi in Wembley. While she was there she was expected to share her time with her well-built, slow-moving uncle, his two teenage sons, who were exact replicas of him, and her aunt, who was a quiet-spoken version of her mother. She saw very little of them. They all blamed it on the way she looked.

In Manchester she was too thin, her skin too pale, her hair too bright. In London in the mid-sixties thin was the only shape to be. And red hair was considered an asset.

Tentatively she started to leave her scarf off. And when she plucked up courage to examine herself in the mirror she saw with a rush of gratitude that her curls were growing back.

All the girls that year were wearing tight blue jeans or tiny mini skirts. When she could afford it out of her allowance, Rachel went down to the King's Road and bought herself the same. It was as if she had been reborn. Her classmates started to notice her and suddenly she had a party to go to every night.

In the old, dark days in Prestwich Rachel had hated parties. She was always the odd girl out, the wallflower. She would hang back in the dark and hope no one noticed her. Now she came out into the light and found she was in demand. There was a queue of boys who wanted to dance with her, and it went to her head.

She lost her virginity to a third-year student six months after she had arrived in London, and for two whole months she believed herself to be in love. Until the next boy. And the one after that.

By the time she moved into her second year at the Central School she had become an *habituée* of the Picasso and the Ad Lib club. She was already cutting too many classes for her tutor's peace of mind. Then she met Nigel Rogers and everything changed.

She ran into Nigel late one night at the Ad Lib. He had somehow become part of the group of people she was with. She found herself drawn to him. He was handsome in a blond, languid sort of way but that wasn't what fascinated her. It was his attitude. Where her contemporaries were pushy and loud, Nigel was cool, almost self-contained. He didn't seem to give a damn about impressing anyone. Even her. She de-

## SCREEN KISSES • 21

cided to find out why. By the end of the evening she had her answer. Nobody impressed Nigel simply because nobody could.

He was the youngest son of an earl. All his life he had been surrounded by money and luxury and people doffing their caps. From an early age people he didn't know very well called him sir and gave him his way. It didn't make him precocious. For he didn't need to prove he was superior. He knew he was.

Rachel and Nigel were total opposites. He had nothing to prove, nothing to defend. She had everything. The attraction was instant. From the moment they saw each other in the Ad Lib, they never left each other alone. She met him every night after classes and they would go dancing or to the cinema, or to his flat in Eaton Square.

She started to learn about a different kind of life. The people Nigel knew moved gracefully and spoke well. They played rugby rather than football, and polo rather than golf. Whatever they were doing, be it jiving in a disco or shooting on their father's estate, they never looked out of place.

At the beginning of her relationship with Nigel, Rachel felt like the ugly duckling she had been when she came down from Manchester. She was pretty, she knew how to handle herself, but the crowd she was moving with now demanded higher standards. Once more she had to learn to fit in. And she learned from the only source available to her. The Central School. Her elocution teacher was astounded when she saw Rachel paying attention. Not just paying attention but staying late after class to work on her vowels. The

## 22 • TRUDI PACTER

movement teacher got another surprise when he found Rachel applying herself. And the mime class couldn't believe its eyes.

After two years at drama school Rachel could have got a job anywhere as a model. She was poised. She was elegant. She had style. Nobody in a million years could have imagined her parents were second-generation Jewish immigrants who lived in Manchester.

There was only one problem. She showed no signs of learning how to act. Whether she read Lady Macbeth or Irma La Douce, she always gave the same performance. Technically there was nothing wrong with it. Her timing was spot on. She pitched her voice well. But when her tutors looked into her eyes they met with a blank stare.

"Try to show emotion," they urged her. "If you give us just one true feeling then we have something to build on."

Obediently she reached inside herself. And found nothing. Somewhere along the way she had lost touch with her feelings. She had groomed herself and schooled herself into the woman she thought people wanted, but in the process she had lost a vital spark. And try as she might she couldn't recover it.

The head of the school discussed Rachel with her uncle. "If your niece doesn't shape up and become an actress," he said, "we have no alternative but to get rid of her. There are hundreds of applicants queueing up to get on to our course. Her place is needed for somebody who really wants to act."

When her uncle told her about his meeting with

## SCREEN KISSES • 23

the head of college Rachel was terrified. Leaving Central School meant going back to Manchester and her parents. Before the prospect hadn't daunted her. She knew her stay in London was only temporary. But now she had found Nigel and Ascot and the Ad Lib club the idea of returning to her roots was unthinkable. She'd have to learn to act. It was her only salvation.

She tried everything: relaxation classes, method acting, the French technique. They all failed her. Finally her tutor gave her one last chance. She would put her through the emotion memory test. If she got something from her, just a spark or a glimmer of true feeling, there would be a reprieve.

They put her on a couch in the middle of the classroom. Around her in a semi-circle sat the other students and beside her sat her tutor, a tall, grey-haired woman who had once been an actress on the West End stage.

"I want you to tell me," she said softly, "about the greatest trauma that ever happened to you. Something so shocking and so private that even now it lives inside you."

"Why should I do that?" asked Rachel.

"Because you want to be an actress," her teacher replied.

Rachel was tempted to tell her to go to hell. Then she thought about her uncle and the warning he had given her. She took a deep breath. "I'll tell you about a bad experience," she said. "The first time I had my hair cut."

Someone at the back of the class sniggered. The

teacher looked patient. If Rachel was playing another one of her games she'd make the session short. There wasn't all day to waste on students who wouldn't apply themselves. She looked at Rachel lying full length on the sofa, her red hair draped around her shoulders. With those looks, she thought, the girl would make a great dramatic actress. What a pity she didn't have it in her. What a waste.

With an effort she concentrated on the task ahead of her. "Tell me what happened when your hair was cut," she instructed. "Bring it all back."

So Rachel started to talk about the afternoon she spent in her father's hairdressing salon after school. In a monotone she described how she had walked into the small, neon-lit room with the long mirror and the round-backed leatherette chairs.

As she talked she went back in time. A year back in time to the Manchester of her childhood. Her own private nightmare.

"What were you wearing?" asked the teacher, prompting her now.

"My school uniform. Is it important?"

"It's all important. Your shoes, the light on your hair, the angle of the scissors in your father's hand. Don't keep anything back. I want to hear it all."

It was like going into a trance. She forgot the rest of the class sitting around her. She forgot the teacher close by her left shoulder. All she could see was the row of round-backed chairs and herself sitting in the middle of them. It was like watching a film in slow motion. There was her father with the thinning shears in his hands. He was turning the chair round now. Swiv-

## SCREEN KISSES • 25

elling it so her back was to the mirror and she couldn't see herself. Couldn't see what he was doing to her.

She felt the scissors go through her hair, cutting into its thickness; and one by one she saw her curls falling to the floor. They fell like feathers, drifting, fluttering, finally blowing away from the chair. She was reminded of her mother plucking a chicken for Friday night dinner. Her father's movements had the same briskness, the same cold-hearted brutality a human being uses when stripping an animal of its coat.

That's how she felt—like an animal. A chicken being prepared for the pot. She felt the bile rise within her. And with it came anger. "Give it back to me," she shouted. "Give me back my hair. Can't you see I'll be cold without it? Can't you see I'll perish?"

She sat bolt upright. Her eyes were burning and her skin was the colour of ash. "Daddy," she said, "Daddy, how could you do it to me?"

There was a silence in the classroom. Then the teacher started to smile. "So," she said softly, "you really do have emotions hidden in there. Maybe we'll make an actress out of you after all."

Once she found she could emote, she did so all over the School. She played every part in *Julius Caesar*—Mark Antony, Calpurnia, Brutus, Portia, even Caesar himself. She caught up with Shaw, Ibsen, Shakespeare and all the other playwrights she had neglected. As she read each play she brought out all her new emotions and tried them on for size.

Nigel found this very boring. "When are you

## 26 • TRUDI PACTER

going to pack in this acting lark and come back to the human race?" he asked her.

"Never," she said. For she had gone past Nigel now. Before she had discovered the theatre he had satisfied her, in and out of bed. Now all that held them together was sex. When they started quarrelling even that started to pall.

He took her to the men's finals at Wimbledon and all she could think about was costume design. In nightclubs she bored everybody by talking about text and sub-text. Afterwards when he took her home they didn't fight. Because there was nothing left to fight about. Instead they made love coldly and mechanically. Afterwards he turned to her. "You weren't really there, were you?" he said sadly.

Her eyes filled with tears. "I'm sorry," she said.

She missed him when he left her. She missed his warmth and the comfort of his body. She even missed some of the parties. And she turned to the theatre for solace.

In her last year at the Central School Rachel learned her craft, and as her confidence grew so did her expertise. She rarely thought about the time when her course would end, so when her tutor started to talk about the passing-out play she woke up with a start. What the hell was she going to do with the rest of her life? she wondered.

She supposed she could get married. But the idea appalled her. She was only twenty-one. She couldn't trade in her life for the sake of security. Not yet. But what other options did she have? It was either that or go back home and live with her parents.

# SCREEN KISSES • 27

Or she could go on the stage. The alternative was so startling, so obvious, she wondered why she hadn't thought of it before. She had only one obstacle to overcome—her father. She knew he would never condone the idea; he had made that clear right from the start. Well, she reasoned, if he won't condone it, somebody will have to make him.

On the night of the passing-out play the whole family came to see her. Her parents came down from Manchester; her father's brother came in from Surbiton; and her Uncle Albert brought his two boys along from Wembley to see her. Her class was putting on *The Taming of the Shrew* and she was to play Kate. She knew that what she did with the character would decide her future, for there were important theatrical agents in the audience that night. And there was her father. He was the one who mattered. If she could impress him, if she could convince him she was good, then her way was clear.

She gave a good performance, she knew that from the way she controlled the audience. She could make them laugh, and she could make them stop laughing. She could make them hold their breath, and she could relieve their tension in an instant. She felt as if she was at the centre of the world and everything she did affected the way it moved.

It seemed to her as if the whole play passed in a matter of minutes. With the curtain came applause. Wave upon wave of approval rose up from the audience and broke over her. She was in her element.

Her Uncle Albert was the first one to come back-

## 28 • TRUDI PACTER

stage to see her. He found her still in her make-up, weeping into a pile of tissues.

He put his arms round her. "What's the matter?" he asked. "You were wonderful just now."

"I know I was wonderful," she sobbed.

He smoothed her hair. "So what's all this about?"

She dried her eyes and looked at her uncle. "It's about my father," she said. "You know he doesn't want me to go on the stage. He put me through all this to get me married off."

The large, pudgy man smiled. "Do you have anyone in mind?"

"Once," she said, "but he went away. Now all I want to do is what you saw me doing tonight."

Albert Finer straightened up and headed towards the door. "Stay where you are," he instructed. "I'll try and talk some sense into your old man."

What makes me do it? Rachel wondered as the train pulled out of Euston. It was a question she asked herself at the beginning of every tour. As always it was prompted by the prospect of where she would be staying. Birmingham, where she was heading, was her least favourite stop. The Millgate Hotel, she groaned inwardly. Coin-in-the-slot fires and lumpy porridge. She considered her cosy London flat. I must be mad, she thought.

But there was another voice inside her that said nothing of the sort, and as the train gathered momentum this was the voice she listened to. "I'm going on tour. I'm going on tour," said the voice. "This tour will be the turning point of my life."

She thought about the other tours, the other turning points in the last six years. There were Manchester and Sheffield, Newcastle and Birmingham. They had all had digs with coin-in-the-slot fires. They all led nowhere.

But the voice clamoured to be heard over her doubts. "This time it will be different," it said. "This time you're playing Laura Cheveley. The glorious bitch. The make-or-break part."

What about last time? she thought. And the time before that? What was wrong with my Portia, my Kate or my Miss Julie? Why didn't I make my name with those roles?

Now the voice was cunning and coy. "Maybe you had the wrong director," it said. "Maybe the man you needed, the man you always needed, was Jeremy Powers. The one who makes stars out of his leading ladies."

She leaned back in her seat and watched the fields flash by. Make me a star, Jeremy Powers, she said to herself. This time, make me a star. Then it will all have been worth it.

As the train pulled into Birmingham Rachel picked up her bags and prepared to disembark. Once more her thoughts returned to her digs. She had played Birmingham before and had stayed at the Millgate Hotel. Another actress had recommended it—not for the gas fires and the lumpy porridge but for the landlady. In the grimy provinces a nice landlady made all the difference. And Sheila was a find. She had been acting as surrogate mother to generations of actresses for some twenty years. Bringing toast to their rooms when they were late, letting them watch her televi-

## SCREEN KISSES • 31

sion, and sharing her booze with them when the money ran out before payday.

Sheila, thought Rachel, as the taxi threaded its way through the grimy backstreets of Birmingham. Sheila with your tight, permed curls and your National Health dentures. I do hope you're still there.

She paid the cab driver in front of a red-brick terraced house in a street that boasted a betting shop and a corner grocer's. On the outside nothing had changed. She sniffed the air as she pushed her way through the door. Old cabbage and the smell of damp. Nothing had changed inside either.

As she walked through the door she noticed with disappointment that Sheila wasn't alone. Sitting on the floor, smoking a cigarette, was an angular young man. He was wearing blue jeans, and there was something about the way they fitted that seemed familiar. Suddenly she knew who he was.

"Richard Roberts," she said, "what are you doing here?"

He looked blank.

"You remember," she said. *"Spotlight.* The audition with Jeremy Powers. When we met you were having a good old moan about what a bastard he'd been."

He put down his cigarette. "Of course," he said, "you're the sexy redhead who wanted to be Laura Cheveley. Did you get it?"

She nodded. "And you?"

He laughed. "Let's put it this way. I got employed, but not playing the part I wanted."

"Don't tell me," she said. "You got landed with the old fart."

## 32 • TRUDI PACTER

They looked at each other and at that moment the bonds between them went deeper than lust or love or even mutual attraction. They were two survivors in a profession where pride took second place to employment. If Richard had been playing the understudy or playing the lead she wouldn't have regarded him any differently. He was a working actor. In the end that was all that counted.

Richard looked at his watch. It was six o'clock. Then he looked at his landlady and at Rachel.

"Come on," he said. "The Fox and Grapes has been open for half an hour already. Time for a drink."

He saw Sheila looking dubious.

"Don't worry, it's on me. To celebrate the beginning of the tour."

The older woman smiled. She and Richard had played this game before when he was last there, and she wasn't having any. If Richard wanted to buy her a drink he could bring her back a bottle from the off-licence. She wasn't going to tag along like a gooseberry while he chatted up Rachel. She gave him an old-fashioned look. "You two go on ahead of me," she said. "I've got work to do here."

They sat awkwardly holding on to their tea cups after Sheila left the room. It was Richard who spoke first. "I'm not making a pass," he said, "but I'm desperate for a beer and I hate drinking alone."

His hair was blonder than she remembered it. And she decided she liked the way he wore his jeans. "Give me a couple of minutes to unpack," she said, "then I'll be ready."

The saloon bar of the Fox and Grapes was already

## SCREEN KISSES • 33

packed when they arrived. Factory workers free from the day's shift were there in their blue jeans drinking hand-pumped beer. Workmen from the printing plant over the road were standing in groups still wearing their grimy, ink-stained overalls. In one corner a local group was tuning up. Rachel looked at her watch. It was nearly seven. In an hour's time, she thought, the singer should arrive. She knew it would probably be one of the girls who worked in the local shopping centre. She'd be singing songs from the war years, or earlier even. And she'd be a little nervous and probably off-key. And round about ten o'clock the rest of the pub would join in and drown her out.

I shouldn't love it, thought Rachel. It's dingy, it's clapped out and you smoke a packet of cigarettes every time you draw breath. Yet there was something about the pub that always reminded her of good times. Birmingham had been her first rep. Her first chance to stand on a real stage in front of a real audience. The people who came to see her were the sort of people she saw tonight—bank managers and clerks. It didn't diminish the quality of their applause. Every night after the theatre she used to come to the pub to drink with them and listen to how the show had gone that night.

When they received her well, she loved them. And when they didn't, she blamed the play, the director or the costume designer. Occasionally she blamed herself, but only occasionally. She knew she was young and had a lot to learn, but she also knew she was good.

They had managed to squeeze themselves into a

corner by the bar and Richard asked her what she wanted to drink. She asked for a small brandy and a bottle of Babycham, and laughed when she saw his expression.

"Don't look so shocked," she said. "I know it's a tart's drink. But I also happen to know that the beer around here tastes like piss. So I have this instead and fantasize it's a champagne cocktail. It's probably the closest I'll ever get to one."

Now it was his turn to laugh. But there was no amusement in the sound. "I wonder if my father said that when he started out in the profession."

She looked at him with curiosity. "Why, who is your father?"

"Edmund Roberts. You probably caught his Richard III at the Old Vic when you were in drama school." Now he had her full attention.

"That Edmund Roberts. I'd no idea."

Into her mind came the image of a tall, commanding man with a shock of white hair and a drinker's paunch. But it wasn't his appearance she remembered so much as his voice. It was strong, full and perfectly pitched, and Edmund Roberts was in total command of it. He could make you cry with that voice then the next minute reduce you to helpless giggles. She had worshipped him while she was at drama school. They all had. And despite rumours of his difficult temperament and his drinking he had never gone down in her estimation. Men like Edmund Roberts were allowed their indiscretions. Their genius gave them that right.

She looked at the tall, lean-hipped man standing beside her and tried in vain to find something of Ed-

## SCREEN KISSES • 35

mund Roberts in him, but there was nothing. Richard was better looking than his father but he didn't have his presence. His voice was a good voice, an actor's voice. But that was all. Edmund Roberts could bring the room to a standstill with one command. His son was merely charming.

For a moment she felt disloyal. Who am I to judge him? she asked herself. I haven't even heard him read. Yet in her heart she knew she didn't have to. The son was not the father.

Richard's voice broke through her thoughts.

"How do you stick it?" he asked her.

She shook her head in confusion. "Stick what?"

"This," he gestured round the pub. "Horrible dives where you drink brandy and Babycham. Draughty theatres. Living out of a suitcase."

She laughed. "It's the first thing I think about when I start a tour. Then I think about the part I'm going to play, and the company, and the theatre. And all the bad things seem to fade into the background. I suppose I must love it."

"That's because it's still all new to you. You should hear my father bellyaching about the conditions he has to work in. It could put you off the provinces for life."

She finished her drink and signalled the bartender for another round. "Then why do you live like this?" she asked. "With your looks and family connections you could get yourself a spot in some comfortable telly sitcom and put your feet up for life."

He looked pained. "What, and prove my father right? He always maintained I'd never stay the course.

In fact he wasn't that keen on my being an actor in the first place. He didn't think I had it in me, so I had to prove him wrong."

"And do you think you will?"

"One day. Maybe. We'll see . . ." Abruptly he changed the subject and started chatting about the other members of the cast and their director, Jeremy Powers. It was as if a screen had come down in front of his eyes blocking out his emotion, his ability to feel.

She had known Richard Roberts only a brief time, but already Rachel felt she had somehow got too close to him. She wondered about the other women who had got close. Had they been shut out after a certain moment? Or had they finally reached him?

She looked at him across the smoke of the saloon bar. His hair was very bright in the half light, and for the first time she noticed his eyes were green, like a cat's.

They were standing very close to each other. So close they were almost touching. He returned the look she gave him. And she drew her breath in. He hadn't said anything. Neither of them had. But she knew that if she wasn't very careful she could find herself sharing this man's bed.

The next morning she hated the face she saw in the bathroom mirror. Red eyes, pallid skin, puffy jowls. I'll never drink again, she swore. Then she giggled and looked quite different.

She turned on the shower and thought about the evening she had spent with Richard Roberts. He had taken her to an Indian restaurant and when they had

## SCREEN KISSES • 37

returned to their digs he hadn't laid a finger on her. Clever bastard, she thought. Waiting for me to make the first move. Well, he can wait a while longer. There's Jeremy Powers to deal with before I can plan my social life.

She stood under the tepid stream of water and tried to concentrate on the read through ahead of her. She had done *An Ideal Husband* at drama school and even then she had wanted to play Mrs Cheveley. She was such a schemer, such a perfect bitch. Only Oscar Wilde could have created a woman who would use blackmail to bring down a cabinet minister. And not give a damn about the consequences.

She thought about the performance she was going to give. Then she thought about the rest of the cast and how they would read their parts that morning. A small shiver went through her.

Judgement day, she thought mournfully. Judgement day in the Green Room. God, how I hate it.

She arrived in the actors' recreation room at the back of the theatre ten minutes late. The coffee machine was already half empty, and the cast and stage management were standing around in nervous little clusters. Nobody knew each other yet and they were eyeing each other suspiciously, like gladiators before a fight. She looked round the room for Richard and found him in one corner deep in conversation with Powers. Better leave well alone, she decided, helping herself to the remains of the coffee. Then she took her place on one of the battered sofas grouped around the room and sized up the competition.

There were two silly-looking girls who appeared

## 38 • TRUDI PACTER

to have just come out of drama school. She noticed they were sitting together, so they had probably been in the same year. Out of the corner of her eye she registered a tall, handsome man whom she immediately recognized. Charles Alcott, the star of a popular TV soap. So that's our leading man, she thought. I wonder if he's any good.

Her inspection was interrupted by their director. Jeremy Powers in jeans and a crumpled suede jacket got to his feet and signalled for them to start. "Take it in your own time," he said. "Don't push it. Nobody's trying to prove anything."

That's what you think, she said under her breath. He had put her on her mettle at the audition when he accused her of temperament. Now she was going to show him she was better than he thought.

She read the first few pages lightly, holding herself in reserve for the big scenes. As she did so she listened to the others. The girls were better than she thought. Alcott was worse. And Richard was a revelation. His stage voice was better than his speaking voice. She could detect echoes of his father in the delivery and timing. But it was a forced performance. He was trying too hard and the notes he hit were phoney ones. She sighed. Nerves, she thought. Hope it doesn't happen to me.

They were coming to the middle of the second act, Mrs Cheveley's first big speech. Rachel tensed herself and pitched in.

At the end of act two there was a silence. She saw admiration on the faces of the others and it felt better

## SCREEN KISSES • 39

than applause. She turned and looked at Jeremy Powers.

"I see you've worked on your part already," he said.

She nodded. "I thought it would help."

"Well, it didn't." There was a sting in the words.

"Why?"

"Because you're going too fast. I wanted you to feel your way into this part. Try it on for size. Experiment with it. What I'm getting from you now is an opening-night performance. And it's not what I want."

She was rattled. She couldn't be any better than she had been just now. She knew that. Yet this man was telling her she was wrong. For the first time in six years she started to doubt herself.

Hands trembling, she fumbled for a cigarette. Before she could light it Powers had done it for her. Then he turned her away from the rest of the room and said quietly, "Look, I don't want to go on with this now. We both need to talk about what you've been doing if it's going to work at all."

"What do you want me to do?"

He paused, thinking, then he said, "Stay behind at the end of this, will you? We'll sort it out then."

She played the third act in a monotone. She'd been made a fool of once that day. There was no way she was going to risk a repeat performance.

When they finally reached the end of the third act the others trooped off to the pub and Rachel was left alone with Jeremy—the man who would decide her future. The director must have sensed her mood,

## 40 • TRUDI PACTER

for instead of making her sit down he asked her if she was hungry.

"Why?" she asked.

"Because it's one o'clock. And if you don't have any other plans I thought we could thrash this thing out over lunch."

She started to feel better. When she found Jeremy was taking her to the Grand some of her confidence started to return. It was easily the smartest hotel in town, with the best restaurant. If he's going to all this trouble, she thought, he can't think I'm a lost cause.

The Grand was a skyscraper building that put her in mind of the Hilton. The carpet in the lobby had the same flashy mixture of primary colours. Modern paintings decorated the walls, and the lifts were fronted in shiny, new-looking chrome. She knew the local captains of industry used the restaurant to talk over their business deals, and when she got to the large, round room on the twenty-fifth floor, she realized why. The place was made for someone with an expense account. A very large expense account.

The menu was full of lobster and chargrilled steak and the wine list was a yard long. She handed the menu in its leather binding to her companion. "Choose for me," she said. "I don't want to be responsible for eating the budget for the next three weeks."

He smiled, and without consulting the list ordered asparagus and butter sauce, followed by grilled steak. "They bring a selection of vegetables," he told her, "unless you wanted a salad."

He didn't wait for her reply. She got the impres-

## SCREEN KISSES • 41

sion that for the thickset man sitting opposite her food was an incidental. He'd been busy playing the gracious host to help her relax. Now that was over he wanted to get down to business.

He asked her about the wicked lady she was playing and seemed genuinely interested in what she had to say. She had given a lot of thought to character and motivation and now she played it all back for the benefit of Jeremy Powers.

When she had finished he smiled and patted her hand. "Fascinating," he said. "I don't see Laura Cheveley that way at all."

She had just speared a piece of steak with her fork. And now she paused, holding it in mid air.

"How do you see her?" she asked.

"You'll find out as we go into rehearsals. Correction: we'll find out together. I don't go in for all this arty-farty business of dissecting the character. It's intellectual but it's cold. I want you to *be* Laura Cheveley. I don't want you to put her on the analyst's couch."

She was panic-stricken. "But I don't work that way. I can't do it. I wouldn't know how to begin."

He took a sip of his claret. "Begin by trusting me. When I first saw you in the audition room I knew you were right for the part. The way you carry yourself. That extraordinary red hair of yours. Wilde could have written it for you."

"But it's not just the way I look," she said despairingly. "I have to understand the woman I'm playing. I have to get inside her. Otherwise I can't give a performance."

## 42 • TRUDI PACTER

He looked at her and smiled. "And just what did you think you were doing at the read through?"

"Trying to put you in your place," she said angrily. "I wanted to convince you that I was an actress. Not some kind of selfish amateur."

Now he laughed out loud. "I'm convinced. With that terrible temper of yours, you'll end up playing Laura Cheveley. You won't be able to stop yourself."

"I don't understand."

He tried to look patient. "Rachel, I chose you not because of what you've already done but because of what I think you can do. I believe you have a talent, otherwise we wouldn't be sitting here. But nobody's done anything with it. Not even you.

"Look, I don't want to put you down but you have to know the truth about yourself. You're perfectly adequate on stage. At times you're better than that. But you give what I call a drama school performance. Most provincial actors do, which is why they stay in the provinces. I think you can do better than that. And whether you like it or not, I'm going to make you do better than that."

She pushed her plate away, the food barely touched. "What do you mean, whether I like it or not?"

"Exactly what I say. I don't expect you to love creating this part. Not all the time anyway. There will be nights when you don't sleep. There will be times when you want to strangle me. But we'll get there in the end. You can depend on that."

She looked at him with mounting distrust and the lines from an old Hollywood movie ran through her

## SCREEN KISSES • 43

head. "Hold on to your seats, folks . . . we're in for a bumpy ride."

She got back to her digs at around eight. After Rachel left the Grand she hadn't felt like talking to anybody. The idea of moping around Birmingham on her own filled her with gloom, so she did what she always did when she was depressed. She went to the movies.

*The Way We Were* was showing at the Metropole and for two hours Rachel was Barbra Streisand, falling slowly and deliciously in love with Robert Redford. She left the Metropole at six and went straight round the corner to the Odeon, where she saw Mia Farrow in *The Great Gatsby.*

When Rachel emerged at ten to eight, she looked into her purse and totted up the cost of the afternoon. She had spent two pounds fifty on four hours of escape. She smiled; it was cheap at the price. I was going to walk out of the play when I left the Grand, she thought. And I was going to tell Jeremy Powers exactly what he could do with his part. Now I'll bide my time.

She decided to go to the pub. There was bound to be somebody from the theatre down there. However, she was disappointed. None of the actors was in either of the bars. Even the stage management had decided to drink elsewhere.

She went into the saloon bar and ordered herself a brandy and Babycham. Somebody would turn up sooner or later. By ten she had consumed two brandies, two Babychams and an entire pack of cigarettes. It was time to call it a day.

## 44 • TRUDI PACTER

I'll make myself some tea, she thought as she got back to her digs, and I'll watch the box. There were worse ways of ending an evening, though for the life of her she couldn't think of any.

The living room looked empty. Then she saw him sitting in a corner. Tall and thin, with a mop of bright blond hair and a permanently sulky expression.

"Richard," she said, "what are you doing here?"

"Waiting for you . . . what does it look like?"

She did a double take. "What on earth for? We didn't have a date or anything, did we?"

He stopped looking sulky. "No, we didn't. But the rest of the crew decided to take off for some fabled steak house out in the country. And I decided to hang on and wait for you."

She threw herself down on the sofa. "So that's where everyone's gone. Have you any idea what I've been doing these last two hours?"

Now he started to grin. "Tell me."

"I've been sitting in the Fox and Grapes," she said, pulling a face.

"I might have guessed. I almost went down there to look for you."

"What stopped you?"

"There are better places to get drunk. Even in this town."

She looked at him. "So you think I want to drown my sorrows?"

He raised an eyebrow. "Don't you? It couldn't have been all that nice having Powers make a fool of you at the read through. And I bet he didn't apologize afterwards either."

## SCREEN KISSES • 45

"No, he didn't," she said with feeling. "If anything it got worse."

He sighed. "Don't say I didn't warn you. I told you the man was a bastard when we first met at the audition."

He thought for a moment, then he said, "If you don't feel like joining the others, I've got an idea that'll cheer you up. There's a rather sordid club at the back end of town where all the gamblers hang out. Last time I was here I used to go there with one of the other actors from the show. They've got an all-night licence and there's even a decent cabaret if you go at the right time."

She was intrigued. "What do you mean by a decent cabaret?"

He gave her a sideways look. "Come with me and see for yourself."

The club was called the Vagabond. They reached it through a maze of twisting back alleyways. From the outside it looked like a workman's pull-up, but once they walked through the café and up a steep flight of stairs they could have been in another world.

The place reminded Rachel of the set of an old Marlene Dietrich film, all tinsel and sequins and pink-tinged mirrors. But it was the bar that held Rachel's eyes, or rather the occupants of the bar. They were all women. And if they weren't for sale, they looked as if they were. Their dresses were shiny and tight with little straps made of rhinestones. Their hair was dyed improbable shades of blonde, and how they balanced on their spiked heels, Rachel couldn't imagine. But balance they did. Around the counter and on the precarious little stools at the back of the room. All the while they toyed with their drinks and cast anxious glances at the men sitting at the tables around the dance floor. There was an air of expectancy in the club, and Rachel noticed no one was dancing.

"What's going on?" she whispered to Richard as they pushed their way to a table.

He grinned. "The cabaret's about to start," he said. "We came just in time."

She was about to ask him more, when the lights went down and there was a roll on the drums from a recording playing behind the curtains. Somebody put on another tape, and now the room was filled with slow, sexy music with a throb in it. Cheap music.

Christ, Rachel thought. I might have known it. He's brought me to see a stripper.

At that moment the girl made her appearance. She was tall and slender and had a Slavic look to her cheekbones—her only European feature. The rest of her came from the Orient.

Her skin, Rachel noticed, was a dark honey colour. And her hair swung down to her waist in a long black curtain. She was wearing a long, simple, white gown that fitted her without being tight. In contrast to the other women in the room the girl had class, though Rachel wondered what the daylight would do to her.

The girl started to play with the long white gloves she was wearing, stroking them and pulling at the fingers. Rachel took a quick look at her companion. He was entranced. She knew he had seen the routine before but there was something about his expression that

## SCREEN KISSES • 47

told her this girl was special. Rachel shrugged and looked back at the stage. Maybe she could learn something.

The girl spent a good five minutes getting out of her gloves. Then she paraded back and forth across the tiny stage like a mannequin showing off the latest fashions. Someone backstage turned up the music and Rachel guessed the stripper was about to get down to business. She was right. In one shimmering movement the girl loosened a fastener and slid out of her dress. Then Rachel found out what all the fuss was about. Standing in front of her was the most perfect body she had ever seen.

The breasts were full and high and Rachel guessed the flimsy bra the stripper wore wasn't giving them any help. She had the longest neck and the longest back she had seen on any woman, and her waist when the eye finally reached it was ridiculously small. If she had been naked she would have looked as erotic as a sculpture. Coldly, classically beautiful. But she wasn't naked. She was wearing the kind of underwear you see in dirty magazines.

Someone had changed the tape again—this time to Ravel's *Boléro*—and every eye in the room was watching the girl. For a moment she stood perfectly still, then she started to sway her hips to the music. On anybody else it would have been a bump and a grind. But this girl had more artistry. Her body rippled and moved under the cheap underwear as if she was being touched by a thousand invisible hands. As if she was being pleasured by the audience itself.

She smiled dreamily and unfastened the hook in

the front of her bra. It fell to the ground and now her breasts were on display. She started to play with them, putting a finger in her mouth then running it around the edge of her nipples until they stood erect. Then she made her way into the audience.

Rachel had heard stories about shows like this but the setting had always been Berlin or Amsterdam. Now she was sitting in the middle of Birmingham watching a naked woman offering herself to the paying customers.

She felt Richard's hand on her arm. "Don't fret," he said. "She doesn't actually let anyone touch her. The whole thing's a big tease."

The girl changed course and started to make her way across to their table. But Rachel had had enough. "I'm off," she said, standing up. "I'll wait for you down in the café."

Then she ran through the dark, smoky club past the girls lined up against the bar until she reached the back door. It was only when she made her way down the narrow staircase that she realized Richard was behind her. "Steady on," he said. "Nobody lit a fire behind you."

But she wasn't listening. The café had filled up since they had arrived, and she pushed and shoved her way through factory workers and cab drivers until she reached the cold, clean air outside. Then she stood stock still, breathing deeply, pushing the smoke out of her lungs, waiting for the beating of her heart to slow down.

Richard was contrite. "I'm sorry it upset you," he said. "I'd no intention of doing that."

## SCREEN KISSES • 49

"It didn't upset me," she said roughly. "That's the problem."

He looked at her, not understanding.

Then she moved closer to him. "You bloody fool," she said, "it turned me on."

He didn't take her in his arms. Or even kiss her. Instead they both walked fast to the main road where they picked up a taxi. Then they headed back to their digs. There was a back entrance to the hotel and that night they used it. Her room on the first floor was the nearest. They climbed the stairs two at a time and pushed their way through the door, shaking with laughter.

"I thought you were meant to be getting me drunk tonight," she giggled.

"I know better ways of drowning your sorrows." And he led her over to the bed and started undressing her.

Other men, unable to control their hunger, had grabbed at her. With Richard there was no desperation. He knew where he was going and was in no hurry to get there. Idly Rachel wondered how many other times he had travelled the same route.

Then as he took off his jeans she stopped wondering. For he was fully erect. And big. So big that she thought there wasn't enough of her to contain him.

She expected him to enter her and she parted her legs. But he smiled and shook his head.

"Not yet," he whispered. "You have to be ready." And, stilling her protests, he began to touch her. He started with her lips, sliding his fingers round her mouth, caressing her face, then stroking her neck.

She started to feel excited. Not the urgent lust she had felt when she was watching the stripper, but a slow tingle that started deep inside her and spread to her lips, her breasts, and between her thighs. Lightly, with great skill, he touched her all over until the tingle became a giant surge of desire. She reached for his penis. Once more he held her back.

"There's more before we get to that."

He kissed her. Gently, experimentally as if she was some delicious fruit and he wanted to savour her taste. Then he ran his tongue down the length of her and parted her legs. It was the first time a man had kissed her there and she was slightly shocked that she enjoyed it so much. Then she felt herself growing tense. And she realized that he knew what she wanted. For now he was facing her and she could feel his cock pushing against her stomach.

"Now," he whispered.

He opened her. First gently, then with such force that it knocked the breath out of her. He thrust into her roughly, rhythmically, and she arched her back to receive his length. All night they pounded against each other, and when the dawn came up they finally fell asleep.

They didn't wake until lunch time. Rachel realized they had missed the first morning of rehearsals. Damn, she thought, that's no way to start. Then she looked at her lover and decided she didn't really care.

"Richard," she said, "I'm sure one day I'll pay for this. But I think I've just fallen in love with you."

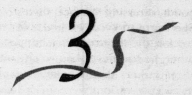

At the beginning they couldn't leave each other alone. For Rachel rehearsals passed in a kind of dream. She would go to the theatre, parrot her lines, then run back to her digs with Richard. He had moved into her room the next day. It wasn't something they talked about; there didn't seem any need. Richard simply piled all his things into the big holdall he travelled with and dumped them on her floor. A few days later Rachel hung his jeans and sweatshirts alongside her things in the tiny closet in the corner of the room.

The place really wasn't big enough for both of them but somehow they made do. In other plays with other men Rachel had held on to her privacy. But Richard wasn't like other men. She felt as if he had

## 52 • TRUDI PACTER

somehow attached himself to her, like a mistletoe or an ivy. And they fed off each other.

As she got to know him he told her how he had grown up in the theatre. Since he was old enough to remember, he had never known any other home. Edmund, his father, didn't believe in owning things. Houses and possessions were for ordinary people. He was an actor, a strolling player, a vagabond putting up wherever he could, providing it was near a theatre.

In the good days they lived in grand hotels—the Gresham in Dublin, the Savoy in London, the Algonquin in New York. Richard worshipped his father. Every night his mother would take him down to the theatre where he was playing. When he was a toddler and too young to understand the dramas they let him go backstage and dress up in the costumes.

Richard continued to worship his father until he grew up and discovered Edmund Roberts was a drunk. He should have seen it coming, he told Rachel. No sober man would have treated his wife so badly, striking out at her for the smallest provocation. No sober man would borrow large amounts of money and forget to pay it back. No sober man would have prompted such pity.

As the drinking got worse, so did the theatres. Instead of London they played Birmingham. Instead of New York and Washington there was Edinburgh and Glasgow. As "A" tours gave way to "B" tours, they stayed in cheap lodgings instead of hotels, and when Edmund got into fights the cast stopped pitying him. Instead they despised him.

Richard learned to grovel, to make excuses. As

## SCREEN KISSES • 53

he grew older he developed a talent for talking his way out of difficult situations. Protecting his father paid off. The family name got him into RADA.

When he graduated, his parents came to see him in his passing-out play.

"What did you think?" Richard asked afterwards. They had gone for a drink at the Garrick Club and Richard leaned back, expecting praise. It didn't come. Instead Edmund spoke his mind.

"You did nothing to make me ashamed," he said, "but you did nothing to make me proud either." Then, seeing his son's face, he relented. "You're a solid actor," he told him. "There'll always be work for you. But don't expect to be a leading man. It isn't in you."

When Rachel heard the story she was horrified.

"What did you say to him?" she asked. "If I had been you I would have got up and walked out."

Richard smiled. "It was tempting," he said. "I'll never forget sitting there and watching this smug old boozer telling me I was no good. And I remembered all the things I'd done for him. All the lies I told. All the fights I dragged him out of."

"So what did you do?" said Rachel.

Abruptly Richard switched off his smile. "Nothing," he said. "I'd talked my way out of too many other bad scenes to let that one throw me. If I'd lost my temper with the old man he wouldn't have talked to me for months. Years maybe. And his name was too big for me to risk it. In this profession, Rachel, you never know when somebody can come in useful. Even your father . . ."

## 54 • TRUDI PACTER

\*     \*     \*

Rachel had never loved before. All her previous affairs had been conveniently fitted around the theatre. She had always kept a part of herself in reserve until she met Richard.

With him she gave everything—her room, her secrets, and finally her heart. It improved her. The tension she always brought with her to rehearsals disappeared. She joined in with the others, helping the slow ones with their lines, laughing at her own mistakes. And she stopped kicking against Jeremy Powers. "If he wants to tell me how to play Laura Cheveley," she confided to Richard, "then let him try. The worst that can happen is that I make a fool of myself in rehearsal."

So she played the character blind the way Powers wanted her to. She stopped trying to analyse what made a bitch. Instead she worked with her feelings and her instincts. I am Laura Cheveley, she told herself in the mirror each morning. And, as she read the part, she started to become her.

For no reason, she began to paint her nails red. She discarded the jeans she normally wore to rehearsals, replacing them with skirts and clingy sweaters. Her heels got higher, her make-up heavier. Nobody noticed the change in her except Jeremy Powers, who watched and waited.

One day in the rehearsal hall it finally happened. One moment she was Rachel Keller playing the bitch. The next moment Rachel Keller disappeared entirely, and what was left was Laura Cheveley. It was as if she had stepped from one body into another, and it hap-

## SCREEN KISSES • 55

pened so effortlessly that she hardly noticed it until the end of the performance when she went back into her own skin.

It was the most exciting thing that had ever happened to her, and the most fulfilling. The rest of the cast caught her excitement and shared it with her. Only Jeremy stood apart from the rest, silent and thoughtful. Finally he walked over to her. "Let's have a cup of coffee," he said. "I want to talk to you about what just happened."

They went through into the Green Room and Jeremy found a table in the corner. "How did you do it?" he asked.

Rachel shrugged and took a sip of her coffee. "I don't know. Does it matter?"

The director smiled. "It's all that matters. Unless you know what it was you did, how can I rely on you to do it again?"

She held the mug between her hands and thought for a moment. Then she shook her head. "It's no good," she said. "I only know how I felt. Not what I did."

"That's a start. Okay, Rachel, tell me how it felt to be Laura Cheveley."

She looked away, and when she spoke again it was as if she was in a dream. "It was like me, but it wasn't me. I was much angrier, much blacker. I wanted to hurt; worse, I wanted to maim. And it didn't bother me. It was as if what I was feeling was perfectly normal."

"Have you ever felt that way before?"

She grinned. "Once, when you made me angry.

And once before, a long time ago, when I quarrelled with my father."

He nodded. "I thought so. There's a lot of anger buried inside you, Rachel. I provoked you once to see if I could make it come to the surface. Now you've found it all on your own, and you've built on it until you got the bitterness that is the core of Laura Cheveley."

She looked at him surprised. "I did that?"

"Unconsciously, yes. What I want you to do next time you play the part is to think about those emotions of yours. I want you to be aware of them growing and changing into something else."

Rachel was worried. "Will it hurt my performance?"

"A bit, in the beginning. But I'll be there to help you through that."

She remembered she had found her emotions once before, when she was at drama school. Then she had called up the memory of losing her thick, red hair. The memory of grief. Yet although she was in touch with her feelings she had never known how to use them.

Now with Jeremy to guide her, she located the furies that drove her once more. But this time she moulded them and directed them to her will. Out of her rage rose the incarnation of the perfect bitch.

Working with the director didn't teach her simply how to play Laura Cheveley. Powers showed her that she had more than just anger at her command. She had warmth and sadness, passion and a deep well

## SCREEN KISSES • 57

of pain. All of these feelings were hers to parade in front of an audience. For now she owned them.

The first-night audience in Birmingham loved her. In Leeds she took three curtain calls. In Newcastle the critics hailed the birth of a new Vanessa Redgrave.

"I think it's time we had a little talk about your future," said Jeremy Powers.

He took her to a small Italian restaurant in the expensive part of town. The walls and the floor were covered in white tiles, and green ferns sprouted from every corner. The place reminded Rachel of a greenhouse. As soon as she sat down at the table, she relaxed.

In the beginning she and Jeremy had been formal with each other, lunching in five-star restaurants, drinking in hotel bars. Now she was comfortable with him. She trusted him. And she was glad he had chosen to take her somewhere that didn't frighten her.

They both ordered pasta and Jeremy asked for a bottle of Frascati. Then he told her what was on his mind. "I've been asked to put on a West End show," he said without preamble. "I'd like you to be in it."

She was stunned and more than a little excited. "What is it?" she asked.

"*Kiss Me Kate*. The Lambton Organization want me to do a revival of the original show, without the music. And I thought of you."

Now she was nervous. "What did you think of me for?" she asked.

"What do you think?"

He couldn't, she thought. I'm too inexperienced.

## 58 • TRUDI PACTER

And I have no name at all. He must have me in mind for one of the cameos.

"You tell me," she said.

The waiter brought the white wine and Jeremy splashed it into the glasses.

"I want you for Kate," he said. "I think you'd be good."

She couldn't believe it. It was too fantastic. Too easy. "What's the catch?" she asked.

He smiled and took a sip from his glass. "Don't be cynical, Rachel. It doesn't suit you. There is no catch. Why should there be?"

"Because I'm unknown," she said quietly. "Nobody's going to queue in the West End to see me."

He leaned back in his chair. "That's not quite true," he said. *"Kiss Me Kate* is a popular show. It has nostalgia. If we hype it up enough, put on a showy production, people will want to come and see it. Star or no star."

"But why me?" she asked. "What did I do to deserve this break?"

"I thought you knew the answer to that," he said. "We're breaking box office records in every town we go to. And it's not due to my brilliant production either. You're carrying this show, Rachel. All on your own. And if you can sell out a provincial tour I don't see why you can't do the same in Shaftesbury Avenue."

The spaghetti arrived. Suddenly Rachel was ravenously hungry. Everything she had ever wanted was happening right now. She was in love. Her career was taking off. Yet there was a tiny doubt at the back of

## SCREEN KISSES • 59

her mind. Something about the situation didn't feel right. She decided to go along with what was happening to her. If there was a problem it was bound to come to the surface sooner or later.

The rest of the evening passed smoothly enough. Jeremy talked about the show and some of the people he was considering for it. After dinner he ordered two glasses of Sambuca, a sweet Italian liqueur with a coffee bean floating in it. The waiter put a match to the glasses and the alcohol and the coffee bean burned and melted together.

When the waiter had left them Jeremy turned to her and looked serious. "I want to ask you something," he said. "It's a personal question and if you don't want to answer me I'll understand."

She was curious. "What's it about?"

"Richard Roberts. How involved are you?"

The alarm bells she had heard earlier on started to sound again. What the hell was Richard to do with anything? She decided to be honest. "Richard's my boyfriend," she said. "I thought that was obvious."

He smiled and for some reason it irritated her. "There's no need to be defensive," he said. "We all have our sleeping arrangements during the run of a play."

"What I have with Richard isn't a sleeping arrangement," she snapped.

"Then what is it?"

"None of your business."

She had intended to put him in his place. To take the knowing look off his face. Instead he seemed to have hardly heard her. He signalled to the waiter for more Sambuca.

"Have you by any chance gone and fallen in love?" he asked.

"What if I have?"

There was a long pause. Then he said, "Because if that's the case you're doing the wrong thing. There is a time and a place to fall in love. And at this stage in your career it's simply not appropriate. Listen to me, Rachel, I'm not knocking love. It's a charming emotion, very life-enhancing. But it's a luxury, and like all luxuries it has to be earned."

She had been right all along. There was a catch. "Are you asking me to ditch Richard?" she asked.

"Just for the run of the play. Once you've established yourself in the West End, you can choose whichever lover you want."

"And until then?" she asked.

"Until then," he said firmly, "you do without." He paused. "Or you could let me help you."

"Look," she said patiently, "I think you're a very good director. The best I've ever worked with. You've made me think and feel in ways I never even dreamed I could. But love. What the hell do you know about it?"

"More than you could ever guess," he said softly.

Suddenly she knew where the whole conversation was leading. "So you're thinking of furthering my education in bed as well as out of it," she said.

"There's no need to be crude."

"Why not? That's what it's about, isn't it? You

## SCREEN KISSES • 61

pick me for the lead in a West End musical and I pay you back in kind."

"Not if you insist on telling the whole restaurant about it."

She realized she had been shouting, and for a moment she felt foolish. She had never made a fuss about sex before. But then no one had asked for her body as collateral before.

"I don't think you understand," she said. "I love Richard. I'm in love with him. I can't just put my feelings on hold to suit you. Or your play. Or my West End reputation. It doesn't work like that."

The waiter arrived with the liqueurs. This time Jeremy waved the flame away. He didn't feel like waiting for his drink. "Richard means a lot to you," he observed.

"Yes, he does."

Jeremy was silent for a moment. Finally he said, "He's not worth it, you know. The man's a lightweight. He's good-looking, I'll give you that. But there are plenty around like Richard Roberts. Weak, charming, ambitious. He'd sell you down the river tomorrow given half a chance. If I offered Richard the same proposition as I offered you this evening, he wouldn't think twice before grabbing it. You wouldn't hear anything about love or finer feelings from the likes of him."

"How can you be so sure?"

"Because I've been around a long time," he said. "Too long."

## 62 • TRUDI PACTER

She looked at him steadily. "You're a cold bastard," she said. "And you don't convince me."

He smiled. "I will," he said.

When she got back Richard had already gone to bed. He had left a light on in the bathroom for her, and when she went to clean her teeth she saw the message scrawled across the mirror.

"Desmond French came backstage after you left. Call him tomorrow."

Underneath he had written a London number. She drew in her breath. Desmond French—the most important agent she'd heard of—and a West End musical all in one evening. It wasn't a bad start.

Mentally she went through the contents of her wardrobe and her elation started to crumble. She owned nothing she wanted Desmond French to see her in. He was too smart, too successful, too glamorous. She could never live up to him.

She saw Richard behind her in the bathroom mirror. "I'm sorry I woke you," she said.

"I wasn't really asleep. I was too excited waiting for you to come back."

She turned round and hugged him. "Desmond French is a bit of a bolt from the blue. What did he have to say?"

"The usual. You were marvellous, lustrous, that sort of thing. I think he wants to make you into a star."

"Did he say so?"

"Of course he didn't say so. But he does want to take you out to lunch in London, so I reckon it's on the cards."

## SCREEN KISSES • 63

She looked around the tiny, cramped Newcastle hotel room where they had both been living for the past week. Her eyes took in the naked light bulb, and travelled down to the faded, chipped lino. She smiled at her lover. "I don't know if I'm quite up to the likes of Desmond French. He handles Sophia Watson and Cathryn Carlisle, not to mention dozens of movie stars. I'm just not in his league."

Richard put his arm round her and led her to bed. "Why don't you do us all a favour and let Desmond French be the judge of that? Incidentally did Jeremy have anything interesting to say tonight?"

She thought about telling him everything. The offer of *Kiss Me Kate*. And the condition he put on it. Then she thought about what he had said about Richard and changed her mind. I don't suppose it will come to anything, she thought. Better let sleeping dogs lie.

Desmond French asked her to have dinner with him, and she arranged it for her night off, so she could stay in London. They were to meet at The Ivy. Now that the moment had come, now she was standing outside the door opposite the Ambassadors Theatre, she had a moment of panic. She hadn't been anywhere near a smart restaurant since her days with Nigel. She was out of practice. Her clothes were more suited to waiting at draughty stations and sitting in front of gas fires. She couldn't even remember what was in style any more.

She came up to date the minute she walked into the big, crowded room. How silly I was to forget, she

## 64 • TRUDI PACTER

thought, looking at the women. There's only one look that's in style at this kind of place. It's called expensive. And I haven't got it.

She left her coat in the tiny cloakroom just inside the door, then she walked up to the head waiter and asked for Desmond French. He hadn't arrived yet, and the waiter asked her if she wanted to go through to the bar. Rachel looked around her. On her right at a big round table was Michael Caine and a party of people. Half way up the restaurant she saw Patrick Lichfield. The bar was chock-a-block. If I sit here, she thought with a certain desperation, I really will be on display. She didn't want that; not the way she was dressed. The shirtwaister that had seemed crisp and businesslike in her tiny London flat looked dowdy in this glamorous place. I look like a hick, she thought. A hick from the provinces on her big night out.

She let the waiter take her to the table, where she sat down and waited uncomfortably for Desmond French.

He arrived ten minutes late. As soon as he came through the door she knew who he was. His hair was jet black, except for two silver-grey wings swept behind his ears. He had a deep tan that spoke of yachts on the Riviera and swimming pools in Los Angeles. There was something theatrical about him. Even though it was warm that autumn, her companion was wearing a vicuna overcoat with an astrakhan collar and a scarlet lining. She imagined he was in his early fifties, and she wondered if he was gay. He has to be, she decided. Heterosexual men aren't that flamboyant.

He came over, introduced himself and sat down

## SCREEN KISSES • 65

without fuss. Then he ordered champagne for them both without asking her if she wanted any. She felt daunted and slightly annoyed. It might be second nature for the beautiful people to have champagne before dinner, but it wasn't second nature for her.

"You didn't even think about it, did you?" she said.

"What didn't I think about?"

"Whether or not I wanted a drink. And whether I even liked champagne."

He apologized immediately and she felt ungracious. Pull yourself together, she told herself. It's not as if you haven't been around. Remember Nigel. He lived in places like this.

The waiter came with the menus. "What do you feel like eating?" French asked.

"You choose," she said weakly. "I don't know the place."

He ordered then looked at her closely. "It's nothing to be ashamed of, you know. If I'd wanted to take a duchess out to dinner I would have invited one. But I didn't. I asked a repertory actress. A hard-working, talented repertory actress. And I'm glad I did."

Rachel started to feel better, and as she did so, the waiter arrived with the champagne. She held her glass up. "Actually I love it," she said. "I just don't get all that much of it in the sort of places where I stay."

He grinned. "I would have thought not. From what I remember, Sheila's favourite drink is port and lemon."

## 66 • TRUDI PACTER

She was surprised. "I didn't know you knew Sheila. Where on earth did you meet her?"

"Same place as you did. The Millgate Hotel. Best rep digs in Birmingham if you can stand the smell of cabbage."

He put a hand up. "Don't ask me what I was doing there. It's quicker to tell you the whole story. I spend twenty-five per cent of my time touring round the provinces looking for talent. Always have done. The kind of artistes I'm looking for don't hang around film sets or TV studios. Or if they do, they're world-class stars and well represented already."

She smiled.

"So that's what you were doing in Newcastle watching *An Ideal Husband.* You were searching for people to put on your books."

The waiter arrived with giant prawns on cracked ice. The agent leaned back as he put the plates down. "You make it sound so simple," he said. "Do you know how many possibles I find on one of my trips? Usually none at all. It can take me a year to find just one actor with a glimmer. So you can see last week was lucky for me."

She looked at him warily. "You think I have potential?" she said.

"Lots of potential. Now eat your prawns and tell me what you've been doing up until now. I want dates, names, places, everything you can remember."

She talked for over an hour. She talked through another glass of champagne, half a bottle of Pouilly Fuissé, grilled liver and bacon with mange-touts, and the sweetest, crispest *crème brûlée* she had ever tasted.

## SCREEN KISSES • 67

"I'm impressed," he said finally. "You seem to have worked hard during these past few years. Though none of it would have come good if you hadn't met Jeremy Powers. He has an eye for talent, and a knack of bringing it out."

"I know," she said. Then she burst into tears.

The agent looked worried. "He didn't rape you or anything, did he? I know Jeremy can be the pits sometimes, but I hardly thought he went in for crimes of violence."

She wiped her eyes. "Of course he didn't rape me," she said crossly. "He wanted to though. As a sort of price for putting me in a West End show."

French seemed relieved and ordered some coffee. "That old thing," he said. "Jeremy's always asking pretty young actresses to go to bed with him. Pretty young actors as well sometimes. And you'd be surprised how many of them take him up on it. Your director is a very influential man. He could star Muffin the Mule in a play and I know at least three managements who would put the piece on."

"Why?"

"Because he's good. Because he's box office. Because everything he puts on the stage is a sell-out success. This is a tough business, Rachel. And everyone who offers you a helping hand is going to ask for something in return. Even me."

She flushed. "You don't mean . . ."

"No, I'm not after your body. Not all of it, at any rate."

"What do you mean, not all of it?" She was suspicious now.

## 68 • TRUDI PACTER

The agent smiled and stirred saccharin into his coffee. "There's only one part of your body that interests me. And that's a purely professional interest. I'm talking about your nose. I want you to alter it."

Her hand flew up to her face. "What's wrong with my nose?"

"It's too long," he said, looking her in the eye. "And it's slightly too broad across the bridge." He took hold of her hand and put it back on the table. "Don't overreact. It's not that bad. If I wasn't thinking of you for the screen it wouldn't matter. But I am. And that nose would never survive a close-up."

She considered for a moment.

"Will it hurt?" she asked.

"Like hell." He smiled. "You'll be swollen. You'll have two black eyes. And after you get out of hospital you'll want to go into hiding for at least three weeks until everything goes back to normal."

She looked doubtful. "I don't think I can do that," she said.

He smiled. "You don't have any alternative. There isn't enough work in the theatre to keep an actress like you alive. West End management are all looking for big names, and you haven't got one. Not yet anyway.

"The only way I can build you into something is to put you into films. And for that you need to make a trip to Harley Street."

"I suppose you know the name of a doctor."

He nodded.

Her hand went up to her face again. "I'm being silly," she said, "but I'm attached to my nose. It might

## SCREEN KISSES • 69

not be my most beautiful feature but I hate the idea of some surgeon messing about with it. I mean, I wouldn't be me any more after he'd finished."

"I thought you were used to being different people."

"Yes," she said, "but not for very long. When the curtain comes down I take my make-up off and go back to my life. It wouldn't be like that if I had the surgery."

"No, it wouldn't. But has it occurred to you that with a new nose you wouldn't be going back to the life you once knew? Everything would be different. You'd be working in a new medium. You'd be earning more money. Even the people you worked with would be different."

She thought about her friends in the theatre. She thought about Richard. And finally she thought about her audience. Could I live without them? she wondered. Would the cold eye of a camera lens give me the same love, the same approval as all those people out there night after night?

Desmond French saw her hesitate. "Why don't you go home and think about it?" he said. "And when you've made up your mind, call me. But don't leave it too long . . ."

The moment she got back she told Richard everything. She told him about Jeremy Powers and about Desmond French. And she asked him for his help.

He laughed at her. "You've got a perfectly nice nose," he said. "I can't see anything wrong with it. If you ask me Desmond French was having you on."

## 70 • TRUDI PACTER

They were taking a stroll along Brighton Pier before a matinée. Summer had long since gone and the sea was dark and choppy, covering them with a fine spray as they walked.

She turned around to face him. "What do you mean, French was having me on?"

He looked irritable. "Every time some man starts raving on about your performance in *An Ideal Husband,* there's always some kind of string attached. First it was Jeremy offering you the West End and then asking you to go to bed with him. Now it's Desmond French. 'I can put you in films, dear,' he says, 'but you'll have to have your nose bobbed.' Rachel, it's a load of old nonsense and you know it. Men are always making promises to young actresses they've no intention of keeping."

They were approaching the end of the pier which housed a mini-fairground. There was a fortune-teller, a coconut shy, and a hall of mirrors. Rachel spotted the Tunnel of Love and grabbed hold of Richard's arm. "Darling, let's have a go on this. Come on, it'll be fun."

But he was having none of it. "Did you hear what I just said, or have you decided to ignore it?"

"I'm not ignoring it. I just don't think you're making any sense and I don't want to have a row with you."

"What do you mean, not making sense?"

"What I said. Look, Desmond French has actresses queueing up to see him. Some girls wait for months and still don't get through his door. But with me it was the other way round. He actually called and

## SCREEN KISSES • 71

asked me out to dinner. Men like Desmond French simply don't go around doing that kind of thing. They don't have the time."

"Every man has time for an adventure. They make the time."

She had never seen him like this before. She took his arm. "Richard, you're being unreasonable. Come on, let's forget it and give the Tunnel of Love a whirl."

But her words were lost in the wind. Richard pulled away from her and walked over to the shooting gallery. He gave the man standing in the booth a pound and grabbed an air gun. Six clay ducks, perched precariously on sticks, moved slowly across the range. Richard took careful aim and pulled the trigger six times.

The ducks went down in rapid succession and somewhere in the background a buzzer started to sound. The fairground trader grinned broadly and shook Richard by the hand. "Well done, lad," he said, "you hit the jackpot first time out. Not many people do that."

Richard scowled. "I hit the jackpot all right. I ended up with everyone else's favourite girl."

He leaned closer to the man who had just congratulated him. "Let me tell you something about jackpots, mate. In real life, nobody gives you any prizes for winning them."

He was silent on the way back to the theatre, and he kept out of Rachel's way before the show. During the interval when everyone was crowded backstage he didn't speak to her at all. And by the time the final curtain came down she was starting to feel furious.

"Bloody prima donna," she muttered under her breath as she made her way back to her dressing room. "He'll be jealous of his own shadow next."

For she realized that was the problem. Richard was uncomfortable with her success and he was taking it out on her. She wondered if he would pick her up from her dressing room that night, like he always did. She decided he probably wouldn't. He didn't seem in the mood for a cosy drink after the show.

She spent a long time taking off her make-up and unhooking the elaborate costume. She was standing in the stiff whalebone corset that formed its base when she heard footsteps outside in the corridor. She grabbed her robe. So he'd decided he was speaking to her after all.

She was opening the tiny fridge provided by the management when he came through the door. "Will you have wine or beer?" she asked.

"Neither," he said abruptly. "I can do without your charity."

She slammed the fridge door shut. "This is a new one," she said. "I didn't hear you talking about charity on all the other nights after the show."

"Maybe I had no idea what a big star you were going to be."

She paused. "So you've revised this afternoon's ideas. You don't think Desmond French was having me on."

He came up to her. "No, I don't think Desmond

## SCREEN KISSES • 73

was having you on. But I do think he'll be having you before you're very much older.''

She slapped him hard round the mouth, her fingers leaving their mark. It took half a second for him to return the blow and instinctively her knee came up. But he was too fast for her. He grabbed her round the waist, knocking her off-balance, and they ended up sprawled across the floor.

"You bastard," she growled through clenched teeth. "You dirty-minded, arrogant bastard."

He started to struggle to his feet and it was then that she realized her robe had come adrift. She was lying there in a tight whalebone corset and a lacy camisole looking like a naughty Victorian postcard. There was a long silence finally broken by Richard.

"You tempt me," he said softly.

"To what?" she asked, matching her voice to his.

He didn't answer her. Instead he knelt down and started to unbuckle his jeans.

"You wouldn't," she said.

He reached for the long cotton bloomers she was wearing and pulled them down around her knees. Then he slid his hand up the silk stockings until he encountered her flesh. She clamped her knees together but he was too strong for her, and too fast. Before she knew what was happening he was astride her. And her legs were parting despite all her objections.

He looked down at her. And she saw he was smiling. "I always wanted to fuck a star," he said.

She felt angry and ashamed. And something else. She felt horny as hell. He started to push his way inside her, and from nowhere she felt a fire in her loins.

## 74 • TRUDI PACTER

She arched her back and he thrust deep into her, pinning her body to the floor with a force she had never felt before. He took her relentlessly and without consideration. She had never been so excited. When the climax came it consumed her.

Much later, when she took the corset off she found she was covered in deep red welts where the bones had bitten into her. But she didn't care. The quarrel between them was over and they were lovers again. Richard never mentioned her career from that moment on. If she worried about her future, she worried about it on her own.

When the tour finished in Torquay, Rachel still hadn't called Desmond French. The surgeon's knife terrified her. She wondered which was worse: going to bed with Jeremy or changing her face permanently.

In the end she did nothing. She steered clear of Jeremy and concentrated on the play. She knew she was good in it. Jeremy Powers had told her so; Desmond French had endorsed his opinion. There was still time for somebody else to come along and discover her.

Nobody came. On the last night Jeremy came up to her and asked her to have a drink with him. He had something to tell her.

Her heart rose. He's changed his mind, she thought. He wanted me for Kate all along. Asking me to go to bed with him was just a try-on.

She smiled into the mirror as she took her make-up off after the play. Rachel Keller smiled back. Rachel Keller with the crooked nose that was slightly too

## SCREEN KISSES • 75

long for the camera. She patted astringent lotion into it. You'll never know what a lucky escape you had, she thought.

Jeremy took her to a wine bar by the seafront. It had a spacious front window with a couple of tables in it. Jeremy led her to one of them. Then he ordered a whisky for himself and a glass of white wine for her. While they waited for their drinks, they talked about the tour. Jeremy had been gratified by the box-office takings and laid their success at the feet of Charles Alcott.

Rachel was surprised. "The last time you bought me a drink," she observed, "you said I was responsible for the show doing so well."

"Then I was mistaken," he replied. "You don't really think the public is flocking in every night to see a bunch of unknowns in an Oscar Wilde drawing room comedy, do you? They're coming to see Charles Alcott, the star of *Fast Money*. I'll grant you he's not the world's greatest actor. But the audience loves him. That man's guaranteed bums on seats. He's keeping us all in business."

She started to feel angry. "Do you always change your mind exactly when it suits you?" she asked. "Or is it just when you're trying to get into somebody's knickers?"

He smiled. "There's no need to lose your temper," he said. "I didn't bring you here to have a shouting match."

"Then why did you bring me here?"

"To talk about the future."

"You mean *Kiss Me Kate*?"

The drinks arrived and he didn't reply. Her heart started to beat faster. He's changed his mind, she thought. He must have done. Otherwise why would he have brought me here? Suddenly she had to know what was on his mind.

"Do I still have the part?" she asked.

He looked at her. "No, actually. I know at the time it seemed a good idea, but things have changed since then.

"The management have asked me to put a big television name in the part. And I've decided to go along with them."

So that's why he was banging on about Charles Alcott, she thought bitterly. "Would it have made any difference if I had gone to bed with you?" she asked.

"Not in the end," he said. Then he saw her face. "There's no need to look at me like that. I'm not a complete bastard. You're still in the play. I'm offering you the understudy's part. With a bit of assistant stage-managing thrown in to justify your salary."

The understudy's part, she thought. He wanted me to go to bed for the understudy's part. She took a sip of her drink to steady her nerves, but the wine tasted sour. "People are pretty expendable as far as you're concerned, aren't they?" she observed.

"Not people," he said slowly. "Actors. When they're on their way up they learn everything they can at my expense. Drain me dry and don't even remember to say thank you. Then when they finally make it, they kick me in the teeth with their temperament. I know you all think I use you. But what the hell do you think you do to me, given half the chance?"

## SCREEN KISSES • 77

"Is that why you invited me out?" she asked. "To accuse me of using you?"

"Not quite. You and I still have some unfinished business between us."

"Like what?"

"Like Richard Roberts."

She remembered the way he had talked about Richard the last time they had dined alone together, and she felt cold.

"What unfinished business do you have with Richard?" she demanded.

He smiled. "I told you once he wasn't worth loving. And I was right. I've proved it."

"How?"

"Let me ask you something. Where did Richard tell you he was going after the tour?"

"He didn't. I assumed he would be on the dole like the rest of us."

Powers smiled and ordered another whisky. "Then he hasn't been all that honest with you. He's coming to work for me in *Kiss Me Kate*."

She felt reality slipping away. "When did that happen?"

"When you went down to London to meet Desmond French. Richard was rather down in the mouth about all the success you were having so I took him out to dinner to cheer him up."

A suspicion started to form in her mind. What was it Desmond French had said to her over dinner? "Jeremy's always asking actresses to go to bed with him. Sometimes he asks actors too."

It can't be, she thought. Richard's not like that.

"Did you offer Richard a part in your show over dinner?" she asked.

"No, I waited until he showed me how much he wanted it."

Her face felt hot. "How did he do that?"

"How do you think?"

She put down her glass. "How could you?" she said. "How could you do it?"

He started to look pleased with himself. "I do it all the time," he said. "For me it's a kind of sport. Don't look so shocked, Rachel. You demonstrate your power every night on stage when you manipulate the audience. I don't have that luxury. So I have to find another way of reminding myself I'm effective."

She felt nauseated. "Does seduction really do that for you?"

"In spades. There's nothing like getting a strong, spirited young animal and making them do what you want. The best candidate on this tour would have been you, of course. But you had other ideas, so I chose the consolation prize."

"You're sick. You know that," she said.

"No sicker than you. We just get turned on by different things."

She decided to ignore the jibe. "Tell me," she said, "what did you offer Richard? It wasn't Petruchio, was it?"

He laughed. "Dear girl. He's not that much fun. Or that talented either. No, Richard's got a small cameo role and he's bloody lucky to get it."

She felt an irrational urge to cry. Then she

## SCREEN KISSES • 79

thought, not yet. Not in front of this bastard. I won't give him that satisfaction.

"You don't really expect me to understudy Kate," she said. "Not now you've told me about Richard."

He shrugged. "Why not? It's a good job. It's in the West End. What have you got to lose?"

She ran through the possibilities. There was her pride. Her self-respect. Then she laughed at herself. What a fool I am, she thought. I lost all those just now when Jeremy told me about Richard.

She sat up very straight in her chair. Then she said, "There's something else I can do. It will change me for ever. And I dare say it will hurt." Nervously her hand went up to her nose. "But I've decided to go through with it, just so I never have to set eyes on you or Richard Roberts again as long as I live."

**B**ob Delaney was looking for money. A lot of money. Twenty-five million dollars' worth of money. And so far there were no volunteers to pick up the tab.

It didn't depress him. Delaney had been making too many films for too many years to be depressed by a little hitch such as no punters for his new project. He'd find a punter. Time was on his side. Time, a great script and a major star.

With these thoughts in mind he pushed his way through the heavy glass entrance doors of Magnum Studios. He was a tall man with fine broad shoulders and a way of walking that reminded you of John Wayne in *True Grit*. With his wavy dark hair and weathered, lived-in face there was something of the cowboy in him. He looked as if he would be more at

## SCREEN KISSES • 81

home in blue jeans and loafers than the dark city suit he was wearing. But Delaney was on his way to ask for money. And he had too much respect for it to turn up looking anything but immaculate.

As he made his way to the elevators he grinned the low, easy, confident grin that was his trademark. With every step he took he saw a familiar face. Bing Crosby, Greer Garson, Sophia Loren, Steve McQueen all gazed down from the walls of the long cool corridor as reminders that Magnum hired the best. Because Magnum could afford the best.

Finally he reached the elevator bank that would take him to the executive suite. As he waited he mentally went through the details of his package.

Top of his list had to be David Price, his star. A product of the Australian film industry, he had made only two major international pictures. But such had been their popularity that right now Price was one of the most bankable properties around, ranking alongside Robert Redford and Paul Newman.

Delaney sent up a silent prayer of thanks to Price's agent, Desmond French. He and the Englishman had been trading favours for some years now, and it was French who had talked Price into doing the picture. I wonder what Desmond is going to want in return for this one, he thought. Then he put the question to the back of his mind. French had never been unreasonable in the past. Whatever he wanted Delaney could doubtless provide.

Bob Delaney never had many problems because he didn't go looking for them. He was the son of an immigrant Dubliner and an American short-order cook, and his Irish roots had given him an easy-going confidence that automatically made people trust him. When he had told CBS Television that he wanted quarter of a million dollars' development money for a desert island movie, they gave it to him. Not because they had any particular enthusiasm for tropical sands and swaying palm trees but because they knew that Delaney would deliver on time and on budget exactly what he was selling them. He hoped Dan Keyser, Magnum's head of production, would feel the same way.

Nervously he hefted the script he was carrying. He had been looking for an excuse to make a desert island picture for a long time. Then during the school holidays he found his son watching an old video. It seemed to cast a spell over the boy. When Chuck had gone to bed Bob took a look at it and found to his surprise that it was an adaptation of *The Admirable Crichton.* Then he sat down and watched it from beginning to end. He started to get excited. This was the desert island picture he had been looking for. It had all the ingredients that audiences seemed to go for today: a snotty English family with their faithful retainer, Crichton; a dramatic shipwreck on a desert island; and the thing he always looked for in his movies—the unexpected. In this case it was the reversal of traditional roles. Crichton the servant became the leader of the shipwrecked party—building shelters, finding food, saving everyone's asses. The snotty family turned into his lackeys making sure their new leader and provider got everything he wanted.

The following morning Chuck found his father

## SCREEN KISSES • 83

had made off with his video. But he didn't protest. It seemed to put his father in a good mood, and Chuck was thankful. Dad had been difficult to reach since he and Chuck's mother divorced. If *Paradise Lagoon* cheered him up then he was welcome to it.

The elevator came to a stop at the seventeenth floor and Delaney got out. He had finally made it to the executive suite. The rest was in the lap of the gods.

Dan Keyser's outer office reminded Bob of the headquarters of a Wall Street bank. Three secretaries all equipped with word processors were working fast and energetically. And a Japanese woman was doing nothing of the sort. Instead she sat, beautiful and immobile, behind a large walnut desk. Occasionally she would answer the telephone. Now and then packages and papers would be delivered to her, but her main task was to receive visitors. This she did with the accomplished poise of a society hostess and Bob wondered, as he always did when he came to this office, whether she hadn't been trained as a Geisha in another life.

Keyser kept him waiting for the statutory ten minutes then the Japanese woman signalled for him to go through. If the outer office was a model of efficiency, the inner sanctum was a shrine to self-indulgence. A bar of antiquated pine ran the length of the room, and opposite the bar was a wall of solid glass that overlooked an ornamental garden. Nobody walked in the garden. Secretaries and other staff were banned from sunning themselves on the lush, green grass, nor were they allowed to smell the roses and jacaranda that crowded the beds. Instead a full-time gardener was employed to manicure this half acre of real estate for the pleasure of one man: Dan Keyser. He owned the view and the visiting rights. It made him feel powerful.

As Bob approached the head of Magnum Studios he started to relax. Getting through to this inner sanctum was such a performance that it was easy to forget that the man he was meeting was not a god or a member of royalty. He was mortal. In some ways too mortal.

If Hollywood decided to make a film about itself and was casting around for a movie mogul they would have picked Dan Keyser simply because he looked the part. He was a large, chubby man given to wearing shiny suits and smoking fat cigars. And the only thing that stopped him being a total cliché was his boyishness. Where other men in his mould were threatening, Dan was affable. He had an open face and a soft voice and people liked him for it.

This was not to say Dan Keyser couldn't be tough when he wanted to. In the fifteen years he had been dealing with Dan, Bob had known about two projects the studio chief had cancelled because they had run over budget. But there was no brutality in his decisions. He canned things for solid business reasons, not to see people squirm.

Because of this, Bob took his script to Dan Keyser first. The two men greeted each other effusively, then the studio chief took Bob over to the far end of his office where there was a sofa and two padded armchairs. According to Hollywood custom they didn't talk about the movie immediately. Instead they

## SCREEN KISSES • 85

went through the social ritual of chitchat about the latest parties and the new releases.

Bob studied his companion closely. He knew that when the fat man was ready to start the meeting he would give him a signal. It came when he reached across the marble table in front of him and selected a cigar from the humidor. Bob had seen Keyser do this a hundred times before in a hundred different meetings. He mentally straightened his shoulders.

"What are you thinking of calling this project?" asked the studio chief casually.

"*Marooned*," said Bob shortly. "Didn't you get the script I sent you?"

Dan waved his cigar in the air. "I get a million scripts every day. You can't expect me to remember the details."

Swiftly Bob sketched out the plot. It was clear to him that the good-humoured man sitting opposite him had never set eyes on his script. Then he explained how much it was going to cost and at that moment he knew he had Dan's complete attention.

"Twenty-five million," he protested. "That's a hell of a lot of dough. Are you sure the picture's worth it?"

Bob tensed. Now was the time to bring David Price into the conversation. The Australian actor was the magic ingredient in Bob's package and the main reason for making the movie. If Dan was hot for him, *Marooned* would get the green light. Bob put his toe in the water.

"I hear Magnum's been chasing around after David Price," he ventured.

## 86 • TRUDI PACTER

Keyser looked deflated. "Chasing is the word," he said. "We don't seem to have anything on offer that interests that Australian bum."

The producer started to smile. "You have if you get involved with *Marooned.*"

Now Keyser smiled. "I know all about you and David Price," he said. "I heard ten days ago you did a deal with Desmond French. Why do you think I agreed to see you so fast? I take it he likes the script."

Bob nodded.

"Then you only have one problem."

"What's that?"

"The female lead." There was a short silence, then the studio head turned to Bob. "Listen," he said softly, "you've got sex, you've got sand and you've got David Price. But that's only half the equation. If you're looking for twenty-five million then you've got to come up with the girl."

Bob stood up. "Do you think I could have something to drink?" he asked.

Keyser indicated the bar. "Help yourself, sweetheart, you know where everything is."

Bob went and poured himself a Perrier. Then he turned to Keyser. "I have no intention of coming up with a girl for *Marooned,*" he said calmly.

Dan looked confused. "Why's that?" he asked.

"Because you've already got one."

The studio head stood up and started to review his files. "There's Belinda Weber," he said half to himself, "but she's already working on a picture. Caris Evans is contracted out to Columbia." Then he paused, frozen to the spot.

## SCREEN KISSES • 87

"You're not thinking of Claudia Graham, are you?" he asked.

Bob took a swig of his mineral water. "That's the girl," he said.

Dan sat down heavily. "Forget it," he said. "The woman's a mistake."

Now Bob was intrigued. "Tell me about it."

"From the top?"

He nodded.

The studio chief walked across to the bar and made himself a Gibson. Bob noticed it was just past four in the afternoon. Whatever Dan had to say about Claudia Graham was going to be bad news.

It was not as hopeless as he thought. Claudia, who ranked alongside Raquel Welch and Brigitte Bardot as a sex symbol, knew a thing or two about acting. There was a brain behind the boobs. There was also a heart, a soul and an ego. And the ego was giving trouble.

For Claudia had little confidence in herself. Her frail self-esteem needed constant reinforcement and she propped it up the only way she knew how—with men.

When she met someone she liked, she couldn't just have a fling or a dalliance. She had to go the whole hog and get married. To date she had been married five times. And husband number five had just walked out on her.

Dan consumed two Gibsons as he told the story. And when he had finished the second, he helped himself to a straight vodka. "I'm getting to the worst part," he explained, gazing mournfully through the

## 88 • TRUDI PACTER

plate glass on to the manicured gardens below. "When Chad filed for divorce, Claudia decided to disappear. Nobody could get hold of the woman. Not only could the studio not reach her, the world couldn't reach her. She refused to see her agent. She wouldn't go to parties. You couldn't even get her on the phone. It was as if she simply ceased to exist. You're not going to believe this but she doesn't even see her therapist any more. So if she was having a nervous breakdown she'll be near the brink of suicide by now."

Bob refused to be downhearted. "It might not be as bad as it looks," he said. "I've handled actresses in my time. Christ, I was married to one for nearly ten years. And I can tell you one thing. None of them ever died from love."

Keyser shook his head. "I wish I could believe you. Claudia's been off the scene for six months now. We're paying out thousands of dollars every month on her contract and we're getting nothing in return. To be perfectly honest with you it would be cheaper for Magnum if she did die."

"Or if she came back to work," said Bob.

The fat man finished his drink and turned to him. "If you can get Claudia back on the set," he said, "Magnum will put up the money for *Marooned*."

Bob looked at him. "And if I can't?"

The bulky studio chief stubbed out the rest of his cigar. "If you can't, there's nothing doing here."

\*     \*     \*

Claudia Graham was not difficult to get hold of. She was impossible. Bob had called her all week. And all week she failed to return his messages.

He tried sending flowers. Still no response. At this point Delaney sat down and considered his options. There weren't any, so he thought about Giselle Pascal. In her own words Giselle was a fixer. In everyone else's she was a procuress. Either way she made money.

Giselle was the kind of girl who needed money. She reminded Bob of a very expensive racing car—nervy, beautiful and costing a bomb to run. He had met her when she first arrived in Hollywood eight years previously and he had been intrigued immediately. But then so had every other man in town. It wasn't her baby-blue eyes or long, flaxen hair that worked the magic. Lots of girls had that going for them. What Giselle had that set her apart from the crowd was her class, and her air of mystery.

She had come from Paris. Anyone could tell that from the way she spoke, the way she walked, the way she wore her clothes. But she hadn't arrived straight from France. Before she came out to the coast she had lived in New York for a few years.

She had trained as an actress and had had one or two small parts on Broadway, but nothing significant. She didn't have that kind of talent, or that kind of need. A man had kept her; a wealthy man with contacts. And when she left him to come out to the coast she kept hold of his contacts. The friends she had met in New York made sure she had a place to stay and plenty of places to go. She began to be seen at all the

## 90 • TRUDI PACTER

best parties, the top country clubs, and the Academy Awards. Men fought each other for her favours, and she could have repeated her New York experience and been expensively kept. But she didn't choose to. This time she wanted to earn a living and be independent.

She considered acting then rejected the idea. Too many beautiful blonds went that route and ended up on the scrapheap. She wanted to do something that made use of her special talents—her chic, her contacts, and her ability to charm the birds off the trees. Eventually Giselle found her niche in life. She made introductions and she took a fee for it. Everyone in Hollywood needed the kind of introductions Giselle could provide, because they all wanted a little bit more than they already had. If a man had money he wanted invitations to the right parties. If he had both money and social cachet, then the chances were he wanted sex. Easy sex. Sex without strings. In the beginning that's how Giselle earned her living. She provided beautiful girls for powerful men with no time to go looking. But Giselle wanted more than to be just another Madame. She was too bright and too socially ambitious for that. So as always she fell back on the laws of supply and demand and started getting the wrong guests into the right parties. To do this she had to cultivate a few powerful Hollywood wives, but that wasn't a problem. Her accent and her chic gave her instant access. Her natural pushiness did the rest.

In the eight years she had been in Hollywood Giselle Pascal had become the most successful hustler in town. If you wanted to go to an "A" list party, meet

## SCREEN KISSES • 91

a powerful producer or fuck a movie star, you called Giselle. For a fee she could arrange any of these things or all of them, depending on your need.

Right now, Bob Delaney's most pressing need was to meet Claudia Graham. Under the right circumstances and for the right length of time. The moment had come to call Giselle.

Giselle arranged to meet Bob at the Hamburger Hamlet on Sunset Boulevard. The Hamlet was famous in Hollywood as the place people with influence met each other to do deals. Bob used it to meet wellknown actors when he was casting a film. As he swung through the doors he marvelled at the audacity of the place. For the Hamburger Hamlet did not pander to the occupants of the film capital. It was a huge, barnlike place, rather like a steak house serving fast food. All the waitresses were elderly granny figures in starched white pinafores, and the only concession the place made to luxury was the roomy leather chairs grouped around each table.

It was in one of these that Bob found Giselle, who had arrived a few minutes early. As always she looked as if she had just stepped out of the pages of *Vogue.* She was dressed in a soft black leather suit that was unmistakably St. Laurent. For this meeting she had chosen plain gold jewellery which she wore around her throat, in her ears and on her fingers. Delaney guessed she had bought it on Rodeo Drive and knew by its cut that it probably cost more than most people's diamonds.

But Giselle was more than just an expensive fashion plate. She knew how to wear the merchandise.

Her pale blonde hair was drawn back from her face and coiled into the nape of her neck. Her face, with its high aristocratic cheekbones and clear blue eyes, could take the severity of the style. Delaney gave a whistle of admiration.

"If I didn't know that behind that pretty face lives a calculating machine, I could fall in love with you," he told her.

Giselle wasn't amused. "Save the sweet talk for the floozies," she said. "You're not buying me lunch to start a flirtation."

Delaney drew in his breath. So she wanted to play it tough? Fine, he thought. Let's find out how tough. He gave her his roaring-boy smile—slow, easy and un-ruffled. "I'm not buying lunch to give myself indigestion either," he said. "So be a good girl and order yourself a drink. We'll start the negotiation when you've finished it and not before."

She looked sour and beckoned over one of the waitresses.

"I'll have a Perrier, no ice, no lemon. My friend will take straight arsenic."

He patted her hand. "Don't be a bitch, it doesn't suit you."

He asked the waitress for a Gibson and when it arrived he raised his glass in a salute. The French woman acknowledged the gesture. Just. Then she got down to business. "Okay," she said, "what's the problem?"

Bob told her about the deal he was trying to fix with Magnum. Then he explained about the trouble he had had locating Claudia Graham. Giselle started

## SCREEN KISSES • 93

to look interested. "Were you thinking of going any-where exotic to make this film?" she asked. "Or will you do it in the studio?"

He laughed. "With the kind of budget I have in mind we go on location. Why do you ask?"

"Because Claudia needs to get away."

Now it was Bob's turn to look interested. "Surely she can't be losing sleep over the latest divorce. I know Chad was her fifth husband but she didn't care about him that much."

"No, it's not the divorce," said Giselle, "though she'd like people to think it is. No, it's something far more serious." She pulled her chair closer to the table and looked around her. Then she lowered her voice. "Look, this has got to be between us. Claudia's a friend of mine. A real friend, not some party contact. So if I tell you what's bugging her, then you've got to promise it goes no further."

He nodded. "You got it. Now tell me what's so terrible about Claudia's life that she has to go into hiding?"

Giselle smiled. "There's nothing terrible about Claudia's life. Magnum's paying her so much money, she'll never have to worry again. What's terrible is her face."

Understanding started to dawn. "You mean the lady had a bad nose job."

Giselle shook her head. "Try higher up."

For a moment Bob looked puzzled. Then he said, "Is it her eyes?"

Giselle nodded. "You've got it. She's had them done twice in the past ten years with no ill effects. So when she was heading for the divorce courts this time she thought she'd cheer herself up and have them done again."

Bob let out a low whistle. "Is she crazy?"

"That's what her plastic surgeon asked her. And she took offence. 'I don't pay you to ask me that sort of question,' she told him. 'I pay you to fix my face.'

"Then she walked out and decided to have the job done in Italy. Rome actually, where no one would see her. And when it was finished she didn't want anyone to see her."

Delaney put his head in his hands. "No wonder she's gone into hiding. Tell me, how bad is it?"

"Not as bad as we first thought. The doctor she usually goes to took pity on her and now you can hardly see the scars, unless you look closely. And there's where you have a problem. Claudia's worried about appearing on film because of the scars. She's fine in mid-shot, but even I don't think she'll survive a close-up."

Bob let his breath out. The problem wasn't as bad as he thought. "If you'd told me she'd had the operation on her tits then there would have been no hope at all. But her eyes we can cope with. Look, the reason Keyser wants her for *Marooned* is for her body. In this kind of desert island caper clothes are kept to a minimum, particularly where the girls are concerned. Who knows, we might even risk a few tasteful nude shots. As long as we get a lot of cover on Claudia's natural assets, we can keep the close-ups to a minimum. If we have to go in close there are things we can do with

# SCREEN KISSES • 95

the lens. I don't have to tell you about lighting camera-men's tricks.''

"No, you don't," she said. "The person you have to convince is Claudia. So if I were you I'd start bending the ear of the best lighting man in town. There'll be a lot of questions to answer when you get together with her."

He grinned, and this time it came from the heart. "So you'll fix it?"

"I'll fix it. Only there's one thing I can't promise. I can't guarantee Claudia's going to like any of this, or even agree to it. All I can do is organize that you get to see her. The rest is up to you."

As soon as she regained consciousness the pain came driving in at her. It was incessant, relentless, and she prayed for sleep to claim her back.

It wasn't Rachel's first visit to hospital. She had had her tonsils out, then her appendix. But this wasn't like those first times. This was worse than anything she had ever known. Why did I agree to have this done? she berated herself. It wasn't necessary. I could have gone on living without it. Then she grimaced through the pain. I could have gone on living without a nose job, she thought, but it wouldn't have been much of a life.

She remembered the night she walked out on Richard. For her it had been a turning point, for she had not just left Richard behind, she had said goodbye

## SCREEN KISSES • 97

to the theatre as well. Her only way forward was the screen. The screen and Desmond French. And for these new masters she had to sacrifice her nose.

Instinctively her hand went up to her face and encountered layers of gauze. From what she could make out, her whole head was wrapped in it. She felt the strings of panic. What if the surgeon had got it wrong? What if the knife had slipped and there had been a terrible mistake?

She was interrupted by the nurse, who told her to stop fiddling with her dressings. "The whole lot's coming off in a week. Then you can touch your face as much as you like."

She looked at Rachel with concern. "Hurts, does it?" she asked.

"You bet it bloody hurts. I feel like a train's just gone over me."

The nurse smiled. "They all say that when they come round. Hang on a minute and I'll give you something for it."

The nurse was back in five minutes with a kidney bowl and a syringe. "Turn over for me," she said patiently. "I'll put the needle in where it won't hurt."

"At this stage, whether or not I hurt is slightly academic, isn't it?"

"Don't let Mr Steel hear you say that," she admonished. "He's very particular about his patients. Wants them to have the best."

"And did I get the best?" Rachel asked. "Did he give me a good nose?"

"He gave you a beautiful nose. That's what you're paying him for, isn't it?"

Rachel gazed at the nurse as she bustled away. That's what I'm paying him for, she thought.

She woke with a start to see Desmond French sitting in the chair by her bed. The jab the nurse had given her must have sent her to sleep. Gingerly she felt her nose under the bandages. The pain was still there but it was duller, more diffuse.

French, she noticed, was wearing a velvet suit and a long scarf knotted round his neck. He was also sporting an expensive-looking suntan and she wondered where he had been since she last saw him.

Perfunctorily he asked her how she felt, as if she had grazed her knee or broken her toe. She realized that in French's world, facial surgery was a mundane matter. The cinematic equivalent of putting on a wig or a layer of greasepaint. She decided she wasn't going to let him get away with it. If he started taking her nose for granted, who knows what he might ask her to have altered next?

She looked up at him. "It does hurt, you know. It hurts like fury actually. The nurse had to come and give me a shot for it."

He patted her hand. "Poor old love," he said, "it must be ghastly for you. Never mind, it's all in a good cause. In three weeks' time you'll look back on this and thank your lucky stars you had it done."

"Why, what happens in three weeks' time?"

"You do your first screen test. So Harold had better have done a good job."

She took a sip of water out of the plastic beaker by her bed.

## SCREEN KISSES • 99

"Is there a reason for moving so fast?"

Desmond looked pleased with himself.

"There is, actually. A friend of mine is doing a remake of *The Admirable Crichton*. It's called *Marooned* or something. Anyway there's a part in it for you."

Despite her discomfort, Rachel was riveted. "Tell me about it," she said.

"It's the juvenile lead. If you remember your Crichton, the family butler was betrothed to the parlour maid, Mabel. She's a nice little thing. Crazy about Crichton and honoured to be chosen to be his bride.

"What's interesting about Mabel is that she gets ditched once everyone's washed up on the desert island and she has to stand by while Crichton falls in love with the family's beautiful daughter. She takes him back in the end, of course. She has to. And how she copes with the changes in her fortunes could be very interesting to watch.

"It's not a part for the average cinema actress. The girls who play the support roles nowadays simply don't have the dramatic range. And the ones who do want to be leading ladies."

Rachel was wide awake now. She had expected Desmond French to get her into films, but not so quickly and in such a showy part. She could hardly believe her luck.

"Do you think I can do it?" she asked.

"With your eyes closed and one hand tied behind your back. Oh, by the way, while we're talking about the film, you'd better organize to be away for at least three months. It's a location job, I'm afraid. You'll be stuck in Bali for most of that time."

## 100 • TRUDI PACTER

She smiled, ignoring the tug of the bandages. "I think I could handle that," she said, "if I force myself." Then a tiny doubt crept into her mind.

"Desmond," she asked, "what makes you so sure I'm going to get this part? The producer or director or whatever hasn't even seen my test."

The agent got up from the chair and smoothed down the pile of his velvet suit. "Let's just say the producer and I have an understanding."

A scruffy man on a motorcycle roared up to the wrought-iron gates at the end of Claudia Graham's driveway. He pressed the entryphone button and gave his name to the maid. The gates parted and Bob Delaney steered his Honda the last few hundred yards to the forecourt of the Spanish-style ranch house. Like all film stars' houses it looked as if it had something to prove. The architect who had designed this residence had spared no effort and no expense making his point. From the pink marble columns that fronted a sweeping verandah to the manicured lawns, the house told you it sheltered someone of importance. Someone who had power, influence and glamour.

Surrounded by all this splendour, Delaney looked strangely out of place. He was wearing sneak-

## 102 • TRUDI PACTER

ers, beat-up blue jeans and a tee-shirt with "New York Pitchers" emblazoned across the front. He was also grinning from ear to ear. So when Claudia Graham made her entrance on the verandah she was momentarily caught off-balance.

She had expected an earnest-looking producer in a dark city suit carrying a briefcase. Instead she was confronted by a handsome, smiling man dressed like a beach bum. The fact that he looked perfectly at ease with himself was beside the point.

Claudia drew in her breath and gave him a look normally reserved for wild animals in a zoo. "You *are* Bob Delaney?" she enquired.

"Absolutely," he replied, extending a hand, "and you I presume are Claudia Graham. Delighted to meet you at long last."

She looked at him with a certain amount of distaste. "I suppose you'd better come and have a drink. The maid has set up a table by the pool."

Then she turned on her heel and led the way along the bougainvillea-covered verandah. As they walked Bob ran his eyes over the actress. He didn't look at her the way most men assess a pretty woman. His was the eye of a trained professional. The body, he observed, was as good as all its advance publicity. She obviously worked out regularly, for the bottom was high and trim, the stomach flat as a board, and her back under the tight-fitting Kamali sundress rippled and moved like an athlete's. He nodded his approval. He always admired a woman who kept fit; it showed she looked after herself.

When they reached the large, oval pool Claudia

## SCREEN KISSES • 103

sat down in a large wicker chair and motioned Bob to do the same. He did as he was bidden. She looked better than he had expected. The doctor who had repaired her face certainly knew what he was doing. If her eyes had been botched it didn't show now. What he saw was a woman in her mid-thirties with alabaster skin and the look of an Egyptian sphinx. There was something catlike about her face with its green, slanting eyes and tip-tilted little nose. He took in her hair and once more he nodded his approval. It was thick and black and she wore it spiralling around her face and neck in curly tendrils. She'll do, he thought, she'll do very nicely. Now all I have to do is convince her of the fact.

She shot him a glance from under thick, black lashes. "What are you staring at?" she asked.

He smiled and leaned back in his chair. "I was looking at the bottle of champagne you put on ice so thoughtfully. And I was wondering if you would be very upset with me if I asked you for a beer."

Despite herself she was amused. "Why, don't you drink champagne, Mr. Delaney? I can assure you it's the best."

"I can see it's the best," he said, "but vintage Bollinger is a little rich for my blood at this time of day. If you've got a Schlitz in the fridge I'd prefer it, if it's all the same to you."

She signalled to the Filipino maid who was hovering nervously by the bar. "Bring my guest a beer," she instructed. Then she turned to Delaney. "Do you always behave like this when you're doing business?" she asked.

## 104 • TRUDI PACTER

"It depends on who I'm doing business with," he told her. "If I'm going to see a studio executive, the answer's no. Executives are very conventional people. They spend their time with desks and paperclips and secretaries. If I didn't fit into their office decor, they wouldn't trust me.

"You, on the other hand, are not a deskbound company slave. You're an artistic, creative talent. I reckoned you were just about bright enough to appreciate me for myself."

Now it was Claudia's turn to smile. And as she smiled, she relaxed. The sight of this big, sweaty man swigging away at the beer her maid had brought reassured her. All her life she had been judged by tight-assed studio men with their tight-assed morals, and all her life she had been found wanting.

This Delaney didn't come on like all the others. To tell the truth he didn't look like he gave a goddamn.

She tested the water. "Giselle told me you wanted to talk about a film you were doing for Magnum."

"Sure I wanted to talk about it. But only if you're interested in coming back to work. Otherwise I'd just as soon drink your beer and wish you good day."

He's tough, she thought. He might look like a pussy cat, but this one's got teeth. And I bet he's not frightened to use them.

"I might be interested," she ventured, "but there are certain conditions about my working."

Bob smiled to himself. He'd dangled the bait and like a trout she'd risen to the surface. The beach bum

## SCREEN KISSES • 105

act was starting to pay off. He made an effort to stay in character.

"I don't know if I'm interested in conditions," he said, "but tell me about them anyway."

She pursed her lips. "Number one, I need to choose the cameraman. Somebody who doesn't know what he's doing can murder an actress. Number two, I need to see rushes. Every day after shooting. And number three, I want the power of veto. If I don't like what you've shot, you don't use it."

He took a long swig of his beer. "You're asking for a hell of a lot, aren't you? Why all the conditions?"

She sat up straight in the wicker chair and smoothed her dress down over her hips.

"Because I'm a star," she said. "And because you need me."

He laughed. "Not that much," he replied. Then before she could get angry, he leaned forward and took her by the arm.

"Tell me what's really bugging you," he said.

She pulled away. "I don't know what you mean."

He got up and walked over to the pool. "Do me a favour and cut the bullshit," he said. "Something's frightening you. Otherwise you wouldn't be avoiding producers like me, and you wouldn't be laying down the law when we do get together to talk about a film."

She paused for a moment considering her options. Then for what seemed like a long time she wrestled with her conscience. Finally she said: "Can I trust you?"

He shrugged. "Maybe," he said. "And maybe not." He turned his face up to the sun and ran a hand through the thick, black thatch. "It's hot," he said. "Do you mind if I take a swim?"

She was completely thrown. They were talking about the starring role in a twenty-five-million-dollar movie and the guy took it into his head to go for a dip.

The actress in her refused to be ruffled. She indicated the pool house at the back of the verandah. "You'll find a towel and a pair of trunks in there. Go help yourself."

Five minutes later he came out in a tiny white pair of briefs. Over his shoulder was slung a towel. Now it was her turn to stare. This Delaney certainly didn't spend all his time sitting in restaurants and projection rooms. He didn't carry an ounce of spare flesh anywhere, yet he was a big man with broad heavy shoulders and the muscles of a boxer. He walked like a boxer too, she noticed. Edgy and wary, poised on the balls of his feet. You might be playing Mr Cool, she thought, but inside that head of yours you're figuring out every move you make.

He walked to the end of the pool, looked down, then slowly and deliberately belly-flopped into the water. The crash he made when he hit the pool sounded like an engine backfiring. She winced. Jesus, she thought, I bet that hurt.

If it did, he showed no signs of it. Instead he crawled rather inexpertly up and down a couple of times. Then he struggled out of the water, shaking himself like an oversized terrier. She tried vainly not to laugh.

## SCREEN KISSES • 107

"I wouldn't put your name forward for the next Olympics," she said.

"If you're looking for an athlete try Muscle Beach," he replied gruffly. "I just make movies for a living."

"Sorry, I didn't mean to be rude. It's just that . . ."

"You expected a clean dive," he finished for her, "followed by a lot of graceful slicing through the water. Listen, lady, I swim to get cool, not to impress people with my social accomplishments. I don't pretend to be perfect. And I don't think you should either. It's no way to live."

She reached for the bottle of champagne in the ice bucket and poured herself a glass. "What are you trying to say?"

"That you're a terrific actress. That you've got charisma, watchability, call it what you like. And that's quite enough to be going on with. You don't need to go cutting your face up to prove you're a beautiful woman. You are a lovely woman with or without the plastic surgery."

She stiffened. "Who told you about the eye job?"

He crossed his fingers and put them behind his back. I'll make this up to you, Giselle, he thought. There's no way I'm going to convince this lady to work for me if I'm not straight with her.

"Giselle told me," he said. "And shall I tell you something? It doesn't matter a damn. If I look closer than you'll let me, I'm sure I could discover a scar. But from where I'm sitting nothing shows. I promise you."

## 108 • TRUDI PACTER

She looked serious. "But can the camera promise me that? Or am I going to look like some kind of monster in close-up?"

He thought for a moment. Then he said, "Claudia, I've got a proposition for you. I told you we're shooting the film in the South Seas. It's a desert island saga and nobody wears too much in those situations. Now here's what I've got in mind. We concentrate on footage of your well-known, well-lusted-after body, and we keep your face in mid-shot. If we need to go in close, then we'll put some gel on the lens."

She took a gulp of her champagne. The ice-cold bubbles prickled the roof of her mouth and she started to feel better. "It sounds great," she said, "but how can I be sure you'll do that?"

"Easy, I'll have it written into your contract. I'll make it a provision that all close-ups have to be personally approved by you. If you spot a scar we won't use the frame."

"You mean that?"

He breathed out and uncrossed his fingers. "Sure I mean it. Well, what do you say?"

"I'm interested. But I need time to think about it."

"Claudia," he said gently, "you haven't got time. I took a meeting with Dan Keyser last week and he's starting to run out of patience. You may think you have a three-picture deal but if you go on stalling like this Magnum's lawyers could just think otherwise."

She put down the champagne and pulled a face. So she had been right about him after all. He was tougher than he let on. Much tougher. Then she

## SCREEN KISSES • 109

thought, what the hell? I know tough guys too. I hire them to protect me.

"Give it a week," she said shortly, "then call my agent. He'll tell you whether or not we're in business." Then she picked up the towel he'd left lying on his chair and threw it at him. "Hurry up and get dressed," she instructed. "I'm expecting someone to come and pick me up in half an hour. And I don't want anyone to get the wrong idea."

The sun was going down when Delaney left, and despite the warmth of the evening Claudia started to shiver. Instinctively she reached down and stroked the smooth, warm coat of the dachshund that lay curled up at her feet. The dog opened its eyes and looked up at her.

"How straightforward you are," she said with affection. "There are no tricks with you. All you want out of life is to love me and to be with me. If only every guy I met was like you."

As if he understood, the dachshund got to his feet and climbed on to her lap. The two of them watched the sun go down over the palm-clad hill.

She had lied to Bob Delaney. There was no one picking her up that night, for she had nowhere to go. Claudia Graham was between parties. Between films. Between men.

When Chad had left her her life had gone into a kind of limbo. She had cancelled all her existing dates and told her secretary not to accept any more. She told her agent she was unavailable until further notice. Then she went to Rome and had her eyes done. It was her usual pattern when her love life went wrong. For she knew her value lay in the way she looked and if a man left her it was time for an overhaul. Only this time it had backfired.

The memory of what the Italian surgeon had done to her made her reach for the champagne bottle and refill her glass. Men, she thought. Even when I pay them they still let me down.

Her mind went back to the first time and the first man. His name was Harry Bach and she remembered his tall leanness and the way his hair seemed to spring from his head in thick, black curls. She remembered the way he beat her up too, but for the moment she preferred not to think about it. Instead she concentrated on their first meeting.

She had been so young then. Fifteen. A high school kid. No wonder I was impressed, she thought. Harry was nearly thirty then and a nightclub comedian. Mummy didn't tell me about men like you, she thought, smiling. And even if she had, I doubt if I would have listened.

She had gone to see him with a group of college kids she hung out with. He was playing at the local dance hall, Orange County's answer to Régine. There was an immediate attraction between them. After the show he had come up to their table and offered to buy her a drink. And she hadn't said no. When he asked her to have supper with him the following night she hadn't said no to that either. You didn't say no to a guy like Harry. So when he took her back to his hotel room and asked her to take off her dress and her pan-

## SCREEN KISSES • 111

ties and lay down on the bed for him she did what she was told.

In the beginning the evenings she spent with Harry in his hotel room were a bit like going back to school. She told him she was a virgin, and he didn't want to take that away from her. Not all at once. Instead he played with her, caressing the budding young breasts and sliding his hands between her legs until she was moist and excited and wanting more.

It went on that way for three nights. She would come to the show and afterwards he'd take her for a quick snack in the coffee shop of his hotel. Then they would go to his room, get undressed and lay on the bed. He would spend hours teasing her with his hands, and every part of her responded to him. Her breasts, her buttocks, between her legs. Even the soles of her feet. On the fourth night she couldn't stand it any more. "Do it to me," she begged him, "just do it. Otherwise you'll drive me crazy."

He put his cock in her hands and she felt for the first time how big and how hard it was. All the excitements he had given her before faded into insignificance. This was what it had been all about. This was what she had wanted from him. She guided him towards her, hoping that he shared her need. Then she stopped worrying. He knew the way after all.

She had read somewhere that it hurt the first time, that you had to learn to enjoy it, and she knew that whoever had written that had got the whole thing wrong. Taking Harry inside her hadn't hurt. Quite the reverse. It was as if all her life she had walked around with one of her senses dead. Now for the first

## 112 • TRUDI PACTER

time she was alive, as if the penetration of Harry's cock had somehow completed a circuit and the light had come on.

The light was extinguished two weeks later when Harry told her the gig in Orange County had come to an end. The next stop was Wichita and he had to be on his way.

"Take me with you," she wailed, "I won't get in the way." But Harry couldn't oblige. Until Claudia's father got in the act, then everything changed.

Claudia's old man was the foreman at the local steelworks. A tall, thin, balding man, he had a timid air, but his mild appearance was deceptive. Bill Graham had the temper of a raging bull, and when he vowed to kill the man who had seduced his underage daughter, Harry Bach knew he meant it. The fact that four heavies from the steelworks had him pinned against the wall of his hotel room had something to do with it.

Harry and Claudia were married the next week in Wichita. There was hardly a shotgun in sight.

The marriage lasted five years, all of which were spent on the road. Harry was strictly a stand-up comic, a remnant from the old vaudeville days. But there was a touch of Lenny Bruce about him which saved him from mediocrity. The other thing that made the act special was Claudia. After eighteen months' touring, Harry started to use her as a feed. The arrangement worked surprisingly well, for Claudia, who had always been mature for her age, had grown into a beauty. There was something about her combination of black hair and green eyes that made every man in the audi-

## SCREEN KISSES • 113

ence sit up straight and pay attention. Harry's line in patter did the rest.

As a double act they were a sensation. As a married couple, they didn't stand a chance. For Harry didn't really like women. That's not to say he didn't like sex. If their life together had been confined to the marital bed things would have worked fine. But they had to live together and work together as well, and that's where things came undone.

Every time Claudia wanted something, whether it was a new dress or an extra meal, Harry was irritated. Her dependence on him reminded him that he was no longer a free agent. And when Harry was irritated he took it out on Claudia. He yelled at her in front of the hotel staff. He frequently ignored her, lapsing into long, silent sulks that could last hours, sometimes days. And when he was drunk he beat her.

Claudia took it all in her stride. She loved her husband despite his temper, and the nights in bed more than made up for the trouble he gave her out of it. Claudia put up with Harry for five years until they hit the big time. When that happened she didn't have to put up with anything she didn't like ever again.

The big break came in Las Vegas. They were spotted by a talent scout from Warner Brothers who left his calling card and summoned them to a meeting after the show. Harry was in heaven. He had schlepped around the summer camp circuit, the Borscht circuit, the second-rate club circuit for nearly eighteen years. He had more than paid his dues. Now he was ready to be discovered.

## 114 • TRUDI PACTER

Unfortunately the talent scout didn't agree. He didn't want to discover Harry Bach; there were too many Harry Bachs out there already. The person he wanted to discover was Claudia Graham. With that hair and those tits she would be a sensation in Hollywood. He arranged a screen test, and despite Harry's protestations Claudia took a plane to Los Angeles and spent a day in front of the cameras. It proved to be the most decisive day of her life.

When Brigitte Bardot, Marilyn Monroe and Raquel Welch first walked on to the studio floor something special happened. The camera fell in love with them. When the Warner executives saw Claudia's screen test they realized the same magic was at work. They signed her on the spot. Three weeks later Harry got into town and discovered he was married to a film starlet. He yelled at Claudia to pack her bags and cancel her contract. They had a date to tour the Catskills; her duty to her marriage had to come first. Claudia was dumbstruck.

"Since when did marriage become important to you?" she asked Harry. "I didn't think you liked the arrangement."

"I'm used to the arrangement," was all he said. "Now hurry and pack. You're needed in the Catskills."

Claudia didn't move. "I'm needed here," she replied. "I start filming in two days' time."

"Like hell you do," he said, making a grab for her. They were standing in a suite of rooms at the Beverly Hills Hotel. From his breath, Claudia knew Harry had been drinking. She also knew that if she

## SCREEN KISSES • 115

stayed where she was, she would end up beaten and bruised which wouldn't look good on film. So she ducked, locked herself in the adjoining bedroom and called her agent.

Harry was escorted from the hotel by two heavies. Three days later he filed for divorce and Claudia was devastated. To her mind she hadn't done anything to deserve such treatment. Sure, she had broken up the act, but that was a business arrangement. What she and Harry had together transcended all that. They were married. They had taken vows in front of a priest. For better or worse, they had promised. For richer or poorer. Now he was going back on those promises just because she wanted to be an actress.

She tried calling him. He put the phone down when he heard her voice. She wrote to him begging him to change his mind. She even offered to give up her new career and follow him to the Catskills. To no avail. Harry Bach had given up on her. He had never wanted to be married and now he saw a way of getting out of it he grabbed it. Urging Claudia to pack her bags and leave Hollywood had simply been a jealous reaction. No, he was better off the way he was, the way he had always been. Fancy-free.

Claudia's divorce was finalized a week after her first film left the cutting room. As yet, cinema audiences had not seen the legend that was to become Claudia Graham, so she had no idea of her desirability or her glamour. All she knew was that she was a woman who had been abandoned by her husband, the man she loved.

She racked her mind for reasons why it had hap-

## 116 • TRUDI PACTER

pened. Had she bored him? Had she looked at another man? Had she failed to satisfy him in bed? Finally, in the depths of her despair, she turned in on herself. Her looks had to be the reason for her failure to keep Harry. She had just turned twenty-one and the schoolgirl freshness that had first attracted him was no longer in evidence. She was a woman now. Ripe and full. Well, she'd soon fix that.

She dieted for a month. At the end of it she had her high school shape back. The end of Claudia's diet coincided with the release of her picture, *Forever Female*. Overnight she was the new sex goddess. There was only one snag. She couldn't make personal appearances. If Hollywood's latest bombshell turned up looking as if she was dying from malnutrition the studio would have lost its investment.

So instead they hid her, giving the official reason that her recent divorce had forced her into seclusion. With her first film, Claudia Graham found herself with the reputation that she was sexy. And that she was trouble. They still think I'm trouble, she thought, looking into the palm-fringed sunset. Absently she patted the little dog which sat curled up in her lap. Then she thought of the film she had half promised to make with Bob Delaney. There had to be easier ways to live, though she couldn't think of any.

Dan Keyser and Bob Delaney were lunching at Ma Maison in Beverly Hills. Despite the fact that the studio boss didn't drink at this hour of the day he had ordered a bottle of champagne. Dom Perignon *premier*

## SCREEN KISSES • 117

*cru.* At 300 bucks a bottle it was the finest and most expensive the movie-set watering hole had on offer.

Dan raised his glass. "To you, Bob, for doing the impossible. And to Claudia Graham for agreeing to it."

Bob took a swig of the wine and tried to look impressed, which was difficult. No matter how many glasses of champagne he had raised in celebration he couldn't stand the stuff. It could have cost 600 bucks a bottle, double the inflated price that Ma Maison was charging, and he would have still winced at the taste. So he thought about Claudia Graham and the terms of her agreement. It made him feel better.

It had been a tough negotiation but in the end they had come to terms. Claudia was to get the hair-dresser and make-up team she always worked with. She was to have final veto on all her costumes. The unit had to provide an air-conditioned trailer of the most advanced design to be at her disposal on the set. And her decision on close-ups was final. The shots were to be taken with soft-focus lenses.

He sighed. It would make the picture look fuzzy if they weren't careful. But they were stuck with it. It wasn't the first time he'd had to make that kind of compromise. There was another provision, though, and that was a one-off. He had to make Claudia's dog comfortable. More than comfortable—the pooch was to have a first-class seat on the plane next to the actress; a cook had to be in attendance to prepare his meals; and a personal vet had to be on call when they were filming.

Bob worked out what it would cost, then he

## 118 • TRUDI PACTER

agreed to it. Whatever it took to please Claudia's dachshund he reckoned it was worth it. At least she hadn't insisted on choosing the cameraman.

He smiled at Dan, who was puffing on his cigar, watching the passing parade of agents and socialites. Ma Maison was the kind of place you went to when you were winning. It reminded him a bit of the beach cafés you find along the Croisette at Cannes. Brightly coloured awnings, pastel tablecloths, a feeling of sunshine and money. People came here to be seen, to be noticed. If life wasn't treating you well, you took your lunch someplace else.

The waiter came across to take their orders and Bob had his usual—a T-bone steak, rare; French fries and beans. Dan ordered a diet salad and looked unhappy.

"My wife," he explained, "she keeps on at me to lose weight."

He started nibbling at the dish of black olives in front of him. Bob wondered about Carla Keyser. Did she really lead this tubby, affable man such a dog's life? Or did he just enjoy complaining about her? He remembered all the jokes he had heard about Dan Keyser, and the one that stuck in his mind was "the son-in-law also rises." For Carla was the only daughter of Magnum's chief shareholder.

When she and Dan met, he was working for a top firm of showbiz lawyers. But he didn't stay a lawyer for long. The moment they got engaged, Dan landed a top job at Magnum. Two years after the wedding he became senior vice-president. When their first son

## SCREEN KISSES • 119

was born he was put in charge of production world-wide.

After that everything changed. For Dan found himself answering to two masters: Carla's father at the studio, and Carla at home. Bob had heard about Carla's charity committees, her industry jamborees, the way she sucked up to anyone remotely near the social elite. But he couldn't imagine Dan being taken in by any of that. He couldn't imagine him going along with it either.

Dan interrupted his thoughts. "Somebody told me you convinced Claudia to come back to work by dressing up like a bum."

Bob raised an eyebrow. "Who told you that?"

"One of my executives. He was probably just jealous he didn't do the job himself."

The Irishman leaned back in his chair. "Your executive wasn't far wrong. I did show up looking down-at-heels, but that's because I didn't want to frighten the lady. You don't really think Claudia would have told me what her real problem was if I'd gone to see her in a chauffeur-driven car with my briefcase under my arm."

Dan looked interested. "What was her real problem?"

"If I tell you, you've got to promise me not to panic."

The fat man held his hand out. "Deal," he said.

Bob told the studio chief about Claudia's experience with the Italian plastic surgeon and the way it made her nervous about close-ups.

Dan shrugged. "She's mad, of course, messing

## 120 • TRUDI PACTER

about with nature like that. She doesn't have to either. Not yet at any rate." He thought for a moment. "Tell me, Bob, do you think she has a problem?"

"Only in her mind. It took me a long time to convince her she wasn't the Phantom of the Opera. On screen or off. But she believed me in the end."

The food arrived, and Keyser attacked his salad like a starving man. "When I hear stories like the one you just told me," he said between mouthfuls, "I wonder what I'm paying my executives for. Why didn't one of them sort out the Claudia mess?"

Bob grinned. "Maybe you should try paying them more."

But Dan suddenly seemed to have lost interest in the studio. All his attention was taken up by something that was happening over the far side of the restaurant. "That blonde over there," he said. "Who is she?"

Bob followed the big man's line of sight. And when he saw who he was staring at, he started to laugh. For sitting in the corner of the restaurant dressed from top to toe in cream silk Chanel was Giselle Pascal.

Dan was irritated. "What's so funny?"

"Nothing." He took a sip of his drink. "It's just that I know the girl you're giving the once-over. As a matter of fact we're old friends."

The studio chief brightened visibly. "Then you won't mind doing a favour for a valuable business contact?"

"You want me to introduce you? With pleasure. Though I can't promise it's going to do you any good.

## SCREEN KISSES • 121

Giselle's not some dumb blonde who's going to drop her pants for a part in a film. She gave up acting a long time ago."

"So what does she do? Has she got a rich husband or something?"

"No, there's no husband on the scene. The lady works for a living. And very profitably. She introduces people. Organizes parties."

"You mean she's some sort of public relations executive."

Again the Irishman laughed. "No, and don't let her hear you say that. She'd be very insulted. Giselle operates on an altogether higher level than any PR. I suppose the best way to describe her is as a kind of power broker. She knows everyone who's anyone in this town. And she knows where the bodies are buried."

"She sounds as if she could be a useful person to have on your side."

"You could say that." Then he saw the look of naked lust on the fat man's face. "Of course it depends what you have in mind."

"What I have in mind," Keyser said roughly, "is none of your business. Just be a pal and introduce me, will you?"

Half an hour later Giselle and her lunch date got up from their table. As they did, Bob raised his hand in a salute and beckoned her over. The French woman whispered something to her companion then made her way across the restaurant. In Ma Maison, where attractiveness was mundane and beauty an everyday occurrence, Giselle was an exception. There was

## 122 • TRUDI PACTER

something haughty about the slant of her cheekbones and the way she carried herself. This girl was class and she knew it. From some of the looks she was getting as she threaded her way through the tightly packed tables, everyone else knew it too.

When she finally reached them she didn't take the chair Bob offered. Instead she hovered like a bright butterfly *en route* for greener pastures. The fact that she was going back to her flat for a lie down and a cup of coffee was not something she wanted anybody to know. In public she was fickle, on the move, in demand. That was how she earned her living.

She looked at her watch. *"Chéri,"* she said, "it's wonderful to see you, but I can't stay longer than a moment."

"Then I won't detain you." Bob smiled. "All I wanted to do was have you meet a friend of mine. Giselle, this is Dan Keyser of Magnum. Dan, Giselle Pascal."

Giselle extended her hand in the direction of the large, cigar-smoking man sitting next to Bob. She knew exactly who he was and she wondered why he had wanted to meet her. Surely Magnum had enough clout not to need the services of a fixer.

Keyser grabbed the pale, thin fingers and planted a kiss on three thousand bucks' worth of gold jewellery. It was a surprisingly accomplished gesture, and instead of backing off Giselle left her hand where it was.

*"Enchantée,"* she murmured. "Nobody told me you had charm as well as power, Mr Keyser."

"Call me Dan."

## SCREEN KISSES • 123

She withdrew her hand. It was becoming clear that Keyser was not looking to employ her in a professional capacity. She observed his wide gold wedding band and decided that she knew what was on his mind.

"I'll remember to do that," she said, ". . . next time we meet. Now if you'll excuse me, I really must run."

Then before either of them could say another word Giselle hurried out of the restaurant. Behind her she left a faint trail of Chanel No. 19. Bob turned to his companion. "Satisfied?" he said.

Keyser looked thoughtful. "Not yet," he replied, "but I will be."

Bob looked at the studio chief with new understanding. So that's how he handled being married to the boss's daughter.

The viewing theatre on Sunset Boulevard was one of those small, twenty-seater affairs the independents used when they didn't want to be hassled by studio executives. Over a mile away from Burbank, it had the grey anonymity Bob associated with porno movie houses. And today it suited his purposes, for he was simply looking at actors.

Behind him at the foot of the projector were reels of footage sent in by agents all over the country, and somewhere hidden in all the film were the half a dozen professionals he was seeking today—support acts for his two stars.

Bob looked across at the chubby, boyish-looking character sitting next to him. Maybe in your hands one of this band of hopefuls will end up a star, he thought.

It's been known to happen. To the casual observer, Delaney's companion looked like a cross between a high school dropout and a biker. He was wearing the delivery-boy uniform of battered jeans, tee-shirt and a black leather bomber jacket. It was the jacket that gave him away. The leather was too soft, too perfect to come from anywhere but Rodeo Drive. Rodeo Drive by way of Armani.

He was called Rick Hamilton and he was one of the trendy new directors emerging from the advertising industry in England.

At first Bob had been suspicious of him. He knew Magnum had Rick under contract and wanted to use him, so as a precaution he screened a couple of his films. He discovered the man had talent, that was for sure. Now all he needed to know was whether Rick could handle talent and understand a budget. Bob decided to buy him lunch.

They met in the Polo Lounge of the Beverly Hills Hotel. If there was such a thing as a gentleman's club for the film industry, then the Polo Lounge was it. It consisted of three rooms, and the one in which you sat determined how important you were.

The first room was for tourists and people who didn't know any better. If you sat there, you'd come for the food and the atmosphere. The second room was much the same, except it favoured the older crowd. The third room was where all the action was. If you were an agent or a movie star, this was where you sat. If you were talking heavy business, or if you were Barbra Streisand, you went one further and took

## SCREEN KISSES • 125

a table in the sunny courtyard that backed on to the third room.

Delaney decided to let Rick's secretary book the table for lunch. He wanted to see what value the town was putting on him that week—or what value Rick was putting on himself.

At first Bob thought the director hadn't shown up. He couldn't find him in the showbiz room and there was no sign of him outside under the trees. After twenty minutes he tried the other two rooms as a desperation measure, and he found Rick down amongst the tourists.

Either he has a sense of humour, thought Bob, or the guy doesn't give a goddamn.

Over lunch he discovered both things applied to Rick Hamilton. At thirty-six—ten years older than he looked—the director was a tall, well-made man with narrow black eyes and an air of the streets about him. He had got into films by way of newsreels, and there was nothing that daunted him. He was used to pushing his way through crowds or being shouted at and when he went into advertising this stood him in good stead. After ten years making thirty-second slots for dog food he had acquired another talent, which took him all the way to Hollywood. He was totally unimpressed by any form of bullshit.

Stars could threaten suicide, the front office could look like pulling the plug, but Rick Hamilton carried on regardless. All he cared about was staying as near to the budget as he could and finishing the film. Nothing else mattered.

His friendship with Bob was instantaneous. They

both saw things the same way, and they could work together without strain. All they needed now was a crew and a cast.

Four hours in the viewing theatre on Sunset Boulevard convinced them both that finding a cast was not going to be easy. They might have signed Claudia Graham and David Price but so far they were on their own. All the second-league players were dogs. They either looked terrific and couldn't act or they looked terrible and couldn't act.

By six, Bob decided to call it a day. "There's just one more piece of film I want to see," he told Rick, "then we'll wind it up. I'll get my girl to call around again tomorrow and see what else she can dredge up. If there's nothing here we'll try New York. I refuse to believe that out of a million unemployed actors in America there's no one right for this film."

Rick pulled out a cigarette and turned to the projectionist. "Roll it in five minutes, will you, love? I want to have a quick word with Bob." Then he turned to Delaney. "Tell me about this last reel you're going to show. You brought it in yourself, didn't you?"

Bob nodded. "It goes under the heading of favours for friends. Our leading man, David Price, has an agent who has a protégée. I said I'd take a look at her."

Rick scratched his head. "I suppose we have to go through the motions, though I don't like it. If this girl is so shit hot, why didn't he put her up in the normal way?"

"Because that's not how agents like Desmond French work. He moved heaven and earth to talk

## SCREEN KISSES • 127

David into this film. Now he expects to be thanked. And if this girl is half way good we have to consider her."

Rick looked doubtful. "I hate it," he said. "What part's she up for?"

"Mabel. The juvenile lead."

Rick laughed. "She'll have a hope," he said. "David Price is a difficult bugger to play against at the best of times. But against a newcomer? He'll eat her for breakfast."

"I know," said Bob, "but at least let's see what she can do. We'll talk about how we're going to get out of giving her the part later."

The director nodded. "Then let's get it over with. By the way you might tell me her name. Just for the record."

Bob looked down the typed list he was holding. "Rachel Keller."

Hamilton pulled a face. "Never heard of her."

They stopped talking as the lights went down in the tiny cinema. The flickering screen in front of them gave out the information that they were about to see a scene from *Gone with the Wind*. Rachel was playing Scarlett O'Hara. Both men leaned forward in their seats. If this kid wanted to make a fool of herself she had certainly chosen the right vehicle. Bob wondered what French could have been thinking of. He had always thought the English agent took a pride in the talent on his books.

Thirty seconds later he stopped thinking about French. In fact he stopped thinking about anything except the girl in front of him on the screen. She wasn't

## 128 • TRUDI PACTER

pretty, not in the accepted way, but she had style. There was something striking about her that drew the eye. In a group of other actors she was the one you wanted to watch. Delaney could see that if this girl was put on screen with David Price she'd give him a run for his money.

He felt Rick dig him in the ribs. "Ten out of ten for watchability," he muttered. "Now let's see if she can act."

Five minutes later neither of them was in any doubt about that. The girl had obviously had experience, though where had she got it? Bob had never seen her on film and he kept his eyes pretty much tuned to all the up-and-coming actresses on the market. If she had been in a TV soap, or even a one-off play for Channel Thirteen, he would have been aware of her. So where did she come from?

It was Rick who finally found the answer. "What's the betting this kid's come out of the English theatre—probably in the provinces."

Bob looked confused. "Why do you say that?"

"Firstly because her agent's British and secondly because of her performance. She's got more depth than you'd expect from a screen actress. This part she's playing, Scarlett O'Hara, she hasn't used any of the usual techniques to get it across. She's dragged her Scarlett up from somewhere inside her. When she acts that girl's showing you some private part of herself, some facet of her character. I should think she'd be very exciting to work with."

"Are you saying we should hire her?"

## SCREEN KISSES • 129

"You bet I am. As fast as you can before someone else grabs her and her price goes up."

Delaney did a fast rethink. For the kind of money he was offering he could buy himself a star name, an obvious box-office attraction. But would a star name have this girl's quality? Then he thought, what am I worrying about? With Claudia Graham and David Price I've got all the box office I need.

He turned to Rick. "OK, I'm with you. Let's put our money on this one. Who knows, you might even make a star out of her."

The director stubbed out his cigarette. "Desmond French will be pleased," he said.

**T**he plane had touched down three times during the twenty-five-hour journey: Dubai, Singapore and finally Jakarta, where Rachel caught the connecting flight to take her on the final lap to Bali. She had expected to feel tired. Garuda Airlines was packed with Indonesian families of all ages and sizes, all of them on the same economy deal as she was. The constant noise, the cramped conditions and the long queues for lavatories would have sapped anyone's strength. Rachel had only managed about three hours' sleep on the journey, yet when she finally landed on Bali she was full of energy.

She didn't know whether it was her new nose that did it, or the fact that she had landed a substantial part in an international movie, but she was filled with such excitement, such optimism that if she had been told

## SCREEN KISSES • 131

to appear on the set in full make-up within an hour of her arrival she would have done so, without worrying. As she walked through the glass doors of the air terminal she couldn't resist a glance at her reflection. Rachel, who had worn wigs, body paint and any manner of theatrical disguises, was still taken aback by one tiny change in her appearance.

She remembered the surprise she had felt when the plaster finally came off. The cosmetic surgeon had told her not to expect anything radically different, so she had been totally unprepared for what she saw. The only clue Dr Steel had given her about her new nose was that it would make her look younger. He had lied to her. It didn't make her look young at all. What it made her look was English. An English rose.

She had never been particularly conscious of her Jewish identity. Her parents might have made a fuss about it, but when she left home to come to London nobody in the Swinging Sixties gave a damn about her origins. So looking Jewish had never bothered her, until one day in an over-decorated Harley Street surgery she discovered she didn't any more.

For a moment she had felt like the victim of a huge confidence trick. Desmond French hadn't been concerned about camera angles at all. He thought she had a Jewish nose, and Barbra Streisand clearly filled Hollywood's non-Aryan quota.

The surgeon caught the expression in her eyes and was worried. "Rachel, there's something the matter, isn't there?" he said. "You don't like your new face."

"It's not that I dislike it," she said, genuinely confused. "It's just that I don't know it. This girl looking back at me in the mirror, she's pretty enough—when the swelling goes down, she will be anyway—but really, she isn't me at all."

He smiled. "She's not that different, you know. She's still got your eyes, and the mouth and chin are the same."

"I know, but they look different with this nose."

He made an effort to look patient. How many people had he had this conversation with? "Look," he said, "the space between your features, the proportions, are as important as the features themselves. I've given you a smaller nose and it's altered the balance of your face. Don't worry, you'll get used to it."

He must think I'm a fool, she thought. She looked at him. "But will my parents get used to it?" she asked. "And what about the rest of the community? They'll think I'm an outcast."

Dr Steel looked alarmed. "I didn't know you had a thing about being Jewish. Desmond French simply told me to give you a face he could sell for the screen. An unbiased face. Looking the other way would have cut down your chances, you know."

"I know that," she said, "and I made up all that stuff about the community and my parents. So there's no need to get in a twist. It's just that I wish you'd told me what you were going to do to me before you did it. I'm not an idiot and it is my face."

"If I'd told you, you might have changed your mind."

"Yes, I might, but don't you think that was my right? Desmond French doesn't own me, and judging

## SCREEN KISSES • 133

by the look of your office you're not going to starve if you lose a patient. Or should I say a customer?"

Then before he could reply she had walked out. The shock of seeing herself permanently altered was profound. She had known this was going to happen to her, but when it did she had no idea how to cope with it. It was as if she had lost an identity and no one had given her another one in its place. She could only look back on who she had been.

Then, as she walked into the bright sweltering day, she wondered if the change was such a bad thing. After all, who was she walking away from? A provincial repertory actress. A small-town girl who never really made it. Now she was earning 700 dollars a day for making a Hollywood film. Any way she looked at it, life could only get better.

Bali was like no landscape she had ever seen before. She had expected a tropical island of the type you see on picture postcards and holiday brochures. Instead she was confronted by a huge, mountainous jungle, criss-crossed by narrow roads. Even the villages bore no resemblance to any settlement she had encountered. The houses were fragile, almost shanty-like, yet among them were huge carved temples decorated with brightly painted birds and dragons which she later learned were ancient gods. She sensed she was in the centre of a civilization far older than her own. She was also aware of a kind of magic.

She came down to earth as the airport taxi approached the grounds of the hotel she had been booked into. Here the landscape changed abruptly.

## 134 • TRUDI PACTER

It was as if she had come upon an oasis in the middle of the desert—an oasis of Western civilization. She was driven past lawns as manicured as tennis courts. Here even the palm trees knew their place, for instead of spreading and straggling haphazardly, they stood smartly to attention along the winding avenue that led to the Nusa Dua Hotel.

At first Rachel thought she had arrived at the biggest Balinese temple in the world. The entrance to the hotel was in the style of the grander places of worship she had passed, and when she went inside, the vast marble hall that greeted her took her breath away. It was arranged in a rectangle around a central staircase. To one side were the usual hotel reception desks, only multiplied by ten. Rachel noticed there was even an airline booking office in the lobby. Beyond the reception and facing the entrance was the reconstruction of a beach bar with thatched roofs and groups of little tables.

All around the hall tourists stood in clusters, like clumps of undergrowth. Like any other travellers in smart hotels, they were ill-at-ease in their new holiday clothes and at a loss to know what to do with their two weeks of enforced leisure.

Rachel elbowed her way through a group sitting disconsolately on their suitcases and tried to catch the attention of one of the uniformed clerks behind the desk. At first she had no luck, then she brought her hand down on a bell. It did the trick. Three clerks hurried over to her and a porter appeared out of nowhere and took hold of her bags. Within five minutes she was checked in and on her way to her room.

## SCREEN KISSES • 135

The bedroom was another surprise. For it wasn't just a place to sleep, it was two rooms—one with a bed and one connecting with it that contained a sofa, a table, a fridge and a couple of easy chairs. Rachel sat down on the bed, luxuriating in the ice-cold air conditioning. This was the kind of suite Joan Crawford had in old movies. A mirrored bathroom lined with mosaic tiles led off the bedroom, and a wall of sliding glass revealed a terrace covered in flowers and creeping vines. Rachel motioned the porter to leave her bags. When he had gone she went through to the other room and opened the fridge. At this moment what she wanted most was to sit on her own private terrace, drink a glass of chilled wine, and enjoy the fact that she had arrived.

Three storeys up in the penthouse suite Bob Delaney and Claudia Graham were having their first confrontation. Claudia had arrived earlier that day to find nothing the way she wanted it. The swimming pool on her large private terrace was empty. Her hairdresser had been put in a room the size of a cupboard. Room service had taken an hour to arrive and didn't seem to have any French champagne. And worst of all, she hadn't been allowed to keep her dog in her room.

"The moment I got here," she told Bob, "some Indonesian in black tails took Oscar away. I thought they were going to find him something to eat, but when I called reception they said he was being kept in kennels. And I couldn't see him."

For a moment, Bob felt defeated. The camera crew and the catering unit had arrived the week be-

## 136 • TRUDI PACTER

fore and had been creating mayhem. Now it was the actors' turn. David Price had arrived first with his wife and their two-year-old son. The boy had instantly become ill with some form of Asian diarrhoea. The following day Price's wife Darleen had come down with the same bug. Now Price was threatening to go home to Sydney unless Bob could produce an American doctor. An Australian from the mainland would not do. Price had come up in the world and refused to have any truck with his countrymen when it came to legal affairs, financial affairs and his health.

In the end, when David's agent started laying down the law, Bob had flown in a man from Los Angeles and put him on the payroll. His experience of location work told him that when the bugs started to strike he needed all the help he could get. The expensive doctor was insurance against stomach upsets, malicious insects, all kinds of fever, gonorrhoea and heart attacks. Bob had just started to feel secure again when Claudia arrived.

"Didn't the manager call you?" he asked her in desperation.

"No, he didn't," she replied. "Nor did room service. Nor did my hairdresser. I dare say she's probably gone and committed suicide by now. In all my days I've never put up in such an inefficient hotel." She walked over to the terrace and gestured towards the empty swimming pool. "What they imagine they expect me to do in that, I have no idea."

A couple of suggestions occurred to Delaney but he suppressed them. I'm the producer of this fiasco,

## SCREEN KISSES • 137

he reminded himself. It's my job to make sure all the crazies are happy and comfortable.

He strode into the dining room and found the fridge. By miracle it contained two splits of Moët. It wasn't vintage Bollinger, but it was champagne, and it was French. He popped the cork on one of the bottles and, wrapping a table napkin round the label, brought it through to the terrace. "Sit down," he commanded, "drink this while it's still cold, and I'll go find the guy who runs the place."

Before Claudia could say another word he was out of the door and on his way down the corridor. It took Bob Delaney ten minutes to discover that the manager was away on his annual holiday. It took him another five to locate his deputy. After that things went relatively smoothly. The hairdresser was found a bigger room. The water was turned on in Claudia's pool. Room service located a crate of Bollinger. The problem was the dog. The undermanager, a young Australian, pointed out that keeping Oscar in the hotel contravened the local health regulations.

Delaney put on his most persuasive manner. "Oscar's a very small dog," he said. "If Miss Graham put him in one of her bathrooms, couldn't you look the other way?"

The Australian shook his head. A regulation was a regulation. It was more than his job was worth to disregard it. Delaney sighed deeply and made his way back to Claudia's room.

When he got there, he discovered a small party in progress. The hairdresser and the make-up man were spread out around the pool drinking the local

## 138 • TRUDI PACTER

beer. Claudia had made a start on the second split of champagne. She had also changed into a bikini and left the top half of it off.

Nothing had prepared Bob for the sight of Claudia without clothes on. When he first met her in Los Angeles he realized she had a good body—a worked-out body—but he hadn't guessed how voluptuous she would be. Even the screen disguised it. He tried not to stare at her breasts, but it was no good. There was something tactile about them, something that invited you to reach out and touch.

He was caught momentarily off-balance. He had come to tell Claudia that she couldn't have her beloved dachshund close to her in her room. It had taken time to summon up the courage to tell her the news to her face. Telling it to her breasts was something he hadn't counted on. He hadn't counted on her reaction either.

"If Oscar isn't good enough for this hotel," she said calmly, "then nor am I."

Then she strode through to the bedroom, got her suitcase out and started flinging her things into it. Delaney knew a crisis when he saw it. With an effort he kept his eyes on Claudia's face. "Hold what you're doing right now," he said. "I'll go and solve the dog problem. Do nothing till I get back."

From the corner of his eye he saw the fat, crinkly-haired make-up man give the thumbs-up sign to his companion. The hairdresser winked in turn to Claudia. Delaney kept his cool. Under other circumstances he would have wrung both their necks. But he was on location in Bali, these inflated assholes were

## SCREEN KISSES • 139

Claudia's inner circle, and Claudia was his star. He summoned up what was left of his dignity and for the second time that day went in search of the hotel management.

This time he didn't beard the undermanager in his office. Instead he took him for a drink in the swimming-pool bar.

The Nusa Dua boasted one of the most spectacular pools in the whole of the island. It was circular and enormous—about a quarter of a mile in diameter. Right in the centre of it, like a jewel in a dancer's navel, was a sunken beach bar. In order to reach it you stepped along a walkway leading from the side of the pool. When you got there, you realized that it was possible to drink a pina colada on a tiny, shaded dance floor by the inside bar. If you were feeling overcome by the sun it was also possible to sit submerged on a barstool buried in the pool where you were served by the outside bar. Delaney decided to stay where it was dry. He liked to have all his clothes on when he was negotiating.

He started the conversation with the good news. The pool on Claudia's terrace was more or less full. Room service had located a supply of her favourite champagne. Claudia's hairdresser was overjoyed with her new room. Then he talked about the dog. At the mention of the dachshund the young Australian ordered himself another beer. "I wish you wouldn't push me on this," he said crossly. "The rules clearly state, no animals in the rooms. There's no way I can get round it."

## 140 • TRUDI PACTER

Delaney cleared his throat. "What if I made it worth your while?"

The young Australian pulled the ring from his can of beer and took a swig. "If you're offering me a bribe, there's nothing doing. I won't be paid off by film companies. And I won't be told how to run my hotel by neurotic starlets."

Delaney leaned back in his chair and let the slow, easy smile spread across his face. "Number one," he said, "Claudia Graham isn't some starlet. She's one of the hottest properties in Hollywood and don't you forget it. Number two, I wasn't offering to pay you off. I was offering to make your life easier."

The undermanager looked curious. "How?" he asked.

"By preventing the mass exodus from this hotel of most of my unit. We're staying here on and off for the next two and a half months. I don't think your manager will be too impressed when he comes back from his holiday if you tell him you've gone and mislaid around seventy bookings."

"You wouldn't do that," he breathed. "You couldn't. Where would you put them all?"

"Listen, sweetheart, I've been in this business a very long time. For your information Bali isn't my first location and it sure as hell won't be my last. I'll find other sleeping arrangements for my unit, you can depend on it."

Outside the beach bar the sun blazed down, making the swimming pool sparkle and the undermanager sweat. "Don't be in such a hurry," he said sharply.

## SCREEN KISSES • 141

"Why don't we have another beer and talk the problem over? Maybe there's a way out of it."

The smile returned to Delaney's face. Only this time it didn't look so friendly.

As if responding to some hidden signal, the waiter came across to their table with two more beers. He also brought with him a dish of olives and a plate of small, spiced sausages.

There are two ways of doing things, Delaney thought to himself. The nice way and the nasty way. He was genuinely sad he had been forced to choose the latter.

It took half an hour for the two men to effect a compromise over Oscar's fate. The Australian hotel man came up with the idea of keeping the dog on Claudia's terrace. It was an open area and technically could not be classed as a room. Delaney ventured that he could convince Claudia that Oscar's new sleeping arrangements were the best she could hope for, so long as the hotel provided a kennel with a soft, cosy bed. As the sun went down the two men shook hands on the deal and the Australian manager returned to his office.

Delaney put his feet up on the side of the pool and considered having a swim. It had been a long, hot day. Tomorrow, he knew, would be longer and hotter. For his director Rick Hamilton had planned some preliminary setups and most of them involved Claudia Graham. He sighed wearily and ordered another beer.

While he was waiting for it his attention was caught by a tall, thin girl walking towards the pool.

Most of the sunbathers had gone in as the dusk approached but even if it had been crowded the girl would have stood out. She was lean, the way a young colt was lean—all angles and long, trembling limbs. Her skin was very white against her black one-piece swimsuit, and her hair was a riot of disorderly red curls. There was something familiar about her. He searched his mind for where he had seen her before. But it was late. He was tired. And the beer was beginning to blur the edges of his mind.

The girl had put her towel down and was walking towards the edge of the pool. When she reached it she stood tall and straight against the setting sun as if resolving how best to get into the water. Then without any warning she put her thumb and forefinger to the end of her nose, closed her eyes and jumped in feet first. There was something awkward and clumsy about the gesture that Bob found endearing. Before she had crashed feet first into the pool he had put her down as just another beautiful bimbo on her summer vacation. Now she intrigued him.

He watched as she made a circuit of the huge azure pool. She was a surprisingly strong swimmer and she clearly enjoyed it, for she got her hair wet and she put her head right under. When she finally came up for air he gave her a wave and pointed towards his glass.

The girl nodded enthusiastically and splashed over to where he was sitting.

"What will it be?" he asked.

"Do they have wine?"

SCREEN KISSES • 143

He pulled a face. "Only Australian. I hear it's a bit rough."

She grinned. "That'll do. I'm not fussy as long as it's cold and wet."

He signalled to the bartender for some wine. Then he remembered the last time a girl had asked him for wine and he felt relieved that this stranger by the pool bore no resemblance to her. Actresses, he thought. They only drink champagne if it's French and they scream for the hairdresser every time they go near a swimming pool. The girl had found her towel and was wiping her face and drying her curls. He noticed she wasn't wearing a scrap of make-up and that cheered him too. There was something natural and unselfconscious about her. He got the impression that she travelled light and lived rough and didn't give a damn for the fashions of the day.

He extended a hand and patted the seat next to him. "Come and sit down. You look as if you could do with it after all that exertion."

She shook her head, scattering the damp red curls over her shoulders.

"Damn right," she said, "I've been travelling for twenty-five hours. And that little lot in the pool has just about finished me off."

"Where did you fly in from?" he asked, mildly curious.

"London," came the reply. "I can't tell you what a treat it is to get away from all that damp and cold."

She didn't have a noticeable accent like a lot of British girls he had met. His trained ear picked up that the pitch was damn near perfect. He looked at her again and suddenly he knew exactly who she was and where he had seen her.

"What did you say your name was?"

She looked him in the eye. "I didn't."

Now he was really interested. "Why won't you tell me who you are?"

"Because you may turn out to be a dreadful bore or the hotel lecher. And if we were on first-name terms, then I'd never get rid of you."

"You're nothing if not direct. Are all English girls so upfront?"

"Only the ones who lead interesting lives."

"And what's so interesting about yours?"

She thought for a moment, then she looked at him from underneath her eyelashes. "The men I know," she said. "Or rather the men who keep me. I suppose you could call me a *poule de luxe.* My lovers are all terribly rich. And they make sure I live in the style that suits me."

He smiled. "What style is that?"

She gestured around her. "This kind of thing. Big hotels, azure swimming pools. The best of everything."

He was tempted to tell her she was lying. He knew exactly who she was. He even knew the size of her cheque. Then he thought, what the hell? If she wanted to play games, he'd go along with it.

He kept a straight face. "How long have you been in this line of business, if that's not too personal a question?"

She took a sip of her wine. "Not at all. You don't know who I am, so a few personal details can't do any

## SCREEN KISSES • 145

harm. I've been in this line of business, as you call it, for about eight years now. And if you're going to ask me what a nice girl like me is doing in a profession like this, I'll tell you. It's easy. I don't have to keep regular hours and I don't have to answer to anybody. Well, not all the time anyway."

Bob tried not to laugh. She had probably played a kept woman in some play, for the lines were coming out too pat. If she'd been the real thing she'd have been as coy as hell. He decided to tell her.

"If you're accustomed to this fat lifestyle, how come you're happy to drink Australian wine? And rough Australian wine at that."

She didn't miss a beat. "Simple," she said. "One of my keepers is an Aussie. A very patriotic one. He uses domestic products wherever possible. As I'm *en route* to see him I thought I'd get into practice for the experience."

He leaned forward. "I admire your dedication," he said. "You can't beat a professional who respects her calling enough to do the job thoroughly."

She raised an eyebrow. "What's your calling?" she asked.

"Nothing glamorous. In fact if I were you I wouldn't give me a second glance. I'm a farmer back in Arizona, where I come from. I'm in cattle mostly, though I keep a couple of herds of sheep as well. In fact now I think of it, you were wise not to tell me your name. After two glasses of Australian wine I'd bore you to tears." He stood up. "No, you had a lucky escape. Chances are if we'd got better acquainted I might even have taken a shine to you."

## 146 • TRUDI PACTER

He put his glass down and got to his feet. "If I don't see you again, have fun in Australia." Then he leaned over, kissed her on the cheek and made his way out of the bar. As he waited for the elevator to take him to his room he rubbed the side of his face thoughtfully. It would be interesting to see how she handled herself when they met again that evening.

Rachel lay in the bath and tried to figure out what she was going to wear. Rick Hamilton had invited everyone in the cast to drinks in his suite, and the prospect filled her with excitement and a certain dread.

What do you wear, she wondered, to meet Hollywood? She imagined it was the showbiz equivalent to being presented at court. Except she wasn't expected to wear a tiara. She went over the contents of her wardrobe in her mind. There were three pairs of jeans, an assortment of cotton shirts, a wraparound cotton skirt and a plain black shift. The shift had been hastily purchased at Harrods and was Desmond French's idea.

"For heaven's sake, dear," he had said, "you've got to take something half way respectable. What if the producer or one of the stars wants you to have dinner? You can't turn up looking like a charity case."

After the way he had lied to her about her nose she had been tempted to tell him that the way she looked on her time off was her business, but she held her fire. He had got her the juvenile lead in a Hollywood film. For that he deserved some respect. So she dipped into her savings and spent over a hundred pounds on the basic, black, raw silk dress. After her

## SCREEN KISSES • 147

bath Rachel took the dress out of the wardrobe and held it up in front of her. It was very smart, there was no denying it. For a welcome party it was probably a better idea than the wraparound skirt, particularly with Claudia Graham around.

Her mind made up, she threw it on the bed and went to work on her face.

She applied the cosmetics in the mindless, automatic way of every actress she had ever known. Panstick, powder, blusher, shadow. It was a ritual she knew by heart. As her fingers did their work, she let her mind wander.

I wonder what Claudia Graham will look like in the flesh, she thought. And David Price. Is he really that tall? And that blond? Or is it just a trick of the light? For a moment while she was applying her lipstick she considered Bob Delaney, the producer—the man in charge of them all. Then she put him out of her mind. He's bound to be fat and boring, she decided. They always are.

When she had finished getting ready, she surveyed herself in the mirror. A tall, angular woman in a black dress stared back at her. She had braided her hair that night and it hung down over one shoulder. Smart, she thought, though a bit on the severe side. She reached down into a drawer and fished out a pair of gold hoops which she fixed through her ears. Then she patted her dress, grabbed her handbag and headed off to the penthouse suite.

The door was opened by a butler holding a tray of drinks in one hand. There was a choice of champagne or a tropical cocktail, which looked long and

## 148 • TRUDI PACTER

cool and was decorated with a spray of exotic flowers. Rachel grabbed a glass, but her first mouthful told her she had made a mistake. What looked like innocent fruit juice tasted like pure alcohol. She forgot about the drink and concentrated on the party.

The guests were dressed up in their best and were standing around in awkward little groups. Rachel was reminded of every read through she had ever been to. The location was more glamorous, the faces were better-known, and nobody was drinking instant coffee, but the tension in the air was the same she had known in Worthing rep when the cast met for the first time. She noticed Claudia Graham holding court in the centre of the room, and she was impressed. She had expected a glamour puss, but Claudia was more than that. There was something mysterious—almost exotic—about her. Perhaps it's her dress, thought Rachel. Then she dismissed the thought. She knew she could have worn the lamé sheath and looked commonplace. No, what was special about Claudia was her glow. There was something luminous about her skin, her eyes, her hair. It was almost as if she carried around her own personal spotlight.

David Price, who was standing next to Claudia, couldn't take his eyes off her. Claudia was ranting on about camera techniques, but she could have been reciting the telephone directory for all it mattered. The Australian was clearly fascinated. I wonder how long it's going to take him to get her into bed, Rachel mused. Her eyes lingered on the rugged shoulders, the shock of white-blond hair, the handsome beach-

## SCREEN KISSES • 149

boy face. She did a swift calculation. I bet he makes it tonight, she thought.

Then she remembered something. David Price had just got married to a woman much younger than him. Was it his second wife or his third? Whichever she was, Rachel didn't give much for her chances.

The door connecting the room with the bathroom opened, and as if on cue David's wife came into the room. She was a slight, blonde woman whom Rachel recognized from the paparazzi pictures. Behind her she trailed a two-year-old. The pair of them looked harassed.

"Howie's been sick," said the blonde to no one in particular.

David looked up from his conversation and waved to his wife and his son. The woman pushed her way across to him, then planting herself in front of him, she demanded, "I want you to call the American doctor."

There was a whine in her voice that spoke of dishwashers and the suburbs. Despite her expensive dress she looked as if she was losing her battle with the calendar.

The child tugged at her arm then let out a long, thin wail. The woman looked desperate. Just then a second man joined them, and as he did the hope returned to her eyes. "There you are," she said, fastening on to his arm. "I've been searching for you everywhere."

Rachel did a double take. That was the same man she had seen at the pool only an hour ago; the man

## 150 • TRUDI PACTER

she had flirted with and lied to. What the hell's he doing here? she thought. He's meant to be a farmer.

It was soon apparent that he was anything but. With a certain efficiency he calmed David Price's wife and sent someone running off to find the doctor. Then he took hold of Claudia's arm and started to talk about costume fittings.

That's no farmer, Rachel thought. The bastard was having me on. As soon as Claudia had disappeared into the crowd, she made her way over to him. "How are things down on the ranch?" she said.

He had very black eyes, and they glittered as he looked at her. "Things are fine on the ranch," he said pleasantly. "How's the action in the boudoir? Or have you brought one of your rich lovers with you?"

"Ouch," she said. "I asked for that. Listen, can we start again? Who exactly are you? And what are you doing at this party?"

He grinned. " 'What are you doing here?' she asks me. I would have thought it was obvious. I'm organizing this show. And I'm cleaning up after everyone's mess."

Her confidence deserted her. "Christ," she said. "You're not who I think you are, are you?"

He extended his hand. "I'm Bob Delaney," he said. "You're Rachel Keller. And this joke has gone on quite long enough."

She suddenly started to feel foolish. She had dismissed this man as fat, bald and not worth talking to. Now she was standing beside him she didn't want to talk to anyone else.

"I guess I owe you an apology," he said softly.

## SCREEN KISSES • 151

"I knew who you were before I picked you up this afternoon. It was wrong of me to let you go on with that ridiculous charade."

She looked at him. "Then why did you?"

"Because I thought you were pretty and natural. And you looked like you were having fun."

He looked at his watch. "I'm going to wind this up in half an hour. If you haven't got any other plans, why don't you have dinner with me tonight? Now you know I'm not the hotel bore you can feel quite safe."

She smiled and made a face. "How do I know you're not the hotel lecher?" she asked.

A chauffeur-driven car was waiting outside the hotel to take them to the restaurant he had reserved. As Rachel settled back into the expensive-smelling leather seats she thought about the last time she had been courted. It had been a cheap curry then and a strip show. She wondered if she would like this any better.

She glanced at the man sitting beside her. He looked tougher and more grown-up than anyone she had known before. Yes, she decided, I think I'm going to like this way better.

He started to talk about the party they had just left. And because she was curious, Rachel asked him about David Price. Only a few years ago he had been an unknown Australian model, a nobody. Now he had a mansion in LA as well as his spread outside Sydney. And he took home nearly as much as Redford. "He must have an extraordinary talent," Rachel said. "I mean to succeed the way he was."

Bob laughed. "I suppose you could say that,

## 152 • TRUDI PACTER

though David's talent isn't all in the acting department. He'd be terrible if you tried to put him on stage, for example. And even his screen performances owe more to the director and the cutting room than they do to him. But none of that matters because David's got star quality. You see it when he walks into a restaurant. Dustin Hoffman could walk into Chasens or the Polo Lounge and hardly anybody would notice. David does the same thing and everyone stands to attention. Sophia Loren has the same kind of charisma. Whatever she does you have to watch her."

Rachel looked interested. "You're saying David succeeded because of his looks?"

"Partly that. And partly because of his push. David's one of those tough Aussies who won't take no for an answer. When he was a model boy trying to be an actor he once sat in a casting director's office for thirty-six hours. He didn't even go home to sleep. In the end the director found him a part just to stop him pestering the receptionist."

She grinned and turned round in her seat. "I'm impressed. Tell me, how long has our leading man been married to the skinny blonde girl?"

Bob fished in his pocket for a cigarette. "Not long. Two or three years. What makes you so interested?"

She paused, wondering how far to go. Finally she decided to be honest. "Because from where I was standing they looked like they had problems."

Bob flicked his lighter to the end of his cigarette and in the flickering brightness she saw he was smiling.

## SCREEN KISSES • 153

"You mean you thought young Darleen was in danger of losing her husband to Claudia, don't you?"

"Yes, I suppose I do."

He put his hand briefly over hers. "I wouldn't worry about her if I were you. Although Darleen might look like a dying swan, she's anything but. Let me tell you how she met David. Or rather how she hooked him." He settled back in his seat. "They ran into each other on a film set in Los Angeles. David was married to his first wife then and Darleen was just the continuity girl. But she was gorgeous to look at then, and David was smitten.

"In the beginning he didn't mean it to be anything serious. He was quite content with the woman he was married to. He had been with her for twenty years, for heaven's sake. So he saw Darleen secretly and didn't make her any promises.

"He might have got away with a discreet fling if Darleen hadn't been so determined. You see, she knew who she was. She knew she was a beautiful nobody. She also grasped the fact that with David she could get to be a somebody. So she went to work on him."

Rachel was surprised. "What on earth could Darleen do that a million others couldn't? There aren't those many new things to do in bed."

"No, there aren't. And that's not how she got him. Darleen won out because she treated David like a king. She became his chauffeur, his butler, his personal masseuse. Nothing was too much trouble for her. Shirley, his wife, was used to fetching and carrying for him but she had been doing it for so long that he took it for granted. Anyway she wasn't as determined as Darleen. Or as young. After a couple of years of being David's personal slave Darleen finally got what she wanted. She became the wife of a movie star. And just to make sure it stuck, she got pregnant immediately afterwards."

Rachel shrugged. "I bet she's regretting that now."

"I wouldn't be so sure. Darleen doesn't have to drag that kid around the way she does, you know. With their kind of money she could afford to hire a fleet of nannies. But she insists on looking after the boy herself because it suits her. David adores the child, and by attaching herself to him the way she does, Darleen constantly reminds him that it was she who was responsible for him being there in the first place."

Rachel grinned. "You mean what Darleen gave, Darleen can also take away."

The car drew up in front of the restaurant. "That's about the size of it," said Bob. "And let me tell you something. If I had to put money on either Darleen or Claudia succeeding with David, right now my money would be on Darleen. She's the one with more to lose."

From the outside the restaurant didn't look like anything special—just a couple of shacks by the side of a dirt track. But when they went through the heavy wooden doors it was as if they had stepped into another world. The hallway was dimly lit and furnished with the ornate wooden carvings that Rachel was beginning to find familiar. She had expected to walk into

## SCREEN KISSES • 155

a restaurant, but instead when they reached the end of the passage they were in the open air again. In front of her Rachel saw the glint of water and realized that she had to cross a stream before she could sit down to dinner. A tiny humpbacked bridge led the way towards the restaurant. When she got there, Rachel realized she was in a garden.

All around her was the heavy scent of tropical flowers, and from the trees she heard the tinkling of chimes. About a dozen tables were set out underneath a fragile-looking wooden structure, and Rachel got the feeling that she was intruding on a culture that was ancient and in some way magical.

They were ushered to seats in the corner of the restaurant by three waitresses who hovered about them like moths. Bob ordered himself a bourbon then he turned to Rachel. "What will you have?"

Before she could answer he said, "Don't let them sell you one of their tropical cocktails. I saw you dickering with one of them at the party, but if you have hopes for your health or your future I'd steer clear of them."

She smiled. "I may be new around here but that much I do know. I think I'll take a glass of wine."

He was an agreeable dinner companion. After their encounter at the pool she hadn't known what to expect, but he was neither a lecher nor a bore. There was a humour about him that she liked. As the evening went on, she realized that Bob's ability to laugh was one of the main reasons for his survival. A movie star could throw a fit of temperament; the entire camera crew could go on strike; his backers in Hollywood

## 156 • TRUDI PACTER

could pull the plug; and all Bob Delaney would do was order another beer and smile at the absurdity of fate.

For it was fate's absurdity that led him into the film business in the first place. His father managed an Irish bar in Gramercy Park, one of the lovely, older sections of Manhattan, and Bob was brought up there, washing glasses, preparing snacks and generally running around for anyone who gave the orders. His father expected Bob to grow up and inherit the running of the bar when he retired. Only it didn't work out that way. Bob Delaney did not see himself running a bar. He didn't have anything against bars. It was just that growing up in New York had given him broader horizons. To his father's fury, he took a job as an office boy in the Moss Hart empire when he left school, and once he had had a taste of the entertainment business he was hooked. After five years he decided he had done enough running around for other people, so he lied about his age and the nature of his job with Moss Hart and applied for the job of junior agent at MCA, one of America's biggest talent agencies. He got it because of his background with Moss Hart, and because the deal that MCA was offering was so threadbare that only a former office boy would want to take it.

Bob started at MCA on fifty dollars a week and a percentage of any business he brought into the agency. In exchange he was provided with the use of half a secretary and an office the size of a broom cupboard. In his first month, he brought in a group of Irish folk singers he found through his father. He built

## SCREEN KISSES • 157

them up as much as he could, but none of them was going to grow fat on it.

So for his next discovery, he looked farther afield. He started visiting the Grand Ole Opry in Nashville, and it was here that he found Cherry Miller.

Like many of her predecessors she was a farmer's daughter. And she sang with the intensity of somebody who had known poverty. Cherry Miller was Bob's first big success. He built her up slowly, booking her into dance halls and vaudeville, then when she was ready he talked a record company into cutting her first single. After that she never looked back.

Bob set up his own agency on the proceeds of Cherry Miller. But even then he saw that if he wanted to make money he had to get involved in the movie business. Two years after he set up, he found a director who wanted a negotiator. They went into business, and in the four years of their partnership the Irish agent organized CBS Television for a series, Warner Brothers for a second feature and United Artists for a star vehicle. The star vehicle involved Shirley MacLaine and Jack Nicholson. It made a great deal of money for everyone involved with it.

For Bob, the best thing about success in America was the rewards it brought. He rented a duplex in the Seventies. When he moved to Los Angeles he had a house with a pool. The girls improved as well. In the past he had dated agents like himself—working girls with ambitions and responsibilities and too little time to listen to his problems. When he became a successful producer every actress in town wanted to know him.

## 158 • TRUDI PACTER

Not run-of-the-mill actresses, but famous ones, women with style and sex appeal.

He ended up marrying the classiest one of them all—the Broadway star Kathy Gordon. Two years into the marriage he realized he had made a mistake. Like the working girls he used to know, Kathy had little time for anyone's problems but her own. In the beginning Bob didn't notice. She had too much sex appeal for him to notice anything very much. She bore him a son, and just as things looked perfect Bob went broke. A film he'd financed ran into weather problems and cleaned him out.

Bob took it on the chin with his customary good humour. After all he had Kathy. Together they would survive. Only Kathy wasn't interested. She had fallen in love with a success, and now Bob wasn't one any more she couldn't handle it. There was a silence between them which was broken only by the demands of her divorce lawyer.

"Kathy Gordon must have made you cynical about actresses," said Rachel. They had reached the coffee stage of dinner and she was starting to feel less in awe of him.

He leaned back in his chair and looked at her. "If I felt that badly about actresses we wouldn't be having dinner now. No, I like girls who earn their living on the stage. I often date them. I just take care not to get involved, that's all."

"How do you mean?"

"You want me to spell it out?"

She nodded.

"OK. In my book, actresses are for affairs.

## SCREEN KISSES • 159

They're very sexy, they're easy-going and they don't get too possessive. They can't really afford to. They move around too much." He paused. "But if you're talking about love, commitment, caring, forget it. I'd sooner shoot myself than marry an actress."

Rachel put down her coffee cup. "And I'd rather shoot myself than have an affair with a film producer."

He signalled the waitress for the bill. "Before you make statements like that," he said, "hadn't you better wait for the film producer to ask you?"

They drove back to the hotel in silence. Outside in the warm night air, the crickets danced and chirped. Inside the car you could cut the air-conditioned atmosphere with a knife. Then when they got to the hotel he took her by the arm and led her to the reception desk.

"I would have asked you up for a nightcap, but I'm worried you might jump to the wrong conclusion. Anyway you've got an early start tomorrow morning. We all have."

The porter handed them the keys to their rooms. Rachel picked hers up. "Thank you for dinner," she said. "It was fun, until you talked about shooting yourself."

He took her by the shoulders and kissed her on the lips lightly, the way you kiss a child. "Don't take it to heart," he said. "It was a pleasant evening. And you're a very pretty girl. I think there'll be less hassle all round if we just leave it like that."

Giselle Pascal lived in a tiny, rather spectacular house cut into the side of a hill midway between Los Angeles and the prosperous suburb of Beverly Hills. She could easily have afforded to live nearer to the movie colony but she didn't choose to. When she failed to make the grade as an actress back in New York she put that part of her life behind her. If she couldn't be a star then she certainly wasn't going to ape their habits.

Instead she carved out her own style. Her house was built on three levels, the topmost being the showpiece. To say it was a penthouse room would have been to denigrate it, for a penthouse implies modern furniture and little imagination. The long, low room with its views of the valley did not fit into that category at all. Giselle had filled it with antiques she had had

## SCREEN KISSES • 161

shipped over specially from Paris, including Empire furniture covered in gilt and elaborate carving. It had an opulent, decadent look to it and she had completed the effect with her choice of paintings. The oils she hung on her walls depicted courtesans in various stages of undress, gamblers getting drunk in bordellos, lovers in the act of coupling. Yet there was nothing tacky about Giselle's paintings. Like the furniture they were old enough to know better.

Giselle didn't begrudge her role in the Hollywood merry-go-round. It kept her in French antiques and designer diamonds. But just occasionally she longed for a little appreciation—a modicum of applause. When Dan Keyser called her a week after they met in Ma Maison her instincts told her that this could be the break she was looking for.

As far as the movie colony was concerned, Keyser was one of the three most powerful men in town. The other two were David Begelman at Columbia and Ray Stark. So when Keyser asked her to have lunch with him she didn't question the reason for his invitation. She accepted it gracefully and took special care with her appearance on the day.

They met at Spago, the unofficial headquarters of the movers and shakers in the industry. Giselle noticed with approval that Dan had a regular table in the window.

Spago was best known for its pizzas and its view over Los Angeles, but its clientele didn't go there for either. They went there to be seen. What made Spago more attractive than its rivals was the sheer difficulty of getting a table. Most evenings there was a queue

## 162 • TRUDI PACTER

of people waiting to sit down, and they weren't just anyone either. Giselle had seen tycoons and movie stars standing in line. So when she was led straight over to Dan Keyser's table by the window, she gave him ten out of ten for clout. Then she sat down and looked at his great, curving nose and black, crinkly hair and gave him three out of ten for looks. Any other girl would have jumped to an immediate conclusion. Homely-looking, powerful men don't ask women they hardly know to lunch unless they are up to no good. However, Giselle liked to back her instincts with hard facts, so she played for time and waited for Dan to make his move. This he did over the *spaghetti alla carbonara*. It did nothing for her appetite.

"I want you to come away with me," he said, looking her in the eye. "This is not something I can explain, but I'm crazy for you."

Giselle was startled. She had heard a fair amount of bullshit but this beat everything. With an effort she kept her temper.

"I'm not an actress or an agent you can buy," she said, "so what can you possibly offer me that I don't already have?"

"I've already told you I'm crazy about you," he protested. "What more do you want?"

She looked at him shrewdly. "More than you're prepared to give. You don't really expect me to believe the hearts and flowers line, do you? I'm not stupid. And I know exactly who you're married to. I even know why you're married. So don't try me."

Now it was Keyser's turn to be startled. He had

## SCREEN KISSES • 163

come to Spago in the spirit of fantasy and romance, as a dashing white knight preparing to sweep a fair lady off her feet. At best he had expected her to capitulate. At worst he thought she'd walk out. What he didn't expect was a negotiation.

It occurred to him to cut his losses and walk out of the restaurant. Then he glanced over at the French girl and caught his breath. Underneath the fine silk chemise she was wearing he could swear she was completely naked. Lust overtook his judgement.

"Giselle," he said thickly. "What is it that you want?"

She didn't hesitate. "Power," she said. "I want people to know who I am." Then she paused. "Look, let me explain something to you. Since I came to Hollywood I've been the girl behind the scenes. If someone wants to throw a charity party or make a movie and they don't know quite how to go about it they come to me. And what I do is put the whole together for them and stand back while they take the glory for it.

"Well, a person can get very bored with that. And I just have."

Keyser looked at her with the beginnings of respect. She was brighter than he had thought. "How do you think you're going to get this power you're talking about?"

She looked at him steadily. "I'm not going to get it," she said. "You're going to get it for me."

He sighed. "How am I going to do that?"

"You're going to make me a star," she said.

He started to interrupt her, but she didn't let

## 164 • TRUDI PACTER

him. "Back in New York," she continued, "I was an actress. I wasn't bad either. Except no one ever knew it, because I didn't get the breaks.

"In the end I changed my career because I didn't want to go on being a failure. But I didn't like giving up the stage, and I'd do anything to go back to it."

"Does that include coming away with me?" he asked.

She nodded.

Dan was bemused. He was used to pretty girls asking him for parts, but none of them had been quite so direct, so adamant.

"What kind of thing did you have in mind?" he asked. He pushed his plate of spaghetti away and searched in his top pocket for a cigar.

She laughed. "Don't look so worried. I'm not asking for you to build a starring vehicle around me. Not yet anyway. I'm prepared to wait for that until I'm more established. No, what I want just now is the second lead in a picture. Preferably a picture that's set up and ready to go. That way I don't have to wait around."

Now Dan had found his cigar he took a long time trimming it and lighting it. "I don't think Magnum has anything with your kind of part in it. Not at the moment anyway. We've got a couple of pictures in development that might fit the bill. But we've got nothing in production that would be right for you."

"I think you have," she said.

"OK, remind me. What is it?"

"*Marooned,* the Claudia Graham–David Price picture."

## SCREEN KISSES • 165

"And what part did you have your eye on?"

"Mabel, the juvenile lead," she said quickly. "It might have been written with me in mind."

"It might have been," said the studio chief. "There's only one problem. The part's been cast. Rick Hamilton picked some British actress for it. As we sit here, the woman's in Bali doing her stuff in front of the cameras. We've already got footage of her."

"But you haven't got that much footage of her," said Giselle. "She doesn't shoot her big scene until nearly the end."

Keyser looked suspicious. "How would you know a thing like that?"

"Because I've seen the script," she said confidently. "Claudia's a very old friend of mine. She showed it to me."

There was a long silence. Dan signalled the waiter to take away the plates, then he ordered coffee for both of them. Finally he said, "This idea for the part in *Marooned,* it didn't come out of the blue, did it? It's been on your mind for quite some time."

"Sure it's been on my mind. So have a lot of things I don't stand a hope in hell of getting. It doesn't mean I can't want them."

He started to get angry. "And now I've come on the scene you expect me to wave a magic wand and give you everything your heart desires."

"Listen, sweetie," she said tightly, "let me remind you of a couple of things. Number one, I didn't invite you to lunch. You asked me. Number two, you didn't ask me for my conversation. You asked me because you wanted to fuck me. In my book that's about as realistic as wanting a part in a Hollywood film."

For the first time he looked at her with a certain curiosity. "You're telling me you're that good?"

She didn't flinch. "Yes," she said.

The waiter arrived with the coffee, and Giselle started to get to her feet. "I really haven't got time for that now," she told him. "I've got to get going."

He motioned her to sit down. "Surely just one cup?" he asked.

But she wouldn't be persuaded. She had said all she was going to say that day. He knew where she stood. Where they both stood. Now it was up to him.

She turned towards the exit, bending her knees and swivelling round on the balls of her feet. The movement was a cross between a twirl and a bunny dip, and there was something incredibly provocative about it. Provocative and submissive. No American girl Dan had ever known would have been seen dead doing it.

He gazed after her as she went through the door. The silk chemise was clinging tightly to the line of her buttocks and he was absolutely certain now she had nothing on underneath it.

It was no good, he thought, mopping his brow. He had to have Giselle Pascal or perish in the attempt.

Bob Delaney was fast asleep when the call came, and for a moment he had no idea where he was. His hand reached across to the bedside table where he knew the phone was and encountered—nothing.

He sat up in bed, shaking his head. What on earth

## SCREEN KISSES • 167

had happened to the phone? Then he remembered he wasn't at home. He was in the Nusa Dua Hotel in Bali. He looked at his watch and the luminous dial told him it was three o'clock in the morning. Who on earth wanted him at that hour?

He reached over to the other side of the bed, switched on the light and located the phone. When he picked it up he was fully awake. "Bob Delaney," he said automatically.

There was a high-pitched whine on the line followed by a crackle. Then the slightly accented, unmistakable voice of Dan Keyser's Japanese secretary came through.

"I have Mr Keyser of Magnum waiting to speak to you."

Bob felt a stab of fury. Didn't the bastard know what time it was in Bali? What on earth was he doing getting him out of bed at this hour?

"OK," he said to the Japanese girl, "put him on." Whatever Keyser wanted there was no point in taking it out on his secretary. She had her instructions, just like he had his.

"Bob," said Keyser, "thank God I managed to get you."

There was no mistaking the urgency in the studio chief's voice. Christ, thought Delaney, there's been a crisis at head office and he wants out of the film. Why else would he wake me up in the middle of the night? He made a rapid review of his arrangements with Magnum. The contracts were all in order and legal. The budget had been cleared. If Keyser wanted out he wasn't going to find it easy.

## 168 • TRUDI PACTER

"Morning, Dan," said Bob cautiously. "What can I do for you?"

"A small favour," said Keyser. "Nothing to make your heart stop."

Delaney's antennae went on red alert. When Keyser played a situation down he knew there was trouble. "What is it?" he asked tightly.

Magnum's head of production came straight to the point. "I want you to replace one of the actors."

"You want me to do what?"

"Make an adjustment to your cast. It's nothing to get excited about. I'm not axeing Claudia or David."

Delaney relaxed a little. So far the movie hadn't been canned. The budget was intact. And the two major stars were still in place.

"Who are you thinking of replacing?" he asked.

"One of the supporting parts. The English girl, what's her name? Rachel something or other."

"Why would you want to get rid of Rachel?" asked Delaney. "She's a good actress. Rick's very keen on her. It's early days yet but he seems to be getting some kind of performance out of her."

"I'm not quarrelling about her ability. You know me better than that. If you say the girl's good, then she's good. It's just it doesn't suit me to have her in *Marooned* right now."

A prickle of alarm started somewhere at the base of Delaney's neck. "Don't tell me," he said, "there's a union problem. The Screen Actors' Guild won't wear a British actress."

"The Guild's fine," replied Keyser more calmly

## SCREEN KISSES • 169

than he felt. "I've already had the lawyer check that out. No, there's something else."

"What else could there be?"

"I want someone else for the part."

Goodbye, Rachel, thought Delaney. And despite himself he felt a genuine pang of regret. She might have told him to go to hell but she was a nice kid. He liked her. Never mind, he thought, if Keyser has a big star lined up for her part, I'm in no position to argue.

"Who have you got?" he asked. "Farrah Fawcett? Faye Dunaway? No, hold on. I can do better than that. You managed to talk Jacqueline Bisset into it, that's why you're ringing me in the middle of the night."

There was a silence and Bob thought something had gone wrong with the connection. He strained his ears but all he picked up was static again. "Dan," he shouted, "are you still there?"

"Of course I'm still here," Dan's voice came booming back. "I was just thinking."

"You mean you want Jackie Bisset?"

"I don't want Jackie Bisset." He was irritated now. "I'm not interested in Jacqueline Bisset. The woman I want for the part is Giselle Pascal."

Bob did a double take. If Keyser had suggested his own wife for the part he couldn't have been more surprised. "You're kidding me," he said. "Giselle's no actress. Anyway she left the business over eight years ago."

"Then that's a loss for the business. I happened to get sight of something she was in back in the Sixties, and I was impressed. More than impressed. So I thought, just to satisfy my own curiosity, why not

## 170 • TRUDI PACTER

give her a test? And shall I tell you something, the chick's dynamite. Handled right she could be another Claudia Graham."

And I bet you're handling her right, thought Delaney. He recalled the scene in Ma Maison when he introduced Keyser to the French woman. Even at that early stage what Keyser wanted to do to Giselle was written all over his fat face. So he's using his influence to get into her pants, thought Delaney. Well, not at my expense he isn't. And not at the expense of my film.

"Dan," said Delaney gently, "forget about Giselle Pascal. Forget about her for *Marooned,* anyway. If I replace Rachel now I run the risk of upsetting Rick. And it's not a risk I'm prepared to take. If you'd told me you'd got Bisset or even Farrah Fawcett then Rick would have had to live with the disruption to his schedule. But Giselle Pascal? Do me a favour. There must be something else you can put her in."

Once more the static crackled in his ear, as if the wires themselves were expressing Dan Keyser's indignation. "There isn't anything else I can put her in," Dan said. "Anyway she specifically asked for the part in *Marooned.* She set her heart on it."

"Then you're going to have to disappoint her. There's no way I'm going to replace a perfectly competent actress to satisfy one of your whims. If you have it in your mind to replace any one of my unit, from the focus puller up, I'll want a good legitimate reason for doing so. And Giselle Pascal's fanny is not a good legitimate reason."

\*    \*    \*

## SCREEN KISSES • 171

The road to Giselle's house sloped sharply upwards with hairpin bends every one hundred yards. Dan Keyser's Silver Cloud was not built for this kind of terrain, and as the custom-built automobile jerked and shuddered its way to the top of the hill Dan wondered for the thousandth time whether this trip was going to be worth it.

Giselle had been ecstatic when he called to tell her he had arranged a screen test at Magnum, and when he told her that Bill Johnson, the British director, was doing it, she was even more pleased. But it wasn't enough. When she came up to see him after the test she made it perfectly clear that she wasn't available until he had spoken to Bob Delaney about the part in *Marooned.*

Now he had done that and Giselle had invited him round for a drink to report on the conversation. He racked his brains for something positive to tell her but he was fresh out of ideas. He could think of no positive way to say that Delaney wasn't buying it. No dice was no dice, however you dressed it up. Giselle was sharp enough to see that.

His mind went back to their lunch at Spago and the way she had teased him. She wore that thin silk dress on purpose, he thought. She must have known that her nipples and the outline of her ass showed through it. He was gripped by a lust so urgent, so uncontrollable that if Giselle had come out of her house right then, he would have taken her where she stood. It was then he made his mind up. He was going to have to lie to the girl. There was no other way.

He got out of the car and told his driver to be

back for him in just over an hour. If she bought his lie it would take at least that long for him to do everything he wanted to her.

Giselle answered the door in a tight black leather skirt, black stockings, strappy black patent sandals and a white silk blouse that gaped at the front. It was clear that she expected good news. It was also clear that she was more than prepared to keep her side of the bargain. Keyser felt a moment of remorse. It would break her heart when he had to tell her about Delaney's decision. He allowed her to lead him inside the house, his eyes wandering along the length of her legs in their sheer black nylon. He wondered if she was wearing a garter belt and whether it would be black as well. The thought of Giselle in a garter belt killed any last regrets. She had led him on too long and too far. Whatever happened next she had coming to her.

He noticed a bottle of champagne resting in an ice bucket and saw with approval that it was Krug.

"Is that for now or later?" he asked.

She smiled, teasing him. "That depends on what you have to tell me."

"Giselle," he said reprovingly, "stop negotiating and open the bottle. I've come to tell you good news. The part's yours if you want it."

"In that case," she said, "I've decided to teach you a very unusual way of drinking champagne. But first," she added, coming closer to him, "I want you to undress me."

He made a move to kiss her, but she was having none of it. "I said undress me," she instructed, "the kissing comes later."

## SCREEN KISSES • 173

It was like taking the wrapping paper off a Christmas present. First you undid the ribbons. He pulled at the tie holding her blouse in place and it parted slowly to reveal naked breasts with high pink nipples. Her tits were heavier than he had imagined and he took one of her rosy nipples between his thumb and forefinger and gave it a squeeze. She slapped his hand. "I said undress me. The touching comes later."

Once more he stifled his frustration. Try playing coy when I get your pants down, he thought. Then nothing's going to stop me.

He pulled the blouse off and turned his attention to her skirt. More wrapping paper. This piece undid with a zipper. He pulled it down, and as the skirt descended round her ankles Dan knew it was Christmas Day. Giselle was wearing a garter belt after all. A garter belt and suspenders and a pair of black lacy pants you could see right through. He could feel his hands sweating as he unrolled her stockings. If she put him through much more of this he'd come in his trousers.

Giselle must have read his mind, for she unsnapped the belt and stepped out of her knickers. Now he could see her clearly. All of her. The tits with the big pink nipples, the curly blonde pubic hair, the opening between her legs.

She sat down on the sofa in front of him and grabbed hold of the open bottle of champagne. "Kneel down," she said, "I'm going to give you something to drink."

Bemused, he did as he was told. Giselle parted her legs and raised both her feet to his shoulders. This is ridiculous, he thought. My face is inches away from

## 174 • TRUDI PACTER

her and all she can talk about is serving me a drink. Then the truth dawned. And as it did, Giselle started pouring the wine. It ran down the length of her body in a thin stream, bubbling between her breasts and over her belly until it trickled deliciously between her legs.

Keyser leaned forward and started lapping up the bubbles. Then he put his tongue inside her and found a more exotic taste.

"Isn't it time you got undressed?" she said slowly. "I've got all sorts of other ideas for you. But I think your clothes might get in the way."

He followed her into the bedroom, shrugging off his jacket and tearing at his tie. On her carpet he left a trail of expensive tailoring until he was completely naked. At first he took her quickly, like a greedy child at Christmas dinner. Then when he was satiated, Giselle started to make love to him. She made love the way Callas sang an opera or Bernhardt delivered Shakespeare: with passion, discipline, and the kind of artistry that comes from having practised a thousand times before.

Dan was dazzled. He'd cheated on Carla before, and with beauties more spectacular than the girl in bed with him now. But none of them could compare with her. He knew with a terrible foreboding that this would not be the last time he would visit her elegant house on the hill. And because he knew it, he climbed out of her bed and started to put on his clothes.

"What's the matter?" she asked. "Did I disappoint you?"

## SCREEN KISSES • 175

"Quite the reverse," he told her, "which is why we have to talk."

There was something serious about the way he said it, so she didn't try to stop him dressing. Instead she shrugged herself into a terry towelling robe and padded after him into the main room.

"Do you mind getting me something to drink? And I don't mean any of that champagne either. What I have to say needs something stronger."

She went over to a cabinet, got out a bottle of bourbon and held it up for his approval. He nodded and she poured three fingers into a crystal glass and added ice. For herself she selected a Perrier, then she carried the drinks across to him where he sat on the sofa. "What do you have to say to me that needs such a strong drink?" she asked.

He patted the sofa and she curled up beside him. "The truth," he said. "Look, Giselle, I don't have to tell you this. If I chose I could walk out of your house and that's the last you'd see of me. But I don't want to end it that way. I want to come back here. Often. Which is why I have to get things straight between us."

She looked at him over the rim of her glass. "Then tell me the worst," she said. "I'm a big girl. I can take it."

He sighed. "Giselle, my love, you didn't get the part. I know I told you you had. But I lied because I wanted you so much."

He expected her to throw her drink at him or burst into tears, but she did neither. All the fight seemed to have gone out of her and she merely

## 176 • TRUDI PACTER

shrugged. "So I lost," she said. "It's not the end of the world. I expect I'll live."

He was seized with a sudden desire to make things right for her. "Don't throw in the towel," he said with more force than he intended. "It's not over yet." He paused. "Look," he said, "when Bob Delaney told me he wouldn't be replacing Rachel Keller in *Marooned* he said it was because he didn't have a legitimate reason to. Now I couldn't argue with that. But if I had a reason to get rid of Keller I'd have her out tomorrow."

She looked confused. "But how on earth do you do that? You can't invent reasons that don't exist."

"No, unfortunately I can't. But what I can do is find out a bit more about Rachel Keller. All I'm looking for is an excuse. She doesn't have to be a criminal for me to get her off the picture."

Giselle started to smile—not the washed-out grimace of resignation she had put on before, but a smile full of optimism. "I think I've got an idea. Tell me, how long do I have to come up with a reason for getting rid of Rachel?"

"About four or five weeks," he replied. "According to the shooting schedule I last saw she doesn't figure in too many scenes until half way through March."

"That's all the time I need. I'll give you a reason to get rid of Rachel Keller, Dan. A perfect reason, all wrapped up and served on a silver plate."

For the first time since they had been together, the studio chief looked nervous. "And what about you, Giselle? Will I have you as well?"

## SCREEN KISSES • 177

She smiled and gave him a sideways glance.
"You'll have to wait and see, won't you?"

When Claudia started work on *Marooned* she made the
vow she always made on these occasions. No more
men. Her last husband had drained her both emotion-
ally and financially. If that's what sex did for you, she
thought, she could happily go without.

Then she met David Price and all her good intentions melted away. David wasn't like all the others.
For a start he was rich. Not rich and boring like a
banker or a landowner. David had money for the
same reason she had money. Talent. Both of them had
the ability to fascinate, to mesmerize. It gave them a
kinship.

When she first met him she had felt an immediate
bond. There was no need to explain herself to him.
She didn't need to tell him how her last agent had
robbed her blind, nor did she have to deny any of her
publicity. He'd been robbed and libelled the same
way she had been. He knew how it felt.

At last, thought Claudia as she climbed into her
sunken bathtub with its tiny, gold, mosaic tiles. At last
I've met a man who truly understands me. She leaned
back and pressed a knob. As she did so, dozens of tiny
underwater jets activated the water so that her whole
body was stroked and caressed by its motion. Soon,
she promised herself, David will be doing this to me.
She thought about the Australian star with his heavily
muscled shoulders and white-blond hair. There was
something earthy about him—almost brutal. She
started to feel an urgent physical need for him. Then

she thought about his wife and her desire faded. Why is it, she wondered, that nothing is exactly the way I want it?

Harry, her first husband, couldn't handle her success. Chad, her last, couldn't handle her intelligence. The men in between she tried not to think about.

They were inadequate, she thought. All of them in some way had failed her. Now there was David— a man she wanted, really wanted. And his wife stood in the way.

Most women faced with this situation would have sighed and reconsidered. But Claudia Graham was not most women; Claudia Graham was a star. And it didn't cross her mind that she should be denied anything she really wanted.

She wondered who she was going to confide in about the situation, for there was no point in falling in love if she couldn't discuss it with her friends. Claudia had two sorts of friends: the ones she socialized with, and the ones she talked to about her love life. This second category included her hairdresser and women she considered her inferiors. Inferiors were in no position to judge her, so they could be trusted with all the details. Claudia's closest confidantes were Fanny, her sister who still lived in Orange County, and Giselle Pascal.

She got out of the bath and wrapped herself in the hotel bathsheet, then she padded across the room to her bedside table where she kept her address book. The time had come to start confiding. She tried Fanny first and found herself talking to her niece. Mummy was out shopping, could she call her back? Claudia

## SCREEN KISSES • 179

said not to worry. Calling Bali was beyond her sister's comprehension. She decided to give Giselle a whirl.

The French woman answered on the second ring. "Claudia," she said, recognizing the voice instantly, "what are you doing calling California? I thought you were meant to be busy filming."

"I am," she said crossly, "but something has happened and I need your advice."

Giselle reached across the table for a cigarette. When Claudia rang and wanted advice, she knew from experience it could only be about one thing. When she called from Bali wanting advice the affair had to be serious. Giselle flicked back her gold Cartier lighter and lit her cigarette. This was going to be a long session.

"Who is he?" she asked cautiously.

"Guess."

Giselle exhaled a thin stream of tobacco smoke. She was in a quandary. The candidates as she saw them were Bob Delaney, Rick Hamilton and David Price, but there was an outside chance it could be none of them. Claudia had been known to fall for the camera operator and occasionally one of the bit players.

"I wouldn't even try," she said after much deliberation. "After Chad it could be anybody."

"Giselle," Claudia said sharply, "since when did I fall for just anybody?"

"I'm sorry," she said quickly, "I didn't realize you were in love."

"Well, I am. And if I tell you his name, you've got to promise to keep it secret."

Giselle decided to take a flyer. "I already know

## 180 • TRUDI PACTER

his name. It's David Price, isn't it? It couldn't be anyone else."

"How did you know?" There was admiration in the voice.

Giselle was tempted to say, because married men are the only lovers you keep secret. But she resisted. Instead she said, "Because I've met David and he could have been made for you."

"Why do you say that?"

"Because he's sensitive, he's talented and he's been through everything you've been through. Darling, I know you. And I know what you need."

Claudia started to feel better. Giselle understood after all. She knew she could rely on her. In a soft voice full of emotion Claudia started to tell her friend about David Price. She told her how they met, how he looked at her, how this man made her feel different from any other she had met.

Giselle listened with half an ear. She had been hearing this story for eight years now and she marvelled at the way the actress deluded herself. Whenever Claudia met a new lover, whether he was a billionaire or a beach boy he always had certain things going for him. And they were always the same things. He turned her on like no one had ever done before. He stimulated her intellectually. And he understood her. The fact that weeks or months later this same guy could turn out to be a pervert and a halfwit had long ceased to surprise Giselle. Oh well, she thought, at least Claudia has fun while it lasts.

"What did you say?" asked Claudia, two continents away.

## SCREEN KISSES • 181

"Nothing, I was just thinking how much fun you could have if it wasn't for David's wife."

There was an edge of steel to Claudia's voice. "I'll find a way to handle David's wife."

Or to dispose of her, thought Giselle. She decided to change the subject. "Claudia," she said, testing the water, "how well do you know Rachel Keller?"

"I've hardly met her. Why?"

"Because I need some information on her. A friend of mine at Magnum wants to know more than Bob Delaney's prepared to tell."

"What kind of things?"

"I'm not quite sure. Though I would think he'd want something juicy. Love affairs, abortions, that kind of thing. From what I know of her she's worked mainly in Europe, so she could have got up to almost anything and nobody would know about it out here."

Claudia was intrigued. "Why all this interest in Rachel Keller? She's a boring little British actress playing a supporting role. My guess is she's got this far because the budget wouldn't stretch to a decent name."

Giselle was tempted to tell her friend the truth about Dan Keyser and his promises, then she thought, no, I'll play her along for a bit. Claudia was too interested in Claudia not to be dangerous. Right now, the wrong word at the wrong time could blow everything.

"Darling, I haven't got a clue why my friend wants the dirt on Rachel. I get hired to provide information, not to ask questions."

"I'm with you. Look, I'll do what I can. Locations

## 182 • TRUDI PACTER

always push you closer to the other actors. I'm bound to get stuck with Rachel sooner or later. When I do, I'll go to work on her."

"Claudia, you're an angel. I'll pay you back on this one, I promise."

"You don't have to promise me anything," said the actress. "I know you well enough to call in a favour when I need one."

She rose out of the sea like a mermaid. Her black hair was wet and curly round her shoulders, her breasts unfettered and glistening with droplets of salt water.

I see what they mean when they call her a screen goddess, thought Rachel. She and Darleen were standing behind a semi-circle of cameras and recording equipment on a long white beach that sloped down to the surf.

Like many of the beaches in Bali it was deserted and gave you the impression that no human being had ever walked there before. The sand stood up in crisp, white ridges like icing sugar, and the sea was so clear that you could wade in to your waist and still see shoals of tiny, coloured fishes swimming along the bottom.

They had been there, sweltering in the sun, since the early afternoon, watching Claudia Graham mastering the art of walking on to the shore. It was more complicated than it looked. On film she had to appear to be wearing next to nothing, yet at the same time she couldn't afford to upset the censors, so the wardrobe department had fixed her up with a grass skirt.

So far Claudia had risen from the sea nearly a dozen times and each time something had been

## SCREEN KISSES • 183

wrong. Water had got into her eyes. Her hair had parted in the wrong place. And when Claudia had finally got her act together the grass skirt had started to play up.

Rick Hamilton, jeans rolled up to his knees, waded over to Claudia. After a brief consultation he returned to the shore and barked a couple of instructions to the lighting cameraman. He had decided to shoot the scene from all angles and to deal with the bits that offended the censors in the cutting room.

On the twelfth take Claudia finally emerged from the sea and went on walking until she got to the beach, where she came face to face with her co-star, David Price. Despite the oppressive heat, the Australian actor looked as fresh as if he had been taking a stroll down Rodeo Drive. His white-blond hair bounced across his brow, his pancake make-up was matt and dry, and his shorts were rumpled only because a fifteen-year-old Indonesian girl had been ironing the creases in since dawn.

When he caught sight of Claudia he looked like he wanted to eat her. Rick started to feel happy. David really believed in his role. He signalled the camera to move in close.

The Australian took hold of Claudia's shoulders and pulled her against him. Then he brought his mouth down on top of hers, forcing her lips apart. They held it like that for forty seconds until Hamilton shouted to cut and print.

Claudia decided to pay no attention. Instead she leaned closer to David Price and started to tease the inside of his mouth with her tongue. Despite the cameras and the presence of his wife the actor responded. The kiss went on for a full two minutes and Claudia noted his response with satisfaction. When they finally broke apart there were cheers and scattered applause from the crew. On the edge of the set Darleen looked white and shaken. Her mouth was set into a thin line of disapproval and her fists were clenched.

Claudia took hold of the wrap the wardrobe girl was offering her and turned back to her co-star. "If you feel like running through that scene again," she said, "stop by my suite at around six tonight. I'll be there on my own."

Claudia had pitched her voice deliberately low and the exchange was not meant to be heard by anyone else. But some trick of the wind took her words and blew them over the palm trees and across the sand to where Darleen was standing.

When David's wife realized what was going on she was momentarily winded. Then she started to make plans. If David thought he was going to get up to anything in that harlot's penthouse tonight, he'd better think again.

At five o'clock David felt one of his headaches coming on. They had finished filming an hour earlier and Darleen had run his bath and laid his clothes out the way she always did after a gruelling day.

He looked with affection at his wife and baby son. It might be a hassle dragging them half way across the world but this way he could be sure of the comforts of home. At forty-six he felt he needed them. He reconsidered. He didn't just need Darleen running

## SCREEN KISSES • 185

around him, he deserved her. The divorce from his first wife had cost him several million bucks and the family home. The least he could expect in return was a little tender loving care.

Then he thought about Claudia and the date he had at six, and he felt himself grow hard. A loving wife was one thing; she was bought and paid for along with the rest of his entourage. But Claudia Graham was quite another.

He remembered the way she had looked on the beach that afternoon—soft, vulnerable, his for the taking. This might be a remote location, he thought, but there are some compensations.

His reverie was interrupted by Darleen. "Darling, I've got some more of that cool fruit juice I gave you when you came in. The doctor says we should drink as much of it as we can in this climate."

He took the tall glass from her hands. Actually he hated the drink, which was sweet and syrupy and had a strange aftertaste. But it would have looked ungrateful to refuse it, and he didn't want that. David didn't want to do anything to arouse his wife's suspicions. So he gulped back the drink and tried not to look sick.

Very soon, he thought, I'll be with Claudia. I can afford to be nice to my wife in the meantime.

When he looked at his watch he saw there was an hour to go before his assignation. He decided to take a shower. Humming faintly to himself, he walked through to the bathroom. The pain hit him when he started to take off his shoes.

It started in his temples where it always started,

## 186 • TRUDI PACTER

and he felt the beginnings of dread. A migraine, he thought. That's all I need.

David had been troubled with migraine headaches since he was in his twenties. The doctors who treated him told him there was no cure. All he could do was to avoid alcohol and cheese. Then the headaches would plague him less often.

So David went permanently on the wagon. He didn't even allow liquor to flavour his fruit salad. So what could have set it off? he wondered. He sat on the edge of the bath and massaged his throbbing temples. Lunch had been innocuous enough, consisting of cold meat, salad and bottled water. He hadn't consumed anything else until he got back to the hotel, when Darleen had given him that sticky fruit juice. He remembered the aftertaste and pulled a face. There had to be something wrong with it.

He called to his wife through the door. "Darleen, when did you order this drink?"

"I didn't order it," she shouted. "It was in the fridge when we got back from the beach. We were all so hot it seemed just what we needed. Why, is there something wrong with it?"

He padded through from the bathroom, picked up the glass of juice and smelled it. "I'm not sure. I had a feeling it might have gone off in the heat. But if you say it's been in the fridge it must have been my imagination."

She smiled. "It must have been."

Half an hour later David was in a cold sweat. A thick band of steel seemed to have settled round his head and was slowly contracting. The pain was excru-

## SCREEN KISSES • 187

ciating and the light was starting to hurt his eyes. He thought about Claudia waiting for him in her suite, but the idea had started to lose its attraction. He didn't even have the energy to call her and cancel their date.

Darleen came into the bedroom in a cotton shift and bare feet. "David," she said, "you're lying down. Is anything the matter?"

He grunted. "I've got one of my heads. If you've made any dinner arrangements for us, you'd better cancel."

She was on her knees beside the bed, her hand resting lightly on his brow. "You're burning up, David. Hold on a moment, I'll go and get an ice pack. It should help a little."

It'll help, he thought grimly, but it won't help enough. Whether I like it or not I'm stuck here for the rest of the day. Claudia will never speak to me again. Then he had an idea. When Darleen came back into the room he motioned her to sit on the bed.

"Sweetheart, I want you to do something for me. I had a six o'clock meeting with Bob and Rick in Claudia's suite. There's no way I can go like this. Would you be an angel and ring through and tell them?"

She lowered the ice pack on to his forehead. Then she let go of it. For reasons best known to herself, Darleen had failed to secure the napkin containing the dozen or so ice cubes. And the whole thing burst open covering her husband with tiny, melting, slithering blocks of ice.

"Darling," she said, fluttering round the room,

## 188 • TRUDI PACTER

"I'm so sorry. I'd no idea it was going to do that. Here, let me help you."

But David had had enough. "Get the maid to clean this up," he told her. "You go and make the call I told you about. And do it fast."

She was out of the room before he had finished speaking. She had little doubt that when she called Claudia's penthouse Claudia, not Delaney or Rick Hamilton, would answer her.

She picked up the phone and asked for the actress's room number, then she settled back and poured herself a large glass of fruit juice from the pitcher on the table. There was no doubt about it. The white rum she had added to it when she took it out of the fridge definitely improved the flavour.

Three days later the whole unit moved up country. Rick had finished shooting the beach scenes, now he wanted backdrops of lush, tropical vegetation. The camera unit, the cast, the catering staff, the hangers-on were all transported and rehoused in a series of large villas with thatched roofs on the side of a hill. The part of the island they had moved to was all hills and ridges and thickly wooded escarpments. The countryside was ideally suited to farming and this was evident lower down the steep slope that housed the villas. A series of terraces was cut into the side of the hill like giant steps and they supported the staple crop of rice. Every morning at dawn the natives went to work on the terraces, cultivating, irrigating, harvesting.

The dawn was the best time of the day. It was still

## SCREEN KISSES • 189

cool enough to move around in comfort and the insects had yet to become active. Of all the discomforts of the location the insects were by far the worst. Scorpions nested and scrambled in the thatch above their heads, and every evening someone would find one of them crawling around a bedroom. If the bedroom belonged to one of the actresses widespread hysteria would result.

Although they looked frightening the scorpions were not the real problem. The real problem was the mosquitoes. There were literally hundreds of them crawling along the woodwork, flying through the air, biting anyone and everyone they came into contact with. In a sense they were an unseen enemy. You could go to bed one night with the fans on and the netting in place and still one or two of them would get through. And one or two were enough to cause untold damage. They crawled into the secret, private crevices of the body and administered their bites. The next day the victim would wake up to find itchy swellings that never seemed to go down. Dr Steibel, the man Bob had flown out from California, was kept working overtime. He issued everyone with evil-smelling insect repellent which worked if you used it. The crew, who didn't give a damn about their personal desirability, stank to high heaven and didn't get bitten. The actors were a different story. Most of them were obsessed with being liked, and they couldn't face wearing the repellent. So they put make-up over their bites and suffered in silence.

For Rachel the insects were the least of her worries. Her main concern was loneliness. She was shar-

## 190 • TRUDI PACTER

ing one of the thatched villas with Claudia, Rick Hamilton and Bob, but none of them had any time for her. Claudia, the only other woman there, retired to her room every evening after dinner and she didn't reappear until the following morning. Rick was too busy with schedules, budgets and the day's rushes to communicate with anyone. And Bob—Bob was distant.

Ever since their first dinner, and their first falling out, they had been polite with each other but nothing more. Rachel knew there was an attraction between them. She felt it every time they were in the same room together. But it was a dangerous attraction. She suspected that if they ever got closer, the involvement would be more serious than a run-of-play affair. She saw herself making compromises, maybe even getting hurt. And she was frightened of what she saw, so she kept away.

The rest of the unit was less complicated. The crew, like all crews on location, went native. Rachel could hardly blame them. The girls in the villages and townships were lithe and beautiful, coloured the palest shade of coffee. They were also poor. The technicians with their free spending ways could have been sent by the devil to tempt them.

A lot of the men set up home with the local girls, moving into tiny thatched cottages in the hills or by the beaches. The rest of them, not wanting to be tied down, went to Kuta. The resort was an hour's drive from the airport and was the only tourist spot on the island. Here on the streets you got a whiff of the open drains, and on every corner there was a honkytonk

## SCREEN KISSES • 191

bar. The girls who hung around in those establishments were either for hire or they were Australian tourists. Either way they were good for a one-night stand.

Rachel wasn't looking for a holiday romance, nor was she in need of a run-of-play affair. So she sat alone, isolated from the rest of the actors by her Englishness and the fact that she was sharing her living quarters with the top brass. The only time she saw anyone was on the set or sometimes at dinner when Rick invited everyone over to eat on their verandah.

It should have been so romantic, thought Rachel one night. Dinner was over. Claudia had gone to bed. And Rick and Bob were huddled together talking about the next day's setup. The verandah which ran all the way round the villa was lit by kerosene lamps and beyond her in the velvet darkness she could hear the sounds of the jungle. Without success she tried to concentrate on her book.

I'm earning 700 dollars a day, she told herself. I'm meeting famous movie stars. I'm getting into films. She sighed. Who am I kidding? she thought. If Desmond called me tomorrow and offered me a season's rep in Darlington, I'd jump at it.

They had been waiting since dawn for the right kind of light. Now the sun had burned its way through the heat haze, Rick was satisfied they had found it. He had had the cameras set up in a clearing at the bottom of a thickly wooded cliff. A hundred yards away a winding stream babbled and chuckled over white pebbles,

## 192 • TRUDI PACTER

and the birds that followed the stream flaunted their exotic plumage on its far banks.

Rick, who had fallen in love with the island, could have sat and watched the scene till the sun was high in the sky. Only his conscience and his pay packet stopped him. With a sigh he turned to his first assistant. "Time to go and fetch the cast," he said.

Escorting the talent wasn't exactly his job. That was the duty of the second assistant. But he decided to be flexible.

Five minutes later he pushed his way through the undergrowth to the set looking defeated. Despite his entreaties, Miss Graham was refusing to budge.

"What the hell's the problem?" demanded Rick. "Did Claudia tell you what's bugging her?"

The first assistant director looked embarrassed. "Actually I didn't manage to speak to Miss Graham. I spoke to her hairdresser. She told me to go away. Apparently Miss Graham isn't in the mood for filming."

Rick clenched and unclenched his fist. Then he looked at the sky through his light meter. The sun looked as if it was shining through crystal that day. Everything around him—the trees, the pebbles in the stream—seemed to have a hard, clear outline as if some illustrator had drawn the jungle clearing with a felt-tip pen. Rick cursed inwardly. He might have to wait another week before he got light like this again. He started to think hard.

Right now it was really down to him to go and have a word with the actress. He was the director and, as far as she was concerned, the ultimate boss. But he

## SCREEN KISSES • 193

couldn't. If he went crawling to her now he would have been seen to have given ground. He knew from experience that once he started pandering to a star's temperament the star had the whip hand. The next time she felt upset for whatever reason, she would come down on him twice as hard. No, he couldn't go and fetch Claudia. He went to look for Bob Delaney.

It took ten minutes to disentangle the producer from a long distance call to New York, another five to explain the problem, and fifteen minutes for Bob to deal with the actress. He needn't have bothered. When Bob tried the door of Claudia's trailer he found it was locked. All he got was the hairdresser telling him no dice.

He marched back to the set, grabbed hold of Rick and went into a hasty conference. Something was bugging Claudia and they needed to know what it was.

"Maybe she doesn't like the script," suggested Bob. Rick produced the Roneoed pages they were filming that day. Quickly he ran through Claudia's two scenes, then he shook his head. "We talked about them last night in her suite and she loved them then. She can't have changed her mind about them overnight. It has to be something else."

He considered for a moment, then he turned to Bob. "Do you think it's the rushes? On most films she makes, she normally gets to see what's been shot."

Bob shook his head. "I've been through that with her a hundred times. I didn't want her to see rushes because of the way she feels about her eye job. One bad shot and she'd have the lighting cameraman off the location in five minutes flat. I didn't want to risk

## 194 • TRUDI PACTER

that, so I did a deal with her. She gets to see the rough cut when it's all over, then if she doesn't like any of her close-ups, we can discuss it like human beings. She didn't have any objections to that in Los Angeles, nor did her agent. So you can rule that one out."

The two men were baffled.

"Do you think there's some personal problem?" asked Rick. "I saw the way she was throwing herself at David during that beach scene. Maybe they're having an affair and Darleen's found out."

Delaney started to look really worried. Scripts could be changed. Cameramen could be replaced if there was no other option. But bed partners were another story, particularly when the bed partner in question was his leading man.

Rick looked into his producer's face and didn't like what he saw. "Maybe we should send David to try and sort this one out."

"Maybe we all pack up and go home," said Delaney. "Don't be an idiot. If what you're saying is true, David is the last person we should send to Claudia at this point."

He looked up to see Rachel and two other actors coming towards him. "Of course," he said, "why didn't I think of it before? What we need right now is the woman's touch." He went up to her and took hold of her arm. "I've got a favour to ask of you," he said. Rachel was curious to know what he wanted, but Bob refused to be drawn until he had walked her down to the banks of the stream and they were out of earshot. Then he turned to her. "I want you to go and see Claudia for me," he said.

## SCREEN KISSES • 195

For a moment she was surprised. "Why, what's the problem?"

He looked deep into the sparkling water as if that might provide some answers, then he shook his head. "Nobody really knows. All that's happening is she's due on the set and she won't leave her trailer."

"Hasn't somebody gone to fetch her?" asked Rachel.

Bob sighed. "We've all tried. But it's no good. The lady won't budge. And the lady won't say why she's not budging."

"So what makes you think Claudia's going to fall in line if I ask her? She's not exactly a bosom pal."

"I know that," said Bob, "but you are another woman. And she could just open up to you."

Rachel looked at him. "You think she's got man problems, don't you?"

"She could have," said the producer cautiously. "You've seen the way she and David have been eyeing each other."

She looked cross. "I suppose you want me to do your dirty work."

He nodded. "Will you?"

She shrugged her shoulders. "What have I got to lose? Claudia can't eat me. And she certainly can't fire me." She picked up a pebble and threw it across the river the way she used to do in her school holidays. The stone bounced three times then it sank. She looked up. "OK, Bob," she said, "I'll have a bash. But don't blame me if it all ends in tears."

She straightened her back and started to make her way towards a line of trees on the other side of the set. There, half hidden by dense foliage, was Claudia's long silver trailer. The structure that housed Magnum's star was big enough to accommodate a bathroom, a bedroom, a kitchen and a living room. Rachel thought of the cramped dressing rooms she had spent half her life in, and despite herself she started to dislike Claudia Graham.

In Rachel's world, when you were wanted on stage you went. You could have raging flu, your mother could have died, you could have lost all your money on a horse, but as long as you could stay upright and remember your lines you went out there and gave a performance.

Hollywood temperament was something Rachel didn't understand. She took a deep breath, tapped on the door and announced herself. If this is nothing else, she told herself, at least it will be an education.

To her surprise Claudia Graham answered. "Yes, Rachel," she said, "what is it you want?"

"I'd like to come in and have a talk. It looks like you've got trouble and I'd like to help."

The actress sounded suspicious. "Are you sure you just want to talk?"

Rachel sighed. "What else can I do? I'm not the producer. I can't order you on to the set."

There was the sound of the key in the lock and the door to the trailer swung inwards. Rachel found herself in a small area that consisted of a fixed table around which on three sides there was window seating. On the other side of the room there was a drinks cabinet and a television set.

Claudia was sitting at the table, looking pale and

## SCREEN KISSES • 197

somehow smaller than Rachel remembered her. The hairdresser and make-up man were standing awkwardly by the bar. Claudia looked at her watch. It was past noon. "Why don't you two go find yourselves something to eat?" she said to her staff. "I don't think I'm going to have much use for you today."

It was then that Rachel noticed that the actress had no make-up on and was still wearing her wrap. Her heart sank. She might have managed to get through the door of the trailer but it didn't look as if she was going to accomplish any more than that. She racked her brains. What was bothering the actress so much that she couldn't even get dressed? Then she told herself to stop being silly. They're all like this in Hollywood, she thought. Claudia's probably got indigestion.

She sat down at the table. "What is it?" she asked. "What's the matter? Come on, you can tell me."

Claudia leaned forward and put her head in her hands. Christ, thought Rachel, she's not crying, is she? There was a silence. Then the actress cleared her throat. "It's Oscar," she whispered. "He died in the night."

So it wasn't anything to do with David, after all. Now Rachel was really out of her depth. Who the hell was Oscar? She decided to investigate. "When were you and Oscar last together?" she ventured.

Claudia looked up. "Before I went to bed," she said. "He'd finished all his food but he still seemed hungry. So I decided to give him a treat. I got a lamb chop from the kitchen and put it in his dish. I thought he'd enjoy chewing on it." Now she really did start to cry. "I was such a fool," she said between sobs. "He didn't chew the bone at all. He swallowed it. Whole. And the damn thing choked him."

"Oscar's your dog," said Rachel, the truth finally dawning. "The little dachshund I've seen wandering around the back of the villa."

The actress tensed. "He was my dog," she said. "Now I've got no one."

For some reason she didn't quite understand Rachel felt sorry for Claudia. The situation was ridiculous, she realized that, but there was something sad about the woman sitting weeping over the other side of the table.

Rachel got up and went over to her. Then because she couldn't think of anything else to do she put her arms round the other woman and attempted to console her.

The weeping went on at full strength for another ten minutes until Claudia finally showed signs of calming down. She pulled away from Rachel and reached for a box of tissues. "Do you know what really cuts me in two?" she asked, dabbing her eyes. Before Rachel could reply she went on. "The whole bloody thing was my fault. I killed Oscar. If I hadn't given him that chop he'd be alive today." She started to cry again. "Rachel, what am I going to do? I'll never get over this."

But Rachel had had enough. She might feel sorry, she might risk being thrown out, but she couldn't go on pandering to this woman's ego. "For heaven's sake," she said, "Of course you'll get over it. You're a huge Hollywood star. You've got money,

## SCREEN KISSES • 199

you've got people running around in circles. Half the men I know are besotted with you."

Claudia looked at her, her expression hardening. "You think that's the way it is," she said. "Well, you've got it wrong. All the people who know me, and the ones who want to know me, only do so because I can be useful to them. If I stopped being famous tomorrow they'd disappear into thin air. And as for the men . . ." She pulled a face. "The men are a crock of shit."

Nervously Rachel helped herself to a cigarette from the pack on the table in front of her. "You can't mean that," she said.

"Why not?" said Claudia. "Do you really think any of my husbands actually loved me? They married me because they thought I was good in bed. Or good for their careers. None of them gave a damn about me.

"Why do you think I was crying my eyes out over that little dog of mine? I cried for him because in his way he loved me. I could look any way I wanted, I could be in a filthy temper with him, I could even ignore him, but it didn't make any difference. He still came when I called."

"Is that what you want," asked Rachel, "someone who comes when you call?"

For the first time that afternoon Claudia smiled. "It will do for a start," she said.

She walked over to the drinks cabinet and peered inside it. There were several bottles of champagne and a quart of Scotch. She took out the whisky and two glasses. "I could use some of this right now," she said. "Will you join me?"

Rachel nodded and Claudia poured out generous measures for both of them. Then she took the drinks over to the table and sat down again.

Rachel looked at Claudia curiously. Even with her eyes swollen and her cheeks flushed she was still lovely. "I find it hard to believe," she said, "that nobody ever cared for you. Surely there must have been someone."

Claudia shook her head. "One of the penalties of the business is that nobody cares. Ever. It's to do with being successful. Men either want to buy you or they're jealous of you."

Rachel thought about Richard Roberts. "I loved someone once who couldn't cope with me being successful."

Claudia looked interested. "Tell me about it."

Rachel was tempted to tell her to mind her own business. Then she thought, why should I? She had been lonely during the past few weeks. There had been no one to talk to, no one to confide in, and she needed a friend. With a certain relief she reached out to the other woman. She told Claudia about her last tour, and how Jeremy Powers had promised to make her into a star. "I should have known my boyfriend wouldn't have liked it," she said. "He was another actor in the company. He had his own ambitions."

Claudia looked at her. "How did it end?" she asked.

For a moment Rachel was embarrassed. Then she took a gulp of her whisky. "Jeremy more or less of-

## SCREEN KISSES • 201

fered me a part in the West End—if I slept with him. I told him no. So he went to my boyfriend and asked the same question."

"Don't tell me," said Claudia, "the boyfriend said yes."

"How did you know that?" asked Rachel.

Claudia smiled. "Because it's one of the oldest stories in the business. It nearly happened to me once." She narrowed her eyes. "We're not that different, you and I. Except I've been around longer."

Rachel was conscious she was being drawn into a conspiracy. She and Claudia were on one side; the rest of the world was on the other. Should I really be doing this? she wondered as the actress brought over the whisky bottle and refilled both their glasses. Then she thought about Bob and the way he'd led her on and left her in the air. She took a swig from her glass. Maybe Claudia is right, she reasoned. Maybe all men are a crock of shit.

Oscar was buried by the side of a paddy field near to the villa where they were all staying. Claudia had chosen to have the ceremony performed at sunset, and Rachel wished she hadn't.

There was something desolate about the rice terraces at this time of day. The water, which all but submerged the growing crop, looked dark and brackish in the light of the setting sun, and the hill which had been crowded with locals earlier was silent and deserted now. Only a handful of people showed up to say goodbye to the little dog.

Bob Delaney was there, as was Rick, who had occasionally bribed Oscar with titbits. The rest of the group was made up of Indonesian staff who used to take him out for walks. It was they who lent the only bright note to the proceedings by turning up with little offerings of rice and fruit. One of them had woven a wreath out of exotic blooms which was placed on the grave. Rachel did her best to keep a straight face. All that we need now, she thought, is a trumpeter to sound the last post.

That evening as dusk fell, Claudia said goodbye to one friend and hello to another. Her new companion, confidante and barrier against loneliness was Rachel. She wasn't Claudia's first choice. The candidate she had had in mind was David Price, but Price wasn't playing. The problem was the Australian heart-throb wasn't up to playing.

Ever since the night David broke his date with Claudia something had gone wrong. First it was a crashing migraine which had gone on a surprisingly long time. Then when they finally migrated up country he had been beset by a thousand little illnesses. He had suffered from the runs, though he was meticulous about sticking to bottled water. Every time he thought he was getting over it, the pains in his lower gut would start again and he would be trapped in his room, not daring to venture too far from the bathroom.

It was uncanny how this particular bug never seemed to bother David while he was on the set. Every morning he would wake up with the dawn refreshed and ready to go to work. And every evening when filming was over the familiar rumbling pains would start again.

## SCREEN KISSES • 203

There were periods of blessed relief when he was free of the bug. He could go for two or even three days without needing to hover near his bathroom. But then, just as he was well enough to think about his glamorous co-star again he would be beset with other troubles. Out of the blue a blinding headache would start and he would be forced to retire to bed early. The insects that plagued the rest of the unit seemed to be specially attracted to him. If he left the repellent off, even for a night, he was doomed. And there were some nights when it was necessary to leave it off. Darleen hated the smell of it on his body. She said it put her off sex. So when David Price wished to consummate his marriage he took his life in his hands.

On camera and during the day David Price portrayed the towheaded hero of the great outdoors, the virile athlete who made women go weak at the knees. In private and at night he fell apart. The only person he would see was Darleen. If it hadn't been for his devoted little wife he would have thrown in the towel and gone home. For in his adversity David had discovered he was married to an angel. Nothing was too much trouble for her. If he wanted his dinner in his room she was always there to eat it with him. Most women would have complained about the boredom of being on location. There was not even the camaraderie of the other members of the unit to cheer her up. But Darleen didn't seem to mind at all. All she wanted to do was to make David's life as comfortable and amusing as she could.

She arranged with the staff for fresh flowers to be put in their room every day. Occasionally they protested that flowers attracted insects but Darleen would have none of it. "They're just making excuses not to work," she insisted, "and I'm not having it. If we have to stay on this uncomfortable island then I want it made as pleasant as possible. And that means fresh flowers, fresh fruit juice in endless supply and gallons of cooling water to bring down the blood temperature."

There were times when David feared his wife was too fierce with the staff, but he didn't dare criticize her. She had his welfare at heart. She was looking after his best interests. The way he was feeling at the moment he needed someone to be there for him.

There were times when Rachel wondered about her friendship with Claudia. Apart from their mutual distrust of men they didn't seem to have that much in common. Unlike all the other actresses Rachel had known, the star seemed to be obsessed with her appearance. Apart from that one time in her trailer Claudia never appeared unless she was in full make-up. They could be having a quiet dinner with her hairdresser, or lying on a beach, but Claudia never left off her blusher, her lip gloss, or the painted lines around her eyes. Rachel was tempted to ask her why she was never off duty, then she thought better of it. She was close to Claudia but she wasn't that close.

She thought about the terrible Hollywood jokes the actress told, and the tacky Hollywood gossip she was always spouting, then she felt ungrateful. Claudia might not be perfect but she had been very kind. If

## SCREEN KISSES • 205

it hadn't been for her Rachel would still be stuck on her verandah trying to read a book.

For Claudia had decided to see something of the island, and Rachel had been invited along for the ride. An air-conditioned ride in a chauffeur-driven limousine.

Each afternoon Rachel and Claudia would climb into the back of the studio's Mercedes and the driver would take them to the villages of Ubud and Mas, which were centres for the local artists and sculptors. The Balinese seemed fond of reproducing their flora and fauna. There were carved wooden models of dozens of different species of birds. Some were done in the ancient fashion with cruel beaks and heraldic wings, while others were surprisingly modern. None of them cost more than a few dollars.

When Claudia and Rachel were not loading themselves down with local art treasures they would stand around and allow themselves to be pestered by urchins peddling sarongs and lengths of silk.

Sometimes they travelled farther afield to Singaradja in the west of the island, where they found deserted beaches of black sand and forests full of bats and strange stripy piglets. On these long trips they would often get the cook to pack a picnic for them. Rachel never thought this was necessary. Every village they went through had some sort of café or restaurant, but Claudia wouldn't go near any of them.

"When you've been on as many locations as I have," she said, "you know to avoid the places where the natives eat. They live here, so whatever they put in their food agrees with them. I guarantee if you or

## 206 • TRUDI PACTER

I even smelled it we'd be in the same state as poor David Price.''

Rachel was puzzled. ''But David doesn't go anywhere. I don't think he's left his villa since we arrived up country. How can he be so ill?''

Claudia looked thoughtful. ''Frankly it beats me too. I can only imagine somebody isn't being too careful about the water he drinks. A lot of the bottled stuff comes straight out of the tap. I always check the seal on the cap is intact before I touch it.''

Now Rachel was thoroughly confused. ''But Darleen's so meticulous. Everything David eats or drinks has to get past her first. She wouldn't let him touch anything that would upset him.''

''Unless it suited her.''

''Now what do you mean by that?''

They were sitting on the sand, drying off after an evening swim. Between them they had consumed the best part of a bottle of wine and Claudia was feeling no pain. ''I'll tell you what I mean,'' she said. ''But first of all, put yourself in Darleen's shoes. She's a rather ordinary girl who by good luck and great timing has landed herself a rich movie star. It's the best thing that's ever happened in her life. Like winning a sweepstake. And she's going to make damn sure she keeps a hold of her winnings.''

''I'm still not with you. Why would she want to make David ill in order to keep him?''

''Because if he's not at his best he'll stay right by her side. David's very easily tempted. And Darleen's no fool. If she thinks David might have it in his mind to stray she'll do her best to make sure he doesn't.''

## SCREEN KISSES • 207

Rachel poured herself the rest of the Sancerre. "You mean she'd poison David to keep him faithful?"

"Damn right she would."

Rachel looked hard at Claudia. "I think you know something I don't. Was David Price by any chance tempted to stray in your direction?"

Claudia ruffled her fingers through her hair and wrinkled her nose, giving the impression of a playful kitten. "What makes you think that?"

"Some of the scenes you played together. The love scenes, I mean. There was one clinch on the beach that made us all wonder."

For a moment Rachel thought it was a trick of the light, but imperceptibly the actress changed. Seconds ago she had been a kitten soft and playful. Now her eyes gleamed like sharp-cut emeralds and there was a hardness about her face. Before she answered, Rachel knew the kitten had become an alley cat. And all the claws were out.

"There was a moment," Claudia said, "when I could have gone for David. It wouldn't have meant anything, but it might have been fun for a while."

"What about Darleen?"

"Darleen wouldn't have made a fuss. She knows better than to upset me or her husband while we're making a film."

Rachel thought about Darleen—blonde, faded, desperately trying to hold on to her husband. "Don't you care about her feelings?" she asked.

Claudia got up and brushed the sand off her legs. "Why should I? She doesn't care about mine." Then she picked up her towel and made her way back to

## 208 • TRUDI PACTER

the car. Rachel followed her, taking her time. Claudia had surprised her, and it wasn't the first time she had done it. One moment she was talking to a friend—a woman not unlike her. Then she'd say something or do something that caught Claudia off guard and the shutters would come down. She wondered if she'd ever understand her.

One of Claudia's obsessions was the future. She collected books by all the popular astrologers and twice a week she phoned her personal medium in Los Angeles. Despite this constant communication she showed little faith in him, and consorted with one of the wardrobe girls, who was able to read the tarot cards. Most evenings when they weren't out, Sandra, the hairdresser, would bring the girl to Claudia's room for a private reading. The actress still wasn't satisfied. "This is meant to be a sacred island," she complained to Rachel, "there's got to be some kind of priest here who can tell me a bit more."

"But what on earth do you want to know?" asked Rachel, mystified. "You're not out of a job. You're not short of admirers. Christ, Claudia, people fantasize about being in your shoes."

But Claudia wouldn't be reassured. She couldn't explain it to Rachel or even to herself, but she was constantly frightened. Usually she could keep it under control. But there were times when the tiniest, most insignificant problems became spectres that haunted her. Then she turned to the fortune-tellers.

Claudia hit the jackpot three days before they left the location to return to the luxury of the Nusa Dua Hotel. The girl who read the tarot cards had been out

# SCREEN KISSES • 209

drinking in Kuta. In one of the bars she had heard about a native woman who could see into the future. She lived in one of the old houses outside Ubud, and it was there that Claudia paid her a visit.

It was one trip that Rachel tried to get out of. She had always had a horror of the occult. She didn't mind the wardrobe girl doing her trick with the tarot cards but she drew the line at anything more advanced than the gypsy at the end of Brighton Pier. But Claudia wouldn't take no for an answer. She had set her heart on having a good look at what life had in store for her, and she wanted company while she did so. In the end Rachel was talked into going along.

"You never know," said Claudia, "you might want to have a go yourself. If this old lady's really good, you'd be a fool if you didn't."

Which is how Rachel found herself driving through the mixture of curio shops, cafés and art galleries that made up the village of Ubud.

There was something dusty and shabby about these Balinese centres. The roads were in constant need of repair and she feared for the lives of the Australian tourists who zoomed up and down them on beat-up mopeds. Someone in one of the cafés had told her there was an accident every day, and she wasn't surprised.

Now as she peered out of the car window Rachel realized they were coming to the outskirts of the village. The shacks and shanties that crowded up against each other were replaced by more substantial houses surrounded by lush gardens. The car pulled up along-

## 210 • TRUDI PACTER

side a high stone wall, and Rachel realized that behind it was the fortune-teller's dwelling.

There was a tiny archway in the stone wall. As she and Claudia walked through it Rachel saw not one building but three. They were rambling, ramshackle affairs built in the style of all the houses on the island. Long wooden timbers supporting a thatched roof.

From the smallest of the houses came a young Balinese. He must have been around eighteen and he was dressed like many of his countrymen in an embroidered jacket over a sarong. "Can I help you?" he asked in perfect English.

Rachel started to feel jittery. There was something unreal about the scene; something that had nothing whatever to do with the civilization she had come from. With an effort she pulled herself together. I'm standing in a garden, she told herself. An ordinary garden with grass and trees and a few ramshackle old buildings. Yet as she lectured herself she could smell incense in the air, and all around her she could hear the tinkling of chimes.

Claudia broke the silence. "We've come to see the old lady who lives here. The one who tells fortunes."

The young man put his hands together and gave a stiff little bow. "If you follow me I will bring you to her."

Rachel thought she detected a slight smile on his face but when she looked at him again he was impassive. This place is getting to me, she thought. And we haven't even met the witch.

He led them into the main house and they walked

## SCREEN KISSES • 211

into some kind of kitchen. All along one wall was a brick oven. The table in front of it was covered with straw panniers in which were piled vegetables and exotic-looking fruits. At the far end of the table, sitting on an upright wooden chair, was the woman they had come to see. Rachel had prepared herself for a wrinkled crone in a shawl. So she was totally unprepared for Martha Chong.

The woman in front of them was clearly not from Indonesia. Rachel guessed that her origins were nearer China. Nor was she withered and ancient. Instead she was around sixty and slightly plump. Her black hair was slicked back in a chignon, her face was crudely made up, and she was wearing a flowing robe of deep-red satin.

Rachel suppressed a giggle. She knew Bali was beginning to attract the tourists, and a lot of the merchandise she had seen in the cheaper shops looked suspiciously as if it had come from Taiwan, but now it seemed the rest of Asia was starting to cotton on to the island's profit potential. Magic, she thought contemptuously. Soothsayers looking into the future. We'd get the same reading in Brighton.

Claudia was more easily impressed. She took hold of the chair the Balinese boy offered her and sat down beside the woman. The introductions were made formally by the young man, who appeared to be her assistant. "This is Martha Chong," he said in his fluent, sing-song English. "She will give you half an hour of her time. And she will listen to anything you have to ask her. But she won't necessarily answer you every time."

## 212 • TRUDI PACTER

"OK," said Claudia, "let's get on with it. My name's Claudia Graham. My friend here is Rachel Keller. We want to know what lies in front of us for the next few years."

The woman produced a pack of cards. Not smart tarot cards like the wardrobe girl's, with their pictures of harlequins and skeletons, but grubby old playing cards that looked as if they once came from Woolworth's. She smiled at Claudia then she started laying out the cards in a circle on the table in front of her.

When she had finished she looked at the cards for about five minutes. Finally she raised her head and stared at Claudia. "Which one of you is the artist?" she asked.

Claudia stared back. "Neither of us," she replied.

"One of you is an artist," insisted the old woman. "A creator of images. A weaver of fantasies. One of you casts spells."

Rachel started to laugh. "Not one of us," she said, "both of us. We're actresses making a film here. Or a fantasy if you like."

Martha Chong looked at her severely. "It is better if you don't mock. Laughter offends the gods."

She laced her fingers together and placed them under her chin, then she examined the cards for a second time. This time when she looked up her expression was worried. "I was right the first time," she said. "There is only one artist. The other is a creator of images. She has no magic."

There was a silence, then she spoke again. "I would like one of you to leave the room. Either, it does not matter."

## SCREEN KISSES • 213

Rachel jumped off the wooden chair. "I'll go," she offered. "I didn't come here to listen to a lot of mumbo jumbo about the future. My agent back home does a better forecast."

The Balinese boy showed her through to an adjoining room. As they left, the Chinese woman picked the cards up and started to shuffle them. Then she laid the pack out in a fresh semi-circle and studied them again. After five minutes she passed a hand over her eyes and shook her head. "It's no good," she said. "I can't do it for one. Your futures are too close. Too mixed up."

She shouted across to her attendant. "Bring the other one back in," she instructed. "I want them to hear it together."

Rachel came back into the room looking faintly irritated. "How long are you going to stay here?" she asked Claudia. "I told you I didn't go in for this sort of thing. Frankly it gives me the creeps."

Martha Chong looked at her. "Sit down and be silent. What I am going to say now has importance for both of you. You would be foolish not to listen. Very foolish."

Claudia took hold of Rachel's hand and squeezed it. "Don't fret, honey," she whispered, "we're together in this. I'll look after you."

There was a silence, then the fortune-teller gathered the cards together and laid them out in a fresh pattern. This time she had less trouble deciphering their message. In a short while she looked up and started to speak.

## 214 • TRUDI PACTER

"One of you will betray the other. And the betrayal will change both your lives."

"Which one?" asked Claudia.

The old woman stared at her impassively. "I cannot tell you that," she said, "but I can say that the one of you who is the artist must fight to protect her art. It is her life force. The reason she is here. Without it she will be destroyed."

"And the other?' said Rachel.

The fortune-teller smiled, and at that moment Rachel had the uncanny feeling she was talking to her alone. "The other has no need for art. She is a mortal woman, like the rest. Her life is with a man."

Claudia started to get excited. "Who will be betrayed," she asked, "the artist or the woman?"

"I told you I wouldn't answer that question. To do so would interfere with the workings of the gods."

Rachel got up from her chair. "I've heard enough of this rubbish," she said. "I'm off. I'll wait for you in the car."

The old Chinese woman folded the cards. "I will not read one future without the other," she said. "Either both of you stay or it is over."

"Rachel," begged Claudia, "do me a favour and stick around for another five minutes. For me."

Rachel was adamant. "Not for you. Not for the gods. Not even for my own mother would I stay here one more second. Sorry, I've had it."

She turned on her heel and walked towards the door. Silently the Balinese followed behind her and showed her out. Claudia reached for her handbag. "How much will that be?"

## SCREEN KISSES • 215

The fortune-teller shook her head. "I don't want your money now," she said. "I want it when this thing is over between you two."

"When will that be?"

"When the artist is reconciled with her art. Then and only then will you be free of each other."

"Listen, lady, you heard what my friend said. We're both actresses, we're in and out of work the whole time. We get reconciled, as you call it, every time one of us lands a part."

The old woman looked patient. "I am not talking about work. I'm talking about art. When the artist reaches her goal she will know it. You will both know it. Then one of you will come and pay me."

Claudia shook her head. "There are too many mysteries here for me. Which one of us will pay you? And how much?"

Martha Chong stood up. "To know that you will have to play the game out to its end." She nodded towards the Balinese boy who had returned and was standing beside the door. "Show the lady out to her car. We have finished our business together. For the moment."

On the drive back to the hotel neither woman said a word. The air conditioning must be working overtime, thought Rachel, as she shivered in the back of the car. Yet she suspected that even if she had been out in the heat and humidity of the day she would still have felt cold.

Finally as they approached Denpasar, Rachel broke the silence.

## 216 • TRUDI PACTER

"You didn't really believe any of that mumbo jumbo?" she asked.

"Why," said Claudia, "did it bother you?"

"You bet it bothered me. According to that old witch you and I are going to be at each other's throats any time now. I hate the idea."

Claudia leaned back on the leather seat and started to smile. "Am I to understand you've never done this kind of thing before?"

"Too right."

"I thought so. Listen, honey, around Greater Los Angeles there isn't just one Martha Chong, there are literally hundreds. And they all say different things. Every now and then I pay them a visit if I'm bored or if I think I'm coming up to a crisis. But I never take any of them seriously. Not unless the forecast is good anyway."

She took out a pack of cigarettes and offered one to Rachel, then she clicked her gold Dunhill twice and took a deep drag on her Kent.

"That old bag," she went on, "was probably stoned out of her tree and thought she'd have a bit of fun with us. After all, what are we? A couple of rich tourists looking to exploit the natives."

Rachel looked relieved. "Thanks for the pep talk. I was starting to get the creeps."

"Well, there's no need. Why should I want to betray you? Or you me? We're friends, for Christ's sake. It's the natives around here I'd be worried about."

Nevertheless, she didn't tell Rachel about the Chinese woman's refusal to take any money. The soothsayers she had met in the past had all been money-grabbing professionals. This one was in a different class. For the first time since they'd met she looked at Rachel with suspicion. Are you the artist, she wondered, or the betrayer?

It was one of those warm, overcast days you get in Los Angeles at the end of February. A mist had rolled in from the sea, covering everything in a thin layer of damp. In this kind of weather the chrome rusted on the custom-built Mercedes in the studio executives' drives and the curl drooped in their wives' expensive hairdos.

Giselle looked out of the window at the stormy sky. Towards the west it was getting brighter, and there was just a promise of sunshine later. It didn't cheer her. Giselle didn't like living on promises.

A month had passed since the beginning of her affair with Dan Keyser. To her surprise she was enjoying the liaison. The studio chief was an intelligent man who liked talking almost as much as he liked making love. Once he had discovered that Giselle had some-

## SCREEN KISSES • 219

thing other than fluff in her head he was delighted. Not only did he have a playmate, he also had a companion. He took full advantage of it.

Most evenings he would stop by her hilltop house, have a drink with her and tell her about his day. In the beginning they made love every time, but on a couple of occasions recently when Giselle's schedule had been tight and she had to rush off to an early evening meeting he had been content just to sit and talk for a few moments.

Nevertheless, she reminded herself, she had started this affair for a reason. And the time for love and small talk was drawing to an end. She needed action. With that in mind, she placed a call to Claudia Graham's suite at the Nusa Dua Hotel in Bali.

Claudia answered on the second ring. "Hi," she said, recognizing Giselle's voice, "how are things with you?"

"Pretty average. And you? Are you having fun in Bali?"

"Not really. The David Price thing died on its feet. The poor guy's been sick ever since he got here. I don't think the food agrees with him."

Giselle tried to sound sympathetic. "I'm sorry to hear that. It sounded so promising. Incidentally, did you manage to get anything out of that English actress I asked you about?"

"Rachel Keller, you mean?"

"That's the one."

There was a pause. "Actually Rachel and I have got pretty close in the past few weeks. So, yes, I do know a couple of things about her."

## 220 • TRUDI PACTER

"Terrific." Giselle tried to keep the excitement out of her voice. "Do you want to tell me about it?"

"On one condition."

"What's that?"

"I want to know why you want the information. And how it's going to be used."

"Are you serious?"

"You bet I'm serious. If I'm going to shove Rachel in the shit, I want to know how deep."

"OK, I'll keep it short. The guy who wants the information is Dan Keyser. He's not happy about Rachel in the part and he wants her off the picture."

"So why doesn't he just fire her? He's got that kind of clout."

"It's not as simple as that. Apparently he did try to fire her but Bob Delaney cut up rough."

"So? Delaney's just the producer. Keyser holds the purse strings. Why doesn't he just fire the girl and have a fight with Delaney afterwards?"

"Because that's not the way Dan does business. He wants a reason to fire the girl. A watertight reason that will convince the front office. Then he'll go over Delaney's head."

Claudia considered for a moment. What Giselle was asking of her was simple enough. Almost at the beginning of her friendship with Rachel the British actress had confessed that she had no experience of film work. All she had ever done was theatre in the English provinces. On that evidence alone Dan could can her.

Then she thought about Martha Chong. One of you will betray the other, she had said. The betrayal

## SCREEN KISSES • 221

will affect the rest of your lives. She shivered. There was no way she was going to have Rachel Keller's blood on her hands.

"I don't know if I want to sell Rachel down the river," she said. "I'm quite fond of her."

Giselle's voice was cold. "That kind of sentiment has never stood in your way before. What's the matter? Are you going soft?"

"No, I'm not going soft." Claudia was irritated. "I just don't want to put another actress out of work. The business is tough enough already without making it worse."

"Don't worry, Rachel will get something else. If she's got the talent and connections to land a juicy part in this film, she shouldn't have any problems finding work."

Claudia sighed. "I wish it was that simple. Rachel's an English actress. She made her reputation on the stage. Nobody in Hollywood knows her from a hole in the wall. No, she needs this part. And I'm not going to help you take it away from her."

There was a silence while Giselle ran the problem through her mind. It was clear from the way Claudia was talking that she had enough on the English actress to bury her, but for some reason she didn't want to deprive the girl of a job. Then Giselle had an idea.

"Claudia," she enquired, "if I could organize for Rachel to land another part in something else, would you be willing to help me?"

Claudia started to smell a rat. There was something wrong about the situation. Why was Dan bending over backwards to spare Rachel's feelings? At her

## 222 • TRUDI PACTER

level you cancelled her contract and asked questions afterwards. No, there had to be something more. She thought for a moment. "Giselle," she said cautiously, "if Dan manages to get rid of Rachel, who's he having in her place?"

"I've no idea."

Claudia didn't believe it. "I think you can do better than that," she said.

"Claudia," said Giselle, "can I trust you?"

The actress laughed. "I don't think you have all that much choice. Unless you tell me who's replacing Rachel the chances are she won't be replaced. Not on my say-so anyway."

Giselle pouted. She had hoped she wouldn't have to tell Claudia the whole story. The less people knew about it the more chance there was of putting it into effect. But the game was up and she knew it. "I'm the one who's replacing Rachel," she said. "Dan wants me for the Mabel part."

She heard a sharp intake of breath at the other end. "What do you mean, you're replacing Rachel? I thought you'd finished with acting a long time ago."

"No," said Giselle evenly, "acting finished with me. Dan's giving me a second chance, that's all."

Claudia started to laugh. "Well, what do you know? Dan Keyser's giving you a second chance nearly ten years after you bombed out. What, might I ask, are you giving Dan in return? Or is that a rude question?"

Giselle sighed. "If you were anyone else, I'd tell you to go to hell. But you're not anyone else. So I'll

## SCREEN KISSES • 223

level with you. Dan and I are close . . . if you see what I mean.''

Claudia saw exactly what she meant. It played havoc with her conscience. She liked Rachel. There was nothing not to like. Rachel was honest and funny, and more important than both these things she was there. But for how long? Rachel was good to have around on the Bali shoot, but when Claudia got home to LA there were other companions. More useful ones.

Claudia and Giselle had known each other nearly seven years now, and they helped each other. If it hadn't been for the French woman she might not be making this film. And Giselle listened to her problems—her man problems. There weren't many other people she trusted.

All her instincts told her to sacrifice Rachel Keller, but there was still something that bothered her. Martha Chong. The Chinese woman had predicted a betrayal with some kind of curse attached. Claudia could do without that. Then she thought about Giselle's idea. If another part could be found for Rachel, one as good as the part she was about to lose, would that be betrayal? Or just a move sideways?

Claudia made up her mind. Love, conscience, betrayal—it was all a matter of interpretation. "Giselle," she said, "I think you could have a future as an actress . . .''

Bob Delaney yawned, stretched and turned on the light over his seat. He had been sitting in the first-class section of the aircraft for over four hours now. In an-

## 224 • TRUDI PACTER

other four he would be coming in to land at Lax, the airport of Los Angeles. He wondered if the sun was shining there.

He turned his mind back twenty-four hours. He had arrived at his production office at the Nusa Dua to find an urgent message from Dan Keyser. The production chief had wanted to talk. Soonest. Bob ordered himself a cup of coffee and wondered about the reason for this sudden communication. On this kind of location he knew to keep heavies like Keyser off his back. He didn't need complications.

Reluctantly he reached for the phone. Whether he liked it or not there were complications. As his hand touched the receiver, the phone rang.

It was Dan Keyser, or rather the supremo's Japanese secretary. "Bob," she tinkled, "I'm glad I caught you. Did you get Mr Keyser's message?"

"About wanting to talk? I ran into it literally this minute. We've only just arrived back from the hills."

"Good," she said. "How soon can you be on a plane?"

Delaney was confused. "Who said anything about a plane? I thought Dan wanted to talk."

"He does, but not on the phone. He wants to see you at the studio."

"Can you tell me what it's about?"

There was a short silence. When the Japanese girl came back on the line she sounded subdued.

"I'm sorry," she said, "Mr Keyser didn't give me any details. He just said he wanted to meet with you. Yesterday."

"OK, I'm with you. Tell him I'll be there as soon

## SCREEN KISSES • 225

as I can. Tomorrow probably. I'll call as soon as I get in."

Now he was winging his way towards Dan Keyser and some sort of confrontation. As yet Bob wasn't unduly worried. So far Rick was keeping to the schedule, and apart from a couple of hiccups they looked like meeting their targets. He felt reasonably confident he could talk his way out of whatever was bugging Keyser.

However, the minute he walked into the studio chief's office he knew he had underestimated the situation. Keyser looked as if he was on the verge of a heart attack. His colour was up, his breath was coming in short pants, and he was pacing up and down the length of his office.

"Dan," Bob said, worried, "what is it?"

The fat man came to a stop in front of him. "You lied to me," he said. "I trusted you and you lied to me."

Bob was caught totally off-balance. "What did I lie to you about?" he asked.

"Rachel Keller."

There was a silence and Bob remembered the last time he had talked to Dan. In the middle of the night the studio chief had got him out of bed to talk about Rachel. And push her off the picture. So that's what it was all about. He racked his brains to think what he could have said about Rachel to get this reaction. Then he had it. The girl hadn't had any screen experience, and he and Rick had fudged her CV to make it look as if she had.

## 226 • TRUDI PACTER

"You're talking about Rachel's background," he said, testing the water.

"You bet I'm talking about her background. Seven lousy years in the English provinces. How does that qualify her to make a Hollywood movie?"

"I would have thought pretty well. Laurence Olivier started on the English stage. So did Vivien Leigh."

The fat man breathed fire. "Not at Magnum they didn't. We don't take apprentices here. We let them get their experience at other studios. Then we take them when they're ready."

"You're saying Rachel isn't ready?"

"Damn sure I am."

"And I suppose Giselle Pascal is?"

There was a short silence. Then Dan motioned over to the pine bar that ran the length of the room.

"What do you say to a drink?" he said. "Then maybe we can discuss this like two civilized human beings."

Bob sighed, walked over to the counter and poured himself a whisky. Straight. No ice. He was in a no-win situation and he knew it.

He had tried to talk Dan out of using Giselle Pascal, but clearly she had made up his mind for him and there was nothing anyone could do about it. He thought about the expensively turned-out blonde and wondered what she did for Keyser that was so special. It had to be something out of the ordinary, otherwise why would Dan have gone to the trouble of finding an excuse to get rid of Rachel?

He cursed himself for not covering his tracks bet-

## SCREEN KISSES • 227

ter. How had Rachel's lack of experience managed to leak out? And so quickly? Then he remembered that Rachel and Claudia had suddenly become friends. I bet Rachel told that bitch all about herself on one of those trips they keep taking. Or maybe over dinner one night. Girlish confidences, he thought. They're worse than pillow talk. He played a hunch. "When did Claudia fill you in about Rachel?" he asked.

Dan smiled. "Claudia didn't fill me in. Giselle did."

"How the fuck does Giselle know everyone's business?" Then he stopped what he was saying. Giselle and Claudia. Of course. They were friends from way back. That's how he had met the actress in the first place—by making sure Giselle got him through the door. He sighed. Now the French woman was leaning on the friendship.

He should have put down his drink and admitted defeat, but something stopped him. He didn't like fixers like Giselle telling him how to do his job. More than that, he didn't want to let Rachel down. He hardly knew her but he'd seen her talent, and her guts. She didn't deserve to be trampled on. A plan started to form in his mind.

"How much time will you give me to reorganize things my end?" he asked.

Keyser ran a hand over his black, crinkly hair. "You mean get rid of the Keller girl?"

Bob nodded.

"How much time do you want?" asked Keyser.

"Two or three days. I have to stop off in London before I get back to the set."

The studio chief smiled. "That much time isn't going to make any difference. I'll tell Giselle to hold her fire until I hear from you."

Bob was puzzled. "What do you mean, hold her fire? Surely Giselle's not going to make an announcement to the *Hollywood Reporter.*"

Once more Keyser smiled. "That's what you think."

Delaney rode the elevator down five floors and stepped out on level twelve. Any resemblance between the executive floor and the space where he maintained his office was purely coincidental. Level twelve, the preserve of Magnum producers and a handful of independents, was a workmanlike affair. The cream-painted corridors were bare of pictures. Any other evidence of interior decoration—green plants, painted blinds, wall hangings—had been put there by the inhabitants themselves. This was the floor where pictures were made. Keyser's domain with its beauty-queen receptionists and million-dollar view was strictly for impressing the punters.

Bob had been allocated a medium-sized room with an adjoining cubicle for a secretary. He would stay there for as long as it took him to put *Marooned* together. His regular secretary, Judy, he would have for longer.

She was surprised to see him when he pushed open the door to his office. "I thought you were meant to be in Bali."

"I was," he said shortly, "until Dan Keyser de-

## SCREEN KISSES • 229

manded an audience. Now you'll have to put up with me for the rest of the day."

He saw the concern on her face and grinned. "Don't fret. There aren't any major dramas. At least not if I can help it." He looked at his watch. "What time will it be in London right now?"

"Coming up to eight in the evening." Judy delivered the information without hesitating. The last four years had taught her time differentials between London, New York and Los Angeles regardless of the season.

Delaney paused, deliberating. "Put a call through to Desmond French," he told her. "At his home number. With any luck I'll catch him before he goes out to dinner."

Five minutes later, the English agent was on the line. Delaney grabbed the phone. "Desmond," he said warmly, "how's business?"

"I take it you're not calling to discuss the state of my balance sheet," came the clipped reply. "To what do I owe the pleasure?"

"Slight problems on *Marooned.* Nothing serious; I need your help."

In London, Desmond French sat down and reached for his glass of whisky and soda. When a Hollywood producer called late in the evening with slight problems, he knew from experience the situation was desperate. "Where are you?" he asked.

"Los Angeles. I had to leave the location for a couple of days to sort something out."

French took a sip of his drink. Then he said,

## 230 • TRUDI PACTER

"Would this 'something' have anything to do with either David or Rachel?"

Delaney came to the point. "It's Rachel actually. Dan Keyser at Magnum wants to take her off the picture and put his girlfriend in her place."

French sounded alarmed. "I hope you told him no dice."

"I tried, but he wasn't having any. He's trying to use Rachel's lack of experience against her. I decided to say nothing until I talked to you."

There was a silence then French said, "Is there anything you can do to stop Dan?"

"Not on my own. But with your help I think I might have a plan. If I catch the last plane out, I could be in London first thing tomorrow morning."

"Fine. I'll clear my diary. When will I see you?"

Delaney thought. "Around ten-thirty. That gives me time to check into the Savoy and take a shower first."

"Good, then ten-thirty it is. I look forward to hearing your plan. It would be a great disappointment if Rachel slipped up this early. I reckon it could put her back a couple of years."

"That's the last thing I want to do," said Delaney. "Don't worry, between us I think we can stop it."

He rang off and turned to Judy, who was waiting in the doorway.

"Get me a seat on the eight o'clock," he instructed. "First class if you can, otherwise club will do. I'm going off home now to take a nap and grab a change of clothes. I should surface around mid-afternoon, so why don't you come up to the apartment

## SCREEN KISSES • 231

then and bring with you all the correspondence you can find on Rachel Keller. You might dig out a copy of her contract as well.''

He grabbed his briefcase and was through the door and half way down the corridor before Judy could say anything. She made her way over to the desk and found an address book. He hadn't told her to book the Savoy, but he'd be as sore as hell if he arrived there and found she hadn't reserved his usual room overlooking the river.

It was lunch time when Bob arrived at Western Towers. He thought about grabbing a hamburger before going up to his apartment, then he thought, the hell with it. It's been a long day, I'll order something from the deli when I get in.

Magnum's driver deposited him in front of the tall skyscraper building in downtown Los Angeles. He turned and instructed the man to pick him up later that afternoon, then he made his way down the glassed-in walkway and through the main doors. There was a sterility about Western Towers that only modern architecture could provide. The glassed-in lobby with its profusion of tropical plants reminded Bob of a very expensive zoo. But the inhabitants of the zoo were nowhere to be seen. Places like this were private and anonymous.

When Bob and Kathy Gordon went their separate ways Bob moved to Western Towers in a bid to get rid of his past. He didn't want a home any more. He wanted a place to keep his clothes, impress his business contacts and lay his head when he was in

## 232 • TRUDI PACTER

town. The penthouse at the top of the Towers answered that need. The previous owner had furnished it with mahogany leather sofas and modern Italian glass and chrome. Bob bought the lot for an exorbitant price and never looked back. There was nothing of himself in the apartment. He had started life again with the slate wiped clean.

He stood by the elevator and contemplated the next few hours. If he sent out for pastrami on rye he could fit lunch in between a shower and a nap. He switched his mind to the contents of his wardrobe. He would need to pack a couple of suits for London. He made a mental note to take an overcoat. Britain was none too warm in the early spring.

He was so busy making plans that when the elevator arrived he hardly noticed the couple that got in with him. When he was asked to recall them, all he could come up with was that they were white, nondescript and wearing jeans. One of them was a woman with lank, brown hair and a pudgy face. Her companion was stocky and heavily built. He might have been a delivery boy, for Bob could not recall seeing him in the building before.

Bob pressed the button for the top floor, and as the elevator started its climb he looked at his companions. They too seemed to be going to the penthouse. He was momentarily confused. His secretary Judy hadn't told him to expect visitors. The girl with the lank hair and the sullen face started to speak. "Do you have the time?" she asked.

Automatically Delaney looked down at the face of his gold Rolex Oyster. It was the last face he saw.

## SCREEN KISSES • 233

\* \* \*

He woke up in a white room that seemed to be revolving slowly around him. His head hurt and throbbed and he was lying down. The outline of a nurse swam into focus and he knew he had to be in a hospital. The nurse must have seen him open his eyes for she hurried over to him.

"Which hospital?" he asked groggily.

"The Cedars of Lebanon." Then she sat down and told him what had happened. "You were mugged at Western Towers. In the elevator. The porter found you and he must have called your office. Your secretary was the one who brought you here."

"Did they take anything?"

"Just your wallet. They went through your briefcase but your secretary says there's nothing missing. She's informed the cops and stopped your credit cards. So you don't have anything to worry about."

He smiled weakly. "When can I get out of here?"

"Not for some time yet. The guy who robbed you gave you a nasty crack on the head. You'll live. But we can't let you go walking around with concussion."

He started to protest but the nurse seemed not to hear him. Instead she produced a syringe and started rubbing his arm with a piece of damp cotton wool. Once more he lost consciousness.

When he opened his eyes again the room had slowed to a standstill and the throbbing in his head had receded to a dull ache. He remembered there had been a nurse and he looked around him to see if she was still there. He discovered he was in a small, private room. To one side of him there was a window with a blind half drawn, and there was a pitcher of water and a glass on a ledge in front of him. Hanging by the bed was a call button. He pressed it and two minutes later the nurse appeared looking worried. "How's the head?" she asked.

Bob grinned. "A medium ache. Nothing like it was."

"What do you see in front of you?" She still looked worried.

"A hospital room. What am I meant to see?"

The nurse ignored the question. "Is it moving in front of you?" He squinted. Then he shook his head.

"No, it's quite still. Why?"

She seemed to relax. "Because the last half dozen times I've been able to get any sense out of you you've been complaining about the moving scenery."

Slowly he put his hand up to his temples and felt the bandages. "It must have been one hell of a knock on the head."

The nurse started to smile. "You could say that, Mr Delaney. It hasn't been an easy few days."

He looked confused. "How long have I been in here?"

"Nearly a week. Don't look so dismayed. You're on the mend now. I'll get Dr Adams to have a look at your head. He'll be able to say how much longer we need to keep you here."

But Bob didn't appear to be listening. Instead he reached over to the phone on his bedside table. Before she could stop him, he was dialing his office. "Hello, Judy," he said, "it's Bob. Yes, of course I'm

## SCREEN KISSES • 235

OK. Quit fussing, will you? I want you to come right over, do you hear me? Bring the mail and the messages. Oh, and pick up the trades. I need to see them."

The phone was taken out of his hand by a skinny young doctor. "That's enough, Mr Delaney. I want to take some tests before you start using the phone."

Bob grinned. "Dr Adams, I presume."

"Very funny. Look, I don't know what Nurse Holden's been telling you, but you've been sick. Dangerously sick. That crack on the head you got gave you massive concussion and you haven't been making too much sense these last few days. Now lie still and look into this tube . . ."

An hour and a half later, Dr Adams wore the same look of relief his nurse had. "You're a very lucky man, Mr Delaney," he said. "I expected some damage. Maybe even a slight loss of balance, but you seem to have got away with it."

Bob started to sit up. "In that case can I see my secretary, Mrs Withers? Judy Withers. I expect she's waiting outside."

The young doctor ran a hand through his unkempt blond hair. "There's no medical reason why you can't. Though it would make me happier if you took it easy, just for the rest of the day."

Delaney looked harassed. "I wish I had the rest of the day."

The *Hollywood Reporter* carried the item on page seven under studio moves. The headline proclaimed, "Changes in *Marooned's* line-up."

Underneath, the story filled in the details. They

## 236 • TRUDI PACTER

were brief and to the point. Rachel Keller, the British unknown playing the major support role in *Marooned* was being replaced by Hollywood veteran, Giselle Pascal.

Delaney poured himself a glass of water and swallowed most of it in one gulp. "Hollywood veteran?" he said to his secretary who was sitting by his bed. "Who did Giselle bribe to print that load of baloney? If she's a veteran I'm Methuselah. The woman's had a couple of cameos on Broadway. Who does she think she's kidding?"

Judy put a hand on his shoulder and tried to push Bob back against the pillows. "Try not to get excited," she said anxiously. "The doctor told me you've been on the danger list. You don't want to make yourself ill all over again."

"If I don't get out of here and on a plane to London in the next few hours I might as well be back on the danger list. Has Bali been in touch?"

Judy made a face. "Rick's been on the phone every day since you had your accident. Everyone's been very worried about you."

"I'm touched, but I'm not the one Rick should be worrying about. Rachel Keller's the one with problems. How's she taking the news of the cast change?"

Again Judy grimaced. "She's not happy, and I don't blame her. Being fired is tough enough, but reading about it in the *Hollywood Reporter* first has to be the pits."

Delaney started to get out of bed. "Is that what she's saying?"

"That's what Rick says she's saying. She can't un-

## SCREEN KISSES • 237

derstand why you didn't tell her she was canned before you left for the coast. Nobody can understand it."

Bob made his way over to the cupboard in the corner of the room and started rummaging around for his clothes.

"I didn't tell Rachel she was out of a job," he said through clenched teeth, "because I didn't know. Dan Keyser gave me that particular news item when I got to the studio. I haven't had too much chance to communicate with her or anyone else since I left him."

Judy looked contrite. "I'm sorry," she said, "I didn't know." She looked despairingly as Delaney started to throw first underwear, then his shirt and finally his suit on to the bed.

"Shall I go and ask the doctor if it's all right for you to get dressed?" she asked.

Delaney turned round and ran a hand across his bandages. "What and ruin his day? Listen, be a good girl and go outside while I get dressed. Then I want you to book me on a plane to London as soon as you can. I'll go back to the apartment and pack a suitcase, and while I'm doing that I want you to get over to Magnum, grab the paperwork and meet me at the airport. Oh, and before you leave the office, put in a call to Desmond French and tell him to expect me. Incidentally, did you call and tell him what happened?"

Judy smiled. "What do you think? Of course I called him. It was one of the first things I did. He offered to come over to LA but I told him not to because I didn't know when you'd be well enough to see him. Now you are I'll call and tell him the news."

Delaney put an arm round her shoulders and ruf-

## 238 • TRUDI PACTER

fled her hair. "I didn't mean to push you around," he said. "The one I should be giving orders to is Giselle Pascal. Of all the tough bitches she takes the prize. But this time she's not going to get away with it. Not if I can help it."

He led Judy across to the door and pushed her gently out into the corridor. "Don't worry about calling the airport, I'll do it myself. Just get across to the office, grab the papers and contact Desmond. I'm going to need him more than he knows."

Rachel had always wondered why the chickens her grandmother kept still ran around when their heads had been cut off. When the news reached her about her firing from *Marooned,* she finally understood it.

No matter how great the shock, the body always goes through the motions. The *Hollywood Reporter* had arrived in Bali on the morning plane and copies had reached the set by noon. Yet despite the story they carried, Rachel finished her lunch and went on working. She sat patiently in make-up and allowed herself to be transformed into Mabel. Then she got into costume and presented herself on the set. Rick was embarrassed.

"You shouldn't have gone to all the trouble," he told her. "After this morning's news, I've decided not to shoot any of your scenes. I'd be wasting everyone's time."

So she had gone back to the trailer, got into her shorts, creamed off her make-up and returned to the hotel. She considered having a swim. After all, she had the time now. Then she remembered the first swim

## SCREEN KISSES • 239

she had taken in the hotel pool. The swim where she had met Bob. And without prompting the tears started.

She cried all afternoon, loudly and without caution. Up in her room there was no one to see her grief or share her disappointment. Then Claudia called and asked her to dinner. Rachel declined the invitation. "I don't want a wake," she said.

"I'm not offering you a wake," said the actress. "I'm offering you a chance to get your act together. That's what friends are for."

Rachel was unconvinced, but she agreed to go. Who knows, she thought, maybe Claudia could tell her where she'd gone wrong?

They had dinner in Claudia's suite, just the two of them. Rachel had expected a rough and ready picnic on a coffee table. They knew each other well enough for that. But Claudia had other ideas. That night she was in the mood for formality and the staff of the Nusa Dua had gone over the top to provide it.

The penthouse suite had its own dining room, and when Rachel took a look at it she knew not to expect a picnic. The long table had been draped with a white lace cloth, decorated with candles and covered with the hotel's silver and cut crystal.

"Are you receiving royalty tonight," enquired Rachel, "or is it just you and me?"

Claudia laughed. "What's the point in having a dining room if you don't use it?"

Rachel pulled a face. "I thought tonight was for comforting a friend. You don't have to show off to me, you know. Anyway, I'm not in the mood for this kind of splash. I haven't got anything to celebrate."

"That's what you think."

Rachel sat down and poured herself a glass of wine. "I'm sorry," she said, "I'm not with you. If I remember it right I've just been thrown off this picture. It's no cause for celebration." She took in Claudia's Bruce Oldfield dress with its enormous shoulder pads. "Are you up to something?"

"I wondered how long it would take you to get there. Of course I'm up to something. I've got some fantastic news. And I wasn't going to give it to you over a TV dinner."

She picked up the silver bell in front of her and rang it. Seconds later four Balinese waiters trooped into the room carrying what appeared to be their dinner. Each man was bearing a silver tray. On the first were bowls of scented water and steaming towels. The second and third brought a series of exotic curries. And on the fourth was a bottle of Bollinger champagne and two tall glasses. When the waiters had set it all down, Rachel turned to her friend. "Suppose you tell me what all this is about?"

Claudia smiled. "It's a party," she said, "to celebrate your new career on Broadway."

Rachel picked up one of the warm damp towels. "Tell me about it from the beginning. And don't miss out any of the details."

Claudia took her time delving around the half dozen or so dishes in front of them. On her plate she put a tiny portion of each curry, then she spooned out a mini-mountain of the rice. Rachel watched her impa-

## SCREEN KISSES • 241

tiently. She knew from experience that the actress would leave most of what was on her plate. She was obsessive about her weight and went through the pantomime of eating for the benefit of the people she was with. Left to herself she existed on cottage cheese and grapefruit. Although she wasn't hungry Rachel dug into the food. This was probably the last extravagant meal Magnum would provide for her and she decided to make the most of it.

After what seemed like for ever, Claudia came to the point. She had had a call from a producer friend of hers a few days earlier. The producer, Len Goldman, was bringing a new play to Broadway and he wanted Claudia for one of the lead parts. But the theatre reminded her uncomfortably of her early, going-nowhere days in vaudeville. Hollywood was where she belonged, so she said no to her producer friend and put herself out of the running.

Then came the news about Rachel, and Claudia had picked up the phone again to her old friend Len and asked him to audition her instead.

It was a plausible story and Claudia told it well. There was only one thing the matter with it. Claudia had never met Len Goldman; he was a friend of Giselle's. But she couldn't tell Rachel that. The English girl knew that Giselle was replacing her, and if she thought Giselle had arranged an audition on Broadway for her she would have suspected a plot.

So Claudia stuck to her lie. She even embroidered it a little. By the time Rachel finds out what's going on, she thought, she'll be out of my life and it won't matter any more.

## 242 • TRUDI PACTER

Rachel went for the story in a big way. "I had no idea," she said to Claudia, "that you could be such a pal. I know actresses are meant to help each other but the truth is we never really do. There's too much competition. How can I thank you?"

Claudia grinned. "By packing your cases and getting on the next plane to New York. Len wants to see you tomorrow, or the next day at the latest. So if I were you I'd move it."

"I'm on my way." Rachel raised her glass of Bollinger, golden and expensive in the cut-glass goblet. "I don't have to ask permission to leave this set. Anyway it will give me a certain satisfaction to pack my bags and push off before they tell me officially."

Claudia looked concerned. "Shouldn't you tell Rick you're going?"

"If I've got the time. Otherwise you tell him. The less communication I have with Magnum, the happier I'll be."

Claudia looked worried. "Come on, Rachel, you can't just disappear into thin air without a reason."

Rachel looked bitter. "Why not? People seem to be doing all sorts of things without reasons these days. Bob fired me for no reason, didn't he?"

There was a pause.

"I think you're being a bit hard on him," said Claudia. "There might be all sorts of political reasons for what he did."

Rachel frowned. "Then why didn't he tell me? Why did I have to read about it in the *Hollywood Reporter*?"

"Maybe his hands were tied."

# SCREEN KISSES • 243

Rachel looked at the American actress sharply. "Look, whose side are you on? I know you're working for Delaney but you don't have to defend the bastard."

Claudia poured herself another glass of champagne. How did I get myself into this? She raged. If I hadn't listened to Giselle, we'd all be getting on with the film and looking forward to going home. Instead I'm in the middle of a first-class drama. If Rachel flounces off the set with no goodbyes and no forwarding address Bob will probably put it down to temperament and forget about her. But what if he doesn't? She remembered the way the producer had been looking at the girl. If he starts to ask questions—worse still, if he gets in touch with her—then it's only a matter of time before he finds out I put her up to going for the Broadway part. With a little help from Giselle.

She shook her head. They had six weeks longer in Bali. Six bumpy weeks.

The worry must have shown on her face. For when she looked up Rachel was staring at her. "Whatever it is, it can't be that bad," she said.

Claudia took a sip of her champagne. "Wanna bet?"

Bob Delaney touched down in London at eight o'clock in the morning, local time. He had had very little sleep on the plane and as he walked through terminal three he felt decidedly groggy. A shower, he thought. A shower and a shave and the kind of English breakfast only the Savoy could provide. Then he would be ready for Desmond French.

## 244 • TRUDI PACTER

The thought of English kippers followed by Oxford marmalade put a spring into his step. In fifteen minutes he had picked up his baggage, cleared customs and was sitting in a taxi on his way to the Savoy. The hotel in the Strand was one of London's grandest. If you were a visitor with money you stayed at any of the establishments in Park Lane—the Hilton, the Grosvenor House, the Dorchester. But if you were a visitor with style and money you stayed at the Savoy. Nubar Gulbenkian, the richest man in the world, lunched there every day when he was in London. Kings and heads of state, playboys and movie stars all had their favourite rooms overlooking the river. So did Bob Delaney, and he was using all the facilities available to him. As well as a full breakfast he had ordered the morning's papers and the services of a shorthand typist and a barber. By ten o'clock he was ready to face Desmond French.

French's offices were a ten-minute walk away in St Martin's Lane. Bob did it in five. When he arrived he wished he'd saved some of his energy, for French's offices did not have a lift. After climbing up four floors jet lag overtook him. He collapsed into a shiny, button-backed leather chair and croaked his name to the receptionist. Seconds later the agent was standing in front of him.

Bob was startled by his appearance. The Desmond French he knew had always been an eccentric dresser but today's outfit took the prize. It wasn't the suit that arrested his attention; it was the fabric. For Desmond French had somehow persuaded his tailor to make him a sharply cut three-piece Savile Row suit

## SCREEN KISSES • 245

in pale-blue denim. Delaney rubbed his hands across his eyes. Normally he would have said something, but today there were more important things to be discussed. He followed the agent into his office.

French hadn't wasted any time. Spread out on his desk was a copy of Rachel's contract with Magnum, and beside it was another document—David Price's contract.

Bob stared at Price's paperwork, then his face broke into a broad grin. "It looks like great minds think alike."

French shrugged. "The Price deal is the only area of manoeuvre."

Bob turned to him. "Do you want to give me your thoughts on the situation?"

The agent sat down behind his desk. "You probably know this already," he said, "but our Australian friend is not all that happy about his stay on Bali."

"What's the matter? The food not suiting him?"

"Not just the food," French said. "The insects bite him in places I couldn't begin to describe. The climate exhausts him and his wife's bored to tears."

Bob started to grin. "Poor man. How he has to suffer for a million bucks a picture."

French put his feet up on the edge of his desk. "I was getting to that. I've known David for a long time. He's a selfish sod, so if I told him he could walk away from Bali, insects, diarrhoea and all, and still get paid—I could almost guarantee he'd jump at it."

"Could he walk away?"

"Now you mention it, he could. The fellow's a bit of a hypochondriac so I slipped an illness clause into his contract." He picked a document off the pile in front of him. "Here," he said, pushing it under Bob's nose. "Turn to page four, paragraph seven. It's all there in writing. If you remember, I had to enforce part of it when David's troubles started. I don't think Magnum would have sent a doctor all the way from Los Angeles if I hadn't screamed very loud indeed."

Bob read through the clause in paragraph seven and nodded his head. "If David wants to he could walk the picture tomorrow."

Desmond smiled. "He won't though. He has this quaint, old-fashioned notion that the show must go on. Unless somebody tells him otherwise he'll struggle through to the end."

Bob laughed shortly. "So who's going to tell him? You or me?"

"Neither of us, I hope. If you handle things the right way with Keyser nobody has to say a word to David."

Bob sat down in front of French's big mahogany desk. "You seem to have the scenario all worked out. What do I say to Dan?"

"I would have thought that was perfectly simple. If Rachel goes, David Price goes right along with her. Both stars are handled by Desmond French. And for Dan Keyser's information, Uncle Desmond is pretty pissed off with the current state of affairs. If the bastard tells you it can't happen, turn to page four of the contract and show him paragraph seven. I think Dan will make the connection."

The jet lag that had threatened to defeat Delaney earlier seemed to have miraculously disappeared.

## SCREEN KISSES • 247

"You crafty son-of-a-gun," he said, "I've got a feeling this could work. Keyser will accuse me of blackmail, of course."

The English agent smiled. "Of course," he said. "How else does the film business work on the West Coast?"

Bob flew back to Los Angeles the same day. There was nothing to keep him in London and he had more important things to do than go sightseeing.

Before he left the Savoy he called his office and got Judy to organize a car at the airport and a meeting at Magnum. The sooner he got to Dan Keyser the better.

He didn't expect trouble from Dan, and he didn't get it. The man was a realist. It had been a fair fight and Bob had won on a technicality. He'd get him some other time, on some other picture.

As he turned to leave, Dan put a hand on the producer's arm. "I hope she's worth it," he said.

Bob looked at him. "What makes you think she isn't?"

"Nothing," said Dan innocently. "Except I heard on the grapevine your little bird's taken off."

Bob started to feel worried. "What do you mean, taken off?"

"What I say. Rachel isn't in Bali any more. As soon as she heard things weren't looking good for her on the film, she got on a plane and took off for New York."

Bob fought down panic. "What the fuck's Rachel doing in New York?"

## 248 • TRUDI PACTER

The fat man smiled. "I don't know. She isn't my problem." Then he saw Bob's face and relented.

"Giselle could probably tell you more than me," he said.

Giselle was surprised to see Bob on her doorstep. "I thought you were in Bali," she said. "What are you doing here?"

"I had an urgent meeting with Dan," he told her. "Aren't you going to invite me in?"

She stepped aside and he walked past her into the drawing room. "Nothing seems to have changed," he observed. "I see you've hung on to the fussy antiques and the porno paintings. I never did understand what you saw in them."

She was irritated. "Did you come here to talk about colour schemes, or was it something else?"

He walked over to a bow-fronted walnut cabinet and helped himself to a drink from a tray she had laid out.

"I came here to talk about Rachel Keller," he said.

For a moment Giselle looked doubtful. "Why do you want to talk about Rachel?" she asked. "I thought that was over and done with."

He wondered how much to tell her. Giselle still thought she was on her way to Bali. She was probably packing and rehearsing her lines. If I let her know the truth, he thought, I'll get nowhere. Rachel could be on the next block and she wouldn't tell me.

He took his drink over to the window. "I've got a slight problem with Rachel's contract," he said. "It's

## SCREEN KISSES • 249

nothing to worry about, but I need to see her to sort it out."

Giselle looked suspicious. "What's wrong with talking to her agent? That's what he's there for."

He threw his drink back in one gulp. "Giselle," he said, looking at her, "you do things your way, I'll do things mine. I said I wanted to see the lady."

She shrugged. "How can I help? I don't even know her."

"I know you don't know her," he said patiently. "But I think you know where she is."

Once more the French woman looked blank. "Why should I?"

Bob lost his temper. "Because whatever's been happening to Rachel these last few weeks, you had a hand in it."

Two bright dots of colour appeared in Giselle's cheeks. "Who the hell told you that?"

"Dan Keyser," he said shortly. "So stop playing games. I want to know where Rachel is and how I can get in touch with her. Then I won't waste any more of your time."

She sat down on an overstuffed velvet chair and ran a hand through her hair. So Bob knew what she'd been up to. That was too bad. "I hope this isn't going to make any difference to the way we work together in Bali," she said. "I mean we're still speaking, aren't we?"

He smiled tightly. "Not if you don't tell me how to find Rachel."

"Very well," she said. "She's staying at the Royalton Hotel on West 44th in New York City. She went

## 250 • TRUDI PACTER

there to audition for a play so she should be there for a day or so. No longer."

He put his glass down. "Did you set this up? The audition, I mean."

She looked defensive. "What if I did?"

"Because it doesn't sound like you. Knowing your form, I would have thought you'd be content with pushing Rachel out of her part. You wouldn't try to find her another."

She shrugged. "You're right. I wasn't all that bothered about Rachel's future. It was Claudia. She seemed to think Rachel should be compensated. So I called a few contacts and did what I could."

He stared at her. Even though it was before lunch time she was heavily made up, and there was a perfection about her that spoke of manicures and expensive hairdressers. He thought about Rachel and the way she didn't seem to try, and for some reason he didn't understand he felt a fierce longing for her. He turned to Giselle. "So you and Claudia are in this together?"

She realized too late that she had said too much. "I think it's time you left," she told him. "I've got a lot to do what with packing and getting organized."

"I won't keep you then." He started to walk towards the door. "By the way, when you see him, do give my regards to Dan."

She hesitated. "I won't be seeing him," she said. "I'm leaving for Bali early tomorrow."

Bob turned and smiled. "I have a feeling you will be seeing Dan later on today. There's something important he has to tell you."

## SCREEN KISSES • 251

Before she could ask him anything else, he banged the door shut behind him and left.

In New York the temperature hovered around freezing. Rachel, curled up in the back of a taxi, huddled deeper into her coat. In her bag she had the address of a hotel on 44th Street. She also had the phone number of the Phoenix theater scrawled on the same sheet of paper. They were her two lifelines in this cold, hostile city. She hoped one of them would save her.

She had spoken to Desmond French before she left Bali. He was as upset about *Marooned* as she was and was going to try and sort something out with Bob. He instructed her to sit tight until he had spoken to him. Then Claudia had come up with this new plan and Rachel had jumped on the first plane to New York.

With any luck she would be working when she spoke to her agent next. She crossed her fingers and prayed. The taxi went through the toll gates and suddenly they were on their way into the city. Rachel had never seen New York before and the sheer size of it made her feel insignificant. The crowds that thronged the streets seemed to have an energy about them that bordered on violence. Rachel dreaded the moment she would have to leave the safety of her yellow cab.

It came faster than she thought. One moment she was five lanes deep in traffic. The next she was standing on the sidewalk outside the Royalton Hotel.

She hefted her bags into the lobby. Nobody came to help her; it wasn't that kind of hotel. There was one man doing the work of five behind the desk, and when

## 252 • TRUDI PACTER

she finally caught his eye she gave him her name. He checked her reservation surprisingly quickly and handed her her key.

Then she was on her own. After a jerky ride in an elevator that had seen better days she found her room. For the first time since she had come to New York she felt better. The room was bigger than she had expected—and nicer. The hotel had been there a long time, and she could see from the fittings and the height of the ceilings that it had known better days.

Claudia had told her that screenwriters often used it. They liked it because it was clean and cheap and they could use the bar of the Algonquin nearby and pretend they were staying there instead. Rachel made a mental note to do the same, and started to unpack.

Five minutes later the receptionist called to say that a package had arrived for her. Rachel asked for it to be sent up, and when she opened it she found it was the script of the play she was auditioning for— *Lili's War.* Claudia must have told her friend Len to expect her. She put a call through to the theatre.

The girl who answered seemed to know who Rachel was, and looked forward to seeing her first thing the next morning. Now all she had to do was read the play.

Three hours later, shaking like a leaf, Rachel put it down. How am I going to get away with it? she asked herself. I can't play Eva. The part doesn't fit.

She had been asked to read for Eva von Sidow, a German countess. It was a chilly role and called for

## SCREEN KISSES • 253

the kind of cruelty she simply didn't feel. Why didn't they want me for Lili? she wondered. I could have done something with that.

*Lili's War* was the fictional account of Lili Drukarz, a Polish resistance fighter. The play covered five years of her lonely struggle against the Third Reich followed by her final betrayal by her employer. The employer was the German countess—the part Rachel was up for. The part she couldn't play.

All day and most of the evening Rachel searched in vain for Eva. She thought about war books she had read, documentaries she had seen, and she looked inside herself for some vestige of the character. But she looked in vain.

Finally she went across the street to an Irish bar and ordered a solitary dinner. She couldn't eat it. This is my last good shot, she told herself. My last chance to work in this country. And I've blown it before I even start.

That night she slept badly, dreaming of Bob Delaney. She was in a courtroom, standing in the dock. Up on the bench, dressed in a wig and gown, was Bob. He was sitting in judgment on her. All night long the evidence against her piled up until finally the time for sentencing came. Somebody handed Bob a piece of paper and he put on a black hood. She was going to die.

She woke shaking and sweating, feeling surprised to find herself in one piece. This won't do, she told herself. I can't fall apart now. Under the shower she pulled herself together. She decided she would play Eva by the book. If she was polished and clever

## 254 • TRUDI PACTER

enough no one would be able to see she didn't believe in the part.

She dressed in the only warm clothes she had brought with her—jeans, an old wool shirt and a Shetland sweater—then she wrapped her coat around her and took a yellow cab across to the Phoenix.

The theatre, west of Broadway, was bigger than any she had ever known before. It lacked the intimacy and old-fashioned grandeur of the establishments on Shaftesbury Avenue in London, yet the moment Rachel walked through the stage door, it was like coming home. Backstage, naked light bulbs lit the dingy corridors. There was no evidence of plaster on the white-painted brickwork, and the smell was the same as it had been in Manchester, Liverpool and Brighton—a mixture of size, old make-up and stale sweat.

Something inside Rachel expanded, and despite the sub-zero temperatures she started to feel warm. She had given her name at the door five minutes earlier, but the theatre had claimed so much of her attention that she hardly noticed the girl who had come to greet her. Her name had to be repeated three times before she realized where she was.

"I'm sorry," she said, turning to the plump girl standing in front of her. "I got carried away. I haven't been inside a theatre for nearly six months."

"It doesn't show," said the girl sourly. "You look like you never left."

Rachel decided to say nothing. The girl was obviously one of the producer's sidekicks, and this was no time to be rude to the help. She followed several paces behind as the girl led the way backstage. It was

## SCREEN KISSES • 255

squalid, the way backstages always were. Rails of costumes from some previous production stood in corners. There was a table to the right of the stage piled with copies of the script. The floor was covered, as usual, with tapes securing cables underfoot.

The producer's girl looked back at Rachel. "Len's out in front," she said. "He left instructions for me to read along with you. So as you're trying out for Eva, I'll do Lili."

For the first time Rachel looked at her companion. She had the carefully dishevelled look that only a lot of money and a lot of time can achieve. Her dark Jane Fonda bob was carefully streaked. Her sweater and skirt were clearly bought as a set. And she shouldn't have been wearing those expensive suede boots in the back of a theatre. Rachel had a vision of this princess with a Brooklyn accent doing Lili, and something in her rebelled. "Len changed his mind at the last moment," she said quickly. "He called me just before I left and asked me to read for Lili. So you go ahead and do Eva's part."

The plump girl started to protest but Rachel had already walked out on to the stage, a copy of the play open in her hand. She had only read it twice yet it was as if she and Lili were old friends. Where do I know you from? she wondered as she spoke lines that sounded familiar, felt emotions that seemed like second nature. It was as if the play was the horse and she was the rider, and she was leading it in every direction she thought it should go.

The plump girl read her part in a monotone, looking nervously into the auditorium as if at any moment somebody would call a halt to what was going on. But nobody did. They read right to the end of the first act then Rachel put down the script.

I might have gone down in flames, she thought, but at least I went down in style. She peered over the footlights and saw a tiny, bearded man in a custom-made suit coming towards her. He extended his hand. "Len Goldman," he said.

Before she could introduce herself he waved his call sheet at her. "It says here you're Rachel Keller, but you can't be. Rachel's trying out for the Eva part."

For a moment she hesitated, then she thought, what can I lose? "I *am* Rachel Keller," she said, "and I'm sorry I just couldn't hack the Eva part, so I read Lili instead. I hope it didn't put you out."

She tried to see how he was taking it but it was difficult to make out his face in the half light. I wonder if he's going to throw me out, she thought. Then she heard him laugh.

"Don't apologize," he called up to her, "you were perfect. If I'd met you beforehand I would never have allowed you to read for Eva. Not in a million years. Come down and let me meet you. I want to find out who you are."

Nervously she made her way down to where he stood. Now she was on the level she realized she was almost the same height as Len Goldman. He introduced her to a tall, grey-haired woman standing behind him.

"This is Rose Andrews," he said. "She's directing *Lili's War*."

The three of them went and sat in the front row,

## SCREEN KISSES • 257

and for the next forty minutes both Rose and Len grilled her about her years in the theatre. They wanted to know where she had worked, where she had learned her technique, how she approached a character. Rachel told them everything. She even included the encounter with Jeremy Powers. When she had finished Goldman turned to her. "I want to ask you one more question," he said. "Do you have a union card?"

She looked surprised. "I suppose so," she said. "Otherwise I couldn't have worked on *Marooned.* Why do you ask?"

"Because I want you for Lili."

She sat stock still while the impact of the words got through to her. Then she felt slightly faint. "Did you mean what I heard you say just now?"

He nodded. "Every word. To be honest I had already shortlisted a couple of American actresses for the part, but they don't begin to come near to you."

She started to smile. "Then I can tell my agent I'm working again."

Rose, the director, leaned forward and patted her hand. "Tell your agent to book you out for a couple of years. After what I heard today we'll be running on Broadway for at least as long as that."

Bob Delaney got into his suite at the Plaza at two o'clock in the afternoon. Wearily he threw his case on the bed then he made his way through to the other room, called room service and ordered a hamburger. Then he did the one thing that had been on his mind since he left the coast that morning. He

## 258 • TRUDI PACTER

dialled the Royalton Hotel and asked to be put through to Rachel Keller.

She sounded out of breath when she answered the phone, and he thanked his lucky stars that he'd managed to catch her. "Rachel," he said, "it's Bob Delaney here. I have to talk to you."

There was a small silence. Then she said, "Why is that?"

"Because I have some news for you. You're back on *Marooned.*" He expected her to be excited, maybe even a little relieved. She was neither.

"I don't know if I want to be back on *Marooned,*" she said. "A lot has happened since then."

He took a deep breath and counted to ten, then he said, "I know you're probably as mad as hell over what's gone on. In your position I would be too. But there's a reason for everything. Look, I'm in New York right now. Why don't you let me buy you dinner tonight and explain it to you?"

"Because I don't want to have dinner with you. Tonight or any other."

He took the receiver away from his ear and stared at it in disbelief. Then he tried again. "Look," he said, "there's been a horrible mix-up here. You weren't meant to be fired from *Marooned* at all. I've just come in from LA and the whole thing's been smoothed over. I'm telling you, we're back in business."

"Mr Delaney," she said, "you might be back in business. But I'm not. I'm due to rehearse a play in two months and I'm going back to England in the meantime."

He started to get annoyed. He'd chased half way

## SCREEN KISSES • 259

across the world for this girl. He'd got mugged trying to help her. And just when he'd made everything come right she took it into her head to down tools.

"What about your contract?" he said. "You do have one, you know."

"Correction," she said, "I *had* a contract. It came to an end when you fired me. The same thing happened to our friendship," she added. Then she put the phone down.

Bob Delaney sat stock still in his chair. He had been so sure of seeing her, so sure she would be overjoyed with his news, that he'd gone and got Judy to reserve a table at the Four Seasons that night. He sighed. What a pity, he thought, I like the Four Seasons. Rachel would have liked the Four Seasons. He got out his address book. Rachel wasn't the only girl in New York.

At seven-fifteen in London the phone rang in Desmond French's apartment. French picked it up hurriedly. He was on his way out to the opera and didn't have any time to spare.

When he heard Rachel's voice on the other end, he reconsidered. "Where the hell are you?" he yelled.

"New York," she said. "There's lots to tell you."

He sat down by the phone. "Make it fast," he said. "I'm a bit pushed."

In the space of sixty seconds Rachel had told him about the play in New York and her conversation with Bob Delaney. He made a swift calculation. If she left the film now, Bob Delaney would never talk to him again. But he'd still be on a percentage of the play.

## 260 • TRUDI PACTER

He sighed. I'm not that kind of gambler, he thought. Anyway I like Delaney. More than I like *Don Giovanni* at Covent Garden. He settled back in the uncomfortable gilt chair. "I'd like to fill you in a bit on the background to your firing," he said. "Maybe you might think differently about Bob Delaney when I've finished."

For the next twenty minutes he told Rachel how Magnum's head of production had tried to replace her with his girlfriend, and how Bob had thwarted him. "He didn't have to stand up for you, you know. A lot of Hollywood producers would have handed over your part to Giselle without a murmur. From what I've heard, she's a perfectly adequate actress. And Bob would have had Dan Keyser in his debt."

Rachel was thrown. "What made him do it?" she asked.

For a moment the line went quiet. Then French said, "Maybe Delaney likes you, Rachel. Or maybe he doesn't like Claudia trying to interfere with his plans."

"What did she have to do with it?"

French laughed shortly. "Didn't you know?" he said. "It was Claudia who tipped the balance against you. She let it be known that you had no screen experience. And that piece of information would have finished you if Bob hadn't stepped in."

Rachel was incredulous. "But Claudia's my friend," she said.

The English agent sighed. "Women like Claudia don't have friends. Claudia used you because you were company for her on a miserable location. You

## SCREEN KISSES • 261

don't really think she'd have anything to do with you once she got back to Los Angeles?''

Rachel was unconvinced. "Then why did she get me that audition on Broadway?'' she asked. "She didn't have to.''

"No, she didn't,'' said Desmond, "but it was probably easy for her. And no doubt she felt guilty about what she had done to you. Listen, Rachel, what would have happened if you hadn't got the part? All Claudia did was to get you an audition. I could have done that for you. You landed the part. Never forget that. Your talent and your determination got you picked for Lili. Claudia had nothing to do with that.''

There was a silence while Rachel thought. Then she said, "But why would Claudia get me pushed off the film? She had nothing against me.''

Desmond chuckled. "Claudia didn't have anything against you, but Giselle did. She wanted your part, remember? And Claudia and Giselle are buddies from way back. It suited Claudia to help Giselle. More than it suited her to help you.''

Sitting in her room at the Royalton, Rachel felt depressed. Despite the difference in their backgrounds, she had liked and trusted Claudia. In this new world she was moving in it clearly didn't pay to trust anyone. "Who told you all this?'' she asked suspiciously.

The agent cleared his throat. "Bob told me when he came over to see me in London. He's been living with the situation for quite some time, poor bastard. Keyser ordered him to replace you with Giselle weeks ago.''

## 262 • TRUDI PACTER

"Damn and blast," said Rachel over the phone. "That's why he didn't say anything. He thought he could stop Magnum from firing me." She thought for a moment. "What am I going to do?" she asked.

"About what?" said Desmond French politely.

"About Bob," said Rachel. "I more or less told him to go to hell. And after everything he did for me."

Desmond looked at his watch. They would be nearly through the first act at Covent Garden. If he hurried he could just make it to his seat before the interval. "If I were you," he said into the phone, "I'd go and find Bob this evening and apologize to him. There's time to finish the film before you do the play."

"But where am I going to find Bob?" yelled Rachel.

"Calm down," said the agent. "I have a plan. When Bob's in New York he goes and has a drink in his father's bar in Gramercy Park. He's there most evenings, around six. Oh, and by the way the pub's called Delaney's, after the family name."

"Where do I find it?"

"Hold on a minute." He rummaged around his desk drawer and extracted an address book. After a few seconds he came back on the line. "Delaney's is on the East Side, around 19th Street. And do me a favour, will you, Rachel? Try and turn up in something other than your old jeans. Look as if you've made an effort."

Rachel sounded doubtful. "I haven't got anything to wear. Unless I go shopping."

"Then go shopping," the agent told her. "With

## SCREEN KISSES • 263

what you're earning on *Marooned* you can bloody well afford it."

Rachel did the best stores at a run. She started in Bloomingdales, where she bought a pair of enormous gold hoops for her ears. The designer rooms defeated her. Everything was either too smart, too neat or too formal.

She dashed over to Saks. The store was in the middle of a toy promotion and on every floor toddlers trailed parcels and specially imported helium balloons. Walt Disney, Mickey Mouse and the Seven Dwarfs were everywhere. Rachel didn't have the heart to ask the way to the dress department.

She decided to try her luck at Bergdorfs. Here she found Ralph Lauren. That season he was pushing the urban cowgirl look—full skirts, tiny cropped jackets and lots of beaten silver buckles. There was something preppy about the look that was alien to Rachel. If she had been American she would have grabbed it. But she wasn't American and neither did she feel it. So reluctantly she took off the Mexican belt, unhooked the skirt and climbed back into her jeans.

Wearily she made her way through to the St Laurent department. It was already four-fifteen and all she had to show for her shopping trip was a pair of hoop earrings. She cast her mind back to her impoverished days in provincial rep. Whenever she arrived in a new town she would waltz around the shopping centre trying things on. In those days when she had had no money for clothes everything she tried on suited her. Now she had all the money in the world yet she could

## 264 • TRUDI PACTER

find nothing. The more expensive clothes she saw, the more depressed she felt. Everything was so obviously aimed at the "ladies who lunch." Suit after dress after coat after jacket was chic, there was no denying that. But nothing she tried on had one ounce of sex appeal. She stormed out of Bergdorfs at four forty-five. I'll try one more store, she thought. Then I'll call it a day. Bob Delaney will just have to see me saying sorry in blue jeans.

Now she had made a decision, she felt better. She took out the guide book she had bought and ran her eye down the list of stores and designer boutiques. She stopped at Henri Bendel, which was just round the corner from where she was standing. If she hurried she could be there in three minutes.

As soon as she walked into Bendel she felt optimistic. The store was younger, less serious than the others she had visited. She wandered through the underwear department and right in front of her, pinned to a board, was a sample of every pair of pants they had in stock. Wispy improbable bikinis of satin, silk and extravagant lace. She bought three pairs all in black, plus a matching bra that hardly existed. Then she bought a garter belt. She suppressed a smile. There's saying sorry and saying sorry, she thought. Bob Delaney saved my job, not my life.

She found herself in the middle of what looked like the designer department. But instead of the long halls and imposing, high-ceilinged rooms she had found before, Bendel's had divided its floor into several totally separate boutiques. In the first she found caftans and oriental-looking dresses. Definitely not

## SCREEN KISSES • 265

her style. She went into another, where everything was tailored. The designer responsible for the collection originated from Maine. She shook her head. Too East Coast.

Next she walked into a room full of leather. There were coats, jackets, soft slinky pants, long swirly skirts. Everything looked expensive and smelled gorgeous. Automatically she turned on her heel. She loved it, she had always aspired to it. But leather was beyond her pocket, there was no point in torturing herself.

Then she turned round and reconsidered. She was a Broadway actress now. She could afford anything she damn well wanted.

She headed back into the boutique and in ten minutes she picked out a pair of slim-fitting pants in pale chocolate brown and a chiffon blouse. Because she couldn't resist it she chose a long jacket to go with the trousers. When she put it on she discovered it was lined in soft brown nutria fur. Bang goes my first three months' salary, she thought. Then she remembered what her agent had said to her. So she stood up straight and walked out of the changing room.

The woman who looked back at her from the full-length mirror was somebody she didn't know. She was used to seeing herself in blue jeans or full costume. This was neither of those things. This was the kind of get-up she'd seen on models in glossy magazines. She thought for a moment. If this look does nothing else, she mused, it could just persuade Bob Delaney to forgive me.

She glanced at her watch. It was five-thirty. The

hotel porter had told her it would take at least twenty minutes to get over to Gramercy Park from mid-town at this time of day. She beckoned the salesgirl over. "Do you take American Express?" she asked. The girl nodded.

"Then I'll have it."

The girl looked impressed. "What, all of it?"

"Everything I'm standing up in. On one condition. You don't make me take it all off again. I have a rather urgent date and I need to jump into a taxi and turn up at the other end looking just like this."

Quarter of an hour later Rachel was still wearing the spoils of her first afternoon of total extravagance: the chocolate brown suit with the chiffon blouse; her new gold earrings; and a pair of matching boots she had picked up on her way out of the store.

She arrived at Delaney's in Gramercy Park on the dot of six. She had expected something rough, a cross between a working man's club and a cabman's pull-up. Instead she found a pretty, almost chintzy neighbourhood bar—the kind of place where families stop by for a quick supper after a working day, or lovers go for a drink before dinner. Tiffany lamps hung over a solid oak bar and the waitresses wore checked pinafores.

As she came through the door, Rachel realized that six was a popular time. The bar was jammed and every table was taken. To start with, she decided, I'll get myself a drink. Then I'll have a look around.

She started to struggle through to the bar when she heard her name called out. The voice was unmis-

## SCREEN KISSES • 267

takably Bob Delaney's, and with something like relief Rachel headed towards him.

Bob was wedged in the corner of the bar, and Rachel's relief at having found him was shortlived. For standing beside him, her arm linked possessively through his, was a blonde. Rachel's first thought was that she must have spent all afternoon at the hairdresser's. She was sporting the sort of streaked, elaborate coiffure that Farrah Fawcett had made popular. It looked tousled and somehow careless, yet Rachel knew that every curl, every escaping tendril had been teased and lacquered into place. She hated her on sight.

The girl looked Rachel up and down with a certain curiosity. Then she looked at Bob. "Who's the glamour girl?" she asked.

Bob seemed amused. "Caroline," he said pleasantly, "meet Rachel Keller. Until a couple of hours ago she was starring in my film." He shrugged. "Then she quit on me. But I don't bear grudges. Rachel, can I get you a drink?"

"No," she said, "let me do this." And before he could say anything she had caught the eye of the bartender and ordered another round for Delaney and his girl. She asked for a beer for herself, then she changed her mind. "Do you serve whisky here?" she asked.

"Only Irish."

"That'll do. Make it a large one and I don't want any ice."

Delaney disengaged himself from the blonde. "To what do I owe this?" he asked.

## 268 • TRUDI PACTER

Rachel drew herself up to her full height. "I had a long talk with Desmond French earlier today," she said softly. "He told me what you'd done for me. So I thought I'd better find you and apologize."

Bob grinned. "What for? Telling me to stuff my job? Or telling me to do the same to my dinner?"

The blonde started to pay attention. "I thought we had a date to eat tonight? You didn't say anything about her."

He gave Caroline's shoulder a reassuring squeeze. "We are having dinner tonight, honey. The lady drinking the Irish has other plans."

Rachel started to feel uncomfortable. "Look," she said, "I don't want to take up your time. But if you haven't found a replacement, I'd love my old part back."

Bob took a pull on his Budweiser. "I'll think about it," he said. "I'm staying at the Plaza until tomorrow. Why don't you give me a call there and maybe we'll talk?" He looked at his watch. "Sweetheart, we've got to run. There are a group of people waiting over at P.J.'s and I don't want to be late for them."

He stood up and kissed Rachel on the cheek. "Thanks for the drink," he said. "Enjoy the rest of your evening." Then he took hold of Caroline's arm and propelled her through the crowd.

Rachel turned back towards the bar counter, and as she did so she felt the beginnings of despair. She'd come all the way down here to explain herself, and when she'd finally made it, Bob hadn't given her a chance.

## SCREEN KISSES • 269

She looked up and caught sight of her reflection in the mirror behind the bar. The expensive new suit she had bought that afternoon made her look glossy and desirable, like a fashion plate. What a waste, she thought bitterly. I could have been wearing jeans for all the impression I made. She drained her glass and thought of ordering another. Then she remembered Delaney's belonged to Bob's father. She'd made a fool of herself with one Delaney tonight. There was no point in putting on a show for the entire family.

It took nearly fifteen minutes to find a taxi. The traffic delayed her another half hour. And when she finally made it back to the Royalton it was time for dinner. She thought of going across the road to the steak house, then she ditched the idea. What she needed was a drink. A private solitary drink, with no one there to judge her. She made her way to the hotel bar.

The bar was badly lit but the soft lights were not there to encourage romance. They were there to disguise the fact that the place was in need of a lick of paint. Yet the rundown room was in keeping with Rachel's mood. If she was going to touch the bottom she didn't want anyone wishing her a nice day.

She walked up to the counter and ordered herself another Irish. The only other occupant of the bar came ambling over towards her. "Are you intent on getting stoned tonight," he asked, "or would you consider having dinner first?"

She whirled round. Standing in front of her was Bob Delaney. "What the hell . . . ?" she said, confused. "I thought you had a date tonight."

## 270 • TRUDI PACTER

"I did have a date. But she walked out on me. She seemed to think you and I had something going and she was just the substitute. She told me she wasn't happy being second choice."

Rachel looked at him. "What did you say to her?"

"I told her the truth. She *was* my second choice."

"That was a bit hard, wasn't it?"

Bob looked at her levelly. "Yes," he said, "but so is life. And I've been trailing around after you for far too long to waste any more time."

She thought back to the first time they had had dinner together. So I was right, she thought. It's not just work he's here to talk about. There's something else as well.

His voice cut across her thoughts. "Have you eaten dinner?" he asked.

"No, actually."

He smiled. "If you're interested I have a table booked at the Four Seasons. We could go there and grab a bite."

She looked at him from underneath her eyelashes. "I'm interested," she said.

The Four Seasons was like no other restaurant she had ever been taken to. A curving staircase led up to the main room, which was dark and imposing and full of important-looking men doing deals. Bob went up to the *maître d'hôtel* and announced himself. Then he turned to Rachel. "Don't worry," he said, "we don't have to eat in here."

He led her past the dark panelling and through

## SCREEN KISSES • 271

an archway. Rachel found herself standing by a swimming pool. It was kidney-shaped and azure blue, and all around it people were sitting and eating dinner. She was dazzled. "Is this one of your regular haunts?" she asked him.

He nodded. "When I've got something to celebrate."

She wondered what he was talking about. Then she realized he was talking about her and she felt flattered.

They sat down at one of the tables and Bob ordered blue point oysters and rare beef for both of them. When she accused him of being a carnivore he laughed and told her all Irishmen were carnivores and she could do with building up.

The food arrived and Rachel found to her surprise that her appetite had returned. She told him about the play she had just auditioned for. Bob had worked with Rose Andrews, the director, some years back. All during dinner they talked about Rose and the production, and Rachel's chances of a Broadway run.

On the surface it was simply another dinner with an attractive man who was spoiling her—except when she looked into his eyes, and then she was lost. They were both lost. Finally she said what was on her mind. "Why did you start ignoring me in Bali? After that first evening we spent with each other."

He looked at her. "You were the one who said she'd rather shoot herself than have an affair with a producer."

"You said the same thing about marrying ano-

## 272 • TRUDI PACTER

ther actress. In fact, if I remember, you were very insulting about actresses."

He put his hand over hers. "That was before I
started falling in love with you."

She dropped her eyes. "I had no idea," she said.

"Stop playing games. You had every idea. What
do you think I've been doing chasing all over the
place getting you your part back? If that doesn't prove
I love you, nothing does."

Just for an instant she saw him the way another
woman—somebody who didn't know him—would
see him. And her eyes took in a powerful, glamorous
producer, one of Hollywood's inner circle. He put
himself on the line for me, she marvelled. He risked
Magnum's displeasure to save my job. Something inside her started to relax. She had been holding her
emotions in check for a long time now. Ever since
Richard. Now it was no longer necessary. Now it was
safe to love, because she was loved in return.

She looked around the restaurant, at the glinting
pool, the fresh flowers on the tables, the chic New
Yorkers out on the town. And she wished they were
anywhere but there.

He must have caught her thoughts and he called
for the bill. As they walked out of the room she wondered what to say. Would he offer her a drink somewhere else? Or take her to a nightclub?

"Where are you staying?" she asked him nervously. He put his arm round her. "With you," he said.

He took her back to the Plaza, and all the way
up in the elevator she didn't dare look at him. This
is silly, she thought. I'm behaving like a teenager. She

thought of all the other seductions—how knowing she had been, how supremely confident—and she wondered what had happened to her.

The elevator stopped at the nineteenth floor. They got out and walked along the corridor to his suite. When Rachel saw the enormous living room with the picture window that overlooked the park she was impressed. She tended to forget that the man with her was a Hollywood producer. All she had ever seen was the man himself.

He didn't offer her a drink, or even a chance to change her mind. He simply took her in his arms and kissed her—moist, fluttering little kisses that suddenly turned serious. She felt a pulse beating in the base of her throat, and at that moment she wanted him more than she had ever wanted anyone in her life. Briefly she pulled away from him. "I'm wearing too much," she said.

He started to unbutton her blouse, slipping his hands inside and exploring the soft, warm flesh with his fingers. "You're not wearing a bra," he said. And she laughed, pulling him towards her as he shrugged off his jacket.

In the big living room they undressed each other. She took off his shirt. He undid her trousers and pushed off her blouse until all that was left was her pants. He slid his hands down her body, lingering over her breasts and the curve of her waist until he reached the thin triangle of silk and elastic. Then gently, with infinite care, he took away her last veil.

She had expected to feel shy, but when he lifted her up and carried her into the bedroom she could only feel a sense of urgency. She wanted him close to her. On top of her. Inside her. And when he laid her on the bed she opened herself to him.

Blindly they reached out for each other—touching, tasting, feeling, until she felt his hardness in her hands. Then Bob took over, parting her legs and thrusting into her with such force that her breath was taken away. As if it had all been planned, she found she moved to his rhythm. Her flesh was his flesh. Her heart, his heart. Her orgasm, his orgasm.

That night she slept in his arms. Several times they woke, and when they did they made love again, falling asleep half in and half out of each other. In the morning when she woke she looked at Bob Delaney and she knew she never wanted to leave him.

# 10

**G**iselle adjusted the seat of her exercise bicycle, set the timer and abandoned herself to twenty minutes of sweat and strain. Normally this was the least favourite part of her workout but today she approached it with the frenzy of an athlete in training.

It was not enthusiasm for this twice-weekly ritual that propelled the pedals at 100 rpm, nor was it high spirits. What drove Giselle to push herself to breaking point was rage.

An hour after Bob had left she had spoken to Dan on the phone, and the moment he told her he couldn't get away from the office to see her she knew something was wrong. Dan could always see her. When he didn't have time, he made time.

As soon as he told her what the problem was

everything fell into place. Of course he couldn't see her. He was too embarrassed. Her first reaction was to tell him to go to hell. But she held off. Dan wasn't any pipsqueak cheating on his wife. Dan was one of the most powerful men in Hollywood, and if she played her cards right she could still get something from him. So she was humble, arranging to see him the day after next when they'd both calmed down. Then she put on her tracksuit and marched down to the gym. She arrived there in the middle of lunch, and she thanked her lucky stars the place was almost empty. That day she didn't have the energy to greet acquaintances. She needed everything she had to concentrate on her future, while working the past out of her system.

She glanced at the timing device between the handlebars of her bike and saw she had fifteen minutes to go. She started to think about Dan.

Right at the beginning, before they had become lovers, he had asked her what she wanted, and she had told him power. She had even told him why. That still hadn't changed. She was sick of running around making things happen for other people. She wanted things to happen for her now. She wanted to be at the centre of the action. But if she couldn't be a star, what could she be?

The bicycle slowed to a halt and, shining with sweat, Giselle climbed down and made her way over to the Nautilus machines. She selected one that strengthened her shoulders, then she set the weight at twenty-five kilos and pulled down on it with all her might.

## SCREEN KISSES • 277

As she did so, Carla Keyser, blonde, pampered, smug, came into view. Dan's wife sometimes came to the gym at lunch times when she couldn't get a private instructor. Giselle let go of the weight and shouted hello to her. Carla didn't seem to have heard. Instead she turned on her heel and stalked across to the running machine.

Giselle sat down hard. Carla had cut her, of that she was sure. She wondered if Keyser's wife knew something, then she thought, impossible. She and Dan had taken care to be discreet. They didn't go anywhere they could be seen together. There were no visits to Chasen's or the Polo Lounge. Apart from that first lunch at Spago Dan had taken her to little ethnic restaurants in Westwood and Santa Monica. No, she was sure Carla knew nothing. All she was doing was behaving like a bitch. Giselle wondered if she had slipped off the social register recently. She sighed and went across to the free weights. Maybe if she did some work on her thigh muscles?

The idea hit her as she came out of a crouch. It was so simple she wondered why she hadn't thought of it before. She could make Dan divorce Carla then marry him herself. She looked across to where the blonde was pumping iron. They were all alone in the gym now and she still hadn't acknowledged Giselle. Silly bitch, she thought. She had it coming. Maybe it was what she needed to bring her down to earth.

Carla had always had big ideas about herself, but then with a father like Jerry Gould, Magnum's biggest shareholder, that was hardly surprising. Carla had always had everything she wanted, and always had the best: the best clothes, the best seats at the best restaurants, the best parties. And when the time came, the best husband money could buy. Giselle considered Dan's two children, Donny and Lenny, and wondered if they would be a tie, but they were in their teens now, and she decided they could cope without a father. Then she thought about Carla. Would she put up a fight? Or would she simply take Dan for all the alimony she could get?

She hefted the weights in her hands and as she did so she started to make plans. Carla would have to be eliminated, that was for sure. But how was she going to do it?

When Carla left the gym it was well past lunch time. In the corner of the room, she noticed Giselle Pascal still hard at work on the long pull machine. She was sweating profusely and there was a slight smile on her face. I wonder what she's up to? Carla thought.

As far as Claudia was concerned, film crews were the worst gossips in the world—worse than hairdressers, worse than out-of-work actors, worse even than journalists. When it came to telling a cockeyed story, film crews were definitely the pits.

By the time Bob Delaney came back to the set stories about Claudia were getting out of all proportion. Rick filled him in on the mood of the crew over dinner that night. They had decided to eat in Bob's suite, and bring each other up to date on the events of the past few weeks.

For the first couple of hours Bob did most of the talking. He told Rick everything that had occurred

## SCREEN KISSES • 279

since he last saw him. Such was the drama of the story that he felt he could get away without telling the English director about the time he spent with Rachel in New York. He reckoned without Rachel. Around midnight there was a tap on the door and in she stumbled, sleepy and missing him. She'd had the taste to get dressed. But her role in Bob's life was all too clear.

He decided to drop any pretence. It had been easy to ignore Rachel when he hadn't been close enough to love her. Now it was too late. He put an arm round her and led her into the room. "The lady says I'm keeping her up," he said to Rick by way of explanation. "How much longer are we going to be?"

Rick looked at his watch. "I'd say another half hour. No, make that forty-five minutes. It'll take that long to tell you what's been going on here." He looked at Bob and Rachel huddled together on the sofa. "You two could have more trouble than you bargained for."

Delaney got up and went over to the bar. "I'm going to have a drink. One last drink before I turn in. How about you two?"

Rick asked for a bourbon. Rachel said she'd have nothing. Delaney brought the ice bucket, two glasses and a bottle to the table. He gestured to the director. "You first," he said, "you look like you could do with it. When you feel like it, you'd better tell me what's bugging you."

Rick gave it to him straight. "Claudia," he said. "The woman's driving me nuts."

The problem had started with the crew. Someone had got hold of the fact that Claudia had been behind

**280 • TRUDI PACTER**

Rachel's firing. After that all hell had broken loose. It wasn't that Rachel was particularly popular. Hardly any of them even knew her. But they were all staunch union members, and as such they stood shoulder to shoulder with the underdog.

Claudia was a rich bitch from Hollywood who drank champagne and looked down on the likes of them. Rachel was her innocent victim. In one version the two women had had a lesbian relationship. In another they had fallen out after a quarrel over David Price. In yet another they were fighting over Bob.

The Irishman took a long pull on his bourbon. "How is Claudia taking all this?"

Rick raised his eyes to heaven. " 'How's Claudia taking it?' he asks me. Like a bloody personal affront, that's how she's taking it. She's behaving as if you, me, every member of the crew, created the situation to make her look a fool."

Delaney looked worried. "Why didn't you tell me about this when I called you from New York?"

"Because, to be honest, I thought it would blow over. When it started, she behaved like a pro and pretended not to notice. Rose above it, so to speak. Then her hairdresser and that lame brain who calls himself a make-up man got into the act. Every time I went into her room they went into a huddle round her like they were protecting her from Count Dracula or something. The pair of them wound her up so tight that she's incapable of rational conversation, let alone giving a performance."

Delaney refilled his glass. It was going to be a long night. "So you *have* tried talking her out of it?"

## SCREEN KISSES • 281

"I've tried, David's tried, even bloody Darleen's tried. And she isn't giving an inch. All she does is sit in her room all day and get tanked up on champagne. She's sending the film over budget. And she's drinking the profits."

Rachel started to pay attention. "Look, why don't I go and see her? Before all this happened we were pretty close friends."

Rick shook his head. "Now all this has blown up you can put that friendship behind you. As far as Claudia's concerned you're the reason for all her troubles."

"But that's ludicrous," said Rachel. "If I remember it right, Claudia was responsible for getting me canned."

Rick rubbed his eyes. "Don't confuse me by telling me the facts, for God's sake. I know Claudia got you canned. And that would have been just fine with her if you'd stayed canned. But you didn't, did you? Sir Galahad over here came riding to the rescue. So back you come, reinstated and holding hands with the producer. Meanwhile, Claudia's got egg all over her face."

He ran his hand through his thick black curls until they seemed to be standing on end. "Look, let me try to explain something to you. Claudia is a star who has been embarrassed. At this stage it doesn't matter who is in the right and who is in the wrong. What matters is that a major Hollywood movie queen has lost face. And you, Rachel Keller, are the reason. So if I were you I would keep well out of her way until this movie

## 282 • TRUDI PACTER

is completed. Otherwise who knows what could happen?''

Delaney turned to Rick, and took the drink out of his hand. "You've had enough of this for one night. How early are you starting tomorrow? And what are you shooting?''

With an effort Rick pulled himself together. "We're out at first light, as usual. Most of the morning I'm shooting around David. Exteriors mostly. I was going to try something with Rachel, but she'll look like hell tomorrow, so I'll leave that for the time being.''

Delaney looked thoughtful. "Are you doing anything with Claudia?''

The Englishman spread his hands. "What do you think?''

Bob stood up and took Rachel by the hand. "Right,'' he said, "we're going to bed. In the morning, whatever she looks like, I want Rachel in make-up. It says on the schedule she's doing a beach scene and I'd like to stay with that. We've wasted enough money already without getting further into the shit.''

Rick walked over to the door. "What about Claudia?''

Bob shrugged. "Leave Claudia to me. I handled her once before when she was playing up. I reckon I can do it again.'' He clapped Rick on the shoulder. "Listen, buster, I'm paid to sort out hysterical actresses. Your job is to get behind the camera and put some decent footage into the can.''

\*     \*     \*

## SCREEN KISSES • 283

The following morning, after Rachel had left for the set, Bob went and took a long swim. He was as graceless and clumsy in the pool of the Nusa Dua as he had been at Claudia Graham's when they first met. It didn't bother him. He needed the exercise to clear his head, not win him applause. He had work to do.

After a shave, a shower and the full hotel breakfast he put on a lightweight suit and made his way to Claudia's penthouse suite. The door was answered by a pudgy blonde clutching a half-empty glass of champagne.

"Hi, Sandra," Bob said cheerfully, pushing past her. "Bit early to start drinking, isn't it?"

The hairdresser frowned. "Claudia isn't working today," she said sulkily. "What else am I supposed to do?"

Bob thought of several alternatives and voiced none of them. If he worked with Claudia on another film he'd be dealing with Sandra again. It was easier to have her on his side.

"Where's Claudia?" he asked, still smiling.

"By the pool," said the girl following him through. "Was she expecting you?"

Bob didn't answer. Instead he walked out on to the terrace. As he had expected, the actress was stretched out naked, worshipping the sun. No matter how many times he saw Claudia displaying herself, the sight always disturbed him. For a moment he remembered Rachel and the night they had just spent together, and he felt a pang of guilt. Then he thought, the hell with it, what I'm feeling right this moment isn't love.

## 284 • TRUDI PACTER

She must have heard him coming, for she got to her feet and wrapped herself in a kanga. Then she offered him coffee.

Bob raised an eyebrow and took in the half-empty bottle of Bollinger behind her. "Is that what you're drinking?"

She laughed. "You don't miss a trick, do you, Bob? You're welcome to join me with the fizz if you like. But I warn you, I start to lose my inhibitions around midday."

She stared at him for a long time without blinking, and the memory of her body—the surprisingly large nipples, the lush, black pubic hair—came back to him. A moment ago she had been lying there open to the sun. Open to anyone who happened to drop in. What is it about this dame? he thought irritably. Every time I set eyes on her I want to fuck the arse off her.

Then he grinned. Me and every other macho man in the Western world. That's why we're paying her a fortune and putting up with her shit.

Claudia looked at him. "What are you smiling about?"

"The thought of taking you out to lunch dressed the way you are."

"Lunch." She ran a hand distractedly through her hair. "I'm not nearly ready to have lunch."

He looked at his watch. "It's half past ten," he said. "That gives you exactly an hour and a half to get your ass into gear. Do you think you can manage it?"

She looked at him suspiciously. "Where were you thinking of going?"

## SCREEN KISSES • 285

"The Oberoy."

The green eyes sparkled. The Oberoy, as far as Claudia was concerned, was worth sobering up and getting dressed for. It was the most stylish and expensive hotel on the island. She knew people who had travelled from California just to stay there.

She started to head towards the bathroom. "Make that two hours," she said, "and you've got yourself a date."

The Oberoy had little in common with Kuta, the resort nearest to it. Kuta was full of beach bars, drunken Australians and funny hats. The Oberoy catered for a different market. Claudia noted that with satisfaction the moment the hired limousine purred up the drive to the main building. All around her she could sense rather than see private chalets surrounded by dense tropical foliage. The rich liked to take their holidays in private. And the Oberoy gave the impression of being a grand oriental house with a few favoured guests.

As they drew up outside Claudia saw peacocks parading across the velvet lawns. She shuddered slightly. I wonder if they're tame, she thought, as Bob helped her out of the car. She had an aversion to birds and was always terrified they would want to fly into her hair. It was as if he had read her thoughts.

"If you don't look at them," he said, holding her arm and steering her towards the entrance, "they'll take no notice of you."

Once she was inside she felt better. This was territory she understood. Aside from the Balinese carving, which was in evidence wherever you looked, she could have been in any de luxe hotel anywhere in the world. The carpets were thick, the servants were obsequious, there was an abundance of fresh flowers. She closed her eyes and breathed in their perfume. She was going to enjoy lunch.

As Bob guided her through to the restaurant, she noted with approval the silver, the crystal, the dazzling white linen, plus that extra ingredient that every top restaurant possessed—the hushed, almost reverent air of an establishment that intended to take a great deal of money off its customers. There was a small cocktail bar in front of the main dining room, and Bob led Claudia to one of the few unoccupied tables there. Before she could ask, a bottle of Bollinger appeared at her elbow.

Claudia settled back in her chair, smoothed her skirt over her knees and started to plan her strategy. Bob was trying hard to please her—almost too hard—and she knew the reason why. News of her unhappiness had finally reached him and he, like the good producer he was, was trying to repair the damage.

She knew, they both knew, that she would come into line. She had to. Her reputation as well as his was riding on this film. The question was, how long was she going to make him suffer? And what price would she extract from him to persuade her to go on with the film?

She glanced at the handsome, good-natured man sitting opposite her, and the memory of the afternoon she had spent with him at her house in Bel Air came back to her. He had come on like a pussycat then—

## SCREEN KISSES • 287

all ingenuous good manners and let-me-solve-your-problems. But underneath the gentlemanly surface he could be lethal, a killer.

Something inside her stirred. The hell with David Price and his prissy little wife, she thought. I think I've found what I'm looking for. She kept the conversation light while the waiter brought the menus and refilled their glasses. Now she had made her plan she was in no hurry. They had the whole afternoon in front of them.

It was nearly two o'clock when they finally got into the dining room, yet no mention had been made of why they were there. Bob behaved as if the whole jaunt was an everyday occurrence. He's too relaxed, she thought savagely. If he tells me one more Hollywood anecdote I'll go crazy. She switched the subject to the film, though she made no reference to what was bothering her. Instead she talked about David and his recurring sickness.

Bob looked at his watch under the table. He had been with her nearly two hours now and she hadn't talked about the Rachel problem. He was more than used to Hollywood actresses and the games they played, which is why he knew she was up to something. If all she wanted was for him to silence the crew, she would have said so. If she had wanted an apology from everyone concerned she would have voiced that too. No, there was something else she wanted. He decided to give her more time. Like all good poker players he knew that it was patience and nerve, rather than cards, that finally won the game.

They spent another twenty minutes talking about

## 288 • TRUDI PACTER

David Price. Then while the food was being served Bob brought the subject back to Hollywood. Ten minutes later Claudia caved in. "I've been having a problem with one of the actresses on the film," she said.

Bob smiled his easy-going producer's smile. "You surprise me," he said. "Who's making you unhappy?"

Claudia pursed her lips. "You know damn well who it is. Everyone on Bali knows who it is."

He put his hand over hers. "Sweetheart, I haven't been on Bali for nearly two weeks now. How would I know what's been going on?"

She looked at him with suspicion. Liar, she thought. My hairdresser told me what you've been up to with Rachel Keller. And I have no doubt whatever she's been telling you her version of events. Well, two can play at that game . . .

For the next half hour Claudia recounted every detail of a story Bob knew by heart. Listening to her tell it filled him with a certain amusement, for she had arranged the facts in such a way that the whole saga looked like an elaborate plot to discredit her, with Rachel at the bottom of it. He didn't bother to argue. Claudia could see things any way she wanted—just as long as she went back to work.

He picked up the bottle of Fleurie and refilled both their glasses. Then he looked her in the eye. "What are you after?" he asked.

For a moment she was confused. "I don't understand."

"Claudia, stop it. You've been made to look a

**SCREEN KISSES • 289**

fool by Giselle Pascal and because she's not here to take the blame, you're shifting it on to Rachel.

"Listen, I don't care who you choose to fall out with. If you want to call Rachel names, go ahead. She's a big girl, she can take care of herself. The problem is, can you? Or are you going to go on sitting around in your suite drinking away your reputation?"

She put her glass down. "It's your reputation too, and don't you forget it. If *Marooned* doesn't get finished, you go down the toilet along with me."

Delaney's expression didn't change. The easy smile stayed in place and he continued to look relaxed. He'd come up in a tougher school than she had and he was about to let her know it.

"Bullshit," he said. "You probably don't know this but from the day you signed your contract I took out insurance on you. So if I have to reshoot all your scenes, I can go ahead and still stay in budget."

The wind went out of her, and with it her advantage. "I suppose you're going to tell me next you've got someone else lined up to take my place."

"Sure I have. You don't think you're the only pair of boobs in Hollywood, do you?"

Now she was worried. "Who is it? I demand to know who's going to take over from me."

Bob considered throwing Raquel Welch's or Farrah Fawcett's name into the ring. Then he thought, no. He could get away with the insurance lie but movie stars were more difficult. All she'd have to do was make a couple of calls and his whole plan would come undone. So he leaned forward and looked conciliatory. "Darling, stop fretting. Nobody's going to replace you. You were my first choice and as far as I'm concerned you still are. Now tell me what the problem is and I'll try and sort it out for you.''

Claudia was finished and she knew it. Delaney had been in the palm of her hand. He would have given her anything she had asked. Now she was the one who was doing the asking. What the hell had gone wrong?

She played her last card. "The problem," she said icily, "is Rachel Keller. Because of her I seem to be a laughing stock with the entire unit. Can you blame me for not wanting to come out of my room?"

"No, I can't. Though to be fair, I don't think it's Rachel's fault. The only thing she wanted was her job, which I managed to salvage for her. If that made you look silly, I'm sorry." He paused. "Look, why don't you let me try to do something about that? If I can squash the rumours and the gossip, then things could just go back to normal."

She looked puzzled. "How are you going to do that?"

"I'm not going to do that. We are going to do that."

She sat up and pulled herself together. "How?"

Delaney felt the tension seeping out of his neck. For a while back there it had been a close call. If Claudia had been allowed to use her power the whole project could have been reduced to a shambles. He had seen it happen on other films with other stars. So far he had never gone down that road. He touched wood and sent up a silent prayer to the gods. Then he turned his attention to Claudia.

## SCREEN KISSES • 291

"What we are going to do, starting tomorrow, is to have lunch." He saw her expression and started to laugh. "No, not here. On the set. My plan is to arrange a lunch table for four every day until we finish filming. For the next three weeks, you, me, Rick Hamilton and Rachel Keller will be seen by every member of the crew to be breaking bread and enjoying each other's company. Do you think you can manage that?"

She nodded.

"Good. If everyone in the unit sees you chatting to Rachel as if nothing whatever had happened, the silly stories will stop."

The actress took a deep breath. "I don't have to go on talking to Rachel after we've had lunch, do I?"

"Of course you don't. As far as I'm concerned you two girls can throw rocks at each other when you're off the set. As long as you do it in private."

Claudia was satisfied for now at any rate. She had not managed to discredit Rachel Keller, nor had she seduced Bob Delaney, but she had managed to save face. She had the rest of her life to achieve her other objectives.

Rick called it a wrap at the end of April, then both he and Bob Delaney went out for a private celebration. There was much to rejoice about. They were bang on schedule, and despite David's health problems, Claudia's temperament and the hiccup with Rachel they had come in well under budget. This fact had not gone unnoticed at Magnum and Dan Keyser had sent them a personal telex of congratulations.

"He doesn't miss a trick," said Rick, who was

well into his third beer. "What's the betting if we had gone over another million dollars he would have put it down to our lack of efficiency rather than his interference? It could easily have cost us that if he'd got away with wishing that Pascal woman on us right in the middle of things."

Delaney signalled the beach bar waiter for another round of drinks. "But he didn't, did he? None of it happened, and it looks like we're away to the races."

"So far," said Rick, touching wood. "We've still got two weeks of interiors to shoot in LA." Then he did a fast estimate of how far they'd come. Most people had had days out with fever or diarrhoea but the doctor from LA had seen to it that everyone, including David Price, and his family, had survived everything else. The only real casualty had been Sandra, Claudia's hairdresser, who had suffered a painful swollen foot from a stinging jellyfish.

Delaney had decided to allow David Price to go home a week earlier than everyone else. Rick had done everything he could with him and the actor was totally drained. The concentration of giving a performance while he was severely under par had exhausted him, but right to the end he had been a pro. The rushes showed he had been adequate. There were no fireworks, but the David Price the audience expected came across. He had given value for money. It was more than they had hoped for.

There were other consolations. Claudia's eye surgery was hardly detectable, even in close-up. She

## SCREEN KISSES • 293

looked gorgeous and had given a surprisingly good account of herself.

However, the star of the show was undoubtedly Rachel. Despite her inexperience, she had lived up to Rick's expectations. There was something about the personality she projected on screen that reached out and touched anyone who was watching.

"When we've got a final cut," said Bob, "I want to be there personally when Keyser sees it."

"Why, do you expect him to say sorry for the Pascal business?"

"No. But whatever he says, he's going to make himself look like a prize asshole."

There was an end-of-term feeling at the airport the next day. Most of the film crew had led lives of dedicated debauchery during their stay on Bali. Everyone, from the actors to the crew, had lived high and lived free. Now they were going home nothing would be the same again. From now on they would be commuting into the studio every day from their own houses instead of living in a luxury hotel. They would be gossiping about the movie colony at large instead of their own private movie colony. The richer ones among them would be eating at La Serre and Spago instead of the Nusa Dua, while the others would grab a Mexican takeaway or a snack at the Rib Shack instead of swanning around the beach bars of Kuta. And they all knew that the moment they touched down at Lax, Bali would be consigned to the scrapbook of their memories.

The odd one out was Rachel. Of the whole unit

she was the only one who wasn't going home. Delaney knew that when they started out and had booked her into the Beverly Wilshire. Now he was homeward bound he started to have second thoughts about the arrangement. Since they had come back from New York they had not spent a night apart. More than once he had been tempted to ask her to stay at his apartment, but something stopped him. He had had no serious commitment since the end of his marriage. He could still remember the pain his wife had inflicted on him when they parted. Kathy could do that to me because I opened myself to her, he thought. Now I'm thinking of doing the same with Rachel, another actress. He remembered the rushes he had seen of her in Bali. She's another Kathy Gordon, he thought. She's got that talent, that quality. He felt uneasy.

What would happen to me, he wondered, if I got in the way of that talent? How would Rachel feel if I asked for a share of all that passion she gives to her audience? No, he thought. I don't want her to come and stay. Not yet. Let the Beverly Wilshire take care of Rachel for the time being.

Rachel was doing very nicely in the grand old hotel at the bottom of Rodeo Drive. She had been installed in one of the suites on the top floor near the sun deck, and was taking advantage of the fact. They had arrived early on Saturday morning and she had taken a cab straight to the hotel. "Give me time to unpack and get my hair washed," she had told Bob. "I'll call you when I feel human again."

She started feeling human the moment she walked through the doors. The Beverly Wilshire was

## SCREEN KISSES • 295

de luxe, but in a very cosy sort of way. There was no glitz, no chandeliers, no white-coated waiters. All there was was wall-to-wall luxury. Either of the two grand restaurants would serve guests round the clock. If you wanted caviar you could have it fast. But they would serve a hamburger at the same speed.

Rachel's bathroom was a monument to indolence. There was a shower that worked at five different pressures and a huge marble bath that could have held her and several close friends. Idly she wondered if people were meant to hold parties there. The pile of fluffy white bath sheets looked far too extravagant for just one person, as did all the bottles of bath oil and shampoo.

Smiling happily she filled the tub up to the top, then she threw three different essences into the water and climbed in.

An hour later she woke up freezing cold. Then she remembered she'd been travelling for over twelve hours. I think I need a longer rest than this, she decided. She dried herself on one of the velvety towels, wrapped herself in the robe the hotel provided and got into bed.

When she opened her eyes again it was two o'clock in the afternoon and she was ravenous. She peered through the curtains at the terrace outside her room. There was hardly anyone on the loungers round the pool, the sun was shining and it looked hot. She had an idea. Picking up the phone, she called room service. "Is there any chance of getting lunch served by the pool?" she asked.

The voice at the other end had a smile in it.

## 296 • TRUDI PACTER

"That's what we normally do on a day like this. What would you like?"

Rachel ordered rare beef, three different salads and an ice cream sundae.

"Will there be anything else?"

"I'd love some fruit."

"Why, have you finished the bowl in your room?"

"I didn't know there was one."

The voice broke into a chuckle. "Every guest has one, compliments of the house. Why don't you take a look at it? And if there's anything extra you want, give me a call."

Rachel put the phone down. This was better than being on holiday.

Outside the temperature was in the mid-seventies—warm enough to try the pool. Rachel had done thirty lengths by the time lunch arrived on a silver tray. She'd forgotten to order anything to drink, but her needs had been anticipated. The meal came complete with Perrier water, Coca-Cola and half a bottle of Californian red wine. If she wanted anything different, the waiter told her, she only had to ask.

There was something decadent about eating lunch at three o'clock in the afternoon beside a swimming pool. For the inhabitants of tinsel town it was too early in the season and too late in the day for such activities, so Rachel had the place to herself. At least she thought she did.

"Feeling human yet?" asked a familiar voice. Rachel looked up and saw Bob standing behind her. She

## SCREEN KISSES • 297

had never seen him in jeans and a tee-shirt and it made him look younger, somehow tougher.

"So much for your promises to call me." He smiled. "If I hadn't come over to find you, I could have been waiting till midnight for the phone to ring."

"Nonsense," she said. "I was going to ring when I'd finished lunch."

"Lunch at this hour? You're due to have drinks at six-thirty."

Now she looked surprised. "Who am I having drinks with in three hours' time? Apart from you, of course."

He sat down beside her on the lounger and put his arm round her waist. "What would you say if I told you Dan Keyser?"

"I'd say you were an unconvincing liar. The man only tried to get me fired less than a month ago."

Bob smiled. "That was yesterday. And yesterday in this town doesn't exist. Dan's having a few people round for drinks tonight, and he asked me to come and bring a date. I thought I'd take you if you didn't have any other plans."

"Do you think that's wise? We made an awful fool out of Dan Keyser."

Bob's grin grew broader. "Of course it isn't wise. But it could be a lot of fun."

Dan and Carla Keyser lived in considerable splendour on a high bluff overlooking the Pacific Ocean. Other studio heads preferred to live among their peers in Beverly Hills, Laurel Canyon or even nearby Malibu.

## 298 • TRUDI PACTER

In his heart of hearts Dan would have liked that too, but Carla wasn't having it. She'd been brought up on big estates with tennis courts and swimming pools and an extra house for the guests, and she wasn't changing her style now.

When Rachel arrived she got the impression not of a house but of a country club, for on the way to the front drive they passed stables, two vast swimming pools and four good-sized tennis courts.

"What did Dan mean exactly when he said he was having a few friends in for drinks?" she asked nervously. "I mean should I have worn a cocktail dress or something?"

Bob smiled. "Why, do you have one?"

She punched him. "That's not the point. I could have gone out and bought one."

He parked the car. Then he turned and looked at her. She was wearing the leather pants she had bought in New York, with a filmy, almost see-through blouse in some kind of leopard print. Her only accessory was her thick mane of red-gold hair. "Whatever they're wearing tonight," he told her, "nobody's going to compete with you. You've got something they don't sell in beauty parlours, believe me."

She believed him all the way to the front door. Then when the butler showed them down the marble hall and through into the conservatory where the party was being held, she began to think he had lied to her. She had never seen so many spectacular women in one place, and she wondered if a talent scout had been specially hired to fill the house with female decoration the way other people hire a florist

## SCREEN KISSES • 299

to do the flowers. The thing she noticed most about the women was the way they glittered. Their dresses were made of lamé, sequins or chiffon with diamanté sewn on to them, and if their clothes didn't catch the light then their jewellery more than made up for it. She saw emeralds crowding out a plunging neckline, diamonds literally cascading from ears, lapels, wrists. It was as if she had stepped into Aladdin's cave, or a scene from the *Arabian Nights*.

She looked in despair at her leather pants, her naked wrists, her ringless fingers. What on earth am I doing here? she asked herself. In the first ten minutes she had managed to get separated from Bob. So many people wanted to shake him by the hand, kiss his cheek, clutch his shoulder, that the party had somehow engulfed him, and she was left standing alone in a crowd of strangers, holding on to a glass of Dom Perignon and trying to look as if she belonged. It was a difficult performance. They didn't teach you Hollywood parties at drama school.

She walked over to the table in the middle of the room where there were canapés and dips. Immediately her eye was caught by the centrepiece. It was a swan made entirely of ice crystals, and nestling in its middle was about five pounds of caviar—great, shiny, black balls, worth a fortune every one of them. She was wondering whether she had the courage to dip into it when her attention was caught by a face she recognized. It belonged to a tall skinny man with dirty blond hair, wearing aggressively tight trousers held up by a crocodile belt. A crocodile belt with a silver buckle.

It can't be, she thought. He might have had enough push to get himself to London, but Beverly Hills? How on earth did he manage it? She pretended she hadn't seen him, but it was too late. Richard Roberts had spotted her and was elbowing his way through the crowd towards her. With something like desperation Rachel looked round for Bob but he seemed to have disappeared. So she jerked her head up, took a deep breath and held out her hand to the first man she had loved.

He took it. Then he pulled her towards him and kissed her on each cheek. "We don't go in for shaking hands in La La land," he said. "Or hasn't anyone told you yet?"

She felt her heart booming like the ocean, and for a second she thought she was going to faint.

Richard had a faint smile on his face. "How long ago was it, Rachel?" he said. "Six months? Eight months, maybe? I never forget a girl who runs out on me."

"And I never forget a man who fucks the management. Particularly when he does it to advance his career."

Anger had made her regain her balance. The room had stopped going round. "Why the hell did you cheat on me?" she blazed at him.

He scooped a pile of caviar on to a biscuit and popped it into his mouth as if he had been doing it for years. "I suppose you're talking about Jeremy," he said. "I don't imagine it occurred to you that he might have been lying. But then you didn't stay around to find out, did you?"

## SCREEN KISSES • 301

She was about to reply when she felt an arm around her shoulders. Bob was back by her side. For the first time since she had walked into this grand, chilly, terrifying room, she felt safe.

"Having a good time, darling?" he asked. "Who's your friend?"

Richard looked shifty. "Rachel and I know each other from England," he said. "We were in a play together."

Bob held her close. "How interesting," he said pleasantly. "I had no idea you were an actor. Have I seen you in anything?"

Richard shook his head. "I wouldn't think so," he said. "My type's right out of fashion in this town."

Rachel was fascinated. "What *are* you doing here, Richard?" she asked.

He looked uncomfortable. "I have a fitness consultancy," he told her. "I go to people's homes and work out with them in their private gyms. Carla here, Mrs Keyser, is a client of mine."

Rachel didn't attempt to conceal her amusement. "Looks as if it pays a lot better than Brighton rep. No wonder you decided to change direction."

Now it was Richard's turn to lose his cool. "I haven't changed direction," he snarled. "I'm resting. Remember the word? It's what actors do between plays. One day it will happen to you, Rachel. And when it does, I'd be very interested to see how you manage to pay the bills."

He turned on his heel and walked off. Bob looked at Rachel. "What was that all about?" he asked, then before she could reply he spun her round and introduced her to a tall, heavy-looking man in a dark silk suit. "Dan," he said evenly, "you haven't met Rachel Keller yet, have you? Let me introduce you. Rachel, this is Dan Keyser, our gracious host."

Rachel smiled nervously. "You're in charge of Magnum. Is that right?"

To her surprise he looked delighted. "She knows who I am," he said, "and she's still talking to me. That's what I call a real professional." He looked her in the eye. "I hear from Rick Hamilton the rushes on you were great. So for once in my life I was wrong. We picked the right girl for the part after all." He gave her what people who worked with him called his deeply sincere look. "Rachel, this is a very hard thing for me to do, but I'm going ahead with it anyway. I want to ask you to forgive me. I know I caused you a lot of pain and a lot of self-doubt, but when you've been around as long as I have you learn that these things happen in this business. We all make mistakes. Nobody's perfect. So how about shaking hands and letting bygones be bygones?"

Rachel stifled an insane desire to giggle. Do I shake his hand? she thought. Or do I tell him to get a new scriptwriter? In the end she put her hand out. There were still two weeks to go before they finished the film and she wasn't taking any chances.

When Keyser finally lumbered over to another group, Rachel turned to Bob. "Have we been here long enough?" she asked in a small voice.

"Why, have you had enough?"

## SCREEN KISSES • 303

She nodded. "Then I'll take you on somewhere nice for dinner. But only on one condition."

"What's that?"

"You tell me what went on between you and Richard Roberts back in England."

Giselle always hated having sex in the Jacuzzi. No matter how careful she was she always ended up getting her hair wet or smudging her carefully applied make-up. But it turned Dan on, so she went along with it.

I wonder if his wife goes in for this, she thought wearily as she changed position for the third time. They had started out in the kitchen. Unintentionally. Giselle had gone in there to fetch another bottle of vodka and had been bending over, rummaging in a cupboard when he surprised her. She was not amused. "Put my skirt back down, will you?" she snapped. "There's plenty of time for that later."

Dan took a step back. "You're beginning to sound like Carla. What's the matter, don't I do anything for you any more?"

## SCREEN KISSES • 305

Giselle realized she had made a wrong move, so she didn't answer him. Instead she stepped out of her pants, took Dan by the hand and led him into the dining room. Once there, she stood with her back to him and leaned across the mahogany table. All that covered her was her silk pleated St Laurent skirt.

"If you want to fuck me from behind," she told him, "at least do it properly." He stepped towards her and pulled the silk skirt up around her waist. Then he looked at her. Her arse was gorgeous, like a ripe peach that parted gently down the centre. He stroked the soft, rounded buttocks. "Lady," he said, "this is your lucky day."

He took her from behind. Then when he had finished he turned her over on the dining-room table and started to unfasten her blouse.

Giselle felt the hard mahogany pressing into her back. When we're married, she thought, the only place we'll be doing this kind of thing will be in bed. She smiled sweetly. "Why are you wasting all your energy in this boring old dining room?" she said. "There are lots more interesting things we can do in the Jacuzzi."

She had heard from at least three of her friends about the party at the Keysers' on Saturday night. Rachel Keller had been there on the arm of Bob Delaney. So that was how she managed to keep her part. Giselle was not unduly annoyed about this. Because she fought dirty herself she accepted those kinds of tactics in other women.

What had upset her about Saturday night was Dan. He had told her about apologizing to Rachel and

## 306 • TRUDI PACTER

she had started to wonder whose side he was on. The next thing she knew, he'd be saying sorry to his wife. No, now was definitely the time to step up the pressure.

With a suitable amount of drama, Giselle confessed to Dan that she had fallen in love with him. She reserved this revelation for a night when Carla thought he was out of town. It was no good talking about a grand passion unless she could be perfectly sure of demonstrating it—which is how she managed to find herself getting wet through in the Jacuzzi.

Later on, in bed, she held him close and whispered soft endearments to him in French.

"Why did you have to tell me you loved me?" he asked.

"Why, doesn't it please you? Doesn't it make you proud to have a woman feel that way about you?"

He inhaled her perfume and felt her soft, delicate body against his. "Of course it does. But it also changes things."

"How?"

"Because if this is a love affair, instead of just an arrangement, I'll start to feel responsible for you."

She nuzzled closer. "Is that so terrible?"

He sat up and reached for the glass of bourbon he had left on the bedside table. "Giselle," he said, taking a sip, "it's terrible all right. Believe me, it's terrible. And shall I tell you what's worse? Now you're bringing love into the picture, I think I'm coming down with it myself. It's like a sickness."

She smiled. The plan was starting to take effect.

## SCREEN KISSES • 307

*"Chéri,"* she said, "I don't like these words. Sickness. Terrible. What's wrong with beautiful? Wonderful?"

"Listen, you choose your words. I'll stick with mine." He took another slug of his bourbon. "I use words like terrible because they describe the situation. Do I have to spell it out, Giselle? I'm married. And Carla isn't any *hausfrau,* either. She's Jerry Gould's daughter. And Jerry calls the shots at Magnum. One word from Carla and I join the ranks of the unemployed."

Giselle looked at him steadily, taking in the great curving nose, the black crinkly hair, the power of the man. "If you wanted to leave Carla," she said slowly, "I mean really leave her and come and live with me, I see no reason why you should be out of work."

Dan laughed. "This love you keep talking about must have made you stupid. Not only will Carla take my job away from me, she'll also walk off with half of everything I own."

"You'll make the money back," said Giselle calmly, "when you start your next job."

Mournfully Dan Keyser finished his drink. "Tell me another fairy story, dumbo. Who the hell would want to employ me, once Magnum throws me out in the street?"

"I don't think I can do without you," said Bob Delaney to Rachel Keller. They were having Sunday lunch at the Beverly Wilshire to celebrate the end of filming.

"I know that," said Rachel drowsily, "but why do you have to pick this moment to tell me?"

## 308 • TRUDI PACTER

Delaney tried hard to look patient. "Because you're going home tomorrow."

"You mean you want to send me on my way with a nice feeling."

Bob took a swig of his Californian Chardonnay. Rachel could be very trying when she wanted to be. "Actually that wasn't my intention," he said. "I mean about sending you on your way. I hate the idea of you leaving."

She looked at him steadily out of wide eyes.

"Well, I can't stay here. This meal alone would set me back a week's wages."

She gestured around the large, airy restaurant to illustrate her point. The hotel didn't fail her. Sunday was something of a feast day at the Beverly Wilshire. Rich suburbanites from Greater Los Angeles came there in droves to sample the buffet, which consisted of every kind of roast meat, fish or fowl in season. To go with the roast the hotel provided a selection of vegetables and fourteen different kinds of salads. The desserts commanded a table of their own.

"I see what you mean," said Bob. "But it doesn't have to be like this. You don't need to go on staying here."

Again the wide-eyed stare. "Why, are you thinking of setting me up in a flat?"

This time he grinned. "Actually I am. There's a lovely penthouse in Western Towers that would suit you perfectly. There's only one problem. I live there too."

"Since when has that been a problem?"

"You mean you like the idea?"

## SCREEN KISSES • 309

Rachel pushed her plate away and rummaged in her bag for a cigarette. Smoking was an occasional habit for her. Something she did when she was worried. "Are you asking me to come and stay for a few weeks? Or are you asking me to move in with you on a permanent basis?"

Bob looked serious. "To be honest I don't know, but I can't face the idea of being without you. So come and live with me, and if I go on feeling this way then let's make it permanent."

She inhaled on her cigarette. "What about me? Am I allowed to have feelings about this change of address?"

"What do you mean?"

"Just this. Back home in London I have a flat and a social life. What you're asking me to do is put that on hold while you make up your mind whether or not you want me in your life."

"That's taking a rather tough line, isn't it?"

"Life's a tough business. A man can say one thing to you and mean something quite different. And sometimes he can go behind your back and you don't know where you are at all."

"You're talking about Richard Roberts."

She looked bitter. "Him and all the other run-of-play affairs."

He took her cigarette from her and stubbed it out. "Listen to me," he said, "this is not a run-of-play affair. It's more than that. At least it is for me. I just didn't know how you felt."

She looked at him levelly. "I love you," she said.

He smiled. "That's all I wanted to hear. Will you

## 310 • TRUDI PACTER

settle with me, Rachel? I mean, will you come and stay with me?"

He felt her gripping his hands. "You really mean that?" she said.

"Yes," he smiled. "I don't have your complexities. I'm a straightforward, old-fashioned Irishman. What you see is what you get."

She took a deep breath. "Should I put my flat on the market?"

He let go of her hands. "If you're thinking of getting married, certainly. I don't want any wife of mine living in two places."

She looked at him, surprised. "Who said anything about getting married?"

"I did, I'm an old-fashioned Irishman, remember? And I'm not fond of these modern, living-together arrangements."

For a moment Rachel thought about the Broadway play waiting for her in two months' time. Then she remembered the promises Desmond French had made her about her future. She wondered if that future included a husband. "This has all come as a surprise," she said weakly. "Would you mind awfully if we put off the wedding for a bit? Till I get used to the idea."

"Of course we can, my darling. I'd no idea it scared you."

She grinned. "Nor had I."

Unbidden into her mind came the image of the Chinese fortune-teller she had seen on Bali. "One of you is the artist," she had said. "A weaver of fantasies,

## SCREEN KISSES • 311

a caster of spells. The other is a mortal woman. Her life is with a man."

Go away, Madame Chong, Rachel thought crossly. Get out of my head, I don't need you here. But try as she might she couldn't banish her from her mind. All evening as she packed and prepared to move to Western Towers, the tarot reader whispered to her. "The artist must fight to protect her art. It is her life force, the reason she is here. Without it she will be destroyed."

They became something of an item around town. Rick Hamilton and his wife Marcie were the first people to invite them over, and after that everyone else followed suit. Rachel discovered that for all its surface glamour Beverly Hills was an essentially suburban community. Couples entertained each other in their homes, be they cottages in Malibu like Rick and Marcie's or vast spreads like the Keysers'. Spago, Ma Maison, La Serre and all the other glitzy eating houses were places where the entertainment industry talked over deals. When they wanted to rub shoulders, they did so in their homes.

Rachel discovered she had a talent for cooking, and when they had people over for dinner she was quite happy to spend all day preparing the food. At first Bob thought she was crazy. "A lot of the people who come here are my clients," he said. "Why don't you let me get a caterer in? It's tax deductible."

But Rachel was adamant. If people were coming to her home she provided the food. Although Bob protested now and then, secretly he was pleased. He

## 312 • TRUDI PACTER

had been worried when she hadn't wanted to get married right away, and he wondered just how committed she was. They had never talked about it, but it was an unspoken question between them—until Rachel discovered cooking, and going to the beach with Marcie, and driving up and down the coast discovering the Californian art community. Rachel didn't paint, but like all truly creative people she liked to observe the way other professionals communicated with the world.

She became fascinated by the fashions of the day. In the past the need to adorn herself had been more than satisfied by the stage. Every night she got into costume, and every night it changed her into someone else. Now there was no theatre, no stage, so she found other ways of dressing up. Georgio's, Armani, St Laurent—all the boutiques around Rodeo Drive became regular haunts. Twice, sometimes three times a week she'd come home clutching a silk knit dress in a Pucci print, a pair of extravagant silver sandals, a Louis Vuitton holdall, the latest creation by Calvin Klein. She became intimate with the names of the designers and discovered that in Hollywood you could get away with wearing anything as long as it wasn't last season's.

Bob viewed this latest passion with a mixture of amusement and alarm. "You're turning into a Hollywood wife," he teased her. "Any minute now you'll start talking about last year's diamonds."

"Actually," she said, "I'm more interested in this year's."

So he went out and bought her three sapphires,

## SCREEN KISSES • 313

the colour of her eyes and had them set into an engagement ring.

"I was only joking about the stones," she said, overwhelmed with the present.

"I wasn't joking about my intentions, so you'd better put it on and get used to wearing it."

They developed a life together—a Californian life. On the mornings Bob was working late, they'd drive out to Huntington beach and play in the surf. Bob had learned to ride the waves when he moved out to the coast, and when Rachel got the hang of it he bought her her own board.

They discovered that they both knew how to play backgammon. That took care of two evenings a week. The rest of the time they'd see friends, watch television, go to the movies. One day Bob took her to see the rough cut of *Marooned*.

They saw it in one of the screening rooms at Magnum and Rachel was mesmerized. She remembered her childhood and her years in rep, where her only escape was to go to the cinema. Now she was part of the moving light show. Yet while she marvelled at the screen, another part of her, a small perfectionist that lived inside her, took stock of the actress she saw. Did I time it right? she asked herself. Did I get too skinny in Bali? Is the make-up too heavy? How am I moving?

She had never seen herself give a performance before, and she learned from it. The next time, she thought, I'll wear my hair shorter, and I'll take dance lessons. I get away with my stage technique—just—because so much of me is in close-up. But I won't get away with it again, and I shouldn't try.

## 314 • TRUDI PACTER

She was quiet on the drive home.

"Is something on your mind?" Bob asked.

"No. Why do you ask?"

"Because it must have been pretty unsettling to see yourself on the screen for the first time."

"Not really," she said, "I think I was good enough." Then she changed the subject. But deep down she *was* unsettled. For the past few weeks she hadn't thought about acting, or the stage. She had all the applause she wanted at home, or at least she thought she did. Now she wasn't sure. In the viewing theatre she had been aware of her audience again. Did I convince them? she had asked herself. Did I entertain them? As she thought about the people who paid to watch her, the excitement of her new life started to fade.

Surfing thrilled her less. Cooking began to bore her. Even Rodeo Drive lost its fascination. She had half decided to duck out of the play on Broadway, for she knew it would disturb her life with Bob. Now she started to reconsider. I might not get this chance again, she thought. She remembered the lights on Broadway and Shaftesbury Avenue, and though she tried not to think about them, they started to haunt her. A week later, when Bob was out at the studio, she called Desmond French in London. "When do they need me in New York?" she asked him.

The following day Desmond French put in a call to Los Angeles. He got Bob on the first try.

"Hi," said Delaney who had just come in from a production meeting. "How's business in London?"

## SCREEN KISSES • 315

"Business in London is fine. How about you? Do you have a final cut on *Marooned*?"

"Not yet, but we're getting there. The film's taking shape better than I originally conceived it. I don't know whether it's Rick or the editor, but we look like we could have a big grosser on our hands."

"And the artists?"

"They all earn their salaries. Rachel does more than that, you'll be gratified to hear. She really is everything we hoped for. I'm glad I decided to fight for her."

There was a silence. In London Desmond lit the end of a panatella cigar and poured himself a cup of tea. Finally he could delay the moment no longer. "Who were you fighting for, Bob," he said, "Rachel the woman or Rachel the actress?"

"The actress of course, what are you getting at?"

"I had a long talk with Rachel yesterday afternoon," the agent said slowly. "I suspected you two had a thing going, but I didn't know it had got so serious."

"Until we had a definite date for the wedding there didn't seem any point in telling the world."

Desmond took a long pull on his cigar. "And do you have a date?"

"Not yet. Listen, why are you asking me this? You're not calling me all the way from London to talk about my private life."

There was another silence, then Desmond spoke. "Actually I am, my old love. Rachel wanted to tell you herself but she got the jitters. So yours truly has been instructed to step into the breach.

## 316 • TRUDI PACTER

"I don't know if she told you, but the girl is committed to doing a play in New York."

Bob felt a familiar leaden feeling in the pit of his stomach. Oh Christ, he thought, I might have known it was too good to last. So she's going ahead with it after all. Aloud he said, "She did mention something about it, now you ask. But that was a while ago. Why, do you have a start date for her?"

"Yes," said the agent shortly. "Rachel goes into rehearsal at the end of July."

Delaney let out his breath. "But that's next week, damn it. That means she's on a plane to New York in forty-eight hours' time."

"I'm sorry, love. I didn't want you to hear it this way. But what could I do? I'm just the agent."

Bob put the phone down. And I'm just the fiancé, he said under his breath. Why the hell couldn't she tell me first?

The moment he walked in the door Rachel knew there was something terribly wrong. She had expected a row, and for the tenth time that day she wondered if she should have got Desmond to do her dirty work. Then she sighed. There was no way she could have told him herself. She would never have got the words out.

She looked at him and saw the darkness in his face. He had taken the news badly. "You spoke to Desmond," she said. It was a statement of fact rather than a question.

"Sure, that's what you wanted me to do, wasn't it?"

## SCREEN KISSES • 317

"Yes," she said. Then she came across to where he stood and put her arms round him. "It's not the end of the world, you know. The play might not run that long. And we can both commute."

He looked at her. "Can we?" he said flatly. He stepped out of her embrace and walked over to the bar. "I'm having a drink," he said. "I think we could both do with one. What will it be?"

She asked for a glass of wine, and Bob poured himself a bourbon over ice. A large one. Then he took the drinks over to the round marble table by the window and set them down. He raised his glass. "Here's to a smash on Broadway. With your talent you deserve it."

He gulped the drink down too quickly, and she knew they were both past pretending. "It's over, isn't it?" she said.

He nodded.

She felt the tears rising into her eyes. "Why, Bob?" she asked. "Why does it have to be this way?"

He sat down on the sofa, nursing his drink. "A long time ago, when we first met, I told you the story of my life. I had a hunch then you might be important to me, so I wanted you to know how things were."

He looked at her, thin and pale in the evening light, and he knew she was hurting. What the hell, he thought, after what you've done to me, why shouldn't you suffer? "Rachel," he said, "you know about the way Kathy tore me apart, so forgive me if I duck out of the dance the second time around."

"I'm not Kathy," she said. "I love you. I don't think she knew the meaning of the word."

## 318 • TRUDI PACTER

"And you're telling me you do? Come off it, darling. You're no different from my ex-wife when the chips are down. What you want, what you both want, is an audience, not a man. You're actresses. Talented actresses. Wonderful actresses. And because of that no man will ever be quite enough for you. You need the applause of a hundred pairs of hands, not just one."

Now she was crying in earnest—silent, bitter tears streaming down her cheeks. "Why are you doing this to me? Is it that easy to turn your feelings off?"

He took a pull on his drink. "I haven't turned my feelings off," he said savagely. "If I had I might have been more polite. Is that what you wanted from me, Rachel? Gentle lies? We'll commute. We'll see each other sometimes. When the play's over it will all be the same as it was." He took a breath. "I'm sorry, I can't do that. I love you, dammit. I want you to be my wife. But I'm not sharing you with the paying customers who buy a seat to see you every night. I'm not standing in line with a cinema audience, a fan club, a hairdresser, an agent, a lawyer and whoever else you choose to surround yourself with. I want to be with a woman, not a public property. It's that simple."

She sat down beside him on the sofa. " 'It's that simple,' he says. It's not that simple. Look, I never met Kathy Gordon, but I've met a couple of other big-time actresses since I came here, and I imagine she's the same. You can't compare me to those women, Bob. I don't go in for fan clubs and entourages. I do what I do because I believe in it. Because in a funny way it fulfils me. I don't go in for the glory and glitz. I never have."

## SCREEN KISSES • 319

He turned to her. "Give yourself a little time, Rachel. You've only just got out of the English provinces. Wait till the newspapers start printing your name across the top of three columns. Wait till you get asked on Johnny Carson. Then you might find the world starts looking different. Already I can see all the signs. If any other girl was leaving her fiancé to go to another town for a year or more, don't you think she would have told him herself? Of course she would. But what did you do? You got your agent to call me.

"In time, Rachel, all the really big decisions in your life will be carried out by agents and lawyers. You won't have to do anything except go out on stage or walk in front of the cameras. And do you know something? That's all you're going to want to do."

She took out a handkerchief and blew her nose. Then she wiped her eyes. "How am I going to cope?" she asked. "How am I going to live without you?"

He smiled. "You'll manage. But I don't know if I will. Nothing as good as you has happened to me in a very long time. You've got your work to comfort you, Rachel. What have I got? Dan Keyser and his studio politics. Hustling another deal. Organizing another location. Filling in time on the Hollywood party circuit. It might have been fun once, but I'm coming up to forty and I want more than that."

Rachel put her glass down. The wine was hardly touched. "Will we see each other after I go?" she asked.

"Sure," he said. "We'll run into each other at industry dinners. When *Marooned* comes out, I'll doubtless see you in the Polo Lounge or Ma Maison on the

## 320 • TRUDI PACTER

arm of whichever jerk the studio lays on to squire you around. Who knows? If I happen to be in New York, I might even come by and catch your show."

"But you won't come and see me afterwards, will you?" she said.

"No, we've hurt each other enough for one lifetime. We don't have to go on repeating the performance."

She touched the side of his face with her hand. "Bob," she said, "I want to ask you for something. One last thing before I pack my bags and get out."

"What's that?"

"I want you to love me. I want it to be the way it was the first time we loved each other in New York. The nights will be lonely without you, Bob. Give me one last thing to remember you by."

**D**an Keyser was sitting in his office going through the month's budget proposals. It was a routine job and demanded little of his attention, which was just as well for his powers of concentration were down to nil.

He also had a headache. Irritably he buzzed through to his Japanese receptionist. "Send me in a pack of Bufferin," he demanded, "and make it fast."

But while he barked the order he knew that Bufferin wasn't going to do anything for him. As yet nobody had patented a remedy for what was bugging him. He had a wife and a mistress. And the wife had discovered the existence of the mistress.

He should have guessed something was amiss the moment he walked in the door last night. Normally Carla would have organized a gathering of friends or family, or they would be going out to an industry dinner. He walked into his dressing room expecting to find his clothes laid out for the evening ahead. Instead he found nothing. He walked over to the door that connected his den with the bedroom. He found it didn't open.

Confused, he banged on the thin partition. "Carla," he yelled, "the goddamn door's stuck. Will you let me in from your side?"

Carla's voice came through loud and clear from their bedroom. "The door isn't stuck, Dan. It's locked."

"Then unlock it, I want to talk to you."

There was an icy edge to her voice. "If you want to talk to me, we'll talk in the living room. I don't want to see you in the bedroom."

Dan started to feel worried. Had his wife gone crazy between breakfast and seven o'clock in the evening? He decided to find out. "Then the living room it is," he said as casually as he could manage. "See you downstairs in five minutes."

He changed into flannels and a sports jacket and descended the polished mahogany staircase to the ostentatious room at the front of the house. When Carla said she wanted to talk to him there he knew he was in trouble. Most evenings before dinner he and Carla would have a drink in the conservatory by the pool. It was an easy, informal area and often their children would join them there.

The living room was a different story. Full of dark wood antique furniture and country house paintings, this was a place they used to impress the chairman of

## SCREEN KISSES • 323

the board and the heads of other Hollywood studios. In a way it was an extension of Dan's office—a place for negotiation. And when Carla told him what was on her mind, Dan knew why she had chosen this arena to confront him.

She had heard about Giselle from the wife of one of his studio executives. Ever since he had tried and failed to get her a part in *Marooned,* studio gossip had been rife. He had been discreet about their relationship; they both had been. But Hollywood was too small a town for even the most discreet liaison.

He had been spotted with Giselle in an out-of-the-way restaurant in Santa Monica on a night when he was meant to be in New York. The man who saw them was one of Magnum's screenwriters, and the secret was out. It was simply a matter of time before Carla heard.

As Dan faced his wife across half an acre of sofa he knew his time was finally up. He gripped his drink in his hand, clenched his teeth round a cigar, and tried to talk his way out of the situation.

"It was one of those things," he told the thin, tight-lipped woman sitting in front of him. "Giselle threw herself at me and I was silly enough to get drawn in. I promise on my life it will never happen again."

Carla surveyed her husband with deep suspicion. She knew she wasn't pretty. With her kind of money and clout she didn't have to be pretty. But she took a pride in her appearance, nevertheless. Her hair was neat and blonde and bobbed to her chin. She was dieted to a size 6. And the plastic surgeon had seen to it

## 324 • TRUDI PACTER

that she didn't look forty-five. Carla Keyser looked respectable, rich and like the kind of woman who should be married to the head of the studio. Her father had known that, which is why he had invested in Dan in the first place. Carla wasn't going to stand by now and see the man she had built up and nurtured get taken over by some French whore.

"You're talking as if this was some one-night stand," she said, taking a sip of her mineral water. "Stop trying to kid me, Dan, will you? I happen to know for a fact that you and this tramp have been seeing each other for at least six months. So don't tell me you're going to suddenly stop calling. I know enough about men to know they don't behave that way."

"So what do you want me to do? I've already said I'm going to put an end to it and you don't believe me. What more do you want?"

Carla considered her options. Right now she could have cheerfully murdered this schlemiel she had brought from nowhere. But there were better solutions. "It's not your life we're talking about," she said grimly, "It's Giselle Pascal's. As long as that hooker is in town you're not safe from her. Even if you meant what you said and cut her off she wouldn't let you go so easily. She'd be ringing up, visiting your office, turning up at parties. I couldn't live with that kind of embarrassment. No, she'll have to leave Los Angeles, and the sooner the better."

Now Dan was really worried. He had hoped that with a little juggling, he could pacify Carla and keep Giselle on the side. Now this was not to be. Carla was going to see to it that Giselle packed her bags. The

## SCREEN KISSES • 325

thought of doing without her filled him with an almost physical pain. Sex with Giselle was like nothing he had ever known. It was an addiction, like alcohol or cocaine. He couldn't allow his wife to cut off his supply.

"How do you suggest I run Giselle out of town?" he asked her. "I'm not the Mafia. I can't threaten her with torture or strangulation. The woman's a free agent. She can do what she damn well likes."

"That's what you think. I've done a little research on Giselle Pascal and she's not as free as you imagine.

"The way I hear it, the woman's a fixer. Her whole business is dependent on the goodwill of this town. If suddenly nobody is talking to Miss Pascal then she's out of business."

Dan took a long pull on his whisky. "Are you suggesting I arrange for Giselle to be on everybody's out list?"

For the first time that evening Carla smiled. "How well you understand me. That's exactly what I had in mind. If there's no business for her in LA, then she has no choice but to go. How else can she live?"

Dan got up and walked over to the window. From there he could see the swimming pools, the tennis courts and the outline of the stable buildings. Either I do without all this, he thought, or I do without Giselle. For a moment he was torn.

"I don't want to ruin Giselle Pascal," he said, "I'm not that kind of bastard."

Carla stayed where she was on the sofa. "Then I'll make it easy for you," she said. "I can ruin Giselle

## 326 • TRUDI PACTER

for you. My word's as good as yours around here. Alternatively you can divorce me."

The word divorce started the headache. He had suffered with it all that evening. He had fallen asleep with it alone in his dressing room. He had woken up with it and taken it with him to the studio. Now as he swallowed the Bufferin his receptionist had brought him he prayed for the pain to stop. But he knew in his heart that it would not. Not until Carla stopped talking about divorce.

His thoughts were interrupted by the telephone. With relief he saw it was not his private line. He didn't feel like seeing his wife or his mistress, let alone talking to them.

His secretary told him she had Milton Harrison of Pan Video on the line. Was he in? Keyser's mind raced. Milton Harrison, the chief stockholder of the TV movie corporation, was not a friend of his. Each knew who the other was but they sat on no committees together, neither did they do business together. So why was Harrison calling him?

Dan made a snap decision. "Tell Milton I'm in a meeting and I'll call him back in ten minutes when I've cleared my office. Then when you've done that, get hold of Mike Lander and get him to come to my office. Pronto."

While he was waiting for Lander, Dan went over in his mind what he knew about Harrison. The man had to be in his early sixties by now—not that anyone could tell. Milton was the kind of man who wore his age the way he wore his clothes—elegantly. He was tall, well over six foot, with iron-grey hair and what

## SCREEN KISSES • 327

Dan thought of as an Ivy-League face. The man was handsome, but he had understated rather than flashy good looks. When Milton smiled, his smile was full of old money and old schools.

Dan thought about the TV tycoon and as he did so he fought down a feeling of burning resentment. The Milton Harrisons of this life always had it easy. While he had been fighting his way out of the Bronx, Milton had been in college learning how to be a gentleman. Dan looked back at his early days as a junior in a large law firm. He was the lowest of the low then, little more than a gofer, and he had fetched and carried for the bosses. How else was he expected to learn his trade?

It was different for Milton Harrison, he thought bitterly. When he started out in television he didn't have to scramble around for a job. His father knew the chairman of the board, and young Milton was placed in a position where he could climb the ladder with dignity. Dan considered Milton's progress through the television jungle. He considered his dignity. Then he smiled. In the end it wasn't Milton's dignity that got him to the top. It was his balls and the brassy way the man handled himself in the boardroom. Outwardly Milton Harrison was the perfect East Coast gentleman. But underneath the well-cut suit there lived a tiger.

When the push came to the shove there wasn't much to choose between his tactics and Milton's. They both knew how to handle the knife, and neither of them cared who they sacrificed to get what they wanted.

## 328 • TRUDI PACTER

Milton Harrison had called because he wanted something. Of that Dan was certain. But what? He racked his brains in vain. Maybe Mike Lander would come up with something. After all, wasn't that why he employed the man?

As if on cue, the thin, rather timorous figure of Lander appeared in Dan's doorway. He shuffled rather than walked towards his boss's desk.

"You wanted something?" he asked.

"I just had a call from Milton Harrison at Pan Video," said Dan shortly. "There's no reason why the guy should contact me. So I want a reason, and I want one fast. What gives at Pan Video right now? Who's fighting who on the board? Is Harrison as secure as he looks to the outside world? Are there any money problems?"

He hurled his questions at Lander in rapid bursts like staccato gunfire, and the man didn't flinch. He was used to this kind of interrogation. It justified his half-a-million-dollar salary.

Officially Mike Lander was Magnum's corporate relations officer—an innocuous title for an innocuous job. But Lander wasn't the patsy he looked. For he had an unofficial role at Magnum—a role nobody talked about, or even knew about. He spied for the company, or to be specific he spied for Dan Keyser.

Dan needed to know what his rivals were up to. He needed to know what didn't appear in the official reports, and what happened behind closed doors. Mike Lander was there to provide the answers.

For the next ten minutes he gave his employer a rundown on Pan Video. He summarized the two last

## SCREEN KISSES • 329

board meetings, named the men who were tipped to move up in the company, and the ones who were on the condemned list. He ran through their production schedules, their staffing levels, he even told Keyser how much the company had on loan from the bank.

The fat man shook his head. "It's interesting stuff, but it's not what I'm looking for. From what you tell me the operation looks solid. They have their ups and downs, but nothing better or worse than any other big corporation. No, I'm looking for a trouble spot. Or a potential trouble spot. Something Harrison could need help with."

Lander scratched the back of his head and tried to look patient. "I was just coming to that," he said. He took a breath. "The problem lies with one man. Phil Katz. Now I don't know if he drinks or keeps a mistress or if he's quietly going insane, but for no good reason the guy's taken his eye off the ball."

Dan caught his breath. "Katz," he said. "He's Pan's head of production, yes?"

Lander nodded. "He is today, though if Harrison's got any sense he won't be tomorrow. Everything the company's making is running way over budget. The films in the pipeline are good stuff, only there's no control. The directors out there making the movies are running rough-shod over Katz and he seems to be letting them get away with it."

Dan smiled. "How old is this Katz?"

The thin man looked uncertain, then he put through a call to his office. When he came off the line he was smiling too. "Katz is coming up for sixty. The guy's due to be put out to grass any second now. I

## 330 • TRUDI PACTER

guess that accounts for the current situation at Pan. If you want me to guess again, I'd say that Harrison is looking around for a replacement."

Keyser leaned back in his chair. "I had that one figured out too." He nodded towards the door. "As always, sweetheart, it's been a pleasure doing business with you. You know to put in for your usual bonus. Oh, and it's high time you and Sylvia came over and had dinner at the house. I'll remind Carla to fix a date when I get home tonight."

When Lander had gone, Dan picked up the phone and told his secretary to connect him with Pan Video in New York. Milton Harrison's personal number. Then he sat back and waited. Seconds later, Harrison came on the line.

"It's been a long time," Keyser effused, "too long. To what do I owe the pleasure?"

Harrison laughed his old money laugh. "I hear on the grapevine you may be in the market for a move."

Bastard, thought Keyser. You don't waste time on small talk, do you? You come straight to the point and drive the knife in. He paused, playing for time. "What makes you think that? The company's doing fine. I'm doing fine. Or do you know something I don't?"

"Not really, old man." Once more the relaxed, easy laugh, as if he was talking about a racing fixture rather than Dan's future. "I just figured you might be interested in earning a little more money. Say double what you're on now."

## SCREEN KISSES • 331

Dan relaxed. "So that's why you think I could be in the mood to move."

"Sure," said Harrison. "Money is always the best reason to do anything. That and freedom."

"What do you mean by freedom?"

There was a silence, and Dan reached in his pocket for a cigar. He had cut it and lit it by the time the other man spoke again. "What I mean is that if you come and work for me, you won't have to answer to your father-in-law any more. It can't be all that comfortable having your boss in the family."

This time Dan laughed. "You can say that again. Though I don't have any complaints about Jerry. He keeps out of my way. I keep out of his . . . except at board meetings and Friday-night dinners."

"I don't have any truck with Friday-night dinners," said Harrison. "Or any other kind of social get-together. If we do business I can promise you one thing. I'll stay out of your private life."

Dan thought quickly. Milton Harrison was offering him the chance to cut Jerry Gould out of the picture once and for all. And with Jerry's hold over him, Carla's went too. Freedom, he thought, the one thing I've been looking for. I wonder what the catch is?

For the next five minutes the two men fenced and probed each other, and found nothing to worry about. Finally Dan said, "Look, I don't want to commit myself at this stage. But I could be interested in talking some more."

"Good," replied Harrison, "I'm coming out to the coast the week after next. What do you say to lunch? I'll be at the Beverly Hills. We could eat in my

## 332 • TRUDI PACTER

suite and keep the whole thing confidential, or we could meet at La Scala. I'll leave it up to you."

They arranged to meet at La Scala. Why not? thought Dan as he put the phone down. I don't have anything to hide. Nevertheless he told his secretary to put all his calls on hold until he told her otherwise. He needed to think about Milton Harrison—and his proposition.

After ten minutes he began to feel uncomfortable. There was something wrong about making plans to leave his office while he was still sitting there. He looked at his watch. It was four-thirty. Tonight at seven he had an awards committee dinner. The thought of a swim in the deep blue pool outside his conservatory suddenly appealed to him. He buzzed through to his secretary. "Tell Johnson to bring the car round to the front," he instructed. "I've decided to go home early tonight."

Then he grabbed hold of his briefcase, straightened his tie and made for the door. As he left he noted that his headache had entirely disappeared. He wondered whether to thank Bufferin or Milton Harrison.

None of the equipment was in use in Carla Keyser's air-conditioned gym by the side of the swimming pool. The rowing machine was at a standstill. The rows of graduated weights lay neatly in their silver holders. The running machine and the trampoline stood silent.

But right at the far end of the gym, underneath the window, one piece of sports aid was taking a hammering—the mat. But Carla was not using it for sit-ups

## SCREEN KISSES • 333

or to stretch her muscles. Carla was using it to attend to her instructor, Richard Roberts.

They were both occupying the soft latex mat, and they were both naked. Carla was kneeling in front of Richard, her hands cupping his balls. His penis in her mouth. And while she ran her tongue up and down the length of it, Richard felt himself growing hard.

Carla wasn't really his type. He liked his women younger and softer. But Carla had other things going for her—like her hunger. Most of the women who had allowed him into their beds acted as if they were doing him a big favour. With Carla it was the other way round. When she had first seen his hard-on through his leotard she had been mesmerized. Whatever he did, wherever he walked, she couldn't take her eyes off it. Finally he had come over to her and kissed her roughly. "Is this what you want?" he asked.

She had nodded, and there was something in her eyes he had never seen before. She looked grateful.

The rich lady with all the class, all the clout, was grateful to him, a lousy out-of-work actor, for showing affection. He decided to find out what else he could do for her.

Taking his time, he started to pull at her exercise suit, rolling it down over her hips and past her knees until finally it was on the floor. All the while Carla just stood there, grateful and a little frightened. She had nothing on apart from a tiny pair of briefs, and as he gently tugged at them she made a token protest.

To his surprise he found it turned him on. OK, Mrs Keyser, he thought, I'll show you what a real man can do. Roughly he tore the pants off her and he saw

## 334 • TRUDI PACTER

to his surprise that she had shaved off her pubic hair.
He couldn't stand it any more. To hell with the nice-
ties, he thought, this lady's asking for it.

He was out of his shorts and when she saw the
size of him, she looked terrified. But it was too late
for second thoughts. Richard pushed her down on to
the floor of the gym and rammed himself into her. He
made no attempt to be gentle. Instead he thrust and
pounded away at the rich bitch underneath him, vent-
ing on her all the anger and frustration of the past
months.

He heard her moan, and with an effort he slowed
down. "I'm sorry," he said, "I didn't mean to hurt
you." She looked at him, her face contorted. "Don't
stop now, dammit," she said.

They climaxed together. And when she
screamed, he knew he had pleased her. Carla Keyser
enjoyed him being rough.

It was the best sex he had ever known. He had
once thought sex with Rachel Keller had been the
tops. Now he knew he was mistaken. Sex with love
as the end product was one thing. Sex with power was
something else, and he preferred it.

With Carla, Richard felt fully in control for the
first time in his life. Outside the gym he was just another Joe, a paid lackey for a rich woman. But when
the doors were closed and there were just the two of
them Richard was the master. He liked to make her
wait before he pleasured her. Sometimes he sent her
on two circuits of the gym, then when she was hot and
sweaty and ready to drop, he'd finally give her what
she wanted. The crueller he was the more she wanted

## SCREEN KISSES • 335

him. There were times when he made her go on her knees and beg him for sex. And when he did that he felt in some way he was evening the score.

For life had not been kind to Richard Roberts. When Rachel had left, he had been furious. Women didn't leave Richard Roberts, he wasn't used to it. When he had calmed down he consoled himself that at least he had the run of *Kiss Me Kate* to look forward to.

Then came the next disappointment. The show closed after three disastrous weeks. The girl Jeremy had chosen for Kate, Jill Irwin, was a well-known TV name, but she didn't wear well on the stage. Where Rachel's fire and passion could stop an audience dead, Jill couldn't even arouse their interest. People stayed away in droves. For fifteen miserable days they played to empty houses on Shaftesbury Avenue. When the show closed everyone was relieved.

The euphoria was temporary, for no work came in—no television, no rep, no pantomimes at the end of the pier. Richard had been associated with a disaster, and because the disaster was so very public nobody wanted to take him on. He decided to try his luck in America. He had heard on the grapevine that Rachel was doing a Hollywood film. If she could succeed in tinsel town, why not him? After all, he had played on the West End stage. If he was vague about the dates, nobody in California need be any the wiser about what really happened.

But he was dogged by bad luck. The agent who took him on knew all about *Kiss Me Kate*. He also knew how Richard got into the show. And the young actor

## 336 • TRUDI PACTER

found himself on the casting couch of every closet queen in LA. It was then he called it quits. Richard didn't mind using people to get to where he wanted to go, but he didn't like men. It was as simple as that. There had to be other ways to succeed in showbusiness. During the next six months he tried everything and failed. There were just too many good-looking, talented young actors in Hollywood—and too few parts.

In order to eat, he worked at a gym at Bel Air. A lot of unemployed actors did the same thing. The work was undemanding, the hours were flexible, and the women loved him showing them how to pump iron. Especially the older women.

He hit on the idea of forming his own consultancy. He knew a lot of rich women had their own private gyms and needed a qualified instructor to take them round—a young, handsome qualified instructor. In a matter of weeks he had a list of half a dozen clients. He found to his surprise that he was pulling in more money showing fat women how to work their Nautilus machines than he ever earned as an actor. He moved from his cheap hotel into a smart apartment block with a pool, he bought some new clothes, the Carla Keyser affair began, and he started to enjoy life. Then he ran into Rachel at one of Carla's flash parties and he saw himself for what he was.

Rachel was with Bob Delaney, one of the town's top producers. And it was obvious even to Richard that they were more than good friends.

His first feeling was one of hurt pride. What was she doing with another man? And so soon after him?

## SCREEN KISSES • 337

Then when he heard about the film she'd made and her offer of the lead in a Broadway play, the hurt turned to resentment.

Rachel was no better than him. He knew that when they were in rep together. But somehow she'd managed to get all the breaks while he'd been left behind. The unfairness of it cut into him like a knife. He deserved success far more than she did. After all, he was the one with the famous father and the theatrical tradition. She was just some upstart from the provinces.

The memory of Rachel's disdain when they had run into each other again sapped his juices. Carla looked up at him anxiously, bringing him back to the present. "What's the matter?" she asked. "Did I do something wrong? You seem to have lost interest."

He focused on the too-thin woman kneeling in front of him. The diamonds in her ears could support a whole troupe of actors for a year. And she was his to command. He felt his cock growing hard again. "Quit talking and open your mouth," he said.

There was the sound of a car in the drive. Swiftly Carla got to her feet and ran over to the window. The car belonged to Dan. Why the hell was he home so early from the studio? She hadn't expected him for another hour at least. In panic she grabbed hold of her robe and wrapped it around her. Then she turned to Richard. "Get dressed," she instructed, "and make it fast. I'm going out in front to talk to my husband. When he walks into the house I want you to vanish. Understand?"

Richard understood only too well. Trying to ignore the ache in his balls he pulled on his shorts, shirt and sneakers. Bitch, he thought as he saw Carla striding towards her husband's Rolls in the sugar-pink robe from Georgio's. Couldn't you have timed it better?

Then as he tied the laces on his sneakers he started to make plans for the day after next when he returned. Carla would pay for this interruption, and pay well. He had ways of making her suffer. They would enjoy every one of them.

Dan was surprised to see his wife in her robe.

"It's a bit late to be in the gym, isn't it?" he said. "I thought you got that kind of thing out of the way before breakfast."

She flushed. "I began a new work-out this week," she lied, "and I still can't get the hang of some of the exercises."

Dan started to feel annoyed. "Don't tell me you're putting in extra time just to impress that new instructor of yours. Haven't you got better things to do?"

Carla pulled a face. "If I don't get it right it throws out my whole routine."

"So get it wrong and let the instructor worry about it. Isn't that what you're paying him for?"

Carla ran a hand through her short, blonde hair. How did I get into this? she thought. Aloud she said, "I guess you're right. I get too wound up about the gym. But that's enough about my day. What brings you home so early? You're not due at the awards dinner until seven."

Dan got out of the car and started to walk towards

## SCREEN KISSES • 339

the house. "I decided to can my last meeting and relax for an hour instead. I had an interesting phone call this afternoon. I wanted to give it some thought away from the office."

Now the conversation had changed direction, Carla began to relax. "Give me a couple of minutes to get changed and I'll organize tea for you. Or maybe you'd like a drink?"

"Tea would be fine," he said shortly. "Maybe you'll join me. It's about time we had a talk about the future. We can't go on like this."

Carla took her time getting dressed. This was one occasion she wanted to savour: the moment her errant husband finally decided to see sense. As soon as she had confronted him with Giselle, she knew he would come into line. What alternative did he have? She held all the trump cards. One word to her father and Dan could kiss goodbye to the fancy job at Magnum. And the fancy pay cheque.

She opened the door to her walk-in closet and studied the array of casual wear. There were tracksuits in that season's stretch towelling. She had them in all shapes and colours. Her eye took in a rail of pants in a variety of weights from linen to twill, a rack of silk shirts, and shelf upon shelf of fine cashmere sweaters, jackets, throws. Sometimes she forgot the sheer volume of her wardrobe. And in her heart she knew she probably wouldn't get round to wearing all of it. But a girl had to be prepared for all occasions, whether it was screwing the help or screwing the husband.

She laughed softly at her own joke as she shook out a new Norma Kamali pantsuit. The designer had

## 340 • TRUDI PACTER

used her favourite tee-shirt fabric to create a sporty outdoor look. Carla nodded her approval; it was exactly what she needed that afternoon.

Half an hour later Carla and Dan Keyser took tea in their large conservatory by the side of the swimming pool. An English butler in full uniform sweated slightly as he decanted Earl Grey tea into bone-china cups and passed around the cucumber sandwiches.

Poor guy, Dan thought as the servant finally made his exit. Why does Carla have to go in for all this nonsense? He looked across at his wife, poised and perfect in one of her designer get-ups, and for a moment he was seized with the impulse to ruffle her feathers. He smiled pleasantly. "You mentioned divorce the other day," he said. "I think we should explore the possibility. After all, you and I haven't exactly been seeing eye to eye recently."

Her face hardened at his words. This was not the way she saw this scene being played. She took a deep breath. "You can't be serious," she said.

Dan leaned forward and looked more closely at his wife. She was definitely worried. Her mouth was set into a hard, thin line and her eyes looked wary. Good, he thought, I've got her on the run. Once again he smiled.

"Why shouldn't I be serious. You said yourself that if I didn't run Giselle Pascal out of town, divorce was the only alternative."

Carla put the delicate china tea cup down on the glass table in front of her. "But you are going to send the little tart on her way, aren't you?" she said evenly.

## SCREEN KISSES • 341

"I don't imagine for one moment you can see any future with her."

Dan settled back in his chair. "Tell me why not?"

Now she was angry. "Do I have to spell it out? If you walk away from me, Magnum will kill you, Dan. Stone dead. And once you're out there in the wilderness it's a very long walk back. If you ever make it."

He sighed. "I wish I could tell you you're beautiful when you're angry, but it's not true. Not now. You're forty-five years old, Carla. You can't afford to lose your temper any more."

But there was no stopping her. "How are you going to face life like a down-and-out?" she asked. "Tell me that. If you get lucky you may scrape by as an independent producer, but every buck you earn I'll take off you in alimony. We're living in the State of California, not some socialist republic. And when you haven't got a pot to piss in I can guarantee your precious Giselle won't stick around to hold your hand."

He leaned forward and patted her hand. "You're going too fast, sweetheart. Who told you I was going to be ruined if I left Magnum?"

"I told you," she snarled. "What else could happen?"

"I could be offered something else. In fact I have been offered something else. That was what my interesting telephone call this afternoon was about. Remember I was talking about it when I came home?"

It was as if she had been hit in the jaw. For the sixteen years she had been married Carla had bullied and patronized her husband. She knew he stayed with her not for love but for what her father could do for him, and she resented it. Now suddenly everything had changed. Dan didn't need her father any more, and for the first time she wondered whether he needed her.

"This job you've been offered," she said in a small voice. "Will you take it?"

Dan shrugged. "I might. It depends on the terms. I'm going to need a big salary if I have to divorce you."

"Who said you have to divorce me?"

"You did."

She moved around uncomfortably on her chair.

"Well, maybe I was a little hasty. I was very upset at the time."

He looked at Carla and for the first time he felt pity for the woman he had married. He could face her anger, he could even cope with her snobbery, but this defeat was something different. It stopped him in his tracks. He had meant to tell her goodbye. He had made up his mind about the whole thing. But now he was faced with it he couldn't do it. I'll let it go for a couple of weeks, he told himself. I'll wait till I've seen Milton. When the job's definite, it'll be easier.

He went over to where Carla was sitting. "I think we've both been hasty," he said. "Why don't we think about it for a bit longer? Try the idea on for size. We do have the children to consider."

She didn't trust him but she went along with it. "The children are important," she said. "And so is your name. All our names. If you go on seeing Giselle Pascal we could have egg on our faces."

## SCREEN KISSES • 343

He looked conciliatory. "I told you right at the beginning it was only a fling. The Giselle thing is over. Finished. I give you my word."

He's lying, she thought. He sees her every night before he comes home from the office. I bet he goes over there some lunch times too. Aloud she said: "Darling, forgive me for doubting you. I know it wasn't important. It's just that I was so jealous."

He felt like a heel. "There's nothing to be jealous about," he said. "Nothing's changed. Now be a good girl and put the whole thing out of your mind." He ambled off in the direction of the pool.

Carla reached across the table to a silver Tiffany box full of her favourite Turkish cigarettes. She selected one and lit it, then she considered her options.

She could put a call through to her lawyer right now and be done with it. She was entitled to half of everything Dan owned, plus the estate. That was a gift from her father. A wedding present, she thought bitterly.

Then she thought, what happens if I don't file for divorce? She had her position in Beverly Hills to think of. Divorced women didn't chair committees or throw charity balls—or at least not so easily. If she stayed married to Dan she looked respectable. It had its advantages.

She puffed on her cigarette. Dan wouldn't have the stature he had today if she hadn't kept up a front. Whatever Giselle got up to, she could never offer Dan the solid, suburban respectability Carla had surrounded him with. She realized it was her biggest asset—more so than the children, or even than her father's influence.

The French cutie doesn't hold all the cards, she thought. Not by a long chalk. Then she thought about Richard, her gym instructor, her own private indulgence. If I'm going to play at Queen Mother, she thought, he'll have to go. There's no way I can risk being found out now.

Richard could tell something was wrong from the moment he arrived at the house. For instead of wearing her usual leotard and Reeboks Carla was all dressed up in linen slacks and a Pucci shirt.

"What's the rich lady look all about?" he teased. "I thought we were training this morning."

She looked embarrassed. "I changed my plans," she said.

He pulled a face. "What's the matter? Are you getting bored with me already? You didn't look bored last time we worked out together." He lowered his voice. "The way I remember it you were giving me your full attention."

She walked out of the house and led him towards the pool area. When she got there, she sat down at a little table with an umbrella over it and motioned him to do the same. "The way it's been between us the last few months," she said, "has got to stop."

He looked surprised. "This is all a bit sudden, isn't it? What's the matter, has your old man found out?"

"No, of course he hasn't." She looked cross.

## SCREEN KISSES • 345

"But the whole thing's getting out of hand. I don't want any trouble.'"

The light began to dawn. "You're talking about the other afternoon when he came back early. Is that what you're worried about?"

She avoided his eyes. "It's some of it."

"But not the whole story," he prompted.

With an effort she straightened up and confronted him. "No, it's not the whole story. Look, I know you're a newcomer here but you have to understand that Hollywood is a very small community. People watch each other more than they do in other places. And they talk."

"You're frightened someone will start talking about us. Is that it?"

She smiled at him. "Well, we haven't been all that careful, have we? Somebody saw us lunching at Bistro Gardens the other week. And you do come to an awful lot of my parties."

He stood up and looked across the expanse of blue water. Then he turned to her. "That doesn't prove anything," he said, "except that we're friends. For all anyone knows I could be your walker."

This time she didn't smile. "One thing I'm sure about, Richard," she said, "is that you're no faggot. The other thing is that I'm not your only girlfriend. I've heard the testimonials of other satisfied clients." She pulled a face. "Maybe that's why I had eyes for you in the first place. I knew all about your talents before I hired you."

"If I'd known you wanted a stud I'd have asked for more money."

## 346 • TRUDI PACTER

She patted his hand. "You cost me quite enough as it is. And before today's out you'll be costing me a great deal more."

Now he was confused. He pushed his fingers through his tallow blond hair and glowered. "First you show me the door. Now you're offering me money. What the hell's going on?"

"I'll tell you what's going on." She fumbled in her shoulder bag for one of her scented Turkish cigarettes, and when she'd lit it she leaned back in her chair. Now she had stopped playing little-girl-lost, she looked older and tougher. "I'm going to make you a business proposition," she said. "And when you've heard me out you're going to realize this is probably the best deal anyone is ever going to offer you."

She took a breath. "How much do you make in a month with this exercise counselling?"

He hesitated for a moment, then he said, "Around a thousand dollars. During the summer it's nearer four."

She nodded. "That's what I thought. OK, this is what I have in mind. Right at this moment it suits me for you to be out of town. I don't care where out of town as long as it's a long, long way from Los Angeles."

He started to protest but she interrupted him. "Just hear me out, will you? If you're prepared to go out of town for, say, a year minimum, then I'll make it worth your while."

He was curious. "What did you have in mind?"

Once more she reached into the Hermes shoulder bag. This time she produced a scrap of paper

## SCREEN KISSES • 347

which she laid on the table in front of him. It was a cheque for two hundred thousand dollars. She looked at him. "Does that interest you?"

He did a double take. Whatever trouble Carla Keyser was in it had to be pretty bad news if she was prepared to give him this kind of money to make himself scarce. He played a hunch.

"Starting another business from scratch somewhere I don't know. That's a heavy number. I'm not sure . . ." He let his voice tail off.

Carla took a long pull on her cigarette, then without changing expression she dipped her hand into her bag and produced another cheque. It was for the same amount. She laid the two pieces of paper in front of him.

"That's my final offer," she said. "You have five seconds to make up your mind."

Richard got to his feet, took hold of the cheques and stuffed them in his pocket. Then he turned on his heel and headed for his hired Chevy. Three days later he was on his way to New York.

As soon as he got into town, he put up in a hotel overlooking the Park. Then he phoned a few contacts and got down to business. He was going back to the theatre. Now he was no longer desperate for work he started to get the breaks. A small-time agent liked his style and took him on, and soon after that he landed a breakfast food commercial. It was the commercial that opened doors, though not the ones he wanted. The world that beckoned Richard was the world of glossy magazines and advertising agencies.

## 348 • TRUDI PACTER

By some quirk of fate, his kind of face was in fashion that season. He looked preppy. For a while he fought against the lure of Madison Avenue, then his agent took him to one side. "I'm going to be honest with you," said Manny Cohen. "For the theatre, I couldn't give you away. You're too lean, too upper-crust-looking for most of the parts on offer. Next year it could change, but right now if you don't take the modelling jobs I don't want you on my books."

Richard didn't need to be told twice. He accepted the inevitable, but on condition that he still went up for every theatrical audition that came along. Manny went along with it, though he frequently told Richard that he needed his head examining. "Nobody on Broadway's going to hire you," he said. "Anyone who takes a chance on your kind of talent has to be a big noise. And frankly I don't have those kinds of contacts."

Richard smiled and thought of Rachel. She was coming into town with *Lili's War* in a week or two. "I have those kinds of contacts," he said.

Rachel was word perfect when she got to Philadelphia. During the three weeks of the try-out she had slowly grown into the part. Now even in her dreams she was Lili, a Polish woman, a resistance worker. It was this departure from the real world that had saved her sanity.

Sitting in her apartment hotel on 72nd Street Rachel cast her mind back to those first agonizing days of rehearsal. In her teens she had read a story by Hans Andersen called *The Little Mermaid*. In it the mermaid was given everything she dreamed of but she had to sacrifice her tail. For the rest of time she couldn't take a step without treading on knives. Now Rachel, rehearsing her first Broadway play, was treading on knives.

She had no idea she could miss a man so much.

## 350 • TRUDI PACTER

Everything she did—eating a hamburger, reading the morning post, playing backgammon with the other members of the cast—all of it felt bad. All of it hurt. Sometimes she caught herself saying Bob's name out loud as if he was still in the room with her, and then she was seized with fits of uncontrollable weeping.

Half a dozen times a day she picked up the phone to call him. Once she even got as far as dialling the number but when she heard his answering machine she rung off. What's the point? she asked herself. Even if she got through, what on earth was she going to say? "I love you, I miss you. I'll give it all up if you take me back." She couldn't give up on Broadway. Not now. She was in too deep.

She clung to the play like a drowning person to a liferaft. And it saved her. When she fixed her mind on Lili she left New York City behind her and went back nearly forty years into a different world. Over the next few weeks Poland during the Second World War became the place where she lived.

She went to the library and took books out on the period, and in her spare hours after rehearsal she sat in her rented apartment and read about Europe under Hitler's occupation. She became familiar with Warsaw, Cracow and the ghettos. There were times when she imagined she could actually smell the poverty and the fear.

She brought her new knowledge to the stage and it added a depth to her performance. Rose Andrews stood by as she sketched out the part. Unlike a lot of directors she didn't impose her own interpretation. Instead she allowed Rachel to use her as a sounding-

## SCREEN KISSES • 351

board. Her faith paid off. By the second week of the try-out, the audiences in Philadelphia were aware that something unusual was happening in the theatre. In the last few days their attitude shifted. They knew they were watching a great performance. Rose Andrews and Len Goldman congratulated each other. They had been right to take a chance on this unknown. She was going to give them a Broadway hit.

Rachel looked around the sparsely furnished apartment and wondered what to do with herself. They had all got back from Philadelphia the night before and New York at the end of August was hotter than ever. But it wasn't just the heat that made her feel uncomfortable, it was the prospect of the next four days before opening night. Rose had laid on rehearsals to fill the time but they did nothing for anyone's nerves. Because the scenery hadn't yet been set up they played the piece in the theatre lounge, and everybody walked through it as if in a dream.

That day, they finished at three and Rachel walked wearily back to the solitude of the apartment building. Briefly she thought of calling Bob, then dismissed the thought. He hadn't been in touch, and there was no way she was going to beg him to come to her opening night. To fill the time she called the janitor. The air conditioning was on the blink and she couldn't cope with the prospect of another night in her stifling bedroom. The janitor didn't hold out much hope. He had called maintenance and they had said they were on their way. What more could he do?

"I can't bear it," she said out loud to the four

## 352 • TRUDI PACTER

walls. "If I have to spend another minute in this place I'll go crazy."

She remembered with longing the large, shady roof terrace that Bob had in LA. Then she had an idea. This building also had a roof. She knew a couple of other actors who used it. Why not her?

She changed into one of the skimpy bikinis she had bought in Los Angeles, piled her hair on top of her head and grabbed a large towel and a couple of cushions. Then she tucked one of her war books under her arm and made her way to the top of the building.

At four o'clock in the afternoon the roof was almost deserted. A group of dancers from a Broadway show were packing up the remains of a picnic before heading for the theatre, and there was a sunbather at the far end listening to a radio. Apart from that she was on her own.

Rachel spread out her towel and arranged the cushions under her head then she lay back and closed her eyes. She must have drifted off to sleep, for the next thing she was aware of was someone gently shaking her shoulder. She shook her head and sat up. Then she wished she hadn't. For kneeling opposite her was the sunbather she had seen earlier. It was Richard Roberts.

She rubbed her eyes. "What on earth . . .?" she said.

"Am I doing here?" he finished for her.

She started to get up, but he put a restraining hand on her arm. "Before you run away, you might give me a couple of minutes to explain myself. It's not as if we haven't been introduced."

## SCREEN KISSES • 353

She pulled a face. "Fat lot of good that did me."

"Come on, Rachel, that's no way to welcome a neighbour."

"What do you mean, neighbour?" She was fully awake now. "You're not living here, are you?"

"Of course I live here. What else brings me to this roof in the middle of the afternoon?"

Without thinking she grinned. "Don't tell me your air conditioner has broken down as well. I could kill that janitor for dragging his feet. Anyone would think he wanted me boiled alive."

Richard produced a bottle of beer seemingly out of nowhere. The beads of moisture on the outside told her it had to be cold. He handed it to her. "Here, take a swig, it will make you feel better."

She was tempted to turn it down. But she was hot and thirsty and the sweat was starting to trickle down her back, so she took the bottle he offered and by the time she had finished it he was already half way through his story.

She didn't forgive him. Not instantly. He had let her down too badly for that. But as the afternoon wore on the past took on less significance. So much had happened to both of them in a year that they could have been different people. When he asked her to have dinner she heard herself saying yes. What harm could it do? she thought. No one has any claim on me. Not any more.

He took her to Joe Allen's and she felt instantly at home. The place was full of actors and people connected with the stage. The bare brick walls were covered with posters of every show in town, and with a

## 354 • TRUDI PACTER

start she recognized a bill advertising her own. He must have seen her face, for he put his arm round her and held her close. "Stop worrying," he said. "In three days' time it won't seem so bad. You'll see."

He handed her a martini, and she made no protest. Right now she needed courage.

A tall, good-looking boy with a couple of willowy chorus girls in tow waved at Richard across the bar. He returned the greeting and beckoned them to join him. The girls had just joined the cast of a new musical. Their escort, Greg Parker, was an actor currently out of work. It didn't seem to bother him, or if it did, he didn't let it show. "Congratulations," he said to Richard, "I hear Health-tex hired you as their new sex symbol."

Rachel was intrigued. "Who are Health-tex, for God's sake?"

Richard drained his martini and looked embarrassed. "They make sweatshirts, tracksuits . . . that sort of thing."

"And you demonstrate the range, is that it?" She sounded amused. "I'd no idea you went in for glamour."

He ordered another round of drinks. "There's more to it than you think. I do a series of television commercials and I promote the goods in the stores. And there's the photographic work."

She was tempted to ask him what had happened to his acting plans but she stopped herself. She remembered all too clearly the time when she had run into him in Los Angeles. He had been working as a gym instructor then because he couldn't get the parts, and

## SCREEN KISSES • 355

she suspected that he was modelling sportswear for much the same reason.

He must have read her thoughts for he sighed deeply and took a pull on his drink. "Who am I kidding?" he said bitterly. "I'm no model boy. I'm an actor, not that anyone's interested. I flog around from audition to audition and every time I get up on the stage nobody wants to know. A lot of the casting directors don't even want to hear me read. I'm not the right type, they say. I look too English. I'm not butch enough. Nowadays in the theatre they want muscle men, not actors."

Rachel put a hand on his arm. "It's always like that before you get the break," she said. "What you need is one person, just one, to recognize your potential and you'll be away."

He looked angry. "How would you know? You land everything you go up for."

She started to deny it, then she stopped herself. "I've been lucky," she said.

One of the waiters came up and told them their table was ready, and Rachel breathed a sigh of relief. The conversation was making her nervous. Up to now she knew she had been very lucky. But in her profession you could never be sure how long luck was going to last. In three days' time she could open to bad notices and the play could close inside a month.

Once more by some act of telepathy he was inside her head. "It's not going to happen," he said. "Not this time. I was passing through Philadelphia and caught one of the try-outs. You're going to be a smash."

She was surprised. "If you saw the play, why didn't you come back and see me?"

He looked past her at the menu that was chalked on the blackboard above her head. "I didn't know if I'd be welcome," he said. "If I hadn't taken you by surprise this afternoon, would you have talked to me? Or would you have cut me?"

She thought about the past. "We never did talk about Jeremy, did we?"

"No, we didn't," he said bitterly. "You chose to believe the first person you heard. If you'd bothered to discuss it with me you might not have stormed off in such a hurry."

She sighed. "What does any of it matter now? We can't turn the clock back."

"Can't we?"

There was a silence between them, and she remembered how it had been once. When she had loved him. "It's too late," she said. "I'm a different person now."

"You mean there's someone else?"

She smiled. "There was someone else. But that's all finished now."

"You're talking about Bob Delaney, the producer I saw you with."

She turned to him and he saw the pain in her eyes. "I don't want to talk about Bob," she said softly. "Not now. Maybe not ever."

He reached for her hand. "I'm not going to push you," he said. "I know better than that. But I'd like you to understand one thing. I'm here when you want me. If you want me. There's no hurry."

## SCREEN KISSES • 357

\* \* \*

For the next few days he never left her side. Each morning he turned up on her doorstep and dragged her out to breakfast on Seventh Avenue. One day he took her to the Carnegie. The next, they went to the Stage where he filled her up with lox and bagels and cream cheese. Then he came with her to rehearsals and sat at the back of the room while she recited her part. It was a hollow performance and everyone there knew it. She was holding herself in reserve for the first night. They knew that too and nobody . . . not Len nor Rose Andrews nor any member of the cast said a word. They didn't dare. Her emotions were too finely balanced.

They kept her away from her dressing room. It was important she didn't see herself in costume until the last minute, but it frustrated her. "Why don't you let me look like Lili?" she demanded. "If I don't look like her, how can I feel like her?" Her questions and demands were met with silence. She could go backstage on the first night. And only then.

The day before the opening she became almost hysterical. She refused to go to Seventh Avenue for breakfast, and when she went to the theatre for a run-through on the set she mistimed all her entrances and started walking into the scenery.

"I'm going to get it wrong," she said to Richard. "I'll open on Broadway and make a fool of myself. Then nobody will want me."

He didn't try to reason with her. There was no point. Instead he walked her round Central Park all afternoon until it grew dark. Then he took her to P.J.

## 358 • TRUDI PACTER

Clarke's and bought her a Bloody Mary which she didn't drink. Finally he took her back to 72nd Street. The temperature was in the high eighties and as they walked down the covered arcade to the old apartment building she sensed thunder in the air.

"Did the janitor get the air conditioning to work?" he asked her.

"Yes," she said dully, "but it broke down again this morning."

He paused before he spoke again. "I don't have that problem in my apartment. Would you be happier sleeping there tonight?"

She looked at him. "Would you be there?"

"If that's what you wanted."

She was tempted. The world had turned on its head today, and she was frightened. More than frightened, she was terrified. The thought of facing the night alone in her stifling bedroom stretched like a wilderness in front of her. She looked at Richard, handsome and familiar, and she remembered how it had been before.

Then she pulled herself up. "I'm sorry," she said. "If I came back tonight I'd only be using you."

They rode up in the elevator in silence. When it stopped at his floor he leaned over and gave her a peck on the cheek. "You know where I am if you want me," he said. Then he walked away.

Rachel continued up to her apartment. Wearily she unlocked the front door and went into her long drawing room. The curtains were drawn and through the plate-glass window she could see all the lights of Manhattan.

## SCREEN KISSES • 359

She poured herself a glass of wine and stood staring at the vista for a long time. Tomorrow, she thought. Tomorrow I could own this town, or be hounded out of it. It was hot in the apartment and she felt the silk dress she was wearing sticking to her legs. She walked through into her bedroom and undressed, then she stood under the shower until she was cool.

Finally she opened the bathroom cabinet and took out the sleeping pills that one of the other actresses had given to her. They were to be used in emergencies, for they guaranteed oblivion. Tonight was an emergency. She filled a tumbler of water and tossed them down. Then she went through the doorway and lay down on her bed.

An hour later she was wide awake. She considered taking more pills then she thought about all the other actresses who had done the same thing. No, she thought. She switched on the bedside lamp and looked at her watch. It was nearly two. If she didn't get some sleep soon she'd be no good at all. She had visions of herself on stage. She was starting her first big speech only she was too tired to remember the words. Dear God, she prayed, don't let that happen to me. I'll be good, I'll do anything you want, only don't let me dry. Not tomorrow.

It's not tomorrow, she realized, panic seizing her. It's today. In three or four hours it would be light outside. Despite the heat of the room her skin felt clammy and cold. What am I going to do? she moaned.

Then suddenly she knew what she was going to do. She reached over to the phone by the side of the

## 360 • TRUDI PACTER

bed and dialled Richard's number. He answered on the second ring. "You can't sleep," he said.

"How did you know?"

"Because I know you."

There was a silence. Finally she said, "I'm frightened of being alone."

"I know that too. And you don't have to be alone any more. I'm coming up."

"Hurry," she said.

It was the same as it had been the first time. He touched her in all the familiar places—her neck, her nipples, her navel, and deep down inside her, between her legs. First he let his tongue travel over her body. Then when he felt her respond he drew back and parted her legs.

He was fully erect now and she noticed he was smiling. But there was something in the smile she didn't recognize. He rammed himself into her. "Once more," he whispered urgently.

The quote echoed through her mind. "Once more unto the breach, dear friends." So that's what I saw in his face, she thought bitterly. Victory.

But her mind and her body were strangely disconnected and her sense of disillusionment refused to spread to her loins. Three times he brought her to a climax, and three times she shuddered and spent herself in his flesh. Afterwards she slept.

When she opened her eyes it was eleven in the morning and the sun was streaming through the windows. She looked across the pillow at the handsome, fair-skinned man sleeping beside her. The smile she

## SCREEN KISSES • 361

had noticed the night before was still on his face. Who are you? she wondered. And what the hell do you want from me? With a start she realized she had lain with him a hundred times before and never asked herself that question. She felt empty. So this wasn't a homecoming after all. It was just another dance with a stranger.

The word spread from Philadelphia to New York then travelled like quicksilver to the coast. The new Len Goldman play, *Lili's War,* had all the makings of a Broadway smash, and the reason for the excitement was the girl from England. She was something special, this unknown, something you don't see very often in the theatre—an original talent.

So Rachel's going to make it, thought Bob. I was right all along. In the last couple of weeks he had gone up ten points in the popularity polls, for he had been the first one to discover this talent. Magnum was duly grateful. *Marooned,* which was originally to have a limited release, suddenly jumped to the top of the schedules.

"If Keller's as hot as everyone says she is," said Dan Keyser, "then we stand to get lucky from her Broadway notices."

Bob refrained from reminding the studio boss that he had done his damnedest to have her replaced. He suspected that Keyser had blocked the incident from his mind anyway. All that concerned him now was that *Marooned* looked set to make money. A damn sight more money than the studio had forecast.

I wish I had Dan's talent for forgetting, thought

Bob. For try as he might he failed to rid himself of Rachel. He had sought solace in work, then in booze, and finally there were girls. For a Hollywood producer they were one of the perks of the job, like luncheon vouchers. And they made about as much impression.

There were bright girls, beautiful girls, old girls, new girls, and none of them meant anything because none of them was Rachel. It dawned on Bob that he might have made a mistake, a vast error of judgement. In the past he had turned his back on women who had bored him or betrayed him. Rachel had done neither. Her only sin was fulfilling a commitment.

He had known before he had taken her to bed that she was doing the play. She hadn't tried to deceive him. Though she would have in the end, he told himself. In the end the theatre would have become her lover, not me.

But as the weeks passed without her he became less convinced. Why do I judge every actress by my ex-wife? he berated himself. Why couldn't I have given Rachel a chance? In the end his instincts got the better of him. Rachel without the theatre was what he wanted, but Rachel with the theatre was better than nothing at all.

He thought of calling her, or writing. Then he had a better idea. He would turn up and surprise her. He planned to arrive on her first night. Experience told him not to disturb her until then. He knew the way actresses were before they opened. Kathy had taught him something.

He got to the theatre at seven, half an hour be-

## SCREEN KISSES • 363

fore curtain up. As soon as he saw the front of the house he knew the insiders had been right. There was the smell of excitement in the air. The first-night audience knew they were going to see something good, something great maybe. A lot of them had gone to their seats early so as not to miss anything.

He thought of Rachel behind the curtain that separated the auditorium from the stage and beyond. She'd be in her dressing room now, made up and in costume, and he wondered if she had received the telegram he sent. He had kept it brief. "Luck and love," he had written, "I hope you get everything you wanted."

Looking round the theatre he was convinced that if she didn't get what she wanted tonight she never would. The place was packed. Everyone was waiting to be convinced.

He didn't realize he was holding his breath until she made her entrance, then he let it out in a long sigh of relief. For right from the first moment she commanded the stage. It put him in mind of the first time he had set eyes on her, in a seedy little viewing theatre on Sunset. Even in her screen test there had been something that compelled you to watch her, and she had it now. It wasn't her face or her voice or even the passion she brought to the part, but rather a combination of all three. As the second act drew to a close he took a look at the rest of the audience and he knew she would be a long time in New York.

Damn you, Rachel, he thought. As if I didn't have enough to deal with, without adding commuting to the list. But his heart quickened at the thought of seeing her again. They would be together tonight, just the two of them. And she would be in his arms, in his bed, where she belonged.

As the lights went up he looked at his watch. It was just before ten. In under an hour the waiting would be over. He calculated the distance between his seat and the exit. If he was quick he could make it through the crowds and to the stage door in under ten minutes. Five if he was lucky. He got up and ambled to the bar. A bourbon would make the time go faster.

At the end of the third act he knew there was no need to wait up for the notices. It wouldn't stop her waiting, of course. No actress he had ever known went to bed until she had seen the judgement on her first night. He resigned himself to a long siege at Sardi's, then he smiled. What am I beefing about? he thought. I'll be with her. We'll share this triumph together. If we have to wait till dawn it won't be too long.

There was a hush as she took her first curtain call, then the audience rose to its feet as one and applauded her. She came back three times that night, and each time she took her bow the people who had come to see her stood and sounded their approval.

It took him longer than he calculated to reach the stage door, and even longer than that to get past it. Tonight everyone in New York wanted to see Rachel. The knowledge warmed him. For he knew that out of all the producers, the backers, the agents, the hangers-on, he was the one who owned her.

He joined the end of a queue outside her dress-

## SCREEN KISSES • 365

ing room and found himself wedged up against Dustin
Hoffman who was in a show that season and Peter
Hall who was producing one.

He and Hoffman exchanged smiles. They had
worked together on a picture once. "Looks like this
one is going to run," Bob said.

"Try stopping it," replied the diminutive actor.

Inside Rachel's dressing room the crush was even
worse, and it took him several minutes before he managed to spot her. She was standing in her dressing
gown, her hair all over the place, still wearing her
stage make-up. He noticed she was thinner and there
was a wide-eyed look about her as if she had just
woken from a dream. For a second he was weak with
love for her, then he pulled himself together and
started to struggle through the wreckage of the party.

Everywhere he looked there were empty champagne bottles and sprays of hothouse flowers, some
of them still in their cellophane wrappers. The walls
were covered in telegrams and for a moment he wondered if his was amongst them. Then Desmond
French found him and pulled him through the crowd
towards her. He saw two men competing for her attention. Anthony Norris, her costar, and someone else
who he recognized but couldn't quite place. The second man was saying something to her in a loud, actor-
ish voice and as he moved closer he realized who it
was.

What the hell's Richard Roberts doing here? he
thought angrily. She told me she buried him ages ago.
He had no intention of listening in to their conversation but it was hard not to.

## 366 • TRUDI PACTER

". . . wonderful tonight," he heard Roberts say, "almost as wonderful as last night."

Despite himself he paid attention. She still hadn't seen him and he noticed she was looking agitated.

"Last night was one of those things," she said, "I think we should try to forget it."

Roberts was the first to see him and something changed in his face. "But you were so passionate last night. So much yourself. How could I ever forget it?"

There was a small silence, then Rachel lifted her head and saw Bob. She closed her eyes and screwed up her face, and when she opened them again he was standing beside her. "I had no idea you were coming," she said faintly. "Why didn't you tell me?"

Delaney looked at her for a long time, then he stared at Richard Roberts. "Would it have made any difference?" he asked.

"You know damn well it would." The colour had gone from her face and he saw for the first time how tired she was. He wondered if it was the play or the young man by her side who had claimed her energy.

"Why didn't you wait?" he said sadly. "If you'd just been patient everything could have been different."

Now she was crying. Silent, bitter tears mixed with mascara and dripped down her cheeks. "But you told me it was over," she sobbed.

He turned on his heel. "It is over. As from this minute you and I don't exist any more. Maybe we never did."

He pushed his way through the crowd that blocked the doorway and she made to follow him, but

Richard put a hand on her arm. "Don't make a fool of yourself. Not tonight, Rachel. It isn't worth it."

She didn't hear him. Nothing registered apart from her loss. Like a sleepwalker she went towards the open door, and no one stood in her way. Then she pushed down the crowded corridor, past the stage door and out on to the street. She saw him fifty yards away hailing a taxi. As it stopped and he reached for the door, she called out his name. He turned and for a moment their eyes met and locked. Then he shook his head and climbed into the cab.

She pulled the thin cotton wrapper tightly around her as she watched him disappear into the traffic. Desmond French found her half an hour later standing on the kerbstone, still and silent as a statue. Gently he put his arm round her and led her back into the warmth of the theatre.

The first-class cabin on Pan Am's morning flight to the West Coast was filling up, but Bob was oblivious to the event. Usually he kept an eye out to see if anyone he knew was travelling, but right now company was the last thing he was looking for.

Morosely he riffled through his copy of the *National Geographic*. He didn't usually have much time for the magazine, but today he chose it over and above all the other reading material on offer. At least there was no chance he would stumble on last night's theatre reviews. He had no wish to read about *Lili's War* or Rachel Keller. That chapter in his life was over. The less he was reminded of it, the sooner he would forget it.

It wasn't easy. In front of him lions and elephants

## SCREEN KISSES • 369

paraded across the pages of his glossy magazine but he hardly saw them. Instead etched on his retina was the image of Rachel in her dressing gown deep in conversation with Richard Roberts. They were talking about the night they had spent together. The night she had betrayed him.

The image was so strong that the young woman by his side had to take the magazine out of his hands before she caught his attention. "I didn't know you were so wrapped up in big game hunting," said Claudia Graham acidly. "I've been sitting here for five minutes and you've totally ignored me. It's like talking to a brick wall."

He passed his hand across his eyes. "What on earth are you doing here?" he said.

She smiled and fluffed her hands through her curly black hair. "One of life's lucky coincidences," she said. "I was visiting friends in the city."

Her words were drowned out by the sound of the engines. With a jolt the plane started to taxi towards the runway.

"We're bang on time," said Claudia, looking at her watch. "In seven hours, with any luck, we'll be touching down at Lax."

But the actress's mind wasn't on her destination. Claudia's concentration was reserved entirely for the journey. If she had planned this moment she couldn't have done better. She had seven hours with Bob Delaney. Seven uninterrupted hours in which to engage him, fascinate him and start to reel him in.

When she had discovered his involvement with Rachel she had kept well clear. Let it run its course,

## 370 • TRUDI PACTER

she thought. Nothing lasts for ever. And she had been right. Two months ago the grand romance had gone down in flames and Rachel had flown to New York.

Still Claudia didn't make her move. It was too soon; the memory was too fresh. Some other woman could provide temporary consolation for Bob. When she moved in she wanted to make a more lasting impression.

As soon as the plane was in the air and the drinks were coming round, she tested his mood. "Your friend Rachel made quite an impression last night. You weren't there, were you?"

He looked at her wearily. "Yes, I was there. No, I won't be going back. And if you don't mind I'd rather not talk about it."

The stewardess stopped at their seats with free champagne and Claudia took two glasses off the tray. She handed one over to Bob. "Drink," she commanded. "You sound like you could do with it."

Bob tried to avoid alcohol on long flights on the grounds that it impaired his judgement. Then he thought about Rachel and changed his mind. He'd been sober when he decided to visit her in New York, and look where that had got him. He downed the drink in one and signalled for another. Then he remembered something. "You like Bollinger, don't you?" he said to Claudia. "How do you feel about sharing a bottle?"

"Fine, as long as we can have it in the lounge. I don't find these cramped little seats all that social."

They wound their way up the spiral staircase with Claudia in the lead, and Bob got an uninterrupted

## SCREEN KISSES • 371

view of long, tapering legs in sheer stockings. Despite himself he felt the stirrings of lust, but he strangled them at birth. Don't be silly, he told himself. You need another actress like you need a hole in the head.

Claudia turned out to be surprisingly good company. His one experience of working with her had made him expect a neurotic, self-centred prima donna. But Claudia wasn't like that at all. She seemed fascinated by the film business—not just the parts of it that affected her, but every aspect. And she was willing to learn. To his astonishment Bob found himself giving a monologue on the wrongs and rights of the industry. When the second bottle of Bollinger arrived, he pulled himself up short. "I'm sorry," he said gruffly. "I'm boring you. I didn't mean to deliver a lecture."

Claudia threw her head back and laughed, and Bob noticed the thin, white column of her neck. Her skin had the kind of glow that reminded him of pearls. He wondered why he had never noticed it before.

"You're not boring me," she said, "you're talking to me about a business I've been in all my life. How could that be dull?"

He stared into his drink. Rachel never talked about the business. He knew she had a passion for it, but it was a solitary passion. A secret love. She hadn't wanted to share it.

He looked up at Claudia. "I didn't say making movies was dull. I was just surprised you enjoyed talking about it, that's all."

Again she laughed. "I don't know where you've been recently, but nobody I know in Hollywood talks about anything else." Then she launched into a story

## 372 • TRUDI PACTER

about a new screenwriter called Sly Stallone. Apparently this character not only wrote the script, he also took the starring role in the picture he was making.

Bob was intrigued. "What's it called?"

"*Rocky* or *Biceps* or something. The buzz around town is it's something special, but I'm reserving judgement until I've been to the preview."

"When is it?"

"Tomorrow night. Why, are you interested?"

"Yes, I am. A writer who thinks he's a movie star is kind of fascinating. I'd like to take a look at him."

"Then come with me if you haven't got any other plans. I've got a couple of tickets."

Bob woke up the next morning with the mother and father of all hangovers. He dimly remembered arriving at Lax in a haze of Bollinger. He'd been drinking with some woman. Claudia Graham, yes, it was all coming back to him. He wondered if she felt as bad as he did that morning.

He thought of calling her, then put the idea out of his mind. No more women, he resolved, especially if they're actresses. And no more booze. He might have bombed out in New York but he still wanted to live.

He was in the shower when the phone rang. After thirty seconds he realized he had forgotten to connect it to the answering service. He swore under his breath then he turned off the water, grabbed a towel and dashed to the phone. It was Claudia.

"Do you want to come by for a drink before the

## SCREEN KISSES • 373

showing," she asked, "or shall we meet at the theatre?"

"What showing?" he said, genuinely surprised. "I don't remember anything about a showing."

He heard an intake of breath on the end of the line and realized he had offended her. "Claudia, I'm sorry. I guess I got a little stoned yesterday. Remind me again what we're meant to be doing."

She started to chatter about a new movie by some unknown called Stallone. Apparently she'd offered to take Bob to the preview that night. He groaned inwardly, and kissed goodbye to all his resolutions. Whether he liked it or not he was up to his ears in actresses and booze.

When he had finished talking to Claudia, Bob rang his secretary and got her to reserve his usual table at Spago. She would expect that. Women like her didn't look forward to eating a hamburger after the movies. He smiled and wondered what she would be wearing. Would it be the quiet diamonds? And something tailored by Cerruti? Or would she put on a show? He thought about the tapering legs in their sheer stockings. Then another image of her swam into his mind. She was sunning herself by a swimming pool in Bali and her breasts were naked and hanging free. He grunted and headed back to the shower. This time he'd turn the cold water on—full on.

At half past eight he was sitting at his table at Spago. It was an "A" table under the window. And despite himself he was amused. The table he usually got was in the main body of the restaurant, as befitted a moderately successful independent producer, but tonight he was getting the treatment. He looked at the woman sitting across from him and he let out a sigh. Next to Liz Taylor and Raquel Welch she was the hottest thing in Hollywood.

Without having to be asked, a waiter appeared with a bottle of vintage Bollinger. Bob raised an eyebrow. "I don't know about you, but after yesterday I think I'll stick to Perrier."

She pouted. "What happened to all those rumours about the wild Irish Delaney? I thought beating up bars and ravishing women was your line of country."

"So that was why you asked me to come to the movies. I'd no idea."

She blushed, and he felt sorry for embarrassing her. In the past twenty-four hours all his ideas about Claudia Graham had gone full circle. Because of her reputation and the way she looked she imagined she ate men like him for breakfast. Now he knew her a little better he realized this wasn't true. She was surprisingly shy. Endearingly so. For their evening together she was wearing a plain black knit dress and a single row of pearls. What had impressed him was that she had worn this outfit knowing where they were dining. Other stars of her stature would have put on a grand display for the Italian restaurant on the hill, for it was the town's premier showplace. Despite himself he was intrigued. As the evening wore on she continued to surprise him. The new head of Fox came over and invited them to join him for coffee after dinner. Most actresses, even famous ones, would have grabbed at the invitation. Claudia said she was tired and could she take a rain check. Because Bob was drinking Perrier she joined him, and by eleven her glass of champagne was barely touched. But what he liked most about her was the way she conducted herself. Most women on a first date flirted and gossiped. Claudia talked about the film they had just gone to see, and once again he was surprised at her grasp of the medium. For she didn't just see the movie from an actress's point of view, her eyes were like a director's eyes, and on occasion a producer's eyes.

"How come you never let on you were such an expert?" he laughed. "This is the first intelligent conversation I've had with an actress in years."

She made a face. "In my position it's not done to know too much about what's going on. It makes people nervous. The actors always think I'm going to steal their scenes, and directors imagine I'm going to walk off with the picture."

She leaned forward and looked into his face, and for the first time he was conscious of her perfume. "The trouble with this business," she said, "is that everyone's so damned insecure. So you end up pussy footing around people's feelings and never really making contact. I know for my own good I have to behave that way. But sometimes it can get very lonely."

He smiled and signalled the waiter for the bill. "I know what you mean," he said, "and I'm glad you decided to be yourself with me tonight."

He had expected her to ask him in for a drink, and when she didn't he was more than a little disap-

## 376 • TRUDI PACTER

pointed. He appreciated her behaving like a lady but she didn't have to go to extremes.

On the next two occasions he took her out he got the same treatment, and after that he got the hint. Claudia Graham liked him, that was for sure. But she liked him the way a sister likes a brother. It wasn't good enough. Worse than that it was starting to drive him crazy. She had teased him with her body back in Bali. Every time he had gone to her suite she had virtually nothing on, and he was a stranger then, a mere colleague. The irony of it took his breath away. Now we're friends, he thought, she suddenly hides herself from me.

The last time they had dinner she had worn a pantsuit and never taken the jacket off. At this week's opening she had opted for a white toga which covered her from neck to ankles. He decided he couldn't stand it any longer. There were other women in Hollywood who were both available and more accommodating. He crossed her off his list, then he got on with his life.

Two weeks later she called him. She was having a little supper party on Sunday night. Could he come? He started to trot out his excuses when she let drop a couple of names—John Ritchie and Alwyn Parker. They virtually ran Magnum's front office, and they were looking forward to seeing him on Sunday night. He asked her what time he was expected then hung up. Now he had a final cut on *Marooned,* he needed all the friends he could get.

He was surprised when she answered the door herself. At this kind of soirée there was usually a Filipino maid or two around, but as he walked through

## SCREEN KISSES • 377

the house there was no sign of any staff. Apart from Claudia there was no sign of anyone at all.

"Am I early?" he asked, looking at his watch. "I thought you said you were having a party?"

And indeed she was dressed for a party. She was wearing a long, black chiffon dress, tight in the waist and full in the skirt. She had filled the low neckline with a magnificent ruby necklace and on her ears were long ruby drops. What a beauty you are, he thought sadly. What a shame you're not for me.

He looked around her lavish drawing room with its low, modern furniture and abstract paintings. The wall of glass in front of her terrace had been pulled to one side, and below them the lights of Bel Air twinkled in the warm September night. Anticipation was in the air, and something else besides. "Where the hell are all the people?" he asked again.

She walked the length of the room then she turned, and the full, filmy skirt floated and billowed out around her. Her face was very pale. In the evening light her hair was almost ebony.

"I lied to you," she said. "There is no party."

"Why did you do that?" He was confused now, and a little angry. He was tired of her games and he wanted to go home.

"I did it because I seem to have fallen in love with you. And I couldn't think of any other way of getting you here." Her voice broke and she looked down. "I'm sorry."

The cynic in him realized he was being manipulated. He had known too many actresses not to suspect a charade. But he was a man as well as a cynic and he

## 378 • TRUDI PACTER

waited for her next move. It happened so quickly it took his breath away.

Her hands flew to a fastening at the top of her dress. In one movement it had come apart and was fluttering about her ankles. Underneath it she was completely naked, all jutting breasts, creamy, white skin and pools of darkness.

She came towards him, the rubies gleaming around her neck. "Take me," she said softly. "Do what you want with me."

He followed her into the bedroom without a word. His hunger was entirely of her making. It was up to her to satisfy it.

They could have been in a different world. Where the house was Californian modern, the boudoir belonged to another century. A vast four poster, swagged and draped with red velvet, dominated the room. He noticed a crystal chandelier suspended from the ceiling, but no light came from it. Instead on two tiny Victorian tables candles flickered from old-fashioned gas mantles. It was a scene straight out of *Moll Flanders,* and he marvelled at her inventiveness.

At the foot of the bed was a *chaise longue* covered in the same red velvet as the curtains round the bed. Claudia lowered herself on to it, arranging her legs provocatively so that part of her was on show, part in shadow. She gestured towards the bathroom. "You can change in there," she said.

He found a silk dressing gown hanging on the back of the door. It was expensive English paisley and the label told him it came from Turnbull & Asser. He wondered how many times she had played this scene.

## SCREEN KISSES • 379

Then the memory of her on the *chaise longue,* the heavy white breasts, the tantalizing shadows blotted out all his doubts.

When he re-entered the bedroom she was lying where he had left her, and he noticed the rubies were still around her neck.

"I thought you might like to take my necklace off yourself," she said.

He leaned towards her, reaching behind her, and as he did so she thrust her soft, white breasts into his face. His mouth found her nipples and as he sucked and feasted upon her she undid the heavy silk dressing gown. His hands were moving now, over the soft curve of her belly, down through the black silky hair and into the moist cleft. She was ready for him. More than ready.

He drew back and watched the candlelight play over the lush, alabaster body. One leg was bent at the knee and for the first time he could see the opening between her legs. He was fully erect now and there was no holding back. Gently he pushed her legs apart, but as he mounted her she intercepted him with her hands. He felt them travelling the length of his cock and then he felt a sudden coolness, a numbness. Christ, he thought, she's using Novocaine to prolong the moment. The last time that had happened to him was in a bordello in Paris. She must have seen his surprise, for she laughed softly. "I've waited a long time for this," she murmured. "Now I want to enjoy it. With a little help we can play all night."

It was nearly breakfast time when she finally let him sleep. And as his breathing became deep and reg-

## 380 • TRUDI PACTER

ular she got up from the bed and made her way through to the bathroom. Once there, she closed the door firmly and locked it behind her. Then she set about creaming her face. She had done it a hundred times before when she came off a set and her fingers were quick and expert. In a matter of minutes last night's face had vanished into her tissues. She doused the clean skin in cold water and followed up with witch hazel, then she started painting again. The Claudia who had greeted her lover-to-be the night before had been mysterious, dramatic, deeply rouged. The girl he would see when he woke up would be fresh, dewy, innocent.

She pursed her lips in concentration as she etched brown pencil along her eyeline. This was going to be her finest role.

Sex with Claudia, Bob reflected, was like a Chinese feast. You came to the table ravenously hungry, you ate extravagantly until you were full up, then an hour or so later you felt as unsatisfied as when you started. Not that it was her fault. Claudia was a wonderful girl—intelligent, understanding, generous. He had never known a woman give so much. For now she had declared herself she held nothing in reserve.

Her friends were his friends, her parties, his parties. He found himself at intimate little dinners with heads of studios, private screenings with Clint Eastwood and Jane Fonda, squash parties with Wall Street bankers. As the man in Claudia Graham's life, he was welcome everywhere, and it went to his head. As an independent producer he had always had to struggle

## SCREEN KISSES • 381

and, no matter how hard he worked, the studios made it clear that he was there on sufferance. Until he took up with Claudia. Then he became everyone's best friend.

Right from the start they saw each other every night. On the rare occasions when he was honest with himself he felt things were moving too fast. He needed time away from her—time for himself. But every time he tried to absent himself for an early night or a late meeting it upset her. "You're bored with me already," she would complain, "I knew it was too good to last."

In the end it wasn't worth the hassle. Claudia needed someone around all the time. She needed someone to take care of her, to escort her to parties, and to satisfy her in bed. And Bob took on the task full time.

It took her two weeks to move him in. At first he would go home every morning and shower and change. Then she stepped up the pressure and he started to keep a couple of suits in her closet. One morning he went into the bathroom and found a new Remington razor of the type he used. He also found his brand of shower gel and shampoo.

"You're too good to me," he protested. "You don't have to buy me things. I have all this stuff at home."

She gave him her best early-morning smile. "Now you have it here. So there's no need to go home."

They didn't discuss their living arrangements because she wouldn't let him. But as time went on she made it more and more difficult for him to get to his flat. Finally one weekend he arrived with a suitcase full of clothes and she covered him with kisses. "You don't know how happy you've made me," she told him. Then she showed him through to the spare room, where the closets were all ready for him. Rows of wooden hangers waited for his jackets, the drawers and shelves had been freshly lined for his shirts, and there was a trouser press for his pants and custom-made trees for his shoes.

He felt as if he had been bought and paid for. She ran to him like a child and flung her arms round his neck. "Do you like it?" she asked. "I tried so hard to please you."

He was tempted to tell her she was trying too hard, but he bit his lip. "It's lovely, darling," he said.

They had been living together for two months when she finally brought up the subject of Rachel. They were sitting by the pool one evening in November. The air was just beginning to get cold and all the trees in the valley below were turning to shades of russet.

It had been a tough day at the studio and Claudia seemed to know this, for she had done everything to make him comfortable. When she heard his car pull into the drive she started to pour him a bourbon—the measure he liked, and the brand he preferred, with just the right quantity of ice. With the drink, there were little biscuits covered in Beluga caviar.

She was wearing pants and a soft mohair sweater that showed off every inch of her curves. Despite all his doubts he was pleased to be back. Then she started

## SCREEN KISSES • 383

to talk about Rachel. "You never told me what pulled you two apart," she said, nibbling a biscuit. "I thought you had a good thing going."

For the first time in two months he felt sad. Since he had been close to Claudia he had managed to keep the memory of Rachel outside his conscious mind—as long as he kept working, and as long as he kept moving. While Claudia distracted him he could forget what it felt like to love. Now she had brought Rachel into the foreground once more, and it disturbed him.

"Do we have to talk about Rachel?" he said testily. "She's past, she's gone, she's yesterday. Can't we leave her there?"

"Yes, if that's where she'll stay. I'm frightened she'll come back one day and take you away from me."

He looked sour. "There's no chance of that."

"Why?" She kept her voice light and inconsequential. "Doesn't she still care for you?"

Bob's expression didn't change. Instead he looked over the valley at the reddening trees and let his breath out. "I suppose it's possible that she cares," he said after a while, "but not enough to give up that damn career of hers."

Once he had started talking about her he couldn't stop. And he found himself telling Claudia how he had asked her to marry him and how she had agreed . . . until the play on Broadway appeared on her horizon. "She knew how I felt about actresses," he said harshly. "I explained that to her the first time we met. So she understood it was marriage to me or her career. She couldn't have both."

## 384 • TRUDI PACTER

"And she chose the theatre," said Claudia. "You don't surprise me."

He was mildly curious. "Why do you say that?" he asked.

She was silent for a while, as if she was struggling with her conscience. Finally she spoke: "You know Rachel and I were close for a while?"

He nodded.

"Well, during that time," she went on, "we visited a fortune-teller in one of the villages in Bali. Some crazy old Chinese lady called Madame Chong. Rachel found her—I've no idea where—and to be honest I didn't want to go and see her. But Rachel was adamant. She wanted to know what lay in front of her. And it meant so much that I went along with her to keep her company. God knows, she needed a friend. Or so I thought." She paused. "Anyway we pitched up to this old shack where this Madame lived. And then something weird happened. She did a kind of tarot reading, but she insisted we both stayed in the room. Apparently there were two lives in her cards and she couldn't tell which was which.

"At that moment I started to get the wind up and I tried to leave, but Rachel wasn't having it. She wanted to know about both lives. She said she'd know which was hers."

Bob looked at her. "And did she?"

Claudia looked shifty. She had changed the story almost out of all recognition. What if Bob had heard the real version? Then she relaxed. The only person who knew the way it was with Madame Chong was

## SCREEN KISSES • 385

Rachel, and it was unlikely she was going to tell him. She went on lying.

"Rachel seemed to know almost immediately which one of the two lives in the cards belonged to her. The fortune-teller told us she saw an artist who would give up everything for her art, and before she could go on talking Rachel started jumping up and down. 'Stop right there,' she said, 'you're talking about me.' "

Claudia made her eyes very wide. "What was really weird about the whole thing was that Rachel was virtually unknown at the time. I was the big star, so she should have been talking about me."

Bob frowned. "You said there were two lives. What did your Madame Chong say about the other one?"

Claudia didn't hesitate. "She said the other one was an ordinary mortal who would settle for a man." She paused. "As it turned out, she was right. Rachel took to the stage. And me . . . I seem to have taken to you."

Bob put his arm round her. "I'm flattered. Though I don't know if I deserve it."

The actress snuggled closer, and when he looked at her he noticed there were tears in her eyes. "Whether or not you deserve it," she said quietly, "I'm all yours, Bob. You know that. I'm not like Rachel. My career could never come in the way of what's really important."

"I'd no idea," he said. "You're such a big star. I always thought your career was what drove you."

She smiled. "You imagined all the men I married were incidentals?"

"Not exactly that. But part of the package . . . if you know what I mean."

She disentangled herself from him. "You really don't understand me, do you?" she said. "I got married all those times because I was looking for love. I was looking for a man to build a home for—someone to cook for, to devote myself to. And if any one of my husbands had been worthy of that I would have given up showbusiness without thinking twice." She leaned forward and brushed her hair back off her face. "I got disappointed every time. Then I found you, and now it's different."

He looked worried. "What exactly do you mean by that remark?"

She took her time answering him. Finally, after what seemed for ever, she said: "If you asked me to marry you, I'd tear up my Actors' Guild card tomorrow."

Christ, he thought, how did I get into this? But it was too late. The tears were pouring down her cheeks and she was beginning to sob in earnest. Claudia was building up to a major scene.

He considered leaving, knowing that if he did it would be for the last time. Then he glanced at the plate of half-eaten biscuits, his favourite bourbon in his favourite glass, the Filipino maid in the doorway waiting to serve dinner. And for no reason at all he felt tired. "Claudia," he said heavily, "Claudia, darling. Will you marry me?"

\*  \*  \*

## SCREEN KISSES • 387

Claudia decided on a quiet wedding. That is, she didn't hire the whole of Spago, book the best room at the Bel Air, or take over the Hollywood Bowl. Instead she decided to get married on a yacht. Marvin Davis, the billionaire real estate baron, had what amounted to a floating hotel moored off Cannes harbour. He and his wife offered Claudia the use of it for her nuptials.

"But it's miles away," protested Bob. "Why in heaven's name do we have to go half way across the world to get married? It's not as if it's your first time. Or mine either."

But Claudia silenced his objections. The whole point of going to the South of France, she explained, was to ensure a quality turnout. Riff-raff and hangers-on wouldn't be able to afford the return fare to Europe. Besides, Grace Kelly got married on the Côte d'Azur, and look what an event that turned out to be. Bob didn't bother to remind her that she wasn't marrying royalty, or that quite a number of his friends might find the trip hard on their pockets, or that Marvin and Joanna Davis were not his favourite people. For there was no point in arguing with Claudia. The prospect of getting married again seemed to have turned her into a different person. Friends he never knew she possessed materialized out of nowhere— hairdressers, dress designers, interior decorators, flower girls, gossip columnists. Every inconsequential person in Greater Los Angeles either rang or turned up on the doorstep. If he had been less busy he might have been irritated. But post-production work on *Marooned* had first claim on his attention. Most days he

## 388 • TRUDI PACTER

was in meetings from dawn until seven at night, sometimes later. So when Claudia announced she was off to Paris to be fitted for her wedding dress he was almost relieved. A few days without the mayhem of their imminent marriage was an attractive prospect. He could catch up on all the movies he had missed, get together with old drinking buddies, indulge his passion for hamburger and onions without feeling like a barbarian.

He disguised his pleasure. "How long will you be away for?" he asked.

"A week, maybe two," she said vaguely. "It depends on Dior. Artists like Marc Bohan can't be hurried."

He was tempted to tell her that any dressmaker could produce on schedule if the price was high enough, but he resisted. Instead he suggested she took her time. "Paris is fun at this time of the year. There are a lot of new things on at the theatre. I heard of a couple of good exhibitions coming up. And you'll have time to catch up with some of your friends. I almost wish I was coming with you."

Her eyes took on a veiled look, as if two shutters were coming down.

"You'd only be in the way," she said flatly. "Anyway Dan tells me you can't take a minute off from the studio."

He shrugged and went through into the other room. He could live without accompanying Claudia to Paris, though it needled him that she didn't want him there. If this was her attitude before the honeymoon, what could he expect afterwards?

## SCREEN KISSES • 389

Then he told himself he was being silly. All women went a little crazy before they got married— all normal women who weren't involved in their careers. It was part of their mystique.

However, Claudia wasn't indulging in some female ritual when she told Bob she didn't want him around on her Paris jaunt. It was more complicated than that. For she wasn't going direct to the French capital. She was going there by way of Bali.

The time had come to settle her account with Madame Chong. When the artist is reconciled with her art, one of you will come and pay me, she had said. Well, Rachel was making a name for herself on Broadway, and that was reconciliation in anybody's language. Except Rachel didn't know about that part of the bargain. Claudia remembered how she had walked out on the fortune-teller. She was so freaked she wouldn't even stay till the end of the session.

In a way she was pleased it had happened that way. For everything the Chinese woman had told them had come true. One of them had betrayed the other. Though it wasn't her fault, Claudia told herself. And the fact that she had stolen Rachel's man didn't make her accountable either. It had all been an accident of fate, and the sooner she paid her dues to the Fates the better.

Claudia arrived at Denpasar in the late afternoon. The airport was hot and humid and packed with Asian families. As she queued to have her passport stamped Claudia felt herself being pushed and buffeted on all sides, yet there was nothing she could do about it. Here she was just another American tourist, with no

## 390 • TRUDI PACTER

knowledge of the local language or customs. For the first time in many years she had to wait in line, and she hated it.

Her pale, fine wool slacks, so perfect in the air-conditioned first-class section of the aircraft, were already starting to feel uncomfortable. The waistband was tight and sweaty round her midriff and the fashionably wide legs were a magnet for the dust and debris that cluttered the arrivals hall. In her mind's eye she could see the suite she had reserved for herself at the Oberoy—cool, spotlessly clean, filled with flowers. As soon as she got there she would ditch the constricting pants, the silk shirt, the cashmere sweater, and stand under an ice-cold shower until she felt human again.

Half an hour later she finally made it through immigration, and half an hour after that she managed to drag her Vuitton suitcases off the carousel and find a porter. The hotel had sent a driver to meet her and she heaved a sigh of relief. The worst was over. Now she could step back into her luxury, air-conditioned world and let other people do things for her. While the driver piled her things into the boot of the Mercedes she looked at her diamond-studded Cartier tank watch. It was nearly five-thirty. In twenty minutes' time she could be taking her shower.

Then an idea came to her. It would take just over half an hour to drive to Ubud. She could see the Chinese fortune-teller there and then and pay what she owed. That would get the whole business over and done with. A stagnant breeze rippled over the forecourt of the terminus building, and a cloud of filth,

## SCREEN KISSES • 391

old sweet wrappings and empty cartons blew up against Claudia's two-thousand-dollar trousers. Her resolve hardened.

She climbed into the back of the leather-upholstered car, slammed the door shut and turned the air conditioning full up. Then she leaned forward and spoke to the driver. "Before we go to the hotel I want you to drive to Ubud. Just outside the town is a house with a high wall. I'll know it when I come to it. Stop there and wait for me."

It had taken the last of her reserves to issue this instruction. Her whole body cried out for the comfort and scented luxury of the Oberoy. But she had travelled half way across the world to get Madame Chong off her conscience. It was now or never.

Night came early in that part of the tropics, and it was pitch black by the time they reached Ubud. Claudia started to panic. What if she couldn't make out where the house was? Just as she decided to give up and go back the car pulled up in front of a high stone wall.

"This is the house of the Chinese woman. The one who tells fortunes," said the driver in the singsong accent of the island. "Is it here that you wanted?"

Claudia was startled. "How did you know? I mean, how did you know who lived here?"

The Balinese smiled. "I was born just a few miles from Ubud. Madame Chong is well known in the village."

A regular little tourist attraction, thought Claudia. But she felt a certain relief. If the woman put her faith in the tourist trade rather than in the gods

## 392 • TRUDI PACTER

it would make her easier to deal with—and to get rid of.

She got out of the car and made her way to the archway that led on to the compound. Minutes after she had rung the doorbell the native boy she remembered from her last visit appeared. She gave him her name quickly and asked to see his employer.

"Do you have an appointment?" he asked.

She considered. "Not really. But I came for a reading last spring and I left owing money. I said I'd be back to settle my account, and here I am."

The boy regarded her with impassive black eyes. "I remember," he said. "Wait here and I'll ask her for you."

For the first time since she embarked on this journey Claudia started to feel foolish. What am I doing here? she asked herself. I'm an internationally famous film star. I'm on my way to Dior to get fitted for my wedding dress. My sixth wedding dress. And I'm standing in the middle of nowhere waiting for some wog to give me permission to see a tarot reader. One day I'll look back at this and laugh.

After ten minutes her sense of humour deserted her. She felt the beginnings of a headache coming on. Where the hell has everyone got to? she wondered.

Then just as she was losing hope of ever seeing him again, the boy reappeared out of the shadows. "You have come too soon," he said. "My mistress says the time is not right to see her."

Claudia lost her temper. "Then tell your mistress from me that she's talking rubbish. It's taken me a day and a night to get here. If she wants more money I'll

## SCREEN KISSES • 393

give her more money, but I won't leave the island without settling this business."

There was a silence. Then the boy said, "Madame knows you have travelled far. And because of that she will see you tomorrow. But she cannot promise to help you."

Then before Claudia could yell some more he was gone. She threw herself into the back of the limousine. OK, I'll come back, she thought grimly, and I'll pay you what you want. But if I don't get satisfaction I'll sue the ass off you. It was an empty threat and she knew it, but there was something familiar, almost consoling, about litigation. She'd been punishing her enemies for years with expensive law suits. The thought of hauling a sixty-year-old Chinese fortune-teller through the criminal courts made her feel less vulnerable. She'd be damned if she'd let the old bitch frighten her.

She was up at seven the next morning, dressed and showered and drinking a breakfast cup of coffee. On her tray there was an assortment of exotic fruits, some toast and freshly baked croissants. Claudia touched none of it. She knew she would have no appetite until she had seen Martha Chong.

At eight-thirty she was sitting in the back of a limousine, being driven through the streets lined with curio shops and higgledy-piggledy cafés that made up the town of Ubud. How seedy it all is, she thought. She stared at the hordes of Australians who made their annual pilgrimage to the island, and she shook her head. I've seen better wood carvings in Sydney, she mused, and better food. It was all junk—a junky island. The sooner she got out of there the happier she would be.

They came to the house with the high wall, and this time the boy who answered her summons took her through the entrance way. As she walked through the overgrown garden she thought she heard the sound of chimes, like distant, enchanted bells, and her spine began to prickle. The boy showed her into the ramshackle building where the fortune-teller lived. It was as if Claudia had never left it. The kitchen table still looked like a market stall with its straw panniers and piles of fruit. The old-fashioned range was as she remembered it. There were hens walking around the floor, and in the corner by a wood-burning stove, a thin, grey cat lay sleeping.

Madame Chong was sitting where Claudia had left her nearly a year ago, in a high-backed chair at the end of the table. And Claudia noticed with a certain surprise that the fortune-teller was even wearing the same dress—a red satin affair with a high neck and a flowing skirt. Her red-painted lips curled up into a smile as Claudia approached. "Where is your friend?" she asked. "The one you came with last time."

When Claudia didn't reply the old woman nodded her head. "Of course," she said. "I should have remembered. The woman you came with is no longer your friend."

Claudia sat down facing her, keeping her handbag on her lap. "I've come to pay what I owe," she said. "I don't want to talk about the past. Or your predictions for the future. Just tell me how much you want and I'll get out."

## SCREEN KISSES • 395

But the tarot reader ignored the question. "So you are the betrayer," she said. "Now I understand. You came here looking for absolution."

The actress started to feel uncomfortable. She was in no mood to be judged, not now, and certainly not by the likes of Martha Chong. "I came here looking to give you dollars. Money. Isn't that what you do this for?"

The Chinese woman looked at Claudia in her designer jeans and heavy silk shirt. "It's not a matter of money," she said. "If it was it would be simpler. This concerns the spirit world. The gods. And they are not so easily appeased." She sighed. "I can't take your dollars. Not yet. Not until the trouble between you and your friend is over."

Claudia stood up and rummaged in her bag.

"Your timing's wrong. It *is* over." She produced a sheaf of bills and threw them on the table. "Count it," she instructed, "then put it away. Before I change my mind."

The old woman spread the money across the wooden table, then she started to laugh. "That's almost three hundred dollars. You must want whatever it is very badly."

"I do," the actress said tightly.

The money lay on the table between them, neither woman making any move to pick it up. Over in the stove a twig spluttered and popped. The cat got up, arched its back and yawned, showing sharp white teeth. Then it curled closer to the warmth and went back to sleep. It was Martha Chong who broke the silence. "You can't be the one who is the artist," she

## 396 • TRUDI PACTER

said. "No artist would try to buy her future." Slowly she got to her feet and took hold of the dollar bills. "This," she said slapping the wodge of money against the edge of the table, "this can do many things. It can buy food and shelter, and the fancy clothes you're wearing. I've even known it to buy time. But never in a million years can it change a destiny. Or buy a life."

"I wasn't trying to buy anyone's life," said Claudia.

The woman looked at her out of narrow, black eyes. "You forget," she told her, "I can see into the future. There is someone close to you at this moment who you would like to possess. A man, perhaps? Yes, I'm almost sure it's a man." She paused, wondering. "What makes you want to bind him so closely? What are you frightened of?"

Something in Claudia snapped. "Shut up, you silly old woman," she shouted. "Just take the money and keep quiet."

Madame Chong didn't seem to hear her. "The problem with you," she said, "is you think you can buy everything. And you're wrong."

She walked over to where the cat was lying by the stove. Close to, he was a mangy animal. His ribs stuck out and his ears were torn from countless fights. She ran her hands over his flanks. "You couldn't even buy my cat with your dollars," she went on. "If this creature didn't want to stay with you nothing on earth could hold him. It's the same with a man. But you don't know it yet."

## SCREEN KISSES • 397

Then as Claudia watched, she took the thick wad of money and piece by piece she fed it into the fire.

Claudia Graham got married for the sixth time on board a yacht in Cannes harbour. Present were the 150 hand-picked guests who could afford the first-class transatlantic air fare. Most of the world's press also attended. They piled into motor launches and buzzed and circled the *Joanna II,* the yacht that bore the name of the owner's wife. The entire ceremony and the reception afterwards were punctuated with the pop of flashguns and the whirring of high-speed film.

The bride, dressed in oyster-pink satin overlaid with Spanish lace, looked radiant throughout. Her life's greatest scenes had been played out in front of the cameras, so it was only fitting that photographers should be present on her wedding day.

The groom was less comfortable. He did not share Claudia's love of publicity—a fact that became apparent even before they left America. They had been dogged by reporters and cameramen from the moment they got into the car to go to the airport. By the time they reached passport control Bob's temper had reached fever pitch. It finally snapped when a TV reporter pushed a microphone too close to his face. Bob turned on the man and landed a punch which laid him out cold, then he strode on to the plane, berating himself all the while for not taking Marvin Davis up on his offer of a private jet.

When they arrived at Nice Bob's mood had not improved. Throughout the flight the first-class cabin had been full of reporters conducting on-the-spot in-

## 398 • TRUDI PACTER

terviews with Claudia. They even solicited the opinions of some of the wedding guests who were travelling with them. However, they left Bob alone. When they got through French customs he knew his problems were temporarily at an end, for Marvin had laid on six trained heavies to escort them to a waiting limousine.

By the time they arrived at Cannes harbour, Bob felt almost grateful to the American tycoon. Then they boarded the *Joanna II* and went through to their stateroom and he stopped feeling grateful. He stopped feeling anything. For when he looked around him, he finally knew he was out of his class. He had expected the sort of cabin you would find on the first-class deck of the *QE2*. Instead he found a bedroom the size of a bowling alley, with teak-lined walls and carpets made of real fur. When he walked in he was so surprised that he actually took off his shoes and socks to see if it wasn't some kind of fake. It wasn't On the morning of his second marriage Bob Delaney found himself treading on wall-to-wall mink. After that all reality was suspended. He resigned himself to spending his wedding night on a giant water bed draped in cloth of gold.

He could have spent hours marvelling at the wonders of his wedding suite, but nobody gave him the time. Marvin and Joanna had laid on a five-course lunch to precede the late-afternoon ceremony, and a couple of dozen carefully selected locals had been invited. Both Princess Caroline and Princess Stephanie were expected, as were the Harold Robbinses, the Adnan Kashoggis, the Leslie Bricusses, Dirk Bogarde

## SCREEN KISSES • 399

and the David Nivens. Even Brigitte Bardot was rumoured to be coming out of hiding to lend support to Claudia Graham.

Of the lady concerned there was no sign. Bob searched high and low for Claudia but without success. She seemed to have disappeared into thin air. Finally his friend Rick Hamilton, who was there as his best man, told him where she was. "She's holed up in the Carlton Hotel," he said, "preparing herself for the great event. On a day like this she can't afford to disappoint her public."

Bob was stunned. "The next thing you'll be telling me is she's bathing in asses' milk."

The cockney film director gave him a grin. "If she thought it might do some good she probably would be. She's already flown in her hairdresser and make-up man a day ahead of her to prepare the ground. Right now she'll be having a manicure, a pedicure, a facial and probably a full-scale massage as well. In three hours' time when she comes up the gangplank you won't recognize her!"

Bob looked around him. The railings surrounding the main deck were garlanded with flowers, and amongst them were dozens of hanging lanterns ready to light up the moment dusk fell. A dance floor had been specially laid over the swimming pool, and all around it were circular tables covered with pink starched cloths and crowned with elaborate arrangements of orchids. He groaned. "I don't know how much more of this I can take. In three hours' time I'll be fed up to here with splendour. Like a Strasbourg goose."

## 400 • TRUDI PACTER

"What you could do with," said Rick, "is a stiff drink somewhere cosy and private and close to the working man. I think I know just the place."

"But what about Brigitte Bardot and Harold Robbins and all the other characters Marvin's got coming to lunch?"

Rick gave him an old-fashioned look. "You don't really think they've come to see you, do you? You're just incidental to this drama. Necessary, but incidental. People who come to this sort of bash come to see each other. They'll chat on about all their mutual chums back in the States. Dish the dirt a bit. Chew over the local scandals. And the minute they see you they'll enquire politely about Claudia, then their eyes will glaze over with boredom. I promise you, my friend, if you and I disappear quietly down the gangplank right now, nobody will even notice we've gone."

Bob needed no further convincing. Five minutes later they were on the waterfront and heading into the town. As they made their way up the winding backstreets Bob noticed how still and hot the air had become. At the base of his skull he could feel the beginnings of a headache. He sighed. Wedding nerves, he told himself. Wedding nerves, a long flight and probably jet lag as well. No wonder he was feeling rough.

He wasn't the only one. In the penthouse suite at the Carlton Claudia lost her temper for the fifth time that day. "Sandra," she yelled, "you're going to have to take the whole thing down and start again. When I said I wanted my hair up I meant straight and severe,

## SCREEN KISSES • 401

like Grace Kelly. Not this fluffy mess. What are you trying to do? Make me look like some Hollywood bimbo?''

Sandra, who had been doing Claudia's hair for seven years, looked confused. She had made her look like Grace Kelly two hairdos ago and the star had hated it. If she went on changing her mind all day they'd never get her to her wedding on time. But, Sandra knew better than to argue. Silently she started undoing the row of pins. What on earth had got into the actress?

Claudia blinked and looked at herself in the full-length mirror. Her eyes prickled and her skin felt hot. She fought down the insane desire to smash something—a crystal goblet, the bottle of champagne on the table, the lamp by the side of the bed.

Take hold of yourself, she thought. You're getting married; it's nothing to lose control over. Lord knows, it's not as if you've never done it before. She looked at her watch. In just half an hour she had to leave the Carlton, and she wasn't even wearing her wedding dress.

Automatically she scrutinized herself in the mirror. Dior had dressed her from the skin out—the white lacy bra and matching pants, the sheer silk stockings, the wisp of suspender belt. Her lingerie alone came to almost a thousand dollars. She didn't begrudge the expense. Today she wanted to look her best, feel her best, be her best. Today nothing was good enough.

\*     \*     \*

As soon as she walked up the gangplank of the *Joanna II* Claudia noticed a restlessness amongst her guests. It wasn't excitement or anticipation. The crowd had an angrier sound than that. She had felt the same fury herself earlier, and it worried her. What was getting into everyone? She looked up into the sky. It was the first time that day that she had thought about something other than herself, and she was surprised at what she saw. Instead of the azure blue she expected, the horizon was full of scudding grey clouds, yet the air all around her was uncomfortably still and hot. She had never known it like this before in the South of France.

She shrugged her shoulders and set her face into a smile for the cameras. The weather was the least of her problems. From the moment the Chinese fortune-teller had thrown her money on the fire she had felt as if some curse had been put on her. There was no logic to it, she knew that. Bob had asked her to marry him and he showed no signs of changing his mind. Under normal circumstances this would have reassured her, but now she was beyond reassurance. Wild imaginings haunted her. Bob might change his mind and cancel the wedding. Rachel might reappear from nowhere and shoot her out of jealousy. Her car might crash. She'd be struck by lightning.

None of it happened. And here she was in the middle of May, dressed in her wedding dress, walking towards her husband-to-be. Standing in front of him was a notary dressed in a black suit, and all around her, covered in jewellery and done up to the nines, were 150 of her dearest friends. She took a deep

## SCREEN KISSES • 403

breath, stood beside Bob and put her hand in his. They exchanged glances and she noticed he looked grey and strained. Then the notary started the ceremony and she held her breath. If he could just get to the end, if she could just hear Bob say his vows and listen to the echo of her own voice, then she knew the spell would be broken.

There was a silence and she glanced down to see Bob slip a slim gold band over her finger. Then he kissed her and held her close. "Congratulations, Mrs Delaney," he said. "I don't speak a word of French, but I think the man in the black suit just pronounced us man and wife."

Relief swept over her. It was finally done. The plan she had set in motion *en route* from New York to Los Angeles had finally come to fruition. Claudia Graham had been reborn as Claudia Delaney. No more film sets, no more costume fittings, no more agents and lawyers bugging the hell out of me, she thought. From now on it's lunch at the Bistro Gardens and queening it at industry dinners. Mentally she hugged herself. That's what I want, she thought. What I've always wanted.

She turned round to face the crowd behind them, and in the forefront, standing alone, she saw Giselle. As always the French woman was a monument to the skills of Chanel—though Claudia noticed that she didn't share the designer's penchant for costume jewellery. The sapphires at her ears, round her neck and adorning her wrists were by Boucheron. Claudia wondered if they had been a present from Dan Keyser. Then she remembered a tearful, emotional telephone

**404 • TRUDI PACTER**

call she had had from Giselle a week ago, and she felt sorry. She took hold of her wedding bouquet, held it aloft and threw it to Giselle. Good luck, darling, she whispered. You of all people could do with it.

The French woman didn't share Claudia's belief in superstition. She caught the posy of white lilies and mimosa, blew a kiss to the bride, and disappeared into the crowd. As soon as she found an unoccupied table she dumped the flowers on it and made her way over to the bar. A drink was what she needed right now, not a talisman.

As she waited for her vodka and tonic her eyes nervously swept the deck. But Dan had been true to his promise and stayed away from the wedding. In the circumstances it was the least he could do.

Giselle cast her mind back to the events of the last three weeks, and as she did she felt regret and a deep sense of failure. If only I hadn't told him, she berated herself. If only I'd kept my secrets to myself I'd be standing here on Dan's arm now, instead of by myself.

She picked up her drink and took a large swallow. The alcohol restored her sense of balance. Who am I kidding? she asked herself. Even if I hadn't told him about Milton Harrison, he'd have found out if he'd taken the job with Pan Video.

Milton, she thought ruefully, of all the men I loved, you were the only one who truly understood me. She remembered the tall man with the iron-grey hair who had been introduced to her at the French Embassy. She had just finished her studies at the Sorbonne and was looking for an adventure. Anything

## SCREEN KISSES • 405

to delay the moment when she would have to decide what to do with her life.

Milton didn't just delay her plans, he stopped her in her tracks. He was running the Paris office of an American TV network then, and when he was transferred to New York he took her with him. Giselle's family and friends threw up their hands in horror. "He'll eat you for breakfast," her mother predicted. "An American, thirty years older than you. What can you be thinking of?"

But Giselle wasn't thinking. Her brain had gone temporarily on hold. It stayed in that position for the five years she lived with Milton. Then one day she woke up and discovered she was twenty-six and her life was going nowhere. She had no job and was living with a man who refused to marry her. But I'm happy, her heart said. Nonsense, she told herself. How can you be happy without marriage, without children, without a future?

That night she put the question to Milton and he laughed. "I always suspected you were a conventional girl underneath," he said.

"What are you going to do about it?" she asked.

"Nothing. I've got grown-up children from my first marriage, and I'm too old for any more babies. Or any more marriages. We're happy the way we are. Why not leave it alone?"

But she couldn't. Time was passing—her life was passing—and it frightened her. "If you don't marry me, I'll have to leave you," she threatened.

"I won't stop you," he said. But there were tears in his eyes.

## 406 • TRUDI PACTER

She left for the coast almost immediately, and for a year she didn't contact him. She needed to find her freedom—and her bearings. Then when she'd established herself she called him, and almost immediately their friendship resumed—at a distance, and between lovers. It wasn't a perfect situation, but it was the best both of them could manage.

She sighed. Maybe that was my mistake, she thought. Asking a man I loved to help me marry a man I didn't. As she helped herself to another vodka, her mind went back to the night she put herself on the line for Dan Keyser. What a fuss he made about sex. All that huffing and puffing and splashing about in Jacuzzis. She made a face. Milton and I could find more joy in a minute than Dan could when he tried all night long, she thought.

All the same, she had told him she loved him and he had returned the compliment, declaring that he wanted to share his life with her . . . if only he could get rid of his wife. Then he had kept her up all night telling her how impossible it was. If Carla went, so did his job at Magnum. And then what would they do for the rent?

The following day Giselle had called Milton. At first he had been reluctant. "What do you want with a man like Keyser?" he had asked. "He's a peasant. An educated peasant, I'll give you that, but not in your class."

Giselle had stuck to her guns. "I want to marry him," she said.

He had laughed. "With all you've got going for

## SCREEN KISSES • 407

you, you still want to be someone's wife. Giselle, Giselle, when will you ever grow up?"

"I didn't ring you to go over old ground," she said sharply. "You don't believe in marriage, I accept that. I accepted it years ago. But that doesn't stop me from wanting it. And having it with somebody else."

There was a silence. "Even Dan Keyser," he said.

"Even Dan Keyser," she replied. "Will you help me?"

"If that's what you want." There was a coldness in his voice. "Actually I could use a man like Keyser right now. My head of production is long due for retirement and the place is in a shambles. OK, Giselle. I'll see what I can do. Only, if I help you I want you to promise me one thing."

"What's that?"

"Don't ask me to the wedding."

He had kept his word and contacted Dan, and it had changed everything. From the moment Milton opened negotiations, Dan became a different man. During the course of their affair he had acted furtively—sneaking up to her house before he went out to dinner with his wife; taking her to out-of-the-way restaurants in the evenings when he was meant to be away; pretending he didn't know her when they met.

Now he didn't want to hide her any more. They lunched at Ma Maison and the Bistro Gardens. When they had dinner it was at the Polo Lounge or the Beverly Wilshire. Once he even took her to Spago. They were an item, and the whole town knew it. Even his wife knew it. And he didn't seem to give a damn.

Then one evening he arrived early and told her

he was staying the night. Normally they arranged this in advance, so she guessed that something out-of-the-ordinary had happened. She was right.

"I got offered a job today," he announced.

She feigned ignorance. "What job?"

"The job I've been telling you about for the past six weeks." He was irritable now. "Don't you listen to anything I tell you?"

"Of course I do, *chéri*. You and Milton Harrison were talking about something over at Pan Video, but there was nothing definite mentioned. Anyway I didn't think you were all that interested."

He helped himself to a drink and came over to where she sat on the sofa. "I was interested, all right," he said. "But on my terms. Until I got them there was no point in making a song and dance about the job."

She smiled. "I take it you got them."

"Sure thing . . . hey, why are you looking at me like that? Do you know something I don't?"

She flung her arms round him. "Yes and no."

Gently he disentangled her, then he took both of her hands in his.

"Before I ask what's in that devious little mind of yours, I've got something important to tell you."

"You're taking the job with Milton."

"Of course I'm taking the job. I'd be a fool not to at the salary he's offering. But there's something else. I'm going to ask Carla for a divorce. How do you feel about becoming the second Mrs Keyser?"

She lowered her eyes. "That would make me very happy."

She looked back on the scene as she swallowed

## SCREEN KISSES • 409

her third vodka. If only I had kept my eyes down and
my face straight, she thought bitterly. But I couldn't,
could I? I had to put that stupid, goddamn smile back
on.

"What are you grinning at?" he had asked.
"What's the big secret?"

She looked him full in the face. "I knew you were
going to get that job."

"How come?"

"Because Milton Harrison and I are friends from
way back. He told me weeks ago he was going to offer
it to you."

She had expected him to be grateful, or tender,
or just plain pleased. What she didn't expect him to
do was get up off the sofa and walk away from her.
"How long have you and Harrison been friends?" he
asked harshly.

"Over ten years. Why are you looking so upset?"

His voice was soft and somehow menacing. "I've
gotten a lot of jobs a lot of different ways. I even had
a woman get me a job once, and I married her for it."
His voice started to rise now. "Goddamn it, Giselle,
the guy who gave me the job at Magnum was the father of the bride. The one who's doing me the big
favour over at Pan Video looks to me like he's screwing the bride."

She went very pale. "It's not like that," she said.
"Milton and I were all over years ago."

He turned round on her, eyes blazing. "So you
*were* fucking him. I knew it was too good to be true."

She got up and hurried over to him. "Look,
you're being ridiculous. All that happened way back

## 410 • TRUDI PACTER

in the past before I met you. Before I even came out to the coast."

He pushed her away. "It doesn't matter to me when you were fucking him," he said wearily. "What matters is that you did. Look, Giselle, do you have any idea how I felt about Carla after she got her father to give me the job at Magnum? I thought I'd be pleased with her. Only I didn't feel that way. Castrated is what I felt. When that dame got me the big job she effectively cut my balls off. And that's exactly what you've just done to me."

She was crying now. Tears of rage and frustration were smudging the perfect make-up job. "But I did it for us, so that we could get married. How else could you survive if you divorced Carla? You told me yourself, no one would pick you up once Magnum threw you in the street."

He knocked back the rest of his drink and regarded her sourly. "So you got your old boyfriend to fix it for you. Very clever. And now instead of being grateful to Carla for the rest of my life I've got to grovel to you instead."

He walked over to the French antique table with the inlaid gilt. Without bothering to look for a coaster, he put his glass down. "Well, I'm not going to grovel to you. Not now. Not ever. Let me tell you something. The moment you told me you'd fixed me the job with Harrison, you and Carla started to look just the same to me. Castrators. Ball-breakers. I could no more get up for you now than I could for Carla. Only Carla's got one advantage that you haven't. She's the mother of my children."

## SCREEN KISSES • 411

He picked his jacket up from the sofa and shrugged his way into it. Then he headed for the door.

"You can't leave me," she sobbed. "Not now."

"Watch me," he said.

And that was the last she had seen of him. He didn't write. He didn't call. And when she tried to contact him she was headed off every time by his secretary. In the end she admitted defeat, and with it came a certain relief. All the scheming, the lying and the chasing were finally over. She might be in her early thirties, she might be without a man, but she had a damn good business going for her in LA, and for the first time in a long while she could call her evenings her own. And her nights.

She looked out over the stormy Mediterranean and raised her vodka in a silent salute. From now on in, she vowed, sex would be a leisure activity. Something she did for pleasure.

She thought about Milton Harrison and something inside her relaxed. Maybe I'll call the old bastard again, she thought. I could do with a few laughs.

As she went to put her glass down and join the rest of the party, a gust of wind snatched her tiny flowered hat and sent it scudding along the deck. What the hell . . . ? she thought. Then she looked up and saw she wasn't the only one who was losing her headgear. Silk fedoras, wisps of lace, extravagant designer concoctions were flying all around her.

She started to make her way to where Claudia was standing, and as she did so all the bottles on the bar behind her went crashing over, splashing the silk Chanel dress and covering her with shards of glass.

She recalled the unnatural stillness of the day—the oppressive heat, the stormy sky, the bad temper of her fellow guests. Of course, she thought. How could I have forgotten? This is the way the mistral starts.

Now the hot, dry wind was sweeping over the deck, driving the wedding party to the cabins below. Only Claudia, her face turned into the storm, showed no signs of leaving. She had grabbed hold of the railing behind her and was beating her skirts down with her other hand. She's calling at something, thought Giselle. What on earth is she doing?

But Claudia was oblivious to her friend or her new husband who were both struggling towards her. "Too late, Madame Chong," she yelled into the wind. "He's mine now. Mine before the notary, before Rachel, before the whole damn world. Nothing can take him away now . . ."

Rachel did her best to forget Bob the moment he walked out of her life. It was her agent, Desmond French, who decided her. He had dried her tears and bought her dinner at Sardi's after the show. She remembered looking at him that night across the large, circular table. All over the cloth and half covering the plates were the morning paper reviews. Ecstatic and admiring. She had fixed Desmond with her eye. "What am I going to do?" she asked.

He smiled and handed her a glass of champagne. "For the next five minutes," he said, "or the next five years?"

She was irritated. "Be serious, will you? You saw what happened tonight. It was a mess. Worse than a mess, it was a complete shambles."

The Englishman smiled and signalled for the waiter. "I take it you're talking about your love life. Everything else looked fine to me."

"Of course I'm talking about my love life. How could Richard behave like that? Just because I spent one miserable night with him. And it was miserable, you know."

He took her hand across the table. "Rachel, you don't have to explain yourself to me. Richard Roberts is like a million other ambitious young actors in this town. He wants work and he can't get it, so he does the next best thing. He hangs around friends of his who *are* working. He was nice to you, darling, because he thought something would rub off. A little success, a little money. Maybe even a little glamour.

"I didn't interfere when I saw what was going on because I knew better. That first night was pretty terrifying for you. You needed someone around, someone close. Richard filled that need. And there's nothing wrong with taking what you need, you know."

"There is if it wrecks the rest of your life."

The waiter arrived, and Desmond ordered for both of them without looking at the menu. After twenty years in the business he knew it by heart. When the waiter had refilled their glasses and gone away, he turned to Rachel. "I think you're taking this too hard," he said. "Of course Bob walked out on you. What the hell did you expect him to do? Any man would have done the same. But if he loves you, Rachel, if he really loves you, he'll get over it. For Christ's sake, the man's been around. He knows the

## SCREEN KISSES • 415

business. He knows actresses. And I'm damn sure he knows all about first nights.

"Look, why don't you put the whole thing out of your mind? Walk away from it. You don't need Richard any more. In fact, right now, you don't need any man around you. You did a great job tonight, but your nerves did it for you. What you have to do now is sustain that marvelous performance, and you're going to need every ounce of concentration to pull it off. From now on, thanks to these," he gestured at the pages of reviews, "you'll be playing to capacity audiences. But a New York audience is like no other in the world. They're used to the best the theatre has to offer, and if you let them down—even for one night— the word will spread and they'll stop coming to see you."

He had her attention now. She was still in pain. Still in shock. But the theatre once more swam into focus. It was all she had now. She owed it to herself to do it justice.

For six months she lived and breathed the play. She woke up in the mornings planning her entrances. Most days she lunched with Rose, the director, and searched for new facets of the character she was portraying. When she wasn't on stage she sat in the theatre hunched over her script, learning everyone else's part as well as her own.

Finally *Lili's War* looked set for a long run, and Rachel heaved a sigh of relief and turned her attention to the rest of her life.

The apartment building had served her well, but she had no wish to make her home there, and a home

## 416 • TRUDI PACTER

was what she needed now. She had sold her London flat while she was still living with Bob in LA, and her furniture was left behind in a warehouse in Shoreditch. For some unaccountable reason she longed to see it all again—the button-back sofa she had bought with her first successful tour money; the silver candlesticks she had inherited from her grandmother; the coffee table in the Harrods sale she had queued all night for; the fur rug that had belonged to her mother; her toaster, her food-mixer, her bed.

If she put them all in one room she suspected they might look like a pile of junk to her now. But they were her things, the possessions she had worked for, the fabric of her life. And she wanted them around her.

She spent her time away from the theatre looking at real estate. She tramped round duplexes on the West Side, penthouses on Fifth, brownstones in the Village. And after three months of looking she finally settled on an airy, rambling apartment in the lower Sixties. Apart from the space, what set it apart from everything else she had seen was its terrace, which ran around two sides of the building. Her bedroom looked over it and so did her main living room. The last owner had been a gardener and there were still tubs on the terrace containing climbing greenery. It was the greenery that clinched the deal. It reminded her of the parks and squares of London. She signed the lease the same day she saw the apartment.

It was another six weeks before she could move in. Her belongings took a month to reach her from London, and no amount of phoning, nagging or

## SCREEN KISSES • 417

bribes from Desmond made them come any faster. When they finally did arrive all her suspicions were confirmed. Not only did her possessions look strangely shabby, but there seemed so few of them. The sofa that filled a whole room of her London flat barely fitted into the corner of her new, smart penthouse.

On the days when she didn't have a matinée Rachel haunted Bloomingdales searching for things to fill her new apartment. Sometimes she went further afield to sale rooms in Brooklyn and Queens, and on these trips she occasionally took Richard. Very occasionally. After her talk with Desmond she had kept him at arm's length. He hadn't protested. After all Rachel was a successful Broadway actress now. She was in a position to grant favours and call the shots, and he took what he could get.

His attitude made their friendship possible. Once Rachel knew she was being used, the emotion went out of it. For her, Richard was a handsome escort. Company on a rainy Sunday. When he wasn't there, she didn't miss him. Performing at the theatre and building her new home filled her life. Desmond had been right. She had no need for a man—no need at all. Then six months later she caught a newsflash. She was watching her new television one morning before a matinée, and her attention was divided between the day's news and a pastrami sandwich. Then she saw her. Claudia Graham in glorious colour in the middle of Rachel's living room. At first she thought the star had signed up for a new movie deal and she went over

## 418 • TRUDI PACTER

and turned the sound up. As she did so, she caught the announcement.

". . . is to marry for the sixth time. The new man in Miss Graham's life is producer Bob Delaney, who met the actress when they worked on a film together in Bali . . ."

The remainder of the flash went by in a blur. Rachel stood rooted to the spot. Claudia Graham and Bob Delaney. Bob Delaney and Claudia Graham. The juxtaposition of names didn't make any sense to her. They knew each other, but there had been no attraction, no interest from either side. So what were they doing together? Why were they seeing each other, marrying each other?

She felt faint and sat down abruptly on her new Bloomingdales sofa. Then, with a kind of numb, professional detachment she tried to figure out how she felt. She remembered an old actor whose mother had just died. The first thing he did was to look in the mirror. Why are you doing that? she had asked him.

"I wanted to see what I looked like when I was grieving," he replied.

Now she was doing the same thing—analysing her emotions, exploring the pain. But all she could feel was disbelief. Although she hadn't heard from Bob, she still clung to the hope that he would come back to her. There had been too much love between them for it to come to nothing. Subconsciously she had waited for him. And what had he done? He'd gone out and found somebody else. Claudia Graham. The vision of the movie star's beautiful, selfish face seemed to fill the room, and Rachel was filled with an

## SCREEN KISSES • 419

unreasonable, unreasoning anger. Bitch, she thought. First you try to push me off a film, then you try to rubbish my reputation, now you steal my man.

If Claudia had been there in the flesh rather than just an image on a screen Rachel knew at that moment she would have murdered her. The sheer intensity of feeling sent a shudder through her. She would have sat there shaking all afternoon if her eye hadn't strayed to the clock. It was one o'clock—an hour and a half before the matinée. She grabbed her coat and made her way to the theatre.

Somehow she got through the performance, but the play didn't block out any of the pain. She was reminded of the time when she was rehearsing in New York. Once more she was the little mermaid treading on knives. The mermaid had had to sacrifice her tail to get what she wanted. Rachel had had to sacrifice her love.

The next few weeks went by in a kind of numbness. Every day she got up, ate her usual breakfast, went through the routine motions of her life. In the evenings she went to the theatre and gave a technically perfect performance—a performance without heart. It wasn't that she had lost the ability to feel. It was simply that she had turned her feelings off until it was safe to feel again.

Rachel came back to life a month after Claudia and Bob married. She read all the reports of it, listened to the news bulletins, watched the ceremony on television. Then when the event was behind her she consigned it to the past. She would never forget Bob but he belonged to yesterday. Today she needed to find a replacement, and she wasn't looking for just anybody. An out-of-work actor would no longer do, and neither would another Broadway player. What Rachel needed was a real man, a man of substance.

She met Teddy Hagerty at a party given in a private room at the 21 Club. As Broadway's newest star she was always being invited to parties, and every morning brought three or four new invitations. Wall Street brokers, Broadway producers, Washington wives all wanted her to grace their celebrations, and more often than not she flicked through the gold-embossed cards and dumped the lot in the dustbin. She had no need to make small talk with strangers. She knew enough people.

Then Bob got married and suddenly her life was empty. It didn't stay that way for long. Sometime during the last year she had forgotten that men found her beautiful. Rediscovering this fact gave her confidence. Then she met Teddy Hagerty.

It was not a formal introduction. In fact they weren't introduced at all. Rachel was standing surrounded by a cluster of people as usual when she saw him. He was easily the most attractive man in the room—tall and thin with ragged black hair and a face that looked as if it laughed a lot. As soon as she could, Rachel caught his eye and smiled. Then she looked away, went on with her conversation and expected him to join her group. When he didn't she was confused. She had given him a signal, hadn't she? It was the way things were done in this town. Why didn't

## SCREEN KISSES • 421

he respond? She decided to forget about him. There were more than enough suitors at this gathering. She already had dinner invitations from a senator and an advertising chief. There was no way she would have to go home alone tonight. Yet he bugged her. She didn't like being ignored.

She disentangled herself from the group she was with and made her way over to the window. Perhaps if she was on her own she would seem more approachable. She stood there for a good three minutes, then she looked into the crowd.

The man with the black hair was about a yard away from her, deep in conversation with a heavy blonde. He must have sensed she was nearby, for he looked up and stared at her. Then he smiled—a friendly open smile, followed by a shrug as he returned his attention to the blonde. By now she was furious. Every man in this room, every man in this town practically, was fighting for her attention. What on earth had gone wrong?

Suddenly she was bored with the party. She thought of taking up one of her dinner invitations, then she realized she wasn't in the mood for dinner. Time I went home, she told herself. Better that than settle for second best.

She threaded her way through the crowd, smiling and murmuring goodbyes, then she ran down the curving, red-carpeted staircase that led to the street. The doorman came towards her and asked if she wanted a taxi, but she shook her head. "It's a lovely night," she said. "I'll walk for a bit."

## 422 • TRUDI PACTER

"I wouldn't do that," said a voice behind her. "You'll risk your life on the streets at this hour."

She turned and saw the black-haired man standing behind her. "What business is that of yours?"

"None at all. I was just being friendly."

"Well, don't bother," she said and pushed her way through the heavy revolving door.

A long black limousine drew up in front of her and a man in red livery jumped out. "Miss Keller," he said, "I've been instructed to drive you home."

She turned round, expecting to see the man from the party behind her but he was gone.

"Who told you to do that?" she asked the chauffeur.

"Why, Mr Hagerty. You were talking with him just now."

She gave up and climbed into the back seat. "Sixty-second and Fifth," she said. Then she leaned back against the expensive leather upholstery and took stock of her surroundings. The car was bigger than she had first thought and furnished entirely in white kid. To one side of her was a telephone. By her fingertips was a bar and she noticed a bottle of champagne had been freshly opened. There was just one glass.

She leaned forward and opened the panel that connected her with the driver.

"Where is your Mr Hagerty?" she asked.

The chauffeur cleared his throat. "He sends his apologies but he had to go on to the Hamptons."

She closed the panel and peered through the

## SCREEN KISSES • 423

smoked-glass window. Curiouser and curiouser, she thought. I wonder what he'll do next.

The following morning she found out. At nine o'clock the flowers started to arrive. By eleven she was knee deep in red roses, arum lilies and mimosa. Each offering came with a plain white card bearing the signature Teddy Hagerty. He didn't send regards, or good wishes, and no reference was made to her silent chauffeur-driven ride home.

At midday the telephone rang. "Will you have lunch with me?" said a voice.

"Who is this?"

There was a chuckle at the other end of the line. "You know perfectly well who it is. Now will you have lunch with me or won't you?"

She took a deep breath. "Where did you have in mind?"

"The pool room at the Four Seasons."

"Too corny," she said.

"OK then, Lutèce."

"A bit elegant for a Tuesday."

"Right, in that case I'll take you to the Russian Tea Room. I'll see you there at one o'clock, or I won't see you at all." Then he put the phone down.

She smiled as she replaced the receiver. It wasn't a very original approach. It could easily have come straight out of the pages of a Victorian novel, but she was intrigued. In this tough, go-getting city, the last thing she expected was to be wooed. There was something endearing about it. She hoped the man lived up to his approach.

He did. Over blinis with sour cream and the best

## 424 • TRUDI PACTER

Beluga, she discovered Teddy Hagerty had an ability she had rarely come across in anyone. He could make her laugh. Seen through his eyes, quite ordinary events took on a new meaning, and she realized she had been taking both life and herself far too seriously.

She was half way through her second glass of ice-cold Stolichnaya when she remembered there was something she hadn't asked him. "How did your chauffeur know who I was? In fact how did he know to offer me a ride home?"

Teddy smiled at her over the rim of his glass. "I have a confession to make," he said. "The whole evening was a put-up job. I fell in love with you when I saw the play last Friday. After that it was a simple matter of tracking you down. I spread a little money around, called in a few favours, and in forty-eight hours I knew exactly where you'd be, when you'd be there, and what I needed to do about it. My chauffeur had been waiting around all evening to take you home."

She shook her head in disbelief. "What if I hadn't liked the look of you?"

He put his glass down and leaned towards her. "It didn't cross my mind," he said. "Women have always liked the look of me."

If anyone else had said it the statement would have sounded outrageous. Coming from Teddy Hagerty it seemed completely natural. Rachel realized why as she found out more about him.

Teddy Hagerty was born to be rich the way other people are born to serve, or to teach, or in Rachel's case to act. The Hagertys' fortunes stemmed from

## SCREEN KISSES • 425

land. They owned prairies in Canada and ranches in Argentina. When he was old enough Teddy was sent away to agricultural college where he learned to farm. After that he attended Harvard Business School where he learned to understand the money generated by his land.

Yet he didn't work. And this fact astounded Rachel. "You mean you don't do anything?" she said. "That's terrible."

He grinned. "What do you mean, terrible? Would it make you feel better if I herded cattle or tilled the prairies? Let me tell you something. Any one of the men I employ does those jobs better than I do. And because they've been raised on the land, they enjoy them better." He took her hand. "Rachel, I didn't grow up on a farm, I grew up in grand houses. I spent my childhood learning to play polo and ski and play tennis. I know about art and old furniture because my family own a lot of both. And I understand money for the same reasons."

She felt herself floundering. "But playing polo and spending money isn't doing anything," she protested.

She saw the beginnings of a smile gathering at the corners of his mouth, and despite herself she was entranced. It was such a good-humoured face, such a sunny face, that she couldn't stay cross with him for long.

"What do you know about playing?" he teased. "From what you've told me all you ever seem to have done is work. Well, I'm going to change all that, start-

## 426 • TRUDI PACTER

ing now. How do you feel about having lunch with me in Paris?"

It was her turn to smile. "You know I can't do that. I'm on stage every night."

"Not on Sunday you're not."

"But Paris is thousands of miles away. We'd never get there and back and have time to have lunch as well. It's just not possible."

"When you have a private plane anything's possible."

They flew to Paris on Saturday night. When the curtain came down Teddy's chauffeur picked her up from the stage door and ferried her out to La Guardia. She had barely enough time to change out of costume before she was hustled out of the theatre, and it bothered her. She was still in her stage make-up and she was conscious that she needed a shower. This was no way to travel, she told herself. I should have insisted on more time.

She needn't have worried. The plane had a fully equipped bathroom complete with a sunken tub and whirlpool Jacuzzi. It also had a bedroom with a double bed. As the plane took off, Rachel got to work on her face, then she had a long, luxurious bath. As she lay in the scented water she remembered that it took approximately eight hours to fly to Paris. They would arrive at midday after flying all night. Despite herself, she thought about the bedroom with the double bed, and for the second time since she met Teddy Hagerty she wondered what was going to happen next.

When she emerged into the cabin Teddy was

## SCREEN KISSES • 427

waiting for her by the bar. She noticed he was drinking a martini and she asked for the same. As he poured from a freshly made pitcher she took stock of the man. She had forgotten how good-looking he was. The skin was pale and stretched tight over high, almost Slavic cheekbones. His dark eyes matched his hair. She noticed how it just touched the top of his collar. As she looked at him the lemony smell of his expensive aftershave reached her.

She had expected him to be formally dressed, yet if anything he was just the opposite. He was wearing a turtle-neck sweater and blue jeans. If it wasn't for the cashmere jacket thrown over the top he could have been any young executive relaxing on a weekend, but the jacket set him apart and made him look rich. She was reminded of certain women she had met, who wore their minks slung over their shoulders like old raincoats. She knew that no matter how successful she became she would never be able to wear a fur like that, and she looked at Teddy with new interest.

He turned and handed her her drink. "Relax," he instructed. "After tonight's performance you've earned it."

Before she could reply, a waiter appeared and handed her a menu. More out of curiosity than hunger she cast her eyes over it. There was asparagus and *foie gras* and oysters out of season. Afterwards there was a choice of fresh salmon or game. She looked at the waiter, then she looked at Teddy. "You can't mean it," she said. "It's not real."

He laughed. "Why don't you put it to the test

and order something? Then you'll find out whether it's real or not."

They dined on oysters followed by roast pheasant. Each course was served with a different château-bottled wine. Just when Rachel thought she couldn't eat any more, the waiter came to the table and made crêpes Suzette—light, paper-thin and swimming in Grand Marnier. She didn't have the heart to refuse them. "You're spoiling me," she protested as he led her over to a leather sofa. On the table in front of it was a bottle of Armagnac and two blown glass brandy balloons.

"That's what you're here for," he said softly. "To be spoilt and fussed and made much of."

She started to protest. "But what about you?"

He smiled. "My turn comes later."

The vintage brandy made her head swim. That and the nearness of Teddy Hagerty. She fought down the urge to touch the smooth, pale cheeks, to bury her face in the blue-black hair. There were five hours to go until they reached Paris. She thought of the bedroom she had glimpsed while she was taking her bath, and she smiled. We have all night ahead of us, she thought, and I don't think either of us is planning to get much sleep.

At some time, she couldn't remember when, he got up and held his hand out to her. "Time we went next door," he said. Wordlessly she followed him through the cabin. They had to be flying over the Atlantic, she calculated. The thought of the ocean, black and stormy below them, and the sleek plane carrying them through the night made her heart beat faster.

## SCREEN KISSES • 429

She expected him to take her in his arms or to lead her over to the bed. He did neither. Instead he caught hold of her hand again and pulled her towards the pale wood closet that lined the whole of one wall.

"I'm going into the bathroom to get undressed," he told her. "It will give you time to change."

Before she could ask him what he meant he had crossed into the other room and closed the door behind him. Time to change, she puzzled. What did he mean? She opened the closet and took a look inside. What she saw took her breath away. She could have been in a theatrical costumier's, except the clothes that hung there were not meant for the kind of productions she played in. There was a French maid's outfit with fishnet stockings and a skirt that had no back to it. There were tart's clothes made out of black rubber, shoes with six-inch heels, and all the paraphernalia of bondage.

Her eyes went back to the bedroom. Teddy was standing in the doorway, wearing a black silk dressing gown. And for the first time since she met him she noticed he wasn't smiling.

Suddenly she felt cold. "Why?" she asked him. "Why me?"

His expression didn't change. "I would have thought that was perfectly obvious. You're an actress. You're good at impersonating other people. I assumed you'd enjoy a bit of dressing up."

Nobody is perfect, thought Claudia. Her hairdresser wasn't perfect, her dressmaker wasn't ideal, and none of her husbands had been easy—including the latest one.

When she had married Bob six months ago she thought he was everything she needed. Now she wasn't so sure. There was his habit of going to bed early. No matter where they were having dinner or whose party they were at, he was ready to go home on the stroke of ten-thirty. She knew he worked hard at the studio—he had to, to get up so early—and she had done her best to understand, but it didn't stop her feeling hard done by. After all, she spent all day making herself beautiful for him and organizing their busy social calendar. The least he could do was show some appreciation.

## SCREEN KISSES • 431

That was something else she didn't like—the fact that he took so much for granted. How much, she wondered, did he think it cost to maintain this lifestyle of theirs? The bill for the flowers, servants, parties, and Rolls came to more than he could earn in a week. Then there were her clothes. Top designers didn't come cheap, not if you wanted the best. And Claudia always had the best. It was her due.

For a while the mounting overheads worried her. Now she wasn't working she couldn't be expected to pay for everything. And Bob couldn't keep her. Unless . . .

Two months after she married him Claudia decided her new husband should change his job. As soon as she knew what had to be done, she went into action. First she lunched with the head man at Fox, then she visited all the other studio heads who owed her favours. Finally something so obvious happened she wondered why she hadn't thought of it before. Dan Keyser took her to one side at a brunch and asked her if Bob would be interested in becoming a senior vice-president at Magnum. Apparently he'd heard on the grapevine that Bob was looking for a move, and he had a job going at a salary that would suit them both perfectly.

She almost jumped out of her skin with joy. Wait till we get home, she thought. Do I have a surprise. But Bob hadn't been overwhelmed like she thought he would be. In fact, he'd been downright difficult. "What do you mean, go to work for Magnum?" he had said. "I don't want to work for a studio. I don't

## 432 • TRUDI PACTER

want to work for anyone except myself. I thought you knew that."

"But think of the money," she protested. "It would make everything so much easier."

He looked confused. "But we're not hard up, are we? You never told me we couldn't manage."

Then she had explained the facts of life—the flower bills, the maintenance of the house, the Rolls with the chauffeur, the prices of Paris couture . . .

At first he had been astounded. Then he asked to see her accountant and she started to breathe easy again. Once Bob knew how much he was costing her he was bound to see sense. Only he didn't. What he expected her to do was to give up the house and go and live somewhere cheaper. "I'd no idea living the way we did cost us so much," he had said. "We'll have to make changes."

She tried telling him that wasn't necessary. She liked living this way. She was used to it. There was only one change that had to be made. Bob would have to go and work for Dan Keyser.

When he wouldn't hear of it she threw a tantrum. It had no effect, so she decided to ignore him for a few days. That didn't work either. So in the end she had moved out and gone to stay at the Beverly Hills. A gesture like that was bound to bring him running. It did. He was round at the hotel to drag her back home within hours of her leaving. Then he had made love to her. Passionate, and delicious. But still he didn't change his mind. He was not on any account going to work for Dan Keyser.

So they compromised. She fired the servants, sold

## SCREEN KISSES • 433

the Rolls and cut down on the parties, and he handed over whatever he earned every month. It was up to Claudia to make ends meet as best she could. It wasn't perfect, but she'd live with it for now. *Marooned* was due to open before Christmas, and with any luck the film would make them both a lot of money.

The sound of voices in the hall jolted her out of her reverie. She looked at her watch. It was nearly six. Bob was home early for a change.

She smiled as her husband came into the room. "Let me make you a drink," she said. "We've just got time for a quick one before I get changed."

There was a question in his eyes. "What the hell are you changing for? You look terrific the way you are."

She put a hand to her mouth. "You don't mean to tell me you've forgotten. We're having dinner with Marvin and Joanna tonight. They booked the Polo Lounge specially."

"How many people are there going to be?"

She paused, mentally counting. "I'd say around a dozen. Why do you ask?"

"Because if it's all the same to you I'd like to cry off tonight. I've had a bitch of a day. All I feel like doing right now is putting my feet up and spending a quiet evening at home."

She pouted. "Darling, do you have to be so *bor*ing?"

He fought down a feeling of irritation. There was something about the way she said *bor*ing in that spoilt-little-girl voice of hers that made him want to hit her. "Give me a break, Claudia. Can't you see I'm tired?"

But she wasn't listening. Instead she started on a litany of complaint about her day. Her new car had broken down and she had been late for her lunch with Carla Keyser, so Spago had given away her favourite table. And when she got home she discovered the dressmaker had made a botch of the evening gown he was making her.

He smiled pleasantly. "Well, that's not a problem any more, is it? We're not going to the Polo Lounge tonight. So there's no need to rack your brains figuring out what to wear."

She screwed her face up in a frown. Christ, she looks old when she does that, he thought, and he sighed. From the moment he had met Claudia she had been full of surprises. Her intelligence was something he hadn't expected. Her agility in bed was a revelation. But there were other things he learned about her too, later on, when they were married and it was too late to reconsider.

He had had no idea she was so untidy—almost sluttish. Before, when they had had servants, he hadn't noticed. But since they had been living on a budget, the washing-up piled up in the sink and the mess in the bathroom had grated on his nerves. Despite himself he compared her to Rachel. She had always managed to keep the place tidy. And she cooked, which was more than Claudia ever did. What was the matter with her?

He asked himself the same question the first time he saw Claudia without make-up. Without the blusher, lip gloss and heavy eyeliner she always wore, she looked like a different person. Rachel without her

## SCREEN KISSES • 435

paint looked like a little girl—vulnerable and a bit
sporty. Claudia simply looked old. With a start he realized she was in her late thirties, and all the expensive
plastic surgery in the world couldn't hide that fact. She
could have her skin tightened and her eyes lifted a
thousand times, but in the bright sunlight Claudia
Graham looked her age.

She saw him looking at her and stopped frown-
ing. "If you really mean to stay home tonight I'd better get on the phone to Joanna and tell her."

She got up and made her way towards the door.
He put his hand out and stopped her. "Look, I don't
want to spoil your fun," he said. "Why don't you go
without me? I'm only going to watch TV and turn in
early, and I don't need you around to hold my hand
while I do that."

She looked down at him. "Are you sure?" she
said doubtfully.

"Sure I'm sure," he said. "You can tell your
friends I'm ill or something. They'll understand."

She threw her arms round his neck. "You're so
good to me," she breathed. Then she hurried through
to the bedroom to start getting ready.

Bob knew from experience it would take her at
least an hour to fix herself up, and when she did she'd
look just like the movie queen he'd married. He
leaned back in his chair and felt an intense weariness.
At least, he consoled himself, she kept her word about
tearing up her Actors' Guild card. I don't have to live
with an actress who puts her career before me, he
thought. But even as the notion went through his
mind, he wondered if it really mattered what she did.

## 436 • TRUDI PACTER

\* \* \*

The cable was waiting for her when she got to the theatre. It came in a buff brown envelope with Western Union stamped all over it. The message inside was terse and to the point.

CALL ME SOONEST RE OSCAR NOMINATIONS.

DAN.

She had opened it when she got to her dressing room, and now she felt hot and slightly giddy. Had *Marooned* been nominated? Or was it one of the actors?

She had seen the ads in *Variety* over the New Year. They had beseeched the members of the American Academy to vote for *Marooned,* and because Dan Keyser was heading the studio, there was nothing tasteful about the full pages in the trades. Instead Magnum was touting for nominations in every category from best director to best supporting actress. Christ, she thought, I wonder if it's me that's been nominated?

The prospect of returning to Los Angeles for the awards ceremony stirred up emotions she thought she had put behind her. She was bound to run into Bob again. Bob and Claudia. And she could do without that. But an Academy Award nomination . . . Could I do without that? she wondered.

She looked at her watch. It was four o'clock in New York, which made it one on the coast. Time I put myself out of my misery, she thought.

## SCREEN KISSES • 437

Five minutes after she placed the call, Dan was on the line. "Hello, stranger," he greeted her. "Long time, no hear. How are things in the Big Apple?"

She didn't waste time on small talk. "Who is it?" she demanded. "Which one of us has got the nomination?"

There was a short silence, then Keyser spoke. "Calm down, Rachel," he said. "One of you hasn't got a nomination. Three of you have. Rick's up for best director. Claudia's on the line for best actress. And you're in for best supporting actress. Congratulations. I'm very proud of you."

She should have seen it coming. From day one *Marooned* had been a box-office smash. The critics raved about it, and the paying customers stood in line round the block to see it. But three nominations—in any year that was good going.

"That's fantastic news," she said. "You must be very pleased."

"Pleased? I'm over the moon. Just one award will send our takings through the roof, and we're not doing badly as it is. But enough about me. The whole world knows how I feel about this film. What about you, Rachel? How does it feel to be a star?"

She laughed. "I'm not a star," she said. "At least not outside of Broadway. I doubt if anyone in tinsel town can even remember my name."

"When you win the nomination they'll know who you are. You can depend on that."

"What makes you so sure I'm going to get it? I'm an unknown quantity on film. I'll bet you any one of

## 438 • TRUDI PACTER

the other actresses in my category is a bigger name than me."

It was Keyser's turn to laugh, and the chuckle boomed into her ear all the way from the West Coast. "I'll tell you what makes me so sure," he said. "The buzz, the grapevine. Everyone in this town is talking about you—producers, agents, directors. To them you're the big new excitement, the unknown who comes in from nowhere and conquers the world. Rachel, you've got it made."

She didn't know what to feel. She was flattered, of course she was flattered. She was enough of an actress for that. But she was also a woman, and that part of her flinched from this new-found fame. What was it that Bob had said when they parted? "Wait till the newspapers start printing your name across the top of three columns. Wait till you get asked on Johnny Carson. Then you might find the world starts looking different."

She shuddered. She hadn't wanted a different world from the one she had. "I suppose you'll want me to come in for the awards ceremony," she said dully.

"You bet that's what I want. Why, is there any problem with that?"

She sighed and put Bob out of her mind. "Not that I can think of. Though I don't know if I can manage more than a flying visit. The theatre won't want to make do with my understudy for longer than one night."

"One night is all I ask of you. Incidentally, are you involved with anyone special at the moment?"

## SCREEN KISSES • 439

What business is that of yours? she thought. Aloud she said, "Why do you ask?"

"Simple. You're going to need an escort. You won't want to brave the line-up on your own. Not with all the TV and press around. So is there anyone you want to bring? Anyone you're fond of?"

She thought about her suitors. And despite herself she smiled. There was an English lord who cared more about the opera than he did about her; a senator who was hooked on the gambling palaces of Nevada; and there was Teddy Hagerty . . .

"No," she said firmly, "there's no one I'm fond of. But I can bring Desmond French if it makes life easier."

She thought she heard a sigh of relief on the other end of the line. "There's no need to do that. David Price is coming into town without Darleen. Apparently the marriage is going through a rough patch. Anyway, to cut a long story short, I don't want him showing up with some doxy on his arm. If you were on your own it would solve my problems to team you both up for the evening."

"Consider your problems solved. I'll look forward to seeing David again. It's been a long time."

She put the phone down and thought some more about Bob Delaney. He'd be there, of course. They both would be. She set her chin. I'm a big girl now, she told herself. And a fine actress. I can convince any man I don't give a damn. Even that louse.

Claudia peered at the traffic through the back window of her camper. Outside on the broad boulevard the

## 440 • TRUDI PACTER

cars were four lanes deep and touching bumpers. All the drivers were banging on their horns, and from where she was sitting the noise was deafening.

Only half an hour to go, she told herself. Only half an hour and then it starts. For the hundredth time that afternoon she checked the view from the other window. Then she leaned back, satisfied with what she saw. From where Claudia was parked, in the forecourt of the Astra Cinema, she got an uninterrupted view of everyone arriving for the Academy Awards. In the next thirty minutes she would be certain to know exactly what Liz Taylor, Barbra Streisand, Vanessa Redgrave, Diane Keaton, and Rachel Keller were wearing. Then she could go into action.

Her eyes swept over the dress rail that took up the entire length of the air-conditioned trailer. Hanging on it were four drop-dead outfits—the violet taffeta from St Laurent, the figure-hugging beaded number from Calvin Klein, the see-through chiffon from Romano Gigli, and the safe little black Dior. When she was quite certain what the competition was up to, and only then, she would decide which of the four outfits she would wear for the awards ceremony. This year she knew without a shadow of a doubt that she would win the best actress category. And when she went up to receive her Oscar she wanted her photograph to be on the front page of every newspaper in the world, which is why she had hired the camper.

Right from the start Bob had been against it. "What do you want to pull a bizarre stunt like that for?" he had asked. "Somebody's bound to get hold

## SCREEN KISSES • 441

of the story, and then you'll make both of us look like fools."

But she was adamant. "This is the last film I'll ever make," she said. "I want to go out in glory. I want my picture on all those front pages."

"If you win an Oscar," he protested, "you'll get it. You don't have to go through all this. You don't have to spy on all the other women in town to make your mark."

She stood her ground. "That's where you're wrong. If Barbra or Liz is wearing something awe-inspiring, then I'm dead. I could win the top award of the year and Barbra or Liz's picture would still make page one. The only way to come out ahead in this circus is to have advance knowledge."

There was no reasoning with her, and after two weeks of bitter argument he had reluctantly gone along with her plans. He would collect her from the camper five minutes before the ceremony started. He just hoped it was all worth it.

Claudia checked her watch. It was four-fifteen. Fifteen minutes to go before the off. Her heart started to thud in her chest. For some reason this year everyone was playing safe. Liza Minnelli had kept the frills to a minimum and even Liz Taylor was opting for a tailored, East Coast look. But what finally decided her was Rachel Keller. The British bitch seemed to have set her heart on attracting attention. First she arrived with David Price, when everyone in town knew his marriage was in trouble. Then she staked her claim on tomorrow's headlines by coming dressed like a man. Claudia marvelled at her cheek. She was wearing

## 442 • TRUDI PACTER

a perfectly tailored tuxedo that looked like it came straight from Dougie Hayward, and instead of looking butch or ridiculous she looked somehow right— as if it was a normal, everyday occurrence to turn up at Hollywood's most prestigious event looking like a male impersonator. Except she didn't. Her indecently red lipstick and all that hair left no one in any doubt whatever that Rachel was all woman.

Well, she hadn't cornered the market in sex. Not while Claudia was around. Her eyes flicked over the dress rail one last time, then she let her instincts make the choice. If everyone was playing it down that year, then she could do just one thing—put on the Ritz. The sheer black chiffon dress from Gigli with its clever beading in the right places had to be the one to go for.

She dressed swiftly, with the skill of a professional. The diamanté earrings and the long black gloves were laid out and ready on the counter in front of her. The high, glittering sandals were standing in line with her other evening shoes. It took her just five minutes to get out of her robe and into the regalia of a sex goddess. Before she left the trailer she took one last look at herself in the full-length mirror. The outline of her body was clearly visible through the filmy fabric. Only the beading at her breasts and across her hips stood between her and indecency. She turned and looked at herself in profile, then she nodded her satisfaction. The strict diet she followed had its rewards. Her stomach was as flat as it had been when she was in her twenties. No one out there could possibly guess her true age, not even her husband.

## SCREEN KISSES • 443

She grabbed her bag and stepped out of the camper. What happened now was a matter of time and chance, but of one thing she was certain. In this dress she was ahead of the game.

David Price pushed Rachel into the lobby of the Astra. They had had a tough time getting there. The press hadn't left them alone all evening.

"Is it true about you and David?" someone had asked her. "Are you the mystery woman behind the break-up?"

If Dan hadn't warned her there was trouble between David and Darleen she would have been thrown. As it was, she kept her face blank and said nothing.

Once they were inside she turned to the tall Australian and got a proper look at him. To her surprise, he had filled out since their days together on Bali. Rachel remembered the man as unhappy and rather neurotic. Today, if he had troubles he bore no trace of them. His hair was bleached nearly white by the sun, he was tanned and fit, and there was warmth in his smile. If she hadn't known he was an actor she would have been taken in.

They made their way through the lobby, stopping at a bar that had been set up for the evening. "I know it's early," said David, "but would you like a drink before we go in?"

She nodded, and when he handed her a glass of champagne she looked grateful. The wine gave her courage, and she asked the question that had been

## 444 • TRUDI PACTER

bugging her since she arrived. "What's all this about you and Darleen splitting up? Surely it can't be true?"

For a moment the Australian's expression shifted and Rachel caught a glimpse of the man she had known on Bali. Neurotic and haunted.

"It's true," he admitted, "but there's nobody else involved. Darleen brought this divorce on herself."

"I don't understand."

He took her arm and steered her into a corner. All around them senior members of the movie industry were being hustled by agents, independent producers, talent scouts. Price was unaffected by the scene. He had more important things on his mind. "Did you know my wife was trying to poison me?" he asked Rachel.

She was astounded. "You're making it up. I thought you and Darleen had one of the best marriages in the business."

He looked sour. "So did I. But it seems I was mistaken. The whole business came out into the open when we were finishing *Marooned*. One of the maids at the hotel filled me in. Darleen had taken against the girl and tried to get her fired. It was the stupidest thing she ever did. That maid had seen my wife preparing my meals and she knew a thing or two about her."

Rachel was intrigued. "Like what?"

"Like the fact that she regularly added rum to my fruit drinks when she knows alcohol gives me a screaming migraine. But it gets worse. You remember the trouble I had with enteritis on Bali?"

Rachel nodded.

"Well, that was a little gift from my dear wife as

## SCREEN KISSES • 445

well. Apparently she put local water into my drinking jug instead of bottled water. And you know how lethal that was."

Rachel took a gulp of her champagne. "But why would Darleen want to do that? It can't have been much fun having a sick husband on her hands."

"It was a damn sight more fun than having an unfaithful one around. She suspected that if I was alive and well I would have been chasing around after Claudia. She actually admitted that when I confronted her with the facts."

The crowds were starting to leave the foyer. Fluffy starlets, nervous actors, well-fed men in dinner jackets all started to pour into the auditorium. As they made their way to their seats, Rachel turned to her companion. "Tell me," she said, "would you have gone after Claudia if you'd been feeling better?"

He smiled, showing his best side. "You bet I would," he said.

They got to their seats and Rachel looked around her. They were five rows from the back with a clear view of the stage. So far so good. She wondered what would happen next. Would she win an Oscar, or would it be somebody else's turn this year? Mentally she ran through the list of nominees, but even as she did so her mind was straying. Damn you, Rick Hamilton, she cursed. If you hadn't called this afternoon I could have concentrated better. She had picked up a message from him when she arrived at the Beverly Wilshire. He had called to invite her to lunch the following day and when she rang back and told him she was going back to New York in the morning he was

## 446 • TRUDI PACTER

disappointed. "Don't the theatre management give you any time off?" he complained.

"Not really," she laughed. "Anyway it's probably for the best. The longer I stay in Los Angeles, the more likely I am to bump into Claudia and Bob."

There was a chuckle at the other end of the line. "I wouldn't worry about those two," he said. "They're not exactly billing and cooing nowadays."

"What do you mean by that?"

"What I say. Claudia's marriage to Bob is no different from her marriage to her other five husbands. A complete shambles. I wouldn't be surprised if they called it quits any moment now. They can't go on fighting in public."

For the rest of the day Rick's words kept coming back to her. The marriage was a shambles . . . wouldn't be surprised if they called it quits. So Bob was going to be free again. The knowledge troubled her.

David Price brought her back to the present. "Rachel, look behind you, for Christ's sake. You'll never guess who just arrived."

She swivelled round in her seat and realized that the rest of the guests in the auditorium were doing the same thing. Claudia Graham had just made the biggest entrance of her life.

At first glance the actress seemed to be wearing very little. Her gown, if you could call it that, was virtually transparent, and the emphasis was all on her body. Rachel marvelled at the juxtaposition of jutting breasts and narrow waist. Rick must have been dreaming, she thought. Claudia does not look like a woman who is about to lose her husband.

## SCREEN KISSES • 447

The actress was trailing quite an entourage, including Dan and Carla Keyser, and Shirley MacLaine. Rachel was going to ask David who he was when she caught sight of Bob.

He was lagging behind the rest of the party, and he looked uncomfortable, as if he didn't belong—or didn't want to. Without meaning to, she smiled, and it was then he caught her eye.

She summoned up every ounce of will to break the stare, but it was impossible. He held her more surely than if he had come down the gangway and taken her in his arms. She knew then that nothing had changed.

They might have gone on looking at each other all evening if it hadn't been for David Price tugging at her sleeve. "Watch out," he warned. "If Claudia catches you making eyes at her husband, she'll murder you."

Rachel changed position and rearranged her face. So what I heard this morning is true, she thought. The marriage *is* in trouble.

Claudia had a ringside seat, Magnum had seen to that. From where she was sitting everyone would have an uninterrupted view of her dress—the hosts, the award winners, the TV cameras. She focused her attention on the stage. The opening cabaret was winding to a close and Warren Beatty was walking down to the podium to present the award for the best director. She tuned out. Best directors didn't interest her. Not tonight. There were only two awards she cared about

## 448 • TRUDI PACTER

in the next hour—best actress and best supporting actress.

As Beatty read out this year's winner, she heard a groan from Bob sitting beside her. "Bad luck," he muttered. "Maybe next year." So Rick hadn't got lucky after all. She didn't feel sorry. *Marooned* might not have landed the best director award, but at least it left the way clear for best actress.

The minutes ticked away slowly. During what seemed like an eternity William Goldman presented the awards for the best original screenplay and the best adapted screenplay. Milos Forman gave out the gong for the best foreign language film and Steven Spielberg announced the winner of the best film. Then she saw Barbra Streisand striding up to the podium and she knew her turn had come.

There were four of them shortlisted for the Oscar—Jacqueline Bisset, Liza Minnelli, Kate Carter and her. Automatically Claudia discounted Kate Carter. The girl had been around for four or five years at best. Her latest film had been a smash but Carter hadn't been on the scene long enough for it to mean anything. Of the other two she felt less sure. They were comers, both of them, but neither had a track record like hers. In the end that was what decided the committee—solid, box-office hits.

Clips from all four women's starring vehicles started to flash on to the screen. Claudia leaned forward as she recognized herself. The judges had chosen some footage of the beach scene and Claudia was thankful. The beach scenes didn't show her in close-

# SCREEN KISSES • 449

up. There was no chance of the tell-tale scars giving her away.

She had seen the film a hundred times before. If asked she could recall every frame of it, yet she was still critical of herself. It was a good performance, there was no doubt of that. But if only Rick had given her a bit more time, a bit longer on camera, she could have improved—even on perfection.

There was applause as the clip came to an end, and Claudia felt reassured. They liked me, she thought. Better than that, they loved me. It's nearly in the bag.

Everything went very still as Barbra Streisand came back to the podium to announce the result. The names were read back to front with the winner coming last. Barbra announced the first name—Jacqueline Bisset. All her supporters, including her studio chief, looked stricken. Then came the second name, Liza Minnelli. Claudia felt her skin prickle. There were two more names to go. Please, God, she thought, don't let mine be next. Barbra looked down at her script. Then she straightened up and looked at the audience. Claudia Graham.

She hardly had time to register her disappointment before the next name came up—the Oscar winner.

"It gives me great pleasure to announce that the winner of this year's Academy Award is . . . Kate Carter."

Claudia heard herself yelling from somewhere far off. "It's a mistake. It's gotta be a mistake. The woman's a dog."

## 450 • TRUDI PACTER

Bob put an arm round her shoulder and pulled her close. "Be quiet," he muttered savagely. "Can't you see everyone's looking at you?"

She swallowed hard. Her face was on fire, and at the back of her throat she could taste the disappointment.

After all this, she thought. After all this hoping and praying and spending money on publicity the prize has to go to Miss Nobody From Nowhere. Kate Carter had made two films, just two films. I've made twenty, thought Claudia, yet she gets to walk off with the prize. It's not fair. She was tempted to cry, then she reconsidered. The dress was still a stunner, and she still had a body worth showing off in it. So all right, she didn't walk off with an Oscar, but when she crossed the foyer on her way out she still had a chance of making some of those front pages.

The rest of the evening passed in a blur. She noted with not very much interest that Dustin Hoffman walked off with best actor, Gene Hackman, best supporting actor, and *Annie Hall* best picture.

Then Mia Farrow came up to announce best supporting actress and Claudia caught her breath. There were five names on the list this time. Rachel Keller had four chances to lose it. She blew them all.

Mia Farrow cleared her throat and smiled at the audience. "I have great pleasure in announcing that Rachel Keller, a newcomer to the screen, has won this year's best supporting actress."

Rachel got up slowly, shaking back the great curtain of red-gold hair. Then, looking tall and thin and terribly alone, she walked up to where Mia Farrow

## SCREEN KISSES • 451

was standing. The two actresses embraced then Farrow stood back, leaving Rachel on her own to address the audience. From where Claudia was sitting she could see the girl shaking, but she felt no sympathy. "Bloody newcomers," she muttered. "What is this love affair Hollywood's having with newcomers?"

On both sides people shushed her as Rachel stammered out her thanks. Claudia shot a glance at Bob and wished she hadn't. Admiration was written all over his face, and there was something else too. If she hadn't known him so well she would have said it was worship, but it couldn't be. It was she he loved, not some skinny, flat-chested English girl.

For no reason at all she felt herself starting to cry. Hot tears welled up in her eyes and came streaming down perfectly powdered cheeks. Bob looked at her anxiously. "What's the matter?" he said. "Rachel's on our side. She won it for us."

"What do you mean she won it for us?" Claudia snapped. "She won it for herself and she won it for the film. What's that got to do with us?"

"If you recall," he said acidly, "I'm on five per cent of *Marooned*'s profits. With Rachel's award pushing them up, that's a lot of housekeeping in anybody's language."

Claudia pulled a face. "Then why don't you go running over to your girlfriend and congratulate her? You know you've been dying to kiss her ass ever since we got here."

There was a pause. Then Bob said: "That's not such a bad idea. When all this is over, I might just do that."

## 452 • TRUDI PACTER

"Don't push me," Claudia said, "or . . ."

"Or what?"

"Or I'll turn round and walk right out of here."

Bob smiled. Then he stood up and made way for his wife. "Be my guest," he said.

Swifty's party was in full swing when Rachel got to Spago. Every year the Hollywood agent hired the restaurant for a party after the awards, and every year people killed for an invitation. Rachel had never met the man, but tonight that wasn't a problem. Tonight she was an Oscar winner and the whole world wanted to meet her. The world and Swifty Lazar.

Dan Keyser, a grateful, gushing Dan Keyser, had supervised their exit from the Astra and they had been mobbed. Rachel had arrived anxious about seeing Bob and self-conscious about being on David Price's arm. She needn't have worried. As far as the crowds and the cameras were concerned she could have been with King Kong and nobody would have taken a blind bit of notice. And Bob? Bob didn't worry her any more. I'll find my way back to you, she thought. I don't have any other place to go. But I'll do it when I'm ready. And on my own terms.

She had never seen Spago so full, or so festive. Every famous face she could remember and some she couldn't crowded in on her, offering congratulations. Wherever she turned someone was opening another bottle of champagne. It reminded her of a first night— or a birthday party. And she was glad she had come. She turned to David who hovered somewhere around her elbow. "Tell me," she asked, "who is the gorgeous blonde with Milton Harrison? I have a feeling I should know her."

The Australian raised an eyebrow. "I hoped you weren't going to ask that."

They were standing by the big picture window at the far end of the restaurant. Below them was the sweep of valley that was Hollywood. Rachel drank in the view, marvelling that tonight she had become part of the landscape.

"Still thinking about the blonde?" asked David.

She turned to him. "Not really. Though you might tell me who she is."

"No problem. It's Giselle Pascal. I believe you and she had something of a run-in a couple of years ago."

Rachel smiled. "You could say that. The bitch only tried to walk off with my part in *Marooned*. If it hadn't been for Bob she might have succeeded."

"Did I hear someone taking my name in vain?"

He appeared as if out of nowhere. And he looked so relaxed, so completely at one with his surroundings, the three of them might have been having a drink after the day's filming. He was over the moon about Rachel's Oscar and told her so. Then he went on to talk about the way Keyser had taken it. "Anyone would think you were his invention the way he goes on about you. I'm having a hard time keeping the truth to myself."

Rachel looked over the room to Giselle, who was wearing close-fitting white jersey and real diamonds. "How about her?"

Bob laughed. "I wouldn't worry about Giselle if

## 454 • TRUDI PACTER

I were you. It's all over between her and Dan. Right now she'll be keeping quiet about the whole drama."

David looked curious. "How long has she known Harrison?"

"About twelve years . . ."

Their voices faded into the background as Rachel's eyes moved around the room. They darted over plates piled high with smoked salmon, crudités and little bouchées. They took in clouds of coloured balloons, groups of dark-suited men, and flamboyantly dressed women. But the person Rachel was looking for was nowhere to be seen. Where has she got to? she wondered. It's not like Claudia to miss a party like this.

Bob cut into her thoughts. "I seem to have lost your attention."

"Not really. I was just wondering where Claudia was."

He looked uncomfortable. "She wasn't feeling too well, so she went home ahead of me."

He saw the question in her eyes and made a wry face. "Actually we had a falling out."

He had laid himself wide open and she couldn't resist a dig. "Has something gone wrong in paradise?" she asked.

He started to look annoyed. "Leave it alone, Rachel."

"Why should I?"

"Because it's nothing to do with you."

She gave him her sweetest smile. "On the contrary, it's everything to do with me."

His eyes darkened and she noticed hard lines

## SCREEN KISSES • 455

around his mouth she hadn't seen before. "Let it go, will you? Claudia's sitting at home because she started to give me hell and I wasn't taking it. If I'm not taking it from her, I'm certainly not taking it from you."

She felt anger bubble up inside her. "Maybe hell is what you deserve," she said very quietly.

"What I deserve," he replied with the same lethal calm, "is consideration and understanding."

She pulled herself up to her full height and took a step backwards. "Tell me," she asked, "what have you done to earn this consideration you talk about? You breeze in and out of my life making promises you can't keep. You get married on a whim and wonder why it isn't working out."

"Who said it isn't working out?"

"I said it isn't working out. The town says it isn't working out. You don't live in the most discreet place in the world. And you didn't marry the quietest woman."

"You're very bitter, aren't you?"

"You bet I'm bitter. Do you have any idea what you put me through?"

He smiled without warmth. "Darling, you've made a marvellous recovery. I hear Teddy Hagerty's a very attentive escort. And if you get bored with him, I'd give money the obliging Richard Roberts is waiting around in the wings."

She looked at him sadly. "Poor little Richard Roberts. What did he ever do, except be there when I needed him? Which is more than I can say for you. How dare you listen to my private conversations then walk away when you didn't like what you overheard?

## 456 • TRUDI PACTER

What business was it of yours what I did on the long, dark nights without you? I was alone, remember. Alone and scared. You can't just turn up when you feel like it and say, 'Delete the last few months of your life. Pretend they didn't happen.' They did happen. I wanted them to happen."

There was dead silence between them, and for a moment she thought he was going to hit her. Then Dan Keyser was at her elbow, all smiles and congratulations. "So how does it feel to be a star?" he asked. "I hear Albert Levinson over at Fox is already talking about a vehicle for you."

She was disoriented. "I had no idea," she said. "Surely it's a bit soon."

He grinned and patted her arm. "Movies are a fast business. A yesterday business. You're hot now. Grab hold of it. You never know how long it's going to last."

He looked at Bob. "You were saying something to the lady. I hope I didn't break anything up."

"Nothing that wasn't broken up a long time ago."

Rachel passed a hand over her eyes. "I'm sorry, I'm done in. Would you two gentlemen excuse me if I called it a night?"

Bob came towards her. "I'll take you home," he said quietly. "Where are you staying?"

She told him the Beverly Wilshire, and allowed him to lead her into one of the Magnum limousines waiting outside the restaurant.

She was silent on the ride back. All her rage had been spent, and now she felt empty, winded. The next

## SCREEN KISSES • 457

move, if there was a next move, had to come from Bob.

When they arrived at the hotel Bob walked her to the foyer. Then after she collected her key he stood and looked at her for a very long time. She had seen him angry before, and she had seen him troubled, but never in her life had she seen him so utterly wretched. His sleek black hair was ruffled and dishevelled, and she noticed a muscle moving in spasm under one eye.

"I think we could both do with a drink," she said gently. "It's only ten-thirty. Why don't you come up?"

He took her arm and they walked into the elevator. There was no strain between them. They were two old friends tired from a long journey, wondering where the road would lead them next.

She let him into the long, low living room of her suite. Out of habit Bob crossed to the bar and poured out a glass of wine for her and a bourbon for himself. Then he took the drinks over to where she was sitting and set them down. "What do you want?" he asked her. "What do you really want?"

Suddenly there was no more fight in her. She looked up at him. "You," she said.

He came and sat beside her on the long white sofa, then he drew her close and kissed her. They kissed for a long time, silently rediscovering each other. She tasted his taste and smelled his familiar smell. Once more she started to lose herself in his warmth.

When they finally pulled apart her heart was beating in her ears and there was no need for any more words. He stood up and led her through to the bed-

## 458 • TRUDI PACTER

room. Then gently, with increasing urgency, he started to undress her.

"What about you?" she said, and started to loosen his tie. But he smiled and stopped her. "Let me," he said.

She stifled his words with her kisses. Then they lay down together and lost themselves in each other.

She had forgotten what it was like to love. And now, as the emotion came back to her, she abandoned herself to it. She let down her hair and wrapped him in it. She curled her legs around his body. And finally she drew him into her. As she did so there was such passion, such heat, that the years between them were wiped away.

When it was over, they slept as they had always slept. In each other's arms.

She woke to find him looking into her face. "What is it?" she asked.

"I love you and I want to marry you."

She held him close. "What about Claudia?"

"Claudia and I were finished a long time ago. Though I don't think she's going to like saying good-bye."

She peered at him, wrinkling her brow. "Why?"

"To know the answer to that, you have to know Claudia." He sat up and lit a cigarette. "She didn't marry me because she loved me, you know. That would have been too straightforward. She married me because she wanted to possess me. The way you possess a Dior dress or a house with a swimming pool. Only more than that. I was Claudia's prize possession

## SCREEN KISSES • 459

and I didn't even know it until I'd lived with her for some time."

"How did you find out?"

"Gradually. It was the little things that gave her away. After some time I noticed she wasn't really all that interested in me. Oh, she listened to what I had to say, but she didn't take it in. What was on her mind the whole time was Claudia Graham. How Claudia looked, how Claudia felt, what Claudia wanted. It was like being a one-man audience to a show that never stopped.

"As long as I was there in the background things were fine. But if I expressed any wants or needs of my own then she turned off."

Rachel grinned. "I heard there were some pretty spectacular fights."

He ran his hand along the length of his jaw. "Not half as spectacular as the one she's going to give me tonight when I call it quits. But I don't really care any more. If I thought I was breaking her heart that would be different. But I'm not. I'm just denting her vanity. She'll find herself another husband soon enough. She always does."

He got up and ordered breakfast for both of them. Then he took a shower. "What time are you getting out of here?" he asked.

"Sometime this afternoon. Why?"

"Because I'll be back before then. I'd like you to wait for me."

She smiled. "Of course I'll wait for you. What are you going to do?"

## 460 • TRUDI PACTER

He looked surprised. "Pack a case and leave home. What do you think I'm going to do?"

She stood looking at the door a long time after he had left. Then slowly she started piling her things into a suitcase. Where will we live? she wondered. Here or New York?

She realized she was going to have to decide whether or not to go on with the play. But as the thought passed through her mind, she remembered she was no longer free to make that decision. If she went back to Bob, became his wife, then her career was finished.

She remembered his face the first time he had walked out of her life. How hard it was, how uncompromising. "I don't want to share you with the paying customers," he said. "I'm not standing in line with a cinema audience, your agent, your lawyer."

Oh Christ, she thought. That audience, those paying customers are part of me. Part of my reason for going on. Without the theatre I'm grounded.

At a stroke, all the loneliness and pain she thought she had left behind her came rushing back. So it wasn't as easy as it seemed after all. They couldn't take up where they had left off. No matter what their bodies told them.

She wondered why they hadn't talked about the theatre the night before. Then she smiled sadly. Hadn't I done enough shouting? she thought. We didn't have to quarrel about the theatre as well.

Part of her, the sane part of her, realized it could never work. Claudia Graham had been a red herring.

## SCREEN KISSES • 461

It wasn't another woman that had come between them—not entirely. The profession had done the damage. The theatre.

She finished her packing in a kind of dream, then she called the airport and booked an earlier plane. She glanced at her watch. It was eleven-thirty. If she hurried she could be out of the hotel before noon. She'd have left town before Bob got back.

She walked through to her living room and went straight over to the bleached pine desk. Then she rummaged through the drawers and found a sheet of paper and an envelope.

Dear Bob [she wrote] By the time you read this I'll be on my way to New York. Don't follow me. There's no point. I found out a long time ago I can't live without the stage. So I'm going to have to learn to live without you. After last night that won't be easy. Try not to hate me.

All my love, Rachel

She sealed the envelope and wrote his name on the outside. When he asked for her at the front desk the porter would give it to him. She thought of his face when he read it, and because she knew him so well, she felt his pain for him. Love, she thought bitterly. What did I ever do to deserve it?

As the plane flew eastwards across the Rockies she was haunted by memories. She was back in the audition rooms of *Spotlight* again. Outside in St Martin's Lane

## 462 • TRUDI PACTER

the theatres were flickering into life. She was twenty-eight and waiting for her big chance.

She thought about Jeremy Powers, Desmond French, Dan Keyser, and all the other men who had judged her. How vulnerable I was, she thought. How vulnerable and willing to please. I would have done anything to get on. Almost anything. She hadn't given in to Jeremy Powers and she was proud of that. Whatever I did, she thought, however I got there, I got there on my terms. There were no compromises.

Her hand went up to her nose and she smiled as she explored the still unfamiliar straightness. Can I count this as a compromise? she wondered. Then she decided she couldn't. The plastic surgery was a superficial change. What she had on her mind went deeper.

She thought about the newly won Oscar nestling at the bottom of her suitcase, and she remembered the surge of victory she felt when she received it. That's what I did it for, she told herself. That's why I put up with the draughty theatres and the grotty digs. If I gave it up now, if I upped sticks and married Bob, then all that would have been in vain. My whole life would have meant nothing at all.

All the way to New York she reminded herself of the validity of what she was doing. Yet as the plane started its descent into Kennedy she still had doubts. If walking out on Bob was for the best, then why did it have to hurt so much?

By the time she got to the theatre she had the beginnings of a headache. She had been held up in the rush-hour traffic, and the combination of the delay and the flight frayed her nerves. She summoned her

## SCREEN KISSES • 463

dresser and asked for aspirin and hot tea. Tonight after the performance she would collapse, she promised herself. Right now she had to get into character.

Methodically she lathered cold cream on to her face then wiped it off. Now she was anonymous—a blank canvas on which she could paint anything she wanted. She painted Lili. Lili's skin was pale, paler than hers. Her face was thinner, her nose longer, her eyes hooded and more shadowed. Rachel worked deftly from a row of wand-shaped greasepaints. There was dark paint and red paint and several tones of flesh. When she was half way through she powdered down the surface of her new face and left her lips blank. They would come last—after she had finished her tea and put out her final cigarette.

She went over to the wardrobe behind her and her dresser followed. She didn't need help to get into costume so she signalled the woman to leave. Then she lifted out the drab serge jacket with its matching long pleated skirt and stared at it for a long time. There was something dated about the cut. Something that said wartime, coupons, austerity. Rachel put on the suit and immediately she felt colder and poorer. Then she turned round and faced the mirror one last time. She was nearly Lili. Very nearly. All she had to do was fix her hair. She wound it back into a flat bun and pinned it tightly to her scalp. Then she lifted the wig from the counter and put it on.

The transformation was total. Now her hair was short and black, and the face beneath was pinched and weary from war. The woman who looked back at her now was no longer Rachel. She was Lili. When she

**464 • TRUDI PACTER**

felt it was with Lili's feelings. When she cried it was with Lili's tears.

She heard the first call and started to apply her lipstick. Soon she would be living Lili's life.

When she took her final curtain call the applause told her everything she wanted to know. The play still worked. Her audience still loved her. For a moment she felt warm and filled to the brim. But only for a moment. When the lights went up and people started filing towards the exits, she was alone once more— back in her own skin.

It would be twenty-four hours before she felt warm again. A night and a whole day long before anyone loved her. She wrapped her arms around herself and walked slowly back to her dressing room.

She saw him the moment she came through the door. He was sitting by the mirror she used—the one surrounded by naked light bulbs—and he was drinking red wine from one of her tooth mugs.

"Why are you here?" she asked. "You got my letter, didn't you?"

"I got your letter," he acknowledged. Then he pushed the open bottle of Beaujolais towards her. "Why don't you help yourself to some of this, then maybe we'll talk about it."

She sat down on the heavy brocade sofa the management provided, and started tugging at her wig. "It's no good, it's not going to work whatever you say." She took the hairpiece off and started unpinning the braid at the nape of her neck.

"Tell me, Rachel," he said quietly, "why isn't it going to work?"

## SCREEN KISSES • 465

She started to feel exasperated. "Look, you read my letter, didn't you? You know all the reasons."

He put his glass down hard on the counter. "To hell with the letter. Letters are for pen pals and acquaintances. When my lover tells me goodbye, I want to hear it from her in person."

The confidence she still carried from the stage started to flow out of her. "Bob," she said shakily, "we had this out a long time ago in Los Angeles. The first time I left you. Do we have to go through it again?"

He stood up, pushing his fingers through unruly black hair. Rachel knew there was no getting out of it. She took a deep breath. "You told me you couldn't live with me if I went on acting. Well, I am going on acting, my darling. I have to. It's not something I can turn off. Any more than I can turn off my feelings for you."

"So that's it," he said. "You go on with the theatre. We live apart. Is that what you want?"

She felt tears gathering in the corners of her eyes. "Of course it isn't what I want. But that's all I have to choose from."

He came up to her and grabbed her roughly by the arm, and she noticed his eyes were angry.

"Has it occurred to you that things might have changed?" he said tightly.

She pulled away, massaging her elbow. "What's changed? What could have changed?"

There was a silence. Then he looked at her and she saw the anger in his eyes had been replaced with pain. "I've changed," he said softly.

She was sitting on the sofa in her stiff wartime costume. Her hair, free from its wig, curled and tangled round her shoulders. She felt unkempt, ill-at-ease, defenceless. She gestured over to the chair he had vacated. "Why don't you sit down and have some more wine? Then you can tell me how you've changed."

He ignored the chair and sat down on the narrow sofa beside her. "You don't believe me," he said.

She felt her heart banging in her chest and she cursed her body for a fool. You were in bed with this man twenty-four hours ago, she thought bitterly, and you can't get out of the habit of making love to him. With an effort she sat up straight and drew her breath in. "Of course I don't believe you," she said. "You're an old-fashioned Irishman, Bob. What you really want is an old-fashioned marriage with an old-fashioned wife. I can't be that for you."

He passed his hands over his face. "An old-fashioned marriage," he said sourly. "Don't laugh, but that's what I had. Claudia and I only got hitched because she said she'd give up the business. And to give the woman her due she stuck to her promise. There was only one problem. I didn't love her. She could have stood on her head and it still wouldn't have worked."

Rachel reached over to the table in front of her for a cigarette, but he took the pack out of her hands. "You don't need those," he said softly.

She looked at him, and once more she felt her body giving way, betraying her. "Why no cigarette?"

"Because I want your full attention."

He took both of her hands in his, and the moment he touched her, she knew she was lost. "I love you,"

## SCREEN KISSES • 467

he said. "Because of that the rest doesn't matter. If you want to dance naked in burlesque, if you want to run for President of the United States, it doesn't bother me. There is only one thing that would upset me. If you left me again."

She pictured herself as she had often pictured herself on stage—as a bystander. An onlooker. And she saw not a brave heroine or a gifted actress but a woman who loved. A woman who was at the mercy of her emotion. "I'll never leave you, Bob," she said. "Not now."

He pulled her close, and finally she knew who she was. She was Rachel Keller. Actress and woman. The searching was over.

In Bali an old Chinese fortune-teller sat stroking her cat and staring into the fire. For a split second one of the timbers burned more brightly than the others, sending a shower of sparks up the chimney.

Martha Chong looked annoyed. "Be quiet, Claudia," she said half to herself. "Can't you see, it's finished between you now?"

The timber glowed even more fiercely, cracking and popping in a series of sharp explosions.

The old woman sighed heavily. "Tourists," she thought. "Why didn't I just shut up and keep the money?"

**Trudi Pacter** is the author of KISS & TELL. A former Fleet Street Women's Editor, she currently divides her time between London, New York, and her family's estate in Leicestershire. She is married to Baronet Sir Nigel Seely.

# HarperPaperbacks *By Mail*

**Ambition—**
*Julie Burchill—*
Young, gorgeous, sensuous Susan Street is not satisfied with being deputy editor of the newspaper. She wants it all, and she'll do it all to fight her way to the top and fulfill her lust for success.

**The Snow Leopard of Shanghai—***Erin Pizzey—*
From the Russian Revolution to China's Cultural Revolution, from the splendor of the Orient to the sins of a Shanghai brothel, here is the breathtaking story of the extraordinary life of an unforgettable woman.

**Champagne—**
*Nicola Thorne—*
Ablaze with the glamor and lust of a glittering industry, fired by the passions of the rich and beautiful, this is the sizzling story of one woman's sudden thrust into jet-set power in a vast international empire.

**Kiss & Tell—**
*Trudi Pacter—*
Kate Kennedy rises from the ashes of abused passion to become queen of the glittering, ruthless world of celebrity journalism. But should she risk her hard-won career for what might be the love of a lifetime?

**Aspen Affair—**
*Burt Hirschfeld—*
Glittering, chilling, erotic, and suspenseful, Aspen Affair carries you up to the rarified world of icy wealth and decadent pleasures—then down to the dark side of the beautiful people who can never get enough.

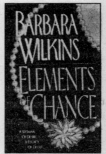

**Elements of Chance—**
*Barbara Wilkins—*
When charismatic billionaire Victor Penn apparently dies in a plane crash, his beautiful widow Valarie is suddenly torn from her privileged world. Alone for the first time, she is caught in a web of rivalries, betrayal, and murder.

*If you like hot, sexy, passionate suspenseful books, you'll love these...*

# 6 novels filled with intrigue, love, deceit and romance

You are sure to enjoy all these exciting novels from Harper Paperbacks.

**Buy 4 or More and $ave**

When you buy 4 or more books from Harper Paperbacks, the postage and handling is **FREE**.

**Visa and MasterCard holders—call 1-800-562-6182 for fastest service!**

MAIL TO: **HarperPaperbacks,
10 East 53rd Street, New York, NY 10022
Attn: Mail Order Division**

Yes, please send me the books I have checked:
- [ ] Ambition (0-06-100048-5) . . . . . . . . . . . . . . .$4.95
- [ ] The Snow Leopard of Shanghai
  (0-06-100037-X) . . . . . . . . . . . . . . . . . . . .$4.95
- [ ] Champagne (0-06-100023-X) . . . . . . . . . . . .$4.95
- [ ] Kiss & Tell (0-06-100022-X) . . . . . . . . . . . . .$4.95
- [ ] Aspen Affair (0-06-100075-2) . . . . . . . . . . . .$4.95
- [ ] Elements of Chance (0-06-100056-6) . . . . . . .$5.50

**SUBTOTAL** . . . . . . . . . . . . . . . . . . . .$_____

**POSTAGE AND HANDLING\*** . . . . . . . . . . . .$_____

**SALES TAX** (NJ, NY, PA residents) . . . . . . .$_____

**TOTAL:** $_____
(Remit in US funds, do not send cash.)

Name_____

Address_____

City_____

State_____ Zip_____

Allow up to 6 weeks delivery.
Prices subject to change.

\*Add $1 postage/handling for up to 3 books...
**FREE postage/handling if you buy 4 or more.**

HP-009-1

MINERAL COUNTY PUBLIC LIBRARY